IN DARKNESS LIGHT SHINES

By
John Galt Robinson

KCM PUBLISHING
A DIVISION OF KCM DIGITAL MEDIA, LLC

CREDITS

Copyright © 2022 by John Galt Robinson
Published by KCM Publishing
A Division of KCM Digital Media, LLC

All Rights Reserved.

This content may not be reproduced in whole or in part, in any form or by any means, electronic or mechanical, including photocopying, recording, or by any information storage and retrieval system now known or hereafter invented, without written permission from the publisher.

This is a work of fiction. Names, characters, businesses, places, events, and incidents are either the products of the author's imagination or used in a fictitious manner. Any resemblance to actual persons, living or dead, or actual events is purely coincidental.

In Darkness Light Shines by John Galt Robinson

ISBN-13: 978-1-955620-15-4
ebook ISBN: 978-1-955620-16-1

First Edition

Publisher: Michael Fabiano
KCM Publishing
www.kcmpublishing.com

KCM Publishing
a division of KCM Digital Media, LLC

To Richard Krysztof, father in law to me, grandfather to our children, godfather to some, friend to many. Your kind heart, generous spirit, hilarious sense of humor and open door are appreciated by all of us more than you know.

Acknowledgements

As always, there are numerous people who contribute their time and talents into these works, and I could not write these novels without them. First and foremost to my Lord and Savior **Jesus Christ**. For I can do all things through Him who gives me strength. I must also acknowledge my amazing wife, **Pam Robinson.** Her love, patience, and support have carried us through nearly thirty years of marriage, three children, three major moves, medical school, and now this new chapter of writing. I could not do this without her and would not want to consider life without her by my side. Next, our three adult children, **Jenna, Luke, and Jordan**, whose admiration and support are priceless to me. To my publisher, **Michael Fabiano of KCM Publishing,** I would not be publishing my fourth novel were it not for your continued guidance and support. A special thank you to my trusted beta readers, **James Blake, David Smith, and Mack Ogburn. Additionally, John "The Chief" Cunningham is a trusted beta reader and a valuable source for all things Navy and political.** Thank you all for your support and honest criticism. You guys are always there for me. Once again, a big thank you to **MJ** for your knowledge and insight into all things federal law enforcement. Along those lines, I would like to thank my friend, attorney **Robert Masella**, for all your help navigating the legal content of this story. **Adam Hergert,** a corrections officer and friend who provided valuable insight and information so we could get the prison portions accurate; you have been a great friend and supporter since **Forces of Redemption** and I most appreciate it. Speaking of great friends and support, to my medical colleagues, **Dr. Tony Buscaglia, Dr. David Ford, and Dr. Ashley McGee**, you have gone out of your way to promote my works and I cannot thank you enough. Closer to home, my brother, **Tom Robinson, is** my IT guru who is always available and willing to help guide me with IT and computer subjects. Another lifelong friend from back home, **Michael DelSignore**, who willingly volunteered to give up valuable time to comb through this manuscript, employing his literary background to provide valuable first editing and criticism; I am beyond grateful. And, finally, to all my readers who have joined me on this journey. Your online reviews, continued support, and encouragement make this a true joy for me. Thank you for being there and for spreading the word. It is through your voice that these books get into the hands of other readers, but it is your encouragement that makes me want to write even better works. Thank you!

Contents

Chapter 1: Buford, Georgia 1

Chapter 2: Cornelius, North Carolina 8

Chapter 3: Air Force One 10

Chapter 4: Air Force One 16

Chapter 5: Atlanta, Georgia 27

Chapter 6: Air Force One 33

Chapter 7: Atlanta, Georgia 40

Chapter 8: South Bend, Indiana 44

Chapter 9: Atlanta, Georgia 47

Chapter 10: Atlanta, Georgia 52

Chapter 11: Alto, Georgia 58

Chapter 12: South Bend, Indiana 61

Chapter 13: Atlanta, Georgia 64

Chapter 14: Alto, Georgia 69

Chapter 15: Alto, Georgia 74

Chapter 16: Grand Island, New York 79

Chapter 17: Atlanta, Georgia 82

Chapter 18: Washington D.C. 86

Chapter 19: Atlanta, Georgia 91

Chapter 20: Alto, Georgia 97

Chapter	Location	Page
Chapter 21:	Atlanta, Georgia	101
Chapter 22:	Washington, D.C.	105
Chapter 23:	Alto, Georgia	108
Chapter 24:	The White House	116
Chapter 25:	Atlanta, Georgia	124
Chapter 26:	Washington, D.C.	128
Chapter 27:	Atlanta, Georgia	134
Chapter 28:	Atlanta, Georgia	137
Chapter 29:	Atlanta, Georgia	140
Chapter 30:	Buford, Georgia	147
Chapter 31:	Virginia Beach, Virginia	151
Chapter 32:	The White House	154
Chapter 33:	Virginia Beach, Virginia	157
Chapter 34:	Atlanta, Georgia	160
Chapter 35:	Washington D.C.	164
Chapter 36:	Alto, Georgia	169
Chapter 37:	Alto, Georgia	174
Chapter 38:	Atlanta, Georgia	178
Chapter 39:	Charlotte, North Carolina	182
Chapter 40:	Air Force One	186
Chapter 41:	Air Force One	193
Chapter 42:	Washington, D.C.	198
Chapter 43:	Washington, D.C.	202
Chapter 44:	Atlanta, Georgia	205
Chapter 45:	Washington, D.C.	210
Chapter 46:	Alexandria, Virginia	214
Chapter 47:	Alexandria, Virginia	220
Chapter 48:	Alexandria, Virginia	228

Chapter 49: McLean, Virginia 234

Chapter 50: Alexandria, Virginia. 239

Chapter 51: Alto, Georgia 243

Chapter 52: Charlotte, North Carolina. 250

Chapter 53: Washington, D.C. 254

Chapter 54: Alto, Georgia 259

Chapter 55: Grand Island, New York. 263

Chapter 56: The White House 266

Chapter 57: Atlanta, Georgia. 273

Chapter 58: Washington, D.C. 283

Chapter 59: Washington, D.C. 287

Chapter 60: Alto, Georgia 291

Chapter 61: Atlanta, Georgia. 294

Chapter 62: Washington, D.C. 300

Chapter 63: The White House 304

Chapter 64: McLean, Virginia 314

Chapter 65: Tysons, Virginia 317

Chapter 66: Washington, D.C. 323

Chapter 67: Washington, D.C. 327

Chapter 68: Washington, D.C. 330

Chapter 69: Washington, D.C. 338

Chapter 70: Washington, D.C. 343

Chapter 71: Washington, D.C. 347

Chapter 72: Alto, Georgia 350

Chapter 73: Alto, Georgia 354

Chapter 74: Alto, Georgia 359

Chapter 75: The White House 364

Chapter 76: Atlanta, Georgia. 372

Chapter 77: Atlanta, Georgia	374
Chapter 78: Atlanta, Georgia	379
Chapter 79: Duluth, Georgia	382
Chapter 80: Duluth, Georgia	388
Chapter 81: Duluth, Georgia	393
Chapter 82: The White House; Six weeks later	397
Chapter 83: Washington, D.C.	403
About the Author	411
Author's Note	412
Forces of Redemption	414
Power City	416
Lost Angels	418

IN DARKNESS
LIGHT SHINES

"You have enemies. Good. That means you have stood up for something, sometime in your life."

– Victor Hugo

Chapter 1

Buford, Georgia

A haphazard collection of police cars and SUVs was strewn about the quiet lakeside neighborhood. A kaleidoscope of flashing blue and red lights accenting white headlights and news camera lights illuminated the surrounding houses. The front lawn and driveway of one particular house was alive with the frenzied movements of numerous federal and local law enforcement officers as they prepared for a potential raid. Cordoned off in the usually quiet residential street, several network news correspondents and their cameramen jostled for position amidst local news affiliates.

Andrew Winkelman, the newly named Special Agent in Charge (SAIC) of the Atlanta FBI Field Office slithered between the television crews and stepped onto the driveway. He was average height and build with a slight bulge at the waistline. He had receding dark hair, with specks of gray, which served to magnify a large forehead and an all but absent chin. He wore grey wool slacks, black dress shoes, and a navy blue FBI windbreaker with matching ball cap.

"Jimmy, how we lookin'?" Winkelman asked as he stepped up to the agent coordinating the raid. His New Jersey accent was as thick as ever despite spending most of his career below the Mason-Dixon Line.

Special Agent James Cleveland leaned on the hood of his black Yukon as he surveyed the scene. He wore a similar windbreaker and ball cap but gave off a more menacing appearance with his six-foot, still mostly muscular frame. He had traces of sandy blond hair on his balding scalp and in his goatee.

"Pretty good, boss," he said handing over a steaming cup of store-bought coffee. "The team is in position and the networks are already reporting live on the scene. If those perps don't come out immediately with their hands up, we just might give the newsies' a good show."

"A newsworthy show is exactly what is expected tonight. Run it by the book but, if they show the slightest bit of hesitation, take em' down hard, Jimmy."

"Will do, sir."

*****

Inside the house, two men and two women stood around the kitchen island. One of the men was furiously typing away on a laptop while the others stared at the live news feed on a flatscreen television in the adjacent living room.

"They've got an assault team lined up and ready to go, Joe. This is seriously shaping up to go full Ruby Ridge on live TV," the man watching the television warned.

Lieutenant Commander Joe O'Shanick, USN, looked up from the laptop and scrutinized the newsfeed. "Stacked and packed and ready to roll, Rammer. They're not playing around. This'll play out for weeks on the news."

"How did they know where to find you?" Stacy Morgan asked. Stacy, a petite blond who looked more like the college cheerleader she once was rather than the practicing OB/GYN she had become. A highly compassionate physician, Stacy tended to wear her emotions on her sleeve as evidenced by the look of concern etched on her face.

"Any number of ways," Joe answered as he continued typing. "I told Special Agent McPherson where we were staying but they could have just as easily tracked our cellphones."

"I just don't understand this. You guys busted Senator Fowler molesting an abducted American woman while he was a guest of the cartel boss and Russian mafia boss who abducted her. Not twenty-four hours ago he was in federal custody and now he's free and it's you two who are being arrested. You risked your lives to rescue those girls! Something is really off here, Joe!" This came from Dr. Christy Tabrizi.

Christy was a practicing Emergency Medicine physician and the most important person in Joe's life. Just earlier this evening they had been discussing their future together, a future that included marriage and children. It was her kitchen they were standing in and her house that was currently being broadcasted on every national news network.

Joe looked up at Christy. In opposition to her close friend, Stacy, Christy stood nearly six feet tall, slender but with an athletic physique. She had long, silky dark hair that framed an exotically unique and, irresistible in Joe's eyes, face that displayed her mixed Iranian and Irish heritage; high cheekbones, a slender nose, delicate chin, and almond-shaped emerald green eyes. She was wearing black athletic leggings and a gray University of Tennessee Volleyball athletic shirt. Christy tended to be more emotionally reserved but her near perpetual, gentle smile currently gave way to a fiery brand of anger and concern.

"You're right, but I can't say this was unexpected," Joe responded. "There's one month to go before the election and Fowler is neck and neck with President Galan. He has some big backers that we now know of; local organized crime, the cartels, Iran, Russia, China, and God knows who else not to mention the backing of his political party and the media. They aren't going to concede anything until they get the presidency back. We know *he's* a crooked politician so we shouldn't be surprised that he has a band of cronies and bureaucrats pulling out all the stops to fuel an alternative narrative for the media. His only chance at avoiding jail is to win the presidency. If he gets the House and Senate, then he's bulletproof. He'll own the DOJ, the media, and the unelected bureaucrats. Congress will support him and thwart any attempt to impeach."

"While in the meantime, we go down as scapegoats," Ramsey added.

Master Chief Matt Ramsey, Special Warfare Operator, United States Navy SEALs, was Joe's platoon Chief Petty Officer and his closest friend. They had served together for years, including several combat deployments. Although Joe was the commanding officer, he wisely valued Ramsey's extensive years in service and wisdom and saw him more as a co-leader and a brother. Both Ramsey and Joe stood six feet four inches, sporting chiseled, muscular physiques sharpened by years of rigorous training and conditioning. He had close cropped sandy blond hair with a matching goatee that he alternated with a walrus-like dropping mustache that have him the look of a Viking. Conversely, Joe had darker features with dark hair, which he inherited from his Filipino mother, while sporting the strong, rugged Irish face and green eyes passed down from his father. Eyes that revealed a compassionate inner soul to Christy but could flash danger to those who crossed him.

A few days ago, Ramsey and Joe had volunteered to help a private investigator, Clay Whitmore, locate and rescue three abducted college girls. The operation, financed by one Charles Courtnall, an extremely wealthy financial investor and the father of one of the girls, had led them to a private island off the coast of Belize, owned by one of the cartels. The op went sideways when, in addition to the three girls, another twelve had been discovered on the island, all of whom were present to serve as sexual slaves for the cartel, Senator Fowler, and several foreign heavy hitters. Joe had literally rescued Courtnall's daughter seconds before Fowler was about to violate her sexually, but then a firefight broke out with the cartel. Fowler had nearly escaped in a helicopter during the melee, but Joe had leapt aboard and pulled him out while it lifted up over the water. Pedro Cardenas, the head of the *Los Fantasma Guerreros* cartel, one of Fowler's biggest backers, had been killed during the firefight along with about a dozen of his soldiers before the girls were successfully transferred to a boat piloted by Courtnall and Christy. Overall, the op had been a success but not without a cost. One of Whitmore's top investigators, Gary Lee, a former Marine who volunteered to assist with the op, had been killed in action. He left behind no family, but he was a good man and the loss was still difficult to accept. Whitmore had suffered a concussion and Joe a gunshot wound through his right triceps muscle, but they had come through it relatively unscathed otherwise. That is until now.

"Scapegoats is the least of our concerns, Rammer," Joe responded as he worked the mousepad on the laptop. "Epstein didn't hang himself."

Ramsey cursed out loud in response to the reference.

"Sorry, ladies," he apologized with his deep voice.

Joe was referring to Jeffrey Epstein, an American financier and convicted sexual offender who owned an island in the Caribbean where it was rumored many well-known celebrities and prominent politicians gathered for exclusive parties and sexual romps. *Ironic.* Upon his arrest for sexual trafficking, Epstein was held in New York City's Metropolitan Correctional Center. Due to his ability to spill the beans on certain high-ranking politicians, many speculated that Epstein would be killed while in jail. Sure enough, a couple of weeks later, he was found dead in his cell under mysterious circumstances. It was quickly ruled a suicide, but many remained skeptical. Strict security procedures had not been followed and not one, but two security cameras that would have caught what happened, mysteriously were not functional that night.

"Joe, are you serious?" Christy asked, the alarm clearly heard in her voice.

"I'm dead serious," Joe said as he clicked off his email and shut the laptop. "It's already started. Special Agent McPherson, the head of the Atlanta Field Office who was heading up the investigation into Fowler was shot assassination style this morning while jogging. Anyone connected to this who could testify against Fowler is going to be a target. Ramsey and I are just the first to be arrested. Whitmore and his entire crew, Courtnall, his family…" Joe paused as the revelation hit him. "…and you, Christy."

Christy stood stoically as Stacy gasped. The magnified weight of their dire circumstances descended up the foursome. From outside, an amplified voice broke the silence.

"Attention in the house! This is Special Agent Winkelman, acting Special Agent in Charge of the FBI Atlanta Field Office. You are ordered to exit the house through the front door, unarmed, with your hands held over your head. Failure to do so will result in armed agents forcibly entering the dwelling and your immediate arrest. You have exactly one minute to comply!"

"Joe!" Christy cried out as she pulled him into a tight hug and buried her head in his chest.

Joe noticed Stacy do the same thing with Ramsey.

"It's alright," Joe tried to sound reassuring as he held her face in both hands and looked into her eyes. "We have the truth on our side. We just have to survive this and let it air in front of a jury. I'm not going to pull punches though, Christy. You're likely going to be a target. You need to keep your head on a swivel. I'll get some guys to keep watch over you while this plays out. Stacy, you too. You weren't involved but as soon as we walk out there, you're going to be on camera with the rest of us. Try to keep your head down and look away from the cameras but you'll likely be lumped in with us anyway. I'm truly sorry, but Rammer and I will see to it you're looked after. That's one of the things I was just working on a few minutes ago."

Joe pulled Christy in for a tight hug and kissed her on the forehead. "It's time to go. C'mon."

A loud crash of splintering wood sounded from the front door. Simultaneously, the great room's French doors that led to her backyard patio came crashing in. Joe spotted two small objects soar through the breached entrance.

"Flash-bang!" He yelled as he pulled Christy down behind the kitchen island and covered her ears. Ramsey did the same with Stacy.

The concussive grenades exploded in a deafening explosion of blinding light. Joe had sealed Christy's eyes with his chest while he closed his own eyes tightly. The kitchen island blocked the majority of the flash, but the loud explosion still left him momentarily stunned with his ears ringing. Joe knew what would come next and continued to lay on the floor as a half dozen federal agents, clad in black tactical gear, carrying Glock pistols and M-4 rifles, surrounded them as they barked commands. An agent kicked Joe, ordering him off of Christy while another did the same to Ramsey.

Joe obediently lay prone on the floor with his hands on the back of his head. A rather large agent put a knee in Joe's back and wrenched his right arm down where he snapped on handcuffs. He followed through with Joe's left arm. Joe was then roughly pulled up onto his knees and brought to a standing position.

Joe looked around and saw the same had been done to Ramsey, Christy, and Stacy. Stacy's face was a mixture of anger and fear, with fear winning out; her big blue eyes beginning to form tears. Christy looked at Joe with a sorrowful expression. Joe knew she blamed herself for asking him and Ramsey to help find the missing girls earlier that week when another girl had told her about the prostitution ring. She had been shot during her escape and died on the table in the operating room. Joe gently shook his head. *It's not your fault. Rammer and I willingly went.*

"I love you," he mouthed the words right before being forcefully spun around.

Two agents grabbed Joe, one on each arm and led him towards the front door. Others did the same with Christy, Ramsey, and Stacy. They emerged to the outside where they were met by another dozen or so federal agents and local law enforcement. Behind them were a row of news cameras and onlookers. The cameras were all lit up with their live feeds, giving the early Georgia night the appearance of daylight in front of Christy's house. The agents led Joe right past the cameras to a waiting SUV. SAIC Winkelman walked up and came to a stop in front of Joe. The news cameras were zeroed in on the two.

"Joseph O'Shanick, you are being placed under arrest for multiple counts of murder, attempted assassination of an elected official, conspiracy to commit murder, the unlawful detainment of an elected official, aggravated assault on an elected official, and grand larceny. You have the following rights: you have the right to remain silent…"

Chapter 2

Cornelius, North Carolina

"The author of *The Lions of Lucerne* share's his last name with what god of mythology?"

"Thor!" Charles Courtnall III said proudly. "And that's a pie for me!"

"Figures," Charles' son Scott said sourly, "Dad would get an Arts and Literature question about one of his favorite authors."

"Hey, what can I say?" Charles teased. "I'm cultured."

"Oh, please!" Charles' wife Jane said rolling her eyes. "This from the guy I had to literally drag to the Van Gogh exhibit last spring! And then, THEN, he hid an earbud in his ear so he could listen to a hockey game!"

"Daddy! You did not!" Tracy Courtnall said in shock.

"He most certainly did!" Jane fired back. "He placed it in his right ear and kept me to his left the entire evening. I caught him when I came out of the restroom and his guard was down. The old sneak!"

"In my defense, it was Game 7 of the Hurricanes playoff series with the Capitals," Charles grinned.

The entire family shared a good laugh at their father's expense. Charles smiled as he looked over at his daughter. Tracy seemed to be in good spirits. Amazing, considering she had just been through a tremendous ordeal, having been abducted while out jogging on her college campus eight days ago. She had been beaten, humiliated, terrified, and nearly raped until Clay Whitmore's team tracked down her location where Joe O'Shanick and Matt Ramsey had led Whitmore's team in her rescue two days ago.

Charles had provided transportation to Belize with his corporation's private jet. He cried tears of joy when O'Shanick handed Tracy into his arms on the beach. They flew home yesterday to a very emotional reunion with their family and many close friends. Mindful of her traumatic experience, Charles and Jane were ready to get her immediately into a psychiatric care facility but Tracy had refused, wanting to sleep in her own bed with her family around her and stating the most therapeutic thing they could do would be to have a family night at home with dinner and games, a favorite family pastime since all three kids were little. Charles looked at her angelic face, her cornsilk blond hair swaying as she laughed along with her brothers and shared a contented smile with Jane. Their family was back together and, for the moment at least, things felt back to normal.

Suddenly, a loud boom emanated from the front entrance. It was followed by another and then a loud crash. Jane screamed. The sound of multiple heavily booted footsteps echoed the hall as Charles protectively grabbed hold of Tracy and his wife. Several men, clad in black Nomex tactical gear and helmets, appeared as they fanned out and cleared the rooms. Four men entered the large kitchen and, pointing their rifles at Charles and his family, ordered them to put their hands in the air. The lead man ordered Charles onto the ground.

"What is the meaning of this?" Charles angrily shouted over the fracas. "Who are you and why are you breaking into my house!?"

The lead man grabbed Charles by the neck and one-handed him to the ground, causing his chair to fall over.

"NO!" Tracy and Jane screamed in unison.

"What are you doing!?" Charles's son Charles IV yelled as he began to stand. He was met with the muzzle of an M-4 leveled at his face with the agent behind it loudly shouting at him to get on the floor. Charles IV swallowed hard and complied.

"Charles Russell Courtnall," the lead agent began, while another agent applied handcuffs to Charles as he was held face down on the floor. "You are being placed under arrest for conspiracy to assassinate a United States Senator, conspiracy to commit murder, and accomplice to murder. You have the right to remain silent…"

Chapter 3

Air Force One

Solitude. The presidency offered many perks. This enormous, lavishly-appointed flying White House was just one of many such perks. He had helicopters, limousines, countless staff who looked after every detail and unlimited access that many only dreamed of, but it all came at a cost. Chief among those costs was solitude.

President Jorge Manuel "Manny" Galan stretched out on one of the plush leather couches that lined each side of the Presidential Suite tucked into the nose of Air Force One. His arms encircled the First Lady, Maria Galan, as she reclined back on him. They snuggled together beneath a warm navy blue blanket with the requisite Air Force One logo.

The two met when both were serving in the Marine Corps. Manny was a young infantry corporal, with the First Marine Division, when Maria, a lance corporal working on the flight line, caught his eye. He'd never forget being instantly mesmerized by her soft facial features, dark almond-shaped eyes, and gentle smile. At the time, Manny had had the looks of a recruiting poster Marine and was a confident and competent squad leader, but he had been tongue-tied around Maria. On many an occasion, he had shied away from asking her out despite the apparent interest she had shown in him. Ultimately, Maria became the one to take the initiative when she suddenly appeared at an on-base chapel service one Sunday and sat down next to Manny. It took him the entire service, but he worked up the nerve to ask if she would like to get lunch together and, to his relief, she said yes with that disarming smile. Six months later, they had married.

The past thirty-six years seemed to have flown by in a blur. They had both put in a full twenty years in the Marine Corps. Manny had finished as a sergeant major, a highly decorated veteran with three combat tours, one in Operation Desert Storm in 1991 and later in Afghanistan and Iraq. Maria had finished as a first sergeant and had also seen time in Operation Desert Storm. They waited several years to have children and, as a family, had lived in Okinawa and Hawaii, but most of their years had been in Camp Pendleton north of San Diego.

Both were of Mexican descent and grew up in different parts of Southern California. Maria in Los Angeles and Manny in San Diego. Both had grown up in poverty.

Raised by his paternal grandmother, Manny and his brother had very little supervision and quickly assimilated into the gang life. At sixteen, he and a fellow gang member were out "trunking," the practice of breaking into car trunks and stealing whatever looked good, when they were collared by a city police officer. They spent a sleepless night in jail before their arraignment the next morning. Prior to the arraignment, the arresting officer met with both of them and made them an offer. It turned out he was a lay pastor at a small inner-city church. If they would both agree to come to Wednesday night youth service for one month, he would see to it the judge dropped their charges. Both boys readily agreed but Manny was the only one who kept to his word. The other never went and began to get involved in heavier crimes and, eventually, wound up in the state prison.

Manny, however, felt obligated to go. He showed up early enough for "Pastor Vincent" to see him walk in and thought he would sit in the back and leave early. However, there had only been twelve youths at the service, and after a brief worship service, Pastor Vincent had them all gather and sit around him as he sat on the steps before the raised platform. There had been no escape.

Surprisingly, this had turned out to be nothing like the church Manny's grandmother had taken him and his brother to on Sundays. Pastor Vincent sat on the steps wearing blue jeans and a polo shirt, biceps bulging through the tight sleeves and simply related to the youths gathered around him. He too had started out in gangs until his best friend had been killed in a fight, stabbed by a rival gang member. He straightened up through a youth outreach program and eventually became a police officer. He didn't so much as teach as he talked about what the kids were dealing with in their lives, how he had lived through much the same thing and how Christ had not only offered him forgiveness but a new purpose. Manny didn't care much about religion, but Pastor Vincent was able to connect with him to the point the Manny came back the following week.

Over the next two years, Pastor Vincent became like a father figure to Manny. He would often have Manny and his brother over to share dinner with his wife and young children. Their house was small but welcoming and Manny soon lost interest in his gang associations and walked away for a better life. Manny knew college would not be an option and, when high school graduation neared, Pastor Vincent played a prominent role in helping Manny choose a life in the Marine Corps.

Manny had always kept in touch with his pastor. Years later, when Manny and Maria settled in as a family at Camp Pendleton and purchased their first car, they became active members of Pastor Vincent's church. Pastor Vincent soon placed them in leadership roles with the growing youth group. Eventually, they became more active in the inner-city community as they reached the twilight of their Marine Corps careers.

Shortly after Manny and Maria retired from the Marine Corps, the local congressman from the district announced he would not run for reelection. With Pastor Vincent's encouragement and Maria's approval, Manny entered into the race for the office. His Marine Corps service and his reputation in the community helped him win in a landslide.

Unlike many politicians, Manny did not have long-term political aspirations; however, he reasoned that, as long as he was in office, he would try to affect the most good he could do for his community and for the country. His career as a Marine Corps non-commissioned officer (NCO) kicked in and he soon became a pragmatic problem solver with a reputation for working with people across the aisle, so long as they were genuine, while charismatically dressing down those who put politics before meaningful action. He had no use for "ticket punchers" in the Corps and certainly had no use for self-serving politicians in Congress. His rising star soon parlayed into a second and then a third term in Congress before the movers and shakers of his party approached him to run for governor of the State of California.

The people of California were growing tired of the incumbent who continued to raise their taxes but did little to solve real problems like crime and the persistent water shortages that were destroying crops and causing water rationing state-wide. The time was ripe for a new candidate and Manny's popularity and reputation led to a narrow but decisive victory. After back-to-back terms, crime was down, water was as available as the state's restrictive environmental regulations would allow, and the people were happier. Manny even worked out a tax cut that had brought in more industry making the port cities and Silicon Valley stronger than ever.

When his second and final term drew to a close, the national party began to court him for a presidential run. Since the president at the time was finishing his second term, the election was wide open, and Manny Galan was the people's choice of his party. His heritage was key to winning key states like California and Texas. Manny won in a close contest and early on had been at least respected if not liked on both sides of the aisle as well as in the red and blue states.

However, his first-term honeymoon was over and the past two years had brought a simmering political cauldron to a boil. The always contentious scene at the southern border had been one of Manny's top priorities. A first generation Mexican-American himself, Manny had a sympathetic knowledge of the many problems people faced in Central America. The abject poverty, drug trafficking, human trafficking, and government corruption had one common denominator: the cartels. Rather than ignore the root cause of the issues that sent hordes of people to flood the border in search of a better life, Manny assembled a coalition that sought to eliminate or at least disable the cartels and restore peace and prosperity to the people of Central America. Over the past year, a coalition of American and local Central American forces had taken the cartels to task in a unique yet determined effort to restore the nations to their people.

As with any military conflict, there had been some bumps in the road along the way and Manny's political opposition had been quick to exploit those for political gain. Chief among them had been Senator Robert Fowler, the senior senator from Arizona who had emerged as the opposition party's challenger in the upcoming election, only a month away. Manny was still well received by many across party lines but, with the media's support and a seemingly limitless financial war chest, Fowler had drawn even going into the final stretch.

That was until a few days ago when Fowler had used a lookalike to evade his Secret Service detail to sneak off to a secret meeting with the head of the *Los Fantasma Guerreros* cartel and several hostile nation government officials. He was brought back in handcuffs by Joe O'Shanick after being found during a rescue of several abducted women who were brought to the island as "entertainment" for Fowler and the others. Needless to say, that pretty much nailed the coffin shut on Fowler's political career, let alone his presidential bid, which made Manny's day trip to Florida unnecessary.

Not that he would have canceled the appearance. Jorge Manny Galan was a president of the people. He eschewed the elitism that often-accompanied political office. Although it was difficult to escape the lofty position the Oval Office elevated him to, Manny made it a point to get out and speak directly to his constituents on a regular basis. Today's rallies were no exception.

They began with a large rally in Miami. He had great support among the hard-working Cuban-Americans, law enforcement, and small business owners, all of whom had shown up in droves. They had a mid-afternoon rally in Tampa and finished the day in Tallahassee. It was good to get out of Washington and it had been a fun day, but it was even more pleasurable to spend a rare moment alone with Maria.

Manny kissed his wife on the top of her head as he gently massaged her shoulders. She signaled her appreciation with a soft soothing voice of encouragement in Spanish. Maria knew what made him tick. Manny closed his eyes and gently smiled as he enjoyed the moment.

"The game's back on," Maria quietly announced.

She may not have eyes in the back of her head, but she always seemed to know what Manny was doing. He opened his eyes and looked up at the large flat screen at the front of the suite. Georgia Tech was hosting Clemson in the game of the week. Clemson was coming off another national championship, but Georgia Tech was strong this year and entering the game undefeated. This was shaping up to be a preview of the ACC Championship game. Manny and Maria had met Clemson's team last winter when they had been invited to the White House. They were very impressed with the players but especially the head coach. Clemson looked to be in good hands for years to come.

However, their son, Tommy had recently matriculated as a freshman at Georgia Tech on a golf scholarship. They were now officially fans of the Ramblin' Wreck. Not that either had a lot of time to watch college football, but just having the game on, knowing Tommy was somewhere in Bobby Dodd Stadium while they watched on TV, gave them a sense of connection. Their older daughter, Lydia, was a junior at Liberty University. Now that Tommy was away as well, they were still getting used to the idea of being empty nesters. Well, if one could consider The White House and empty nest or even a nest for that matter.

As if to prove that point, an urgent knock came at the door,

"Mr. President," the muffled voice of Jonathon James "JJ" Embry, President Galan's Chief of Staff, came through the door. "We have a situation."

Chapter 4

Air Force One

*G*alan let his head fall back and groaned. Maria patted his forearm, threw the blanket aside, and sat up. She glanced at her watch.

"That was a whole thirty-seven minutes," she said with mock excitement.

"Better than the fifteen I predicted," Manny said as he swung his legs off the couch and stood.

He was barefoot wearing gym shorts and a Phenom Elite t-shirt. The fitted athletic cut revealed his broad shoulders, narrow waist, and bulging biceps built up during his years in the Marine Corps and maintained by daily workouts in the White House gym. Maria worked out every morning with her husband, it was one of their daily rituals, one of their only times alone together for that matter, and she looked equally fit in Navy blue leggings and white American Flag tank top. Manny's suit and Maria's dress had been carefully hung in a small closet. The two retired Marines stepped over to the closet and re-donned their respective finery in under two minutes.

The president and first lady emerged from their suite appearing fresh and dapper. Chief of Staff Embry leaned against a bulkhead, reading a document on his iPad. He still possessed his thin, athletic build from his college baseball days at Stanford. He wore a navy blue suit, starched white shirt, and a bright red tie. Embry had been Galan's most trusted advisor since his first term as California's governor. He looked up at his boss and spoke.

"Conference room," he said as he turned and headed down the passageway.

"Can Maria join us?" Galan asked.

"Definitely," Embry answered as he hurried along.

Those two bits of information tipped Galan off that this was a political issue, most likely campaign oriented. The fact that it was being held in the conference room rather than the Presidential Office, where Galan preferred to discuss most matters, meant that the meeting would involve several staff and/or Cabinet members. If Maria was allowed to attend, it wasn't a national security issue necessitating a security clearance and the fact that Embry wanted her presence indicated it was likely campaign oriented as she had a very keen eye for political matters affecting her husband.

Galan wondered what it could be. With Fowler's recent arrest, his presidential bid was derailed. More like a train wreck. Good. Galan never cared for the man. Fowler was the poster child for corrupt politicians. How he was able to bamboozle enough people to repeatedly vote him into office was beyond comprehension. A fawning media and a slick marketing campaign were all Galan could think of, but he preferred not to think of it at all. The mere thought of the political machine made him sick. Why couldn't we return to the days when ordinary citizens served a couple of terms and then returned to their regular lives to live within the system they had presided over? Wasn't that what the Framers of the Constitution envisioned? They certainly had not intended for there to be an establishment ruling class elite, yet that's what so much of Washington had become. *So laments the man campaigning for his second term as president.* Galan laughed to himself as he considered the irony. Not that he had ever wanted to hold political office. He really hadn't. It was about as desirable to him cleaning one's house. An unenjoyable but necessary endeavor to preserve one's house. He simply found few others whom he could trust to do the job.

Galan entered the conference room where several of his staff stood waiting. He politely nodded his acknowledgment and motioned them into their seats. He held a chair out for Maria and took his own seat at the head of the table. Looking around, he saw Embry along with campaign chairman, Kim Pritchard, and her assistant, Loni Chang. Across the table from them sat Steve Nelson, the head of Galan's Secret Service detail, Tabitha Reynolds, the assistant White House press secretary, Aaron Sprole, chief political advisor, and Martin Espinoza, his assistant chief of staff.

Galan looked up at the flat screens mounted on the bulkhead and saw nearly his entire cabinet, chief among them Attorney General Preston Jacobs. Standing in the room were various other staffers, Secret Service agents, and his speech writer, Alison McMasters. No one was smiling. Absent were the Joint Chiefs of Staff so he didn't think they were at war, but something was definitely up.

"What do we have JJ?" Galan asked his Chief of Staff.

"I think it would be best to show you, Mr. President," Embry said as he picked up a remote and pointed it at a large screen. "This was recorded just a few minutes ago."

The screen came to life with Senator Fowler, wearing a dark, tailored suit, walking up to a podium. He was flanked by his running mate and several prominent party members including the speaker of the house. The headline at the bottom of the screen read:

Presidential Challenger Senator Robert Fowler cleared of all charges.

Fowler's face was a dark scowl as he gripped the podium. He leaned into the microphone and began to speak with an inflamed tone.

"My fellow Americans, it is with grave concern that I address you tonight. The events of the last thirty-six hours have been unsettling to say the least but, more accurately, and sadly, will go down as one of darker moments in our history; however, the preliminary reports have been grossly erroneous. I stand before this great country of ours to set the record straight. Due to the enormous weight of the situation, I feel it is my duty to do so with utmost candor. The simple fact is, we have a criminal dictator in the White House. Yesterday, I was wrongfully placed under arrest on false charges after a failed attempt was made on my life. The charges falsely stated that I was consorting with Pedro Cardenas, the head of the *Los Fantasma Guerreros* cartel along with representatives of several nations. Those reports are wrong. The truth is, I was *confronting* Pedro Cardenas and his associates! I was letting them know that I was onto their nefarious scheme with Jorge Galan in his so-called war on the cartels. A war in which he has virtually eliminated all of the competing cartels while allowing *Los Fantasma Guerreros* to thrive in return for their support. The fact is, I was there to call them out and negotiate a real solution; one that's fair for all parties and protects our children from the influx of drugs. One that involves diplomacy rather than spending trillions of taxpayer dollars and the countless lives of our brave men and women who have been sent by Galan to clear a path for his favored cartel!"

Embry looked over at his boss. President Galan sat stoically in his chair as he watched the screen.

"But, sadly, there is widespread corruption within the Galan administration. People who reject honest and open diplomacy while seeking to advance their personal agendas of power and enrichment. I couldn't take it anymore. Something had to be done to stop the needless war that was propping up the cartel. A war that was taking the lives of innocent people and our brave men and women. Therefore, I decided that, even if it cost me a shot at the presidency, I had to make it my mission to put a stop to the corruption and the needless sacrifice of our sons and daughters. I swore an oath to uphold our Constitution. Unlike my opponent, I consider that a sacred oath; therefore, I felt it to be my duty to act. If I failed to act, I wouldn't be worthy to lead this great nation, so I was willing to risk this campaign to do what was right. The problem is, Jorge Galan doesn't want this arrangement he has with the cartel to be disrupted and certainly not exposed. I knew they would do everything in their power to stop me on such a mission, so I couldn't let anybody know, not even my Secret Service detail. I had to act alone and in complete secrecy. I had to elude my Secret Service detail and fly by private aircraft to a discreet meeting where I confronted Pedro Cardenas and his associates. And I did it! I had this worked out! We worked out a peaceful solution that would have put an end to Jorge Galan's private but costly war! A solution that enlisted the help of nations that we have previously been at odds with but would and can soon work together with for mutual benefit. *That's* true diplomacy folks! *That's* how a real president would act if he were to put America first!"

Fowler paused. He dramatically looked down at the podium and slowly shook his head. "Oh, what might have been," he lamented.

Around the Air Force One conference room, no one spoke, no one guffawed. President Galan remained motionless in his chair, one arm on the table as he continued to watch. Maria saw the telltale tightness in his clenched jaw but remained quiet, knowing he was processing what he was hearing.

"We were so close, folks," Fowler continued as his voice cranked. "So close but then this corrupt organization reared its ugly head. Somehow, Galan and his organization got wind of what I was doing. Don't ask me how. I acted alone and have no idea; although, I speculate Cardenas tipped him off. However the leak occurred, a small team of commandos raided the island and disrupted the meeting just as we had reached an agreement. They killed dozens of men in the process including foreign dignitaries and nearly killed me on more than one occasion. I still can't believe I'm alive other than by divine protection. I think it was Galan's goal to wipe out every last person on that island and leave no evidence behind. Was this to cover up his corruption or was this a deliberate attempt to eliminate me as I pulled even in the electoral race with only a month to go? I suspect it's both, but I cannot say for certain."

Fowler paused briefly and then glared at the camera.

"What I *can* say is that it is inconceivable that a sitting president, a man sworn to uphold the Constitution, could even consider, let alone actually send his personal hit squad to assassinate the challenger to his presidency. A United States Senator, no less! The fact that Galan would have any American citizen savagely killed to preserve his reign of power should be immediate grounds for his arrest but, since we cannot arrest a sitting president, these actions should at the very least be grounds for impeachment. Therefore, I call upon my fellow citizens in the House of Representatives to open an inquiry into Articles of Impeachment immediately! It is their patriotic duty to act. Never, in all my years of service to the American people, have I seen such an egregious and unconscionable act come from the White House! Jorge

Galan claims to be fighting the cartels of Central and South America? He is more tyrannical, more *criminal* than all of the cartel leaders combined!" Fowler emphasized his last point by pounding his fist on the podium.

"Look," he said switching to a more somber tone as he leaned forward on the podium. "This is not the way we do things. We are Americans. We are just and we are fair. This, what these men have done, what Galan has done, this is a tremendous black eye on our nation's history. These are dark days…dark days, folks. But, as president, I promise I will lead us into better days. That's not just a campaign slogan, people. It's a promise. Now, I'll take your questions."

A flurry of questions arose from the press. Fowler pointed at a reporter off camera and called her name. "Yes, Joanne."

"Senator Fowler, in your statement, you alluded to the President's hit squad. Could you be more specific and what exactly did they do?"

"Thank you, Joanne. Yes, I did refer to Galan's hit squad. Now, whereas I cannot tell you just how many people are on this hit squad or who all they may be, I *can* tell you that I was personally attacked and assaulted by two Navy SEALs personally known to the president. I personally witnessed them brutally kill, in cold blood, several high-ranking foreign dignitaries. We are all familiar with these two men. They have found their way in and out of the press on several occasions over the past year, often for very sketchy reasons."

Galan tensed knowing where this was leading.

"I'm talking about Navy SEALs Lieutenant Commander Joseph O'Shanick and Master Chief Petty Officer Matthew Ramsey."

The screen briefly changed to side-by-side images of Joe and Ramsey's official service pictures. It was readily apparent that the press had been briefed ahead of time. This was no spontaneous press conference.

"As you may recall," Fowler continued as the screen returned to his live feed. "Lieutenant Commander O'Shanick made the news a few months ago after being rolled up in a multiple murder arrest with a known drug and prostitution ring. He somehow got out of the charges but the exact details of the incident and those regarding his involvement have been kept hidden from the public. A year ago,

O'Shanick and Master Chief Ramsey were personally awarded medals for their involvement in an incident with the cartels in Central America. It doesn't take a genius to connect the dots and realize that O'Shanick is Jorge Galan's personal henchman much like Heinrich Himmler was to Adolf Hitler in Nazi Germany. This man personally smashed my knee with a gun, shot two foreign dignitaries inside a flying helicopter, attempted to shoot me, and then pulled me out of the helicopter to fall from a height of over a hundred feet. After realizing I survived the fall, he then tried to strangle me in the water. His accomplice, Chief Matt Ramsey, threatened to throw me off a yacht in the middle of the Caribbean before narrowly missing me when he hurled a knife in my direction. I have personally spoken to the acting Special Agent in Charge of the FBI's Atlanta Field Office, Andrew Winkelman, regarding these incidents and he is in the process of having these two rogue Navy SEALs arrested and prosecuted as we speak."

The press erupted with more questions, most of them obviously scripted prior to the press conference. Fowler continued to pour it on about Galan's corruption and calling for his impeachment. A signals officer appeared at the door. He quietly walked in and whispered into Embry's ear. Embry nodded solemnly and the officer walked back out. Fowler's press conference ended a few minutes later. All eyes focused on their president.

"Mr. President," Embry spoke up. "I've just been informed that there are more developments."

Embry pointed the remote and switched the adjacent screens to other live news feeds. Over the next ten minutes, the entire room sat in repulsed silence as they watched alternating feeds of the simultaneous raids on the private residences of Dr. Christy Tabrizi, Charles Courtnall III, and Clay Whitmore. The news was particularly focused on O'Shanick and Ramsey. President Galan squinted his eyes shut and pinched the bridge of his nose to ward off a developing headache. He had been briefed on what went down in Belize, particularly Fowler's involvement. O'Shanick and Ramsey should be given a medal. Their selfless act of bravery had rescued a dozen or so innocent girls, restored several families, drove another nail into the inevitable coffin of the LFG cartel, and saved the American citizens from a treasonous

President who would sell them out to a dark globalist cabal. Or should have.

Did Fowler really have a chance to pull this off? Not without a lot of help. It would be his word against the testimony of two decorated Navy SEALs, a well-respected financial investor, a physician, and several girls who were abducted and sold into the sex slave industry. He *did* have the media, but would that be enough? Not a chance. There had to be something else. *What does that pompous sleezeball have up his sleeve?* Galan was going to have to rely on his tactical acumen to stay ahead, lest Fowler outmaneuver him on the political battlefield. With a month to go, Fowler would have to employ a dazzling smoke and mirrors act to spin a narrative that would keep him out of prison and sway the voters. But at what cost? This would likely further divide a nation that had already been divided by identity politics, ideological differences, and an increasingly volatile cancel culture. Not to mention the lives of those directly involved. In order to prevail, Fowler and his cronies would have to ensure the testimonies of the victims and their rescuers were discredited, spun, or kept from the public altogether. It would be the political version of a Hail Mary play but, as Galan looked at the televised coverage of O'Shanick and Ramsey being arrested along with the other innocent and heroic people, he knew the ball had already been snapped and the play was in motion.

Galan bit his lip in concentration as his eyes switched from one screen to another. Three different raids, all carried out simultaneously on live network news and in dramatic fashion no less. This was planned out and well-coordinated. *Madre de Dios!* Galan bolted upright in his chair.

"Preston!" Galan spoke with urgency looking at his Attorney General Preston Jacobs, on the secure video conference.

Jacobs knew what President Galan was asking just by the tone. He and Galan had known each other for years going back to when he was an attorney with the JAG Corps at Camp Pendleton. For years, Jacobs had successfully defended many of Galan's Marines. Most had been young, only a year or two out on their own, fueled up on alcohol and testosterone, who had wound up in the brig after throwing hands in the wrong place. A few had been more serious, but Jacobs and Galan had seen eye to eye that a little correction was the remedy rather than a criminal record. They had been in the business of making Marines and, just as important, good citizens, spouses, and parents. Jacobs had gone on to serve in private practice as both a defense and prosecuting attorney until Galan convinced him to run for Attorney General in California. He had served two terms with honor and distinction and was a natural pick to head up the Department of Justice.

"Mr. President, I am learning this, as you are, with no foreknowledge. I offer no excuses, sir. I have been completely blindsided, but I have already put my people into action."

"Those are *your* agents arresting brave American heroes on national news! If you weren't made aware of this, then, somebody saw fit to keep you in the dark and you have some serious housecleaning to do. May I *suggest* you start with Director Snyder! In fact, I want him patched in on this conference," Galan looked over at the signals officer and nodded. The signals officer ducked out of the conference room to make it happen.

"In the meantime, Preston," Galan continued. "It goes without saying that SAIC McPherson's homicide is likely connected to all of this. If they are willing to take a Federal Agent out, they will go after O'Shanick, Ramsey, and every last one involved. I don't want any mishaps while these people are in jail, and I don't want their families threatened either. See to it they are well looked after while we sort this mess out."

"I'm already on it, sir."

"I know you are, Preston," Galan said, lowering his voice. "And I know I'm coming down on you hard, but we have just been fired upon and we need to assess the situation as rapidly as possible and return fire."

"Yes, Mr. President," Jacobs answered, his square jaw clenched with a look of determination.

The image of FBI Director, Francis Snyder appeared on the screen. His tie was crooked, and he had the glassy eyes of someone who has been drinking. His image wobbled betraying the fact that he was conferencing on his smart phone from what appeared to be the lobby of a very upscale hotel.

"Frank, nice of you to join us," Galan said by way of greeting. "Where might you be?"

"I'm in South Bend for the Michigan game," Snyder said trying to sound sober. "How may I be of service, Mr. President?"

Galan leaned froward, dropped his chin and raised his eyebrows in shock. "You have got to be kidding me! One of your SAIC's was murdered this morning and you're three sheets to the wind at a post-game party?!"

"Sir," Snyder began in protest. "I've already named assistant SAIC Winkelman as acting SAIC of the Atlanta Field office and I've dispatched a team of agents to Atlanta to assist with the investigation as well as delegated several to poke around in DC. I have it under control and I've only had two beers. I swear!"

"BRAVO SIERRA, Frank!" Galan fired back. "I'm a Marine. I know a drunk when I see one. Since you have everything under control, perhaps you could explain to me why your agents just arrested the people who busted Senator Fowler, while he walks a free man, wearing a Brooks Brothers suit, demanding my impeachment on national TV?"

"Sir?" Snyder's glassy eyes now sported a deer in the headlights look.

"You heard me, Frank." Galan stared into the camera. "Are you telling me that you are unaware that your outfit has cleared Senator Fowler of all charges and let him walk while making a show of arresting the two Navy SEALs, the private investigator, and the father of one of the girls who was abducted by the Russian mafia?"

"Sir," Snyder's face became pale as he swallowed hard. "I can honestly tell you that this is the first I've heard of this. I offer no excuses. I have no idea how this could have happened, but I assure you I will find out. This is my department and I take full responsibility."

Galan stared at his FBI director. Snyder was a holdover from the previous administration and a member of the opposite party. Unlike many politicians, Galan was not a party loyalist. He was a patriot and a pragmatic problem solver. If people wanted to join him in solving real issues and making this world a better place, he could care less what their party affiliation was. Upon taking office, Galan interviewed and assessed all of the sitting department directors. Snyder had impressed him as a straight shooter, impartial and reliable. He was an Irish-Catholic family man who had spent a career in law enforcement and seemed well suited to run the FBI. Consequently, Galan saw no reason to replace him simply for being a previous administration holdover. He preferred to assemble the right team as opposed to playing political favoritism.

However, this was unacceptable. Galan was briefed on the Fowler arrest. He knew the facts. There was absolutely no reason Fowler should be walking free while honorable people like Joe O'Shanick and Matt Ramsey took the fall. A Special Agent in Charge had been murdered and a virtual coup de tat was being carried out by agents under Snyder's command and he was not only clueless but blitzed at a college football weekend. Galan believed in forgiveness, that everyone is human and prone to mistakes, Galan knew he would be where he was were it not for forgiveness and second chances, but this was irresponsible and Snyder had to be held accountable.

"Frank, you're in no condition to handle anything appropriately tonight. I'm extremely disappointed in you. I want you to go back to your hotel room before you embarrass this administration any more than you already have. Sober up, go to church tomorrow, and then compose your resignation letter. I will expect it on my desk Monday morning. You're dismissed."

"But, sir, I…"

"You're dismissed, Frank" Galan spoke more evenly.

Snyder swallowed and nodded glumly. His other arm appeared and moved toward the screen and then his feed deleted from the teleconference.

Galan looked at the signals officer. "Once this meeting is over, I will need to speak with FBI Deputy Director Wickenheiser."

"You don't want him now, sir?" Jacobs asked.

"No," Galan shook his head. "Either he didn't know or he's in on it. Won't help us now. We need to move on and plan our response."

Chapter 5

Atlanta, Georgia

The room was cold. Likely on purpose. It didn't help that Joe was wearing cargo shorts and a t-shirt. The arresting agents had handcuffed him to the table and left him there to chill, literally. It was a tactic. Joe had used it as well in Afghanistan. He could take it.

A major part of his BUD/S training was cold endurance. The Pacific Ocean off Coronado usually ranged from 55-60 degrees. The air temperature was often below 70 and dropped into the fifties at night. And it was almost always windy. Most of their twenty-seven weeks of training was either spent in the water or running wet and covered with sand in the cold blowing air. No one is ever fully prepared to endure the physical pain and mental challenges of BUD/S, and few survived it, but it was the never ending cold that Joe had found the most challenging. Treading water at night to the brink of hypothermia only to climb out for pushups and flutter kicks on a cold metal pier while sadistic BUD/s instructors sprayed cold water on them until it was time to jump back into the bay was more than nearly any sane person could endure. Yet he had and he would endure this, whatever this was.

The sudden turn of events had been as chaotic as they were shocking. A little over an hour ago, he had been snuggled up with Christy, sitting around a bonfire, looking out over the calm water of Lake Lanier, with Ramsey, Stacy and Christy's neighbor. It had been a perfect night and a nice decompress following the events of the previous three days. Events that had led them to a tiny island off the coast of Belize where they had not only rescued a dozen girls being trafficked as sex slaves but took down a cartel leader and busted that corrupt Senator Fowler in the middle of everything. It had been a good op. Still was. Joe knew they had done the right thing. Now, he sat in a small room, chained to a metal table while they tried to make him sweat, chill rather.

Whiskey Tango Foxtrot!

How in the world did Fowler wiggle off that hook? The fact that he was able to pin this on Galan and get federal agents to round Joe and everyone else up in front of waiting news cameras was alarming. This went way up the food chain and involved a lot of players. The fact that it was well planned and coordinated and also executed in less than twenty-four hours spoke volumes of the level of involvement. Some might call it a "Deep State," but Joe had seen bureaucracy and corruption sweep through the government like a plague. The higher the level of government, the worse the disease. Years of scandals, political backbiting, identity politics of division, and countless wars directed by politicians who tied the hands of the warriors they sent into battle had left a sour taste in Joe's mouth towards government in general. President Galan and a handful of senators and congressmen the rare exceptions.

So what is Fowler's plan? Or whoever is backing him. Joe was convinced they had rock solid evidence of many offenses to hang Fowler, treason chief among them. How had he turned all that around and how could they believe they could beat this legally?

Joe's thoughts were interrupted by the door opening. Special Agent Cleveland walked in. He remained standing as he slowly shut the door while glaring at Joe. The shades were drawn but Joe spotted at least two cameras up near the ceiling.

"You just went from hero to zero, dipwad," Cleveland sneered. "How you like them apples?"

Joe silently stared up at the agent. His green eyes betraying no emotions.

"This would be a good time to come clean," Cleveland offered.

Joe remained calm and quiet.

"Failure to speak is an admission of guilt in my book, you treasonous slime. Now's your chance to speak if you want to change my mind," he said as he dropped a pen and legal pad down on the table. "If you cooperate, the judge might just be willing to let you out on bail."

"That judge is gonna put *you* in jail if you persist without my attorney," Joe answered.

"Yeah, good luck with that," Cleveland snickered. "No decent attorney is gonna touch your case with a ten-foot pole. A big loss on national TV? Ain't happening, hero. You'll get whatever public defender comes up next in the rotation. Maybe he or she is true believer and will fight to get you a reduced sentence and maybe you'll get some law school bottom dweller who couldn't get hired by a real firm. Either way, you're facing some hard time. On the other hand, if you tell us what we need to know, now, we will recommend a light sentence for your cooperation."

"I'd like to call an attorney please," Joe spoke directly.

"It's your funeral," Cleveland said as he opened the door and stepped out, slamming it shut behind him.

Bad cop, Joe thought to himself as the door reverberated in the small quiet room.

The minutes ticked by in silence as Joe thought about who best to call for an attorney. He would start with his dad. His parents were now likely aware that he had been arrested. It was all over national news. Even if they hadn't been watching TV, somebody had surely called them. His mother would have her friends praying right now while his dad was probably on the phone with his sailing buddy, Tom Brinkworth, a defense attorney back home. "Brinks," as Joe's dad called him, had helped Joe with his legal issues last June when he had his run in with the mafia. If he couldn't help out down in Atlanta, he might be able to point them to someone who could. Hopefully, he would be able to represent Ramsey, Christy, and Stacy as well. Man, what a mess.

The door opened and a smaller man with a missing chin and big forehead stepped in wearing a grey suit and blue tie with yellow stripes.

This will be the good cop, Joe thought to himself.

"Lieutenant Commander O'Shanick, my name is Andrew Winkelman, the acting Special Agent in Charge of the Atlanta Field

Office," he said as he pulled out a metal chair opposite Joe and sat down. "Would you mind if I ask you a few questions?"

"Once I have adequate legal counsel present, I will be happy to answer your questions, sir."

"I see," Winkelman nodded as he folded his hands together on the table. "Well, it is certainly your right to have an attorney. We will have one appointed for you, but it will not be until tomorrow and it may be another day or two before you are able to be represented before the federal magistrate for your bond hearing and arraignment."

"I understand but I would like to contact my own attorney to represent me along with Master Chief Ramsey, Doctor Tabrizi, and Doctor Morgan."

"Well, let me inform you that there is currently no arrest warrant for Dr. Morgan and she was released at the scene. In regard to you, Master Chief Ramsey, and Dr. Tabrizi, yes, you are free to arrange for any representation you like, but let me caution you, this will be a high-profile case that will garner national attention. You and your associates are being charged with a number of serious federal crimes and the evidence is strongly against you. I highly doubt many attorneys, worth their salt, will look at this and willingly choose to risk their reputation by representing a nationally, scratch that, *internationally* broadcast case that has a near certain chance of conviction. So, I'll tell you what," Winkelman said as he leaned forward and lowered his voice. "You seem like a smart guy. I think you know that the Department of Justice is after the president. They can likely nail him without your testimony; however, a signed confession from either you or one of your two associates would go a long way toward wrapping this up quickly and sparing the nation of a rather drawn out and likely divisive political circus. No one wants that. I'm sure you would prefer not to spend the next few years the subject of national scrutiny while you rot in a prison cell facing a life sentence. I think the federal prosecutors would be willing to keep your exposure minimal and offer a significantly reduced sentence were you to provide such a confession. What do you say?"

"I'm not saying or doing anything without an attorney present," Joe answered.

"Hmm," Winkelman said as he steepled his fingers under what passed for his chin. "I'm surprised to hear that, Mr. O'Shanick. I understand you graduated near the top of your class at the Naval Academy. That tells me you are an intelligent man. I don't understand why you would want to take the fall for a corrupt president who ordered you to commit such heinous crimes."

Joe fought the urge to speak out. There had been no such order and President Galan had absolutely no involvement in that rescue operation whatsoever. The feds *had* to know that and were just trying to bait him into a confession. He wanted so much to set Winkelman straight, but he was not well versed in the legal realm and did not know whether speaking out would help or hurt his cause. Better to wait for an attorney.

"Perhaps Mr. Ramsey or Dr. Tabrizi would be willing be willing to sign a confession instead. That would leave you hanging out to dry, but it would at least get one or both of them a reduced sentence. Possibly even immunity," Winkelman raised his eyebrows with a slight grin of enticement.

Joe merely shrugged his shoulders in response. He wasn't taking the bait and he wasn't signing his name to a lie. Neither would Ramsey or Christy. Of that, Joe was certain.

"Of course, Mr. O'Shanick, if it were *you* who was to sign a confession indicating you were ordered by President Galan, then it's likely all three of you could receive immunity. The Department of Justice isn't all that interested in prosecuting two decorated war heroes who were merely following orders. Nor are they interested in prosecuting a highly respected physician who was simply there to provide medical support. They are more interested in taking down a corrupt administration, which I think you and I can both agree that would be in the best interest of our country. After all, you and I both swore an oath to protect and defend the Constitution. Isn't that right?" Winkelman tilted his head in expectation.

Joe simply stared back and said nothing. These guys were clearly going after President Galan. If they had any shred of evidence, they wouldn't be trying to entice Joe into signing his name to a false confession. Wasn't that right? The fact that they were able to spring Fowler so quickly gave him pause. Charges had been leveled at Joe, Ramsey, and Christy out of nowhere and then their subsequent arrests were pulled off in dramatic fashion in front of TC crews from nearly every major network. Joe was also mindful that the weak-chinned man sitting across from him had just replaced his boss who had been shot, assassination style, while out for his morning run on a golf course. There was definitely a well-coordinated movement at play. Despite the testimonies and evidence in their favor, could he along with Ramsey and Christy be found guilty and imprisoned for their roles in a rescue operation? Was this actually possible? The events of the last twenty-four hours seemed to indicate that. Winkelman had quickly sweetened the deal and now an immunity offer was being made. Should he consider it? If not for him for Ramsey, his closest friend and brother in combat? What about Christy? Could Joe bear the thought of the woman he loved, the most honorable and altruistic person he knew, spending the rest of her life in prison? No, he couldn't, but he also could not even consider selling out an honorable president, certainly the finest Commander in Chief Joe had ever served under, by signing his name to a lie. That was a no go for sure.

Winkelman pushed the legal pad and pen over to Joe. "One last chance, Mr. O'Shanick. Your signed confession and the three of you walk with immunity. This offer is only good tonight."

Joe looked down at the pad. He pushed it back across the table, leaned back in his chair and glared at Winkelman defiantly.

Chapter 6

Air Force One

"Mr. President?" The signals officer spoke from the door. "FBI Deputy Director Wickenheiser is ready to join the meeting."

"Let's have him," Galan answered.

Galan drained the rest of his coffee and set the China cup back down on its saucer. That would have to be it. He would likely be up for a while after they got back to Washington, but he wanted to be able to fall asleep when the time finally came. He looked to the screen on the bulkhead and saw FBI Deputy Director Wickenheiser appear among the others.

"James, thank you for joining us on such short notice," Galan said in greeting. "Please tell me you have a handle on what's going on over there."

"Indeed I do, Mr. President," Wickenheiser answered. He was average build, mid-forties, mostly bald with just a trace of sandy blond hair. His round glasses made him look more like an accountant than the career federal law enforcement officer he was.

"Good, because your immediate superior has been asleep at the wheel. I am strongly considering naming you acting FBI director come Monday morning depending on what I see out of you these next thirty-six hours. So tell me what you know," Galan finished.

"Mr. President, let me begin by saying that everything that transpired over the past twenty-four hours has been on my watch. The fact the Director Snyder was unaware is on me. I kept him out of the loop, sir."

"Explain, please," Galan said as he motioned for Wickenheiser to continue.

"Mr. President, Director Snyder has been doing an outstanding job running the Bureau. He is a perfectionist and utterly devoted to his job but, as a result, which leaves him often burning the candle at both ends. He planned this weekend at Notre Dame with his friends last spring. Nevertheless, upon Senator Fowler's arrest, he was going to cancel his trip so he could remain in town to oversee the process. I knew how much that trip meant to him and, even more so, how much he needed just a weekend to get away and let his hair down, so to speak. I told him I would handle things and encouraged him to go. I purposefully kept him out of the loop just to give him one day to enjoy without the hassles of work. So, if I may, sir, please don't hold this against him. Director Snyder was not being derelict in his duties. He is one of the finest men to ever run the Bureau and if you're looking for someone to place in your crosshairs, then it should be me, sir."

"I admire your loyalty, James, and I'll take what you've said into consideration," Galan answered. "Now, please walk me through the events of the last twenty-four hours. How in the world is Robert Fowler a free man, calling for my impeachment, while the two decorated Navy SEALs who busted his rear end are in jail?"

"Well, sir, to put it simply, the most recent evidence has dictated the course of events over the past twenty-four hours."

"What *evidence* are you referring to," Galan asked keeping his voice calm. "I was briefed on what went down in Belize and what Fowler was wrapped up in. He was caught trying to rape an abducted American citizen while a guest of the LFG cartel at their own version of Epstein Island!"

"I understand, sir," Wickenheiser continued unfazed. "Yes, the preliminary evidence and testimonies appeared damning to Senator Fowler, but we've since learned more and things are not as they originally seemed."

"Try me," Galan challenged.

"Well, sir, first off, we have conflicting testimonies. On one hand there's the testimony of Lieutenant Commander O'Shanick and Master Chief Ramsey, while, on the other hand we have the testimony of a sitting United States senator, who happens to be your opponent. He makes a convincing case that you sent Ramsey and O'Shanick after him. Now, I…"

"Deputy Director Wickenheiser, I did nothing of the sort and there is *no* evidence to suggest otherwise," Galan said firmly.

"Mr. President, I understand your frustration and I'm not out to get you, but it is my sworn duty to remain impartial and to follow the evidence. Having said that, yes, on the surface, it seems Senator Fowler was found in a very compromising position. However, he maintains that he was there in a diplomatic role."

"And you believe that Bravo Sierra?" Galan asked incredulously.

"Sir, it's my job to reserve judgment until all of the facts have been considered but the fact is, it's his word against O'Shanick and Ramsey's and there is an island full of dead bodies and there are several dead foreign dignitaries and that doesn't paint a flattering picture of your two SEALs who had no business being there in the first place."

"They were there helping rescue several girls who were *abducted* by the cartels to be used as sex slaves, three of whom are American Citizens!"

"Be that as it may, sir," Wickenheiser continued, "they had no relationship with these women, they were not acting in any official capacity, they *illegally* invaded a foreign nation and killed over a dozen people who were there legally. O'Shanick and Ramsey had no right to be there and, as such, any testimony they might have against Senator Fowler will be unlikely to hold up in a court of law and that's *if* said testimonies would even be allowed. Conversely, sir, I have the sworn statement of a sitting and well-respected United States senator, who was an invited guest on a diplomatic mission, who is an eyewitness to the murder of over a dozen people including an Iranian deputy defense minister and the personal advisor to China's president. The senator also testifies to O'Shanick physically assaulting him, throwing him out of a helicopter, and attempting to drown him. The sworn statement O'Shanick gave to SAIC McPherson is nearly identical with the exception that he states he wasn't trying to kill Senator Fowler. Furthermore, we have been provided with the sworn statement of the helicopter pilot who witnessed it all. I had no choice but to release Senator Fowler and arrest O'Shanick and Ramsey, sir."

"Along with Dr. Tabrizi, Charles Courtnall, and the team of private investigators he hired to locate and rescue his *daughter* who was abducted from a college campus and sold to the cartel!" Galan retorted. "Have you even considered what they witnessed? How does the statement of a corrupt senator who was found molesting a girl on a cartel-owned island outweigh that of two decorated Navy SEALs, a physician, a highly-respected businessman, his victimized daughter, and a reputable private investigator?!"

JJ Embry had been silently taking notes as he followed the back and forth between his boss and the assistant FBI director. He caught President Galan's eye and subtly motioned with his hand for Galan to ease his escalating rhetoric.

"Mr. President," Wickenheiser continued. "With all due respect, none of the people you just named saw anything. Dr. Tabrizi and Mr. Courtnall were waiting offshore in a boat. Mr. Whitmore and Miss Courtnall both suffered concussions. The only eyewitness testimony is from O'Shanick and Ramsey, the two men who admitted to killing everyone."

"To save over a dozen young girls who were being held as sex slaves!" Galan shot back. "One of whom was nearly raped by the senator whom *you* let go! And you favor his word over those of the honorable men and a woman who risked their lives to rescue those women!"

Aaron Sprole, President Galan's chief political advisor, joined JJ Embry in trying to subtly motion for their boss to remain calm. President Galan was a principled man and a seasoned combat veteran who remained calm in a storm, but he was also a passionate man, fiercely loyal and protective of those with whom he served. Good people had been arrested, the *wrong* people and it was inflaming Galan's dedication to the point of affecting his demeanor. Like Embry, Sprole could see this was going to be the political fight of the century and he did not want his boss's righteous passion to lead to a single destructive move, no matter how properly motivated he may be.

"Mr. President," Wickenheiser responded calmly. "I don't favor anyone. I weigh the evidence and, in this case, the scale tips in favor of Senator Fowler and my actions were based on that. I don't like arresting decorated heroes like Lieutenant Commander O'Shanick and Master Chief Ramsey, but I was compelled to do so by the evidence. We will continue to investigate and, if the evidence ultimately exonerates them, then I will be more than happy to drop their charges. In the meantime, the Bureau must pursue this investigation without prejudice as I would hope you expect us to."

Galan took a deep breath to calm his rising anger. He looked directly into the camera and spoke. "Mr. Wickenheiser, when you say, 'without prejudice,' does that include preplanned coordination with network news agencies so they can be present to televise your agents dramatically raiding private residences and arresting these people on live TV?"

"No, sir, it certainly does not. I have no idea how the media found out, but I am looking into it. Someone leaked it. We had several operations ongoing simultaneously, involving numerous agents and personnel. The leak could have come from anywhere, sir."

"Very well," Galan sighed. "Find it and fix it ASAP, Deputy Director Wickenheiser. I'll take your comments regarding Director Snyder under advisement. In the meantime, you are to report any new developments directly to Attorney General Jacobs. I'm sure we will be speaking again soon. You're dismissed for now."

"Thank you, Mr. President," Wickenheiser said before his feed was disconnected.

"Thoughts?" Galan said as he leaned back in his chair.

Political Advisor Sprole immediately spoke up. "Sir, I know Deputy Director Wickenheiser comes across as fair and impartial, but he and Director Snyder are both holdovers from the previous administration and I don't trust him as far as I can throw him. The FBI just launched the biggest October surprise in the history of elections, and he is currently the one at the controls."

"I'm going to second that, Mr. President," Attorney General Jacobs chimed in. "Up 'til now, I've always considered him to be a straight shooter but, like you, I have seen all of the evidence he is referring to and we come to vastly different conclusions. There are any number of ways he could have acted on this, but he chose the most damaging way. I was willing to give him the doubt and see how he proceeded until he played off the raids being covered by the media. True, a number of people were involved but at the local level. I'm willing to venture that only a handful of people had knowledge that three separate raids were being conducted and even fewer knew the precise times and locations. I think the leak came directly from his office. I'm not so sure I would be in a rush to promote him to the director's office."

"Along those lines, sir," Embry spoke up. "I think firing Director Snyder would be the wrong move at this time."

"I'm reconsidering that myself, JJ," Galan answered as he inclined his head to one side. "But I'm interested to hear your reasons."

"Well, first off, I think Aaron and Attorney General Jacobs are correct in their assessment of Wickenheiser. He's running this operation and, no matter what he says, what they did was a direct attack on this administration underscoring what Fowler said in his speech tonight. Second, if you were to fire Director Snyder in response to this political stunt, it would immediately be spun to make you look like you're trying to stack the deck in your favor. Third, Director Snyder *has* been doing a good job and probably was kept out of the loop by his subordinates. Maybe Wickenheiser was trying to give his boss a weekend off or maybe he knew Snyder would not go for the stunt they pulled tonight. Regardless, Snyder might just be the only one you can trust among the FBI brass right now. I'd rather take our chances with him in the top seat than turn things over to Wickenheiser. We'll keep a close watch on him and, if he turns out to be less than stellar, we can always get rid of him at a later date."

"Is anyone else concerned that Wickenheiser went to bat for Snyder and actually encouraged me not to hold him accountable?" Galan asked.

"Yes, sir, I thought about that too," Sprole replied. "If he really is operating on behalf of the Fowler campaign, then he isn't interested in having you name him the new director. He would rather ensure a Fowler win and get his new title with the winning organization. No baggage that way and perhaps a bigger title."

Several heads nodded in response. Galan reclined in his chair, one hand resting upon the table, eyes narrowed in thought. He slowly nodded.

"Alright, Snyder stays for now."

"Would you like me to notify him, Mr. President?" Jacobs asked.

"No, Preston. I'll call him myself. Tomorrow morning. I want him to lose a little sleep over this. It's still his Bureau, a major arrest occurred and an SAIC was killed on his watch, not to mention the events of this evening. Even those his staff may have kept him out of the loop, he needs to remain more vigilant. I want to make sure he gets that message. If he really is a straight shooter, I suspect he will return to his desk ready to clean house and see to it his shop is running clean. If that's the case, he may be one of our best allies when all this is said and done."

Chapter 7

Atlanta, Georgia

Midtown Atlanta was lit up in a dazzling array of well-lit modern architecture. Joe sat in the back of the Bureau car and watched the cityscape fly by as the headed south on I-75/85. They passed the IBM tower to their left while the Georgia Tech campus approached on their right including the former Olympic Village just beyond. Further ahead, the skyscrapers of downtown Atlanta loomed, shining brightly against the dark night.

He had no idea where they were headed. Nobody was saying much of anything. He hadn't seen Ramsey or Christy since they had been arrested at Christy's house. After refusing to answer Winkelman's questions, Joe had been given his one phone call. His father assured him he would arrange for an attorney and that his entire family was praying for him and his friends. They were going to need it.

Joe was averse to conspiracy theories but this sure seemed like he was in the middle of one. Here he was, a day after bringing home a treasonous senator whom they caught in the act while rescuing a dozen abducted girls and now he was in handcuffs along with his friends who helped him? Outrageous! They had Fowler dead to rights; Tupolev, Cardenas, and the cartel as well. Fowler didn't spring himself and reverse the charges to result in all of these arrests. He had to have friends in high places. A lot of them and they had to be everywhere. The FBI, the Department of Justice, courts, media, Congress, everywhere. Should he be surprised? For nearly his entire life he had seen the nation becoming more and more polarized. He had been a child when Bill Clinton was president but, even then, it had seemed like there was so much tribalism between Democrats and Republicans and that had only been further broken down by identity politics. With the brief exception of the terrorist attacks on 9/11, many people had stopped being Americans in favor victim groups and status groups. They had surrendered individual thought and critical thinking for groupthink and animosity toward those outside their defined group. The ensuing power struggle had ushered in an abandonment of moral decency and respect. Ultimately that had led to an ends-justify-the-means pursuit of dominancy. If SAIC McPherson's murder was a part of this, then it had already reached a survival of the fittest contest and there would be no rules. No one was safe in this winner take all contest. At least no one who still stood for decency and morality.

President Galan did not have a "hit squad" and he wasn't ordering the death of people like some organized crime boss. He would follow the rules of a decent society. So would those who worked for him. Would that prevail against Fowler and whatever cabal was backing him? Joe hoped so. He wanted to believe that good ultimately triumphed over evil. The question was, would it?

His thoughts turned to Christy as they exited onto I-20 heading east. His "Epstein didn't kill himself" reference to Ramsey had not been in jest. If McPherson could be targeted for execution, the people who could put Fowler away certainly would be targets. There were ample opportunities to be targeted for death in jail. After all, jails weren't filled with choirboys. These were violent offenders, gang members, and the like, many of them repeat offenders. Those with lengthy sentences had nothing to lose and killed for fun. Others had affiliations that made them obligated to carry out orders. Yes, Joe and Ramsey would be marked. They knew to keep their heads on a swivel. But what about Christy? She had been with them in Belize. She had provided medical care to the victims. She had been aboard when Tupolev was captured and later Fowler. Her testimony alone could put both men away for a long time. She would definitely be a target.

After only a mile, Special Agent Cleveland, quietly exited off I-20 onto SE Boulevard while Joe continued to dwell on Christy.

He and Ramsey were highly-trained special warfare operators. They were highly skilled in hand-to-hand combat, situational awareness, and knew how to kill. Despite all of that, they were still facing steep odds of survival, if actually marked for death in a prison. The cartel affiliates alone would be clawing all over each other for a chance to take out the man who took down several cartel heads including the notorious "El Serpiente," Hector Cruz. A well-armed platoon of his SEALs might be able to handle them, but just he and Ramsey against numerous hardened criminals? That was an entirely different matter. But what about Christy? She wasn't a trained warrior. She was a physician. A compassionate healer with a gentle heart. Not that she couldn't handle herself. Joe had seen her do so on several occasions, but could she survive in a prison if marked for death? He didn't want to think about it.

Just a couple of days ago, he had nearly asked her to marry him. They had talked about it several times and knew that's where they were headed. He had simply decided to wait so he could ask her in a traditional and honorable way. She deserved that. She was the most honorable and amazing woman he had ever met. The fact that she was interested in a knuckle dragging pipe hitter like him still blew his mind, but he wasn't about to question it. He knew it was beyond him. In fact, he truly believed their entire relationship had been a divine appointment.

They had met, last year, during a blown rescue op and ultimately had escaped together. Despite her exquisite beauty, he had originally been turned off by her devout Christian faith. Joe was an agnostic, if not an atheist at the time, but over the past year, a friendship had developed. A friendship where Christy had humbly demonstrated her genuine faith. A faith she had lovingly and effectively proven to Joe was based, not on a hope or blind trust but on ample evidence. Joe now believed. He had seen the evidence. Christ was real and He is who He said He is. He had placed Christy in Joe's life to communicate that life altering truth to his hardened prideful heart. But that wasn't all. He had given them an amazing relationship and the promise of a bright future together. Joe had actually seen a vision of he and Christy with their future children. They had even discussed adopting two of the girls they had rescued from the sex trafficking rings. Had it all just been wishful thinking? Would they ever get out of these charges to live the future they had envisioned.

Joe was convinced that the truth was on their side. They had evidence and the corroborating testimony of several people to not only exonerate themselves but to bring Senator Fowler to justice. They just had to make it to the courtroom. They had to survive.

The car approached McDonough Boulevard Southeast. A large gothic building loomed ahead, lit up brightly. They crossed the intersection and drove through the entrance, which was flanked by two large white arches that matched the building. A sign read:

United States Penitentiary
Atlanta

Chapter 8

South Bend, Indiana

The storied campus of the University of Notre Dame was abuzz with activity as thousands of students and alumni lingered late into the evening following their team's victory over Michigan. The stadium lights were still on, washing the surrounding campus in their glow. Nestled in the heart of the tree-lined campus, the Morris Inn sat just a short walk from the stadium. The opulent hotel kept busy hosting weddings and conferences year-round and sold out every home game weekend.

Frank Snyder sat at the corner of the Morris Inn's upscale bar. Save for the nearly empty glass in front of him, he was alone. His law school reunion, being held in a large conference room down the hall, had begun to dwindle. Several of his classmates had invited him to go with them to hit up some of their old watering holes but Frank had declined. He had lost his celebratory mood after his video chat with President Galan.

His wife, Lynn, had called him within minutes after he had hung up with the president. She had seen the news reports and immediately called him to get the real story. An attorney herself, she worked for a large lobbying firm in Washington that stood to gain a lot were there to be a Fowler White House. Her initial excitement quickly dissipated when she sensed the despair in her husband's voice on the other end of the line. After a few moments of inquisition and badgering, Frank had told her what happened. Lynn had given him an earful. Her private lobbying salary far outweighed what he had been earning as the FBI's director but that didn't stop her from reminding him that they had three children attending a costly private school on top of a multimillion-dollar house to pay for in McLean, Virginia. No longer having a husband running the FBI, a well-known husband who also had a personal relationship with the president, would put a hurt on her lobbying position. Although that certainly was true, he suspected she was more concerned about her status in the pecking order of the Washington elites. He tried to calm her down by emphasizing that President Galan was allowing him to resign which should allow him to fetch a well-paying job in the private sector or even on the speaking circuit but she wasn't having any of it tonight. She abruptly told him to enjoy his night at Notre Dame because things were going to be frigid when he arrived back home. He briefly considered trying to get in contact with President Galan and begging for another chance but doubted the president would even take his call.

Frank looked down at the other end of the bar where a spry fifty-ish appearing bartender named Jimmy stood wearing black pants with a matching vest over a white shirt with a blue and gold striped tie. He was animatedly relating a story to a well-dressed group of Fighting Irish fans. He finished his story to the roaring laughter of his captive audience and looked over at Frank who signaled for a refill. He reached up to the top shelf, grabbed a bottle and trotted over to Frank's corner. A stunning petite blond woman slid into the seat that shared the corner as Jimmy began to pour a double measure into Frank's glass. Her long hair was pulled up revealing sharp facial features, a small nose, and dazzling blue eyes. She wore a short dark leather jacket over a conservative but stylish white button-down blouse. Her athletic, pixie-like appearance reminded Frank of an Olympic figure skater.

"What'll ya have, me jewel?" Jimmy asked with his native Irish lilt.

"I think I try what he is having," she answered with a Russian accent looking over at Frank with a questioning look.

"Connemara?" Frank questioned back.

"And what is dat?"

"It's a twelve-year-old peated single malt Irish Whiskey, lass. Guaranteed to make your blue eyes as green as Dublin in springtime," Jimmy charmed as he held up the bottle in display.

"Is good, *da?*" she asked, looking at Frank who simply nodded back.

"*Da,*" she said pointing down at the bar. "I try. When in Rome, they say."

Jimmy placed a glass on the bar and poured her a single measure. He watched as she took a sip and nodded her approval. Jimmy smiled in return and poured another measure. He turned and began to head back to the other end.

"Where you going, Meester Irishman?" she asked.

Jimmy stopped and turned back to see the woman place three crisp hundred-dollar bills on the bar.

"Leave the bottle with us," she looked over at Frank and coyly smiled.

Jimmy placed the bottle down between them, winked at Frank, and returned to the other end of the bar.

Chapter 9

Atlanta, Georgia

Senator Robert Fowler exited his limousine and, favoring his right knee, slowly climbed the stairs into his campaign aircraft. He stepped into the modified 737, shrugged out of his suit coat, and handed it to a waiting attendant. He loosened his tie as he dropped into his customary seat near the front of the plane. He was average build with a slight bulge at the waistline. His once sandy blond hair was mostly gray, a shaggy medium length that did not hold up well under the makeup artists hairspray. His face was tanned and weathered from years of playing golf in the Arizona sun.

Theron Belknap, Fowler's chief of staff, handed over a crystal rocks glass, with a double measure of Maker's Mark, as he sat down in the adjacent seat. They clinked glasses and sipped their drinks in silence as the rest of the entourage finished boarding. The fact that they were *both* sitting here and still on the campaign trail, was not lost on them. Fowler looked over at his chief of staff and cracked a grin.

"We're gonna owe a lot of people, aren't we?" he asked.

"It's a considerable list and it's only begun, Robert," Belknap replied somberly. There's a lot of work to be done if we're going to fix this mess."

"Just get me across that finish line. We only have a month to go. Once I'm in the White House, we're set," Fowler said as he flashed a cocksure smile.

"*A month?*" Belknap whispered harshly. "It only took you a *day* to nearly sink this campaign you idiot! I *told* you to stay home. I even offered to arrange for a couple of girls to entertain you at your condo in Flagstaff, but you wouldn't even do that! Instead, you had to sneak off to the cartel's orgy island where you got caught with your pants down with a kidnapped American! Do you have *any* idea the strings we had to pull to spring you?"

"Yes, Theron, I…"

"Do you have any idea how many palms I had to grease in the last twenty-four hours? How many political chips I had to cash in?" Belknap stabbed the air with his index finger pointed at Fowler. Something caught his eye, and he looked up the aisle. "Speaking of which, one of those chips just boarded the plane. We'll talk about this later. For now, play nice!"

A portly man with thick gray hair waddled up to the seating area. He wore a light blue and white pinstriped seersucker suit with a light blue bow tie. He smiled brightly, displaying artificially whitened teeth that served to point out his bulbous red nose.

"Well, if it isn't my honorable colleague from Georgia!" Fowler charmed. "To what do we owe the pleasure, Senator Williams?"

"Well, I was wondering if I might hitch a ride with you up to Washington. Seems like we're going to have quite the busy day tomorrow and I'd just as soon get a start on things tonight. May I?" Williams drawled, gesturing towards the empty seat across from Fowler.

"Why, we'd be delighted," Fowler said pouring the charm on a bit too thick. "Can I interest you in a libation?" Fowler asked holding up his already half drank bourbon.

"You're too kind, Senator," Williams said as he dropped his flabby bulk down into the large seat facing his colleague.

Belknap signaled the flight attendant to come take Williams' order as another portly man dressed in a charcoal gray suit appeared and sat down next to Senator Williams. His name was Drake Beaumont, Senator Fowler's campaign chairman. He looked similar to Senator Williams in many respects, the one exception being his gray hair was thinning at a rapid pace.

"Just got an early poll back," Beaumont announced cheerfully, as he accepted drinks from the flight attendant and handed one to Williams. "Tonight's events seem to be having the desired effect. We've pulled even with Galan!" Nobody verbalized the word *president* when referring to Jorge Galan. Fowler had given strict instructions.

With strained effort, Senator Williams leaned forward and fist bumped Fowler. "Now that's good news!"

"Yes, it is," Fowler nodded at the small group and held up his drink. "And I know you three have been instrumental in resurrecting this campaign. I know I wouldn't be here without you. Each of you. Thank you," he said somberly. His face broke into a smile. "Now here's to a Fowler White House!"

"Here, here!" The men proclaimed as they clinked glasses.

Fowler drained his glass and silently vowed to himself to nurse the next one as the flight attendant handed him a full glass. He made no pretense of trying not to look at his eyes lasciviously followed the brunette's shapely form up the aisle. Belknap quietly cleared his throat and nudged his boss back into the matter at hand.

"Okay," Fowler said as he sat back and crossed his legs. "So where do we go from here?"

"Well, sir," Beaumont said as he leaned in and spoke quietly while the plane began its taxi. "From my end, we need to put your incident in the rearview mirror while we focus on making Galan look like the corrupt one. I've been on the phone all day with every major and minor media outlet and they're all on board. So long as nothing materializes in the courtroom, they will ignore the matter altogether while focusing the narrative as Galan's collusion with the cartel. For the next month, the footage of Galan's stooges being arrested will play on every newscast until they become the poster children for a corrupt Galan administration."

"Which means they can never step foot inside a courtroom or talk to any press," Belknap cautioned as he looked across to Senator Williams. "Nothing. We can't have any chance of anything swaying public opinion."

"It's being handled," Williams nodded confidently. "Which brings up another issue. The governor is willing to play ball, but she is going to expect something big in return and HUD won't cut it."

"Oh c'mon, Jeff," Fowler began acting annoyed. "HUD is still a cabinet spot. Don't make me give her a higher spot where I would actually have to regularly interact with that miserable frumpopotamus. I'm not giving her SecState when most of this is a federal issue that's out of her control. There isn't that much she can do. We all know this is you trying to keep your son out of jail from his hooker getting killed at his house."

"No, you listen here, Robert!" Senator Williams sat up straight, face beet red, pointing a chubby finger at Fowler. "That *hooker* died in a hospital after being shot by one of Tupolev's minions. She happened to be one of those girls Tupolev's organization abducted from various college campuses. Those same girls *you* were caught with in Tupolev's and the cartel's company. An incident that I and many others, Governor Maynard-Worthington included, are all trying to make disappear for *your* benefit. If she were to ask for vice president, you would have no choice but to give it to her, but she's not about to ask you to change your ticket at the last minute. She will settle for secretary of state and she will settle for nothing less."

Fowler sat speechless, not knowing whether to be angry or take heed. Belknap stepped in.

"If she does her part and helps us get Senator Fowler across the finish line, secretary of state will be hers," Belknap said. "But that means, nothing, and I mean nothing of what really went on down in Belize can come to light. No courts, no press, no books, nothing. O'Shanick, Ramsey, Courtnall, the chick doctor, the investigator, they get buried and they don't come up for air. Ever, as far as I'm concerned. The entire incident needs to go away. You do that and you and the governor will enjoy the good graces of the Fowler administration. Now, we need your reassurance that you can handle this."

"Now, I have no sway over in North Carolina where Courtnall and the investigator are being held; Georgia is my state. Everything has already been set in motion. The SEALs have been separated and expedited to the general population at the Federal Penitentiary in Atlanta. They won't even have the customary few days in receiving and processing. In fact, they may already be with the inmates as we speak. And not just any inmates, mind you," Williams held his index finger up to expound on a point. "They will be housed among the most violent murderers, rapists, and gang members. Tupolev and the cartels have people on the inside. O'Shanick and Ramsey won't live to see the courtroom. Same goes for Dr. Tabrizi. Governor Maynard-Worthington assures me that the warden will place her in gen-pop with the most ruthless women in her facility. She won't stand a chance."

"And we can be sure this won't blow back on us?" Fowler asked.

"Leave it to us, Jeff," Williams leaned back and sipped his drink. "Dead men tell no tales."

"And what do you want out of all of this?" Fowler asked.

"Senate Majority leader, your cooperation of every major effort we undertake, and unrestricted access to your office."

"We're both in the same party, Jeff," Fowler nodded. "I don't have any problem with any of that, so long as you see to it all my justice appointments are confirmed and all of my proposals sail through."

"There, you see?" Williams flashed his campaign smile. "It looks like we both have a vested interest in getting you over the finish line."

Fowler grunted in acknowledgment.

"Oh," Williams winced. "Tupolev will be expecting a pardon the first week you're in office.

Fowler pinched the bridge of his nose and grimaced. "Of course, but if this blows up in our faces and word gets out, we'll all go down together," he warned.

"Then I guess we will just have to pool our resources and make sure that doesn't happen then," Williams said, steely eyed as he peered at Fowler over his drink. "Won't we?"

Chapter 10

Atlanta, Georgia

𝐁 uilt in 1902, United States Penitentiary, Atlanta has been home to some of the most notorious and dangerous criminals in the nation. The infamous Chicago gangster, Al Capone once served time at USP Atlanta. Despite many additions and upgrades over the century, the facility remained a notoriously miserable place for one to serve one's sentence. Cold and drafty during the winter, unbearably hot during the summer, and dangerous. Always dangerous.

Joe had been moved through the Receiving and Classification center in record time. Usually, this process often entailed several days of finger printing, physical and mental health exams, observation, and strip searches. However, in Joe's case, the process had been expedited on order from the warden. A little more than two hours after arrival and Joe was wearing a pair of khaki prison scrubs while standing alone in a small room with his hands and feet shackled in cuffs.

The room was bright white and barren. Joe had been standing in here for at least ten minutes. It was a guess. His watch had been taken along with his clothes, wallet, and cell phone. He had entered through a heavy steel door which had slammed shut behind him, the sound still resonating in the barren cinder black walled room. Another large steel door loomed ominously up ahead. Still no sign of Ramsey. Had they been kept separated on purpose or had he been taken to another facility? And what about Christy? Had she also been forced to strip and subjected to a body cavity search? Probably. Joe bristled at the thought of it. She had done nothing wrong. None of them had. They were pawns in a political chess match. It bothered him to no end to think that she was caught up in this. They had evidence and they had the truth. That should be enough. That used to be enough, but would it be? The fact that he was standing here, cuffed and shackled, waiting to be led to his cell, caused him to wonder. When he walked through that door, would he ever walk out? What would he encounter on the other side. He had seen several documentaries. He had heard tales from those who had been in prison. From what he had heard, Survival Evasion Resistance and Escape (SERE) school would seem like a walk in the park.

Joe's thoughts were interrupted by an electronic buzz. A side door opened, and a tall muscular black corrections officer (CO) stepped into the room. He towered over Joe's six-foot-four-inch frame. The door shut with a metallic thud while the CO silently sized Joe up and down. He pointed toward the door ahead.

"Start walking," he said with a deep voice.

Joe began to shuffle in his chains. The officer came alongside, reached behind Joe, and grabbed the free end of a chain that hung from Joe's belt harness. Joe felt like he was a dog on a leash. As they neared the door, another electronic buzz rang out followed by the metallic click of a hidden deadbolt. The big officer pushed the door open, and they entered a narrow hallway with a door at the far end. Joe began to walk but the CO grabbed him by the shoulder, turning Joe until they were facing each other. Joe looked at his security badge and saw the man's name was Trenton.

"There are no cameras or microphones in here," the large man spoke in hushed tones. "If we don't walk out of here within a minute, they'll suspect something so listen up. I served four years in the Corps. Infantry."

"Sandbox?" Joe asked.

"That's right. Sometimes side by side with you SEALs and often under the cover of your snipers. I know who you are. I know you're one of the good guys and I think these charges are total BS. But someone way up has it in for you and your friend. The warden gave us strict orders to expedite your intake and put you into gen-pop. I have no control over that, but I have *never* seen something like this before. The warden is a good guy, for the most part, and wouldn't do this unless someone was telling him to do so. Someone *way* up the food chain, but then I think you know already know that."

Joe nodded his understanding.

"What that means, Mr. O'Shanick is, watch your back. In any book, you're a model citizen and a low risk for violence and escape. You should be in a minimal security facility or even the camp here. *Not* gen-pop and certainly not here! You and Mr. Ramsey are being housed with the lifers. The worst of the worst. The only reason I can figure is someone doesn't want you to survive to tell your side of the story. You hearin' me?"

Joe nodded again.

"Good, then listen up," Trenton said as he turned Joe towards the door and began walking. "A lot of cons in here join a gang. They don't think they can survive on their own. Don't fall for that. Keep your mouth shut, don't draw attention to yourself, and keep your head on a swivel. Most of the place is wired with cameras but the bathrooms and stairwells are blind spots. That's where ninety percent of the hits take place. Avoid them as much as you can. The only other friend you've got here is Mr. Ramsey and we have been ordered to keep you two separated as much as possible. Once you walk through that door, you're on your own. Some of the officers know about you and are on your side but they have to toe the line or risk getting canned. I'll do what I can, but my hands are tied and it won't be much. If you do get in a fight, and you likely will, use your skills to injure them but *don't* kill no one. That will ruin any chance you have of walking a free man. But know this, most of these guys are lifers. They got nothing to lose. When they fight, they fight to kill and most of em' have shanks. We do what we can, but the cons are very creative. Assume they're packed. That's all I got for you, Mr. O'Shanick. Godspeed. I'll be praying for you."

"Thank you," Joe said quietly as they reached the door.

Trenton pulled out a large key and inserted it into the lock. He turned the key, opened the door, and led Joe into the dimly lit cell block. They stood in a barred-in buffer zone. Another CO sat behind a desk in a fortified room. Joe saw him press a button and another buzzer sounded. Trenton pushed the barred door open, and they stepped into an open area. Three floors of jail cells lined a wide corridor that stretched almost the length of a football field.

Joe instantly felt a chill. Whether it was a cold cell block or the adrenaline induced fight or flight response kicking in, he wasn't sure. He suspected it was the latter. Joe and Ramsey were highly trained warriors. They were trained for special warfare, combat operations, and hand to hand combat but this was something entirely different. They were walking into a foreign environment, a target on their backs, unarmed, badly outnumbered and, having just been told they could not kill someone trying to kill them, severely handicapped by the rules of engagement. *Actually, it's not all that different, is it Joe?*

Joe looked around as they walked down the corridor. Absent was the welcoming committee of inmates lined up to jeer and taunt as so often depicted in Hollywood. Instead, other than the sounds of snoring, it was mostly quiet. A few cells emitted the soft glow of reading lights. As they walked, Joe looked into one cell and saw a man lying on his bunk watching a baseball game, listening to in with headphones. It looked peaceful enough. A little over halfway down the corridor, Trenton brought them to a halt. A thin man lay supine on the bottom bunk. He appeared to be reading, his bespectacled face aglow from a tablet. He casually glanced at Joe for a few seconds before returning to whatever he was looking at.

"This is you," Trenton said as he produced a ring full of keys and proceeded to remove Joe's leg shackles and waist harness.

He gently held Joe's cuffs as he called out, "Open up 118!"

A buzz sounded and the barred door slid open.

"Step in, wait for the door, to close then present your hands through the slot and I'll remove your cuffs."

Without uttering a sound. Joe stepped in and waited.

"Close 118!" Trenton called out.

Joe glanced over his shoulder as the heavily barred door slid shut. The resultant clang rang loud within the narrow confines of the cell which Joe guessed was roughly six feet wide and eight feet long. He stepped up to the door and slid his cuffed hands through the slot.

Trenton worked the key and removed the cuffs. Joe remained there, looking out through the bars.

"Wake up's at 0600. Report to the clothing room at 0615 and you will be issued your clothing, bedding, and towel. They rushed you in here tonight, so you'll have to make due with just a mattress. Breakfast for this unit is 0700. Report to the commissary after that for your basic hygiene supplies. Keep your head down and walk a straight line. God be with you, sir," Trenton finished with a solemn nod and walked off.

Joe turned and surveyed the cell. He stretched out his arms. As expected, he could touch both sides at the same time. Good thing he didn't have a large cellmate. He leaned down and extended his right hand.

"I'm Joe."

The thin man glanced over at Joe and shook his hand and in a barely audible tone said, "Benny, but there's no talking after lights out. This your first time?"

"Correct."

"Yeah, I thought so," Benny said looking Joe over. "That's alright, you'll get used to it. I'll give you the 411 in the morning. Better hit the rack before the guards hear us. Rule number one; don't give the bulls a reason to harass you."

"Thanks," Joe responded dryly.

"You don't snore, do you?" Benny asked as he stared at his tablet.

"No."

"Good. My last cellmate snored. Big, fat, hairy guy. I never slept."

"What happened to him?" Joe asked. "He get out?"

"No, I strangled him," he answered nonchalantly. "I couldn't take the snoring anymore."

"Yeah, I get that," Joe replied with the same nonchalance.

Benny didn't look like he could strangle a hen, but Joe knew many small SEALs who were tough as nails and just as lethal. *Sleep with one eye open.*

He climbed up into the top bunk and stretched out. Most people would have a hard time sleeping on a thin bare mattress without a pillow or blanket. As a SEAL with several combat tours under his belt, he was used to sleeping under far worse conditions. He could usually be asleep within minutes regardless of comfort level or circumstance. Not tonight. The events of the last few hours kept buzzing around him like a swarm of bees. Just a few hours ago, he was curled up with Christy by the fireside, imagining how he was going to propose to her while she dozed off with her head on his lap. Now he lay in this earth-bound purgatory, wondering if they would ever see each other again.

Chapter 11

Alto, Georgia

Christy was jolted awake when the prisoner transport truck ground to a halt. She wasn't sure how long she'd been asleep, but it felt like only a few minutes at best. She hadn't slept since her arrest. After the initial questioning, which she had refused without a lawyer present, she had been placed in a holding cell with a few other arrestees. Normally a calm person in a storm, the product of her training as an emergency medicine physician, Christy had been uncharacteristically scared from the moment the FBI agents placed her in handcuffs. It was understandable. The entire ordeal of being arrested and placed in handcuffs, at gunpoint, was a novel experience. Within a matter of minutes, her rather pleasant existence had come crumbling down around her. Stacy had been let go at the scene, but knowing Joe and Ramsey had been arrested, for something she had gotten them into, weighed on her more heavily than her own arrest.

After refusing to answer questions, she had been allowed to call her father who assured her he would get to work on obtaining a defense attorney. Christy had been returned to the holding cell where she had remained for a number of sleepless hours. Earlier this morning, a guess as her watch had been taken from her, a couple of uninformed officers came into her cell and informed her she was being transported. When she asked where, they refused to answer but forced her into handcuffs and leg shackles. They had then led her, shuffling in her chains, out to this truck where she was forced to climb, more like fall into, the back. Several prison inmates were already seated inside on one of two benches lining the side of the transport truck. Christy had managed to get to her feet and find a vacant seat along one side. She was immediately met with a very foul odor; a mixture of sweat, body odor, and stale urine that overwhelmed the vehicle's interior. The lurching motion of the drive over the next one or two hours, combined with the strong odor and her newfound anxiety, threatened to make her nauseated. Were it not for the fact that she often encountered much worse smells at work, she may have succumbed to the nausea.

The back doors swung open, and she was immediately blinded by several bright lights illuminating the truck's interior. Squinting into the lights, Christy was able to discern the silhouettes of several large female corrections officers as they immediately began shouting for the transferees to disembark the truck. Their dark silhouettes topped with ball caps gave them a demonic look as they continued to shout their orders. Christy stood and crouched at the edge as she tried to figure how to navigate the three-foot drop while in shackles.

"Let's go! Move it!" The officers shouted.

Seeing no other way, Christy carefully jumped to the ground. She nearly tumbled forward upon landing but managed to keep to her feet. A rather rotund older inmate who followed her down didn't fare as well. The officers pulled the inmate to her feet revealing a copiously bleeding forehead laceration. The others kept filing out of the truck and they were led in a precession up a sidewalk and through a set of steel doors.

They were led into a brightly lit room with white painted cinder block walls. The screaming officers continued their tirade as they removed each woman's shackles and ordered them to stand in line against a wall. The women were then ordered to remove all of their clothing and stand in place. The room was cold enough with the doors open on this cool fall morning, but Christy found herself shivering more from the brutal humiliation of being forced to stand naked with ten other women as the officers began to conduct extremely thorough body searches, all the while continuing to scream at the transferees. Christy, feeling completely violated after being searched, stood stoically against the wall until the last woman was searched. Once that was done, two officers came down the line spraying large amounts of foam into each woman's cupped hands and ordering them to apply it liberally from head to toe and throughout their hair, covering every last inch. More officers came by with a bag of clothes for each inmate and began screaming at them to dress quickly. Christy quickly donned a cheap pair of panties and bra, obviously used, and then removed a large white jumpsuit from the white mesh laundry bag. She held it up in front of her. It had several old stains and reeked of a strong, musty odor. Upon examining the garment, Christy had to fight back tears as the ever-present reality of her situation was brought painfully up to another level. There were large blue letters stenciled on the back that read *Department of Corrections.*

Chapter 12

South Bend, Indiana

Frank Snyder awoke to the sound of his phone vibrating. His hotel room was dark save for the morning glow peaking around the room-darkening curtains. He looked on the nightstand but his phone wasn't there. He sat up to look for the telltale glow of the screen and immediately regretted it when the throbbing pain of a headache struck him like a bolt of lightning. The vibrating stopped. He knew he should get up and check to see who had called him but the thought of sitting up again put that idea on hold; instead, he lay on his back and pulled the adjacent pillow over his eyes in a desperate effort to sleep off his hangover.

The faint smell of perfume emanating from the pillow startled him into a full state of wakefulness. *That blond woman in the bar! What was her name? Katerina!* The realization hit him like a boxer's punch as he suddenly recalled the events of last night. Top shelf Irish Whiskey had been followed by top shelf Russian vodka which led to…*No!*

Snyder shuddered. His mind raced. A wave of emotions, shame mixed with fear and regret, washed over him like a tidal wave. He and Lynn had been married for twenty-one years. Not once, not ever had he been unfaithful. Sure, Lynn was career-minded and controlling but Frank remained utterly devoted to her and their children. He recalled their phone conversation last night. She was already upset with him for losing his position as the FBI director. That would pale in comparison to this. How would he ever explain this? He couldn't. Lynn could never find out. Frank tossed the pillow aside and sat up. His headache was still present, but he ignored it for the moment as he searched, in the dim light, to see if Katerina was still there. He turned on the bedside lamp. The soft light was blinding in his current state. He took a moment to adjust and then began to search the room in earnest for any trace of the woman. She was gone. No note, no discarded clothing. Nothing. Gone.

My wallet! Snyder found his pants draped over a chair. His wallet was still in the back pocket. He rifled through it praying she hadn't taken his license or credit cards, anything that could identify him or cause a major embarrassment. Everything seemed to be in its proper place. Even his cash was still there.

"Oh, thank God!" he cried in relief.

Maybe it was just an innocent encounter. Poor choice of words. An accidental encounter. Maybe she too was married and, like him, had a momentary lapse of reason during a drunken state. He sure hoped so. He didn't need a woman stalking him. Hopefully, she was equally regretful and looking to put this indiscretion in her rearview mirror and never speak of it again. The fact she was already gone was a good sign.

Wait! Does she know who I am? Snyder racked his brain and didn't recall ever telling her who he was, but the entire night was a fog, and he couldn't be sure. He had managed to stay out of the mainstream press for the lion's share of his tenure as the FBI director and, as a result, was not instantly recognizable to most. He dismissed the thought. There was no way to know, and it wasn't worth worrying about; besides, as of tomorrow, he would no longer be the director. His only concern was making sure Lynn never found out.

His phone began to vibrate again. He followed the sound and located his phone which was lying face down on the dresser. He picked it up and instantly recognized the number for the White House Communications Office as the source of the call. Snyder pressed the green button and held the phone up to his ear.

"Director Snyder," he spoke softly, trying not to sound hungover.

"Please hold for the president," came a generic voice over the line.

"Frank," came President Galan's business-like tone less than minute later.

"Yes, Mr. President?"

"Frank, I want to start off by apologizing. I discussed the matter with Deputy Director Wickenheiser, in which he informed me that he purposefully kept you out of the loop with the intentions of wanting to let you have a true weekend off. Considering the magnitude of the situation, I think he should have let you know, but I respect his intentions. He spoke very highly of you and accepted full responsibility for what transpired last night. That being said, I was wrong to have demanded your resignation. Please accept my sincere apology and I hope you will be willing to remain aboard. I have always considered you a fair man and you have always conducted yourself with the utmost of integrity."

That last word stung. Snyder was ever so grateful this was not a video chat. He was certain President Galan would have seen the guilt he was feeling. He took a calming breath as he struggled to keep his hands from shaking while holding the phone. Should he come clean with the truth or proceed as is? He could also resign for undisclosed reasons. If Lynn found out the president had offered, correct that, *asked* him stay on and he resigned anyway? Lynn would have his head. Whatever he decided, he would have to decide it right now. There would be no turning back.

"No apology necessary, sir. I would likely have done the same thing were I in your shoes. I will gladly stay on as FBI director."

"Good," President Galan responded. "I'm glad to hear that, Frank. We have a lot to work through with this mess and I will need an honest and impartial man to help me navigate the waters. When will you be back in town?"

"This afternoon, sir," Snyder responded still shaking.

"Very well," Galan answered. "Take some time with your family tonight. Get fully briefed tomorrow morning and come meet me for lunch in the West Wing tomorrow at noon. We'll figure this thing out with the attorney general."

"Will do, Mr. President. Thank you."

"Thank you, Frank," Galan said before the line went dead. Snyder's hands were still shaking as he set the phone back down.

Chapter 13

Atlanta, Georgia

Morning wake up had come with the loud rumble of all the cell doors sliding open. As promised, Benny had provided Joe with a basic rundown of what the daily routine was along with what life was like inside "The Big A." All in all, it wasn't anything he couldn't handle. Life had been far more difficult during BUD/S, and during Plebe Year at the Naval Academy for that matter. Not that he wanted to spend any length of time here. With some time to kill before morning chow, Joe decided he would try to locate Ramsey. He didn't know whether or not they were in the same cell block. Trenton had told him they were ordered to keep the two separated, but Joe also knew he was purposefully thrown into the most violent cell block for a reason. If the goal was to have them both eliminated, then perhaps Ramsey was here as well.

Joe stepped out and began walking down the block, casting glances in each cell as he walked. Khaki-clad inmates were everywhere. Some in their cells, some huddled together in small groups in the common area and more seated around tables in the day room at the end of the block. So far there had been no sign of his close friend. He crossed to the other side and began walking down the opposite block. At the second cell, he stopped. Taking up almost the entire space between the bed and shelf-lined wall was an immense man. His back was to Joe, but he must have stood six feet seven inches and weighed close to 400 pounds. A solid mixture of muscle and fat. His head was shaved bald revealing pale white skin with several folds in the back of his neck which quickly disappeared into his shoulders. The tattoo of a Cobra's head protruded above the neckline of his white t-shirt. Ramsey stood at the back of the cell facing the man. From Joe's perspective, it appeared to be a standoff.

"Mornin' Rammer," Joe said cheerfully as he stepped into the cell. "You settling in alright?"

The large man turned to face Joe. In addition to shaving his scalp, the behemoth also shaved his eyebrows. He had dark allergy "shiners" under his eyes giving him quite a menacing look that matched his sneer.

"Morning, Joe," Ramsey replied happily. "Yes, King Kong Bundy and I were just going over the house rules. He thought that, being the bigger man, he should get both mattresses and that I would be just fine without a mattress. I was just explaining to him why that wouldn't fly."

"Move along, Pumpkin, before I squash you," the large man growled menacingly as he stared down at Joe.

Joe stood toe to toe staring up at the man. Joe immediately noticed the man's breath reeked of one who didn't know the purpose of a toothbrush. Joe watched the man's breathing, his hand shot up in a flash, clamping down on the man's throat at the end of an exhale. With his airway cut off and no air in his lungs, the man panicked and desperately tried to claw at Joe's hand but suddenly had no strength. His eyes bulged in fear as Joe forced him to his knees.

"Sucks not being able to breath, doesn't it?" Joe spoke quietly so as not to draw attention from outside the sell. "I've got news for you, Uncle Fester. I'm doing you a favor. I'm the merciful one. I'm going to let go in a second and let you live." Joe cocked his head in Ramsey's direction, "He isn't as merciful. Mess with him and you'll be lucky if you live to regret it. Are we clear?"

The large man nodded in desperation. Joe could tell he was on the verge of passing out. With a violent shove, he let go. The King Kong Bundy lookalike clutched his throat as he leaned back on his bunk gasping for air.

"That was lesson one, Uncle Fester," Joe said leaning into the man's face. "I need you to show me you understood it."

Fester squinted his eyes as he retreated from Joe and nodded.

"Good, but I'm going to need a little reassurance from you. To prove to us that you're gonna behave, I think you should skip morning chow, remain back here and straighten the place up for your new roommate. If we see you at chow, then we will know lesson one didn't sink in and that will force us to move to lesson two. Are we clear, Fester?"

He nodded once more.

"Good. C'mon, Rammer," Joe gestured as he stepped back out into the common area.

Despite Joe's attempt to avoid drawing attention, a small group of onlookers had gathered outside the cell. Joe and Ramsey glared at them as they walked out, and the onlookers stepped out of the way.

"That oughta buy us a little breathing room," Joe muttered.

The lineup for morning chow had begun. Joe and Ramsey took their place in line and filed into the mess hall. They reached a small rectangular cutout in the wall where each was handed a plastic tray with powdered eggs, watery grits, breakfast sausage, and bread.

"We ate better at BUD/S," Ramsey commented in reference to the grueling twenty-seven-week selection course in Coronado they endured to become SEALs.

"Actually, I thought we had good chow at BUD/S other than when we were fed MRE's and boiled eggs in the Tijuana mud flats. That mud got into everything and made it all taste like decayed earth and sewage," Joe replied as they found an empty table and sat down.

"That's what I was referring to. Even *that* was better than this slop," Ramsey looked around and lowered his voice. "We shouldn't be here, Joe. This is a total setup."

"I hear you, Rammer. I'd much rather be wet and sandy on a fourteen-mile run than be trapped here in this hellhole. The officer who brought me in last night confirmed as much. He said to lay low and watch our sixes."

"Like how you just said hello to my cellmate back there?" Ramsey ribbed as he took a plastic spork full of scrambled eggs. "You know I could have handled that."

"I have no doubt," Joe answered. "I was just trying to keep from having too much attention drawn on us. Besides, if you mess somebody up in a fight, you get thrown into what's known as the SHU."

"The shoe?" Ramsey looked up with his eyebrows raised.

"Yeah, only it's an acronym spelled SHU which stands for *segregated housing unit*. It's solitary confinement and you're kept in your cell twenty-three hours a day. I need you out here with me. If we were thrown into here to get schwacked, the only way we're going to make it out of here alive is to stick together. Cover each other's six."

"If that's their plan, then maybe they don't want to put us in the SHU where no one can get to us in the first place," Ramsey suggested.

Joe thought about that as he finished his eggs and took a sip of coffee. "True, but if one of us winds up there, it leaves the other out here flying solo. We need to avoid that."

"Any idea on how long we'll be in here?" Ramsey asked. "I mean, I thought we were innocent until proven guilty. I swear I read that somewhere."

"Hopefully, we'll find something out when we talk to our attorneys."

"When do you think that'll be, Joe? I haven't heard a thing. Aren't we supposed to at least have a bond hearing or an arraignment before being tossed in prison? I've never heard of anything like this!"

"One would think so, Rammer. But you know as well as I do that there are some serious forces at play here. Today's Sunday so I doubt we'll hear from any attorney today. Hopefully tomorrow though."

Ramsey didn't reply. He waited for Joe to look up at him and subtly indicated with his eyes that they were drawing attention. Joe subtly glanced in the direction Ramsey had indicated and saw two tables of Latinos staring menacingly at him and Ramsey. Gang-related tattoos covered every square inch of visible skin, including their faces and scalps.

"That didn't take long," Joe commented.

"You think that's who has been tasked to take us out?" Ramsey asked.

"Possibly. Could be anyone. Even if the people backing Fowler weren't targeting us, the cartel gangs would still be after us once they learned who we are. You and I have both, personally, been involved with the demise of the last three leaders of *Los Fantasma Guerreros,* along with dozens of their *soldados,* it only makes sense that we would be targets."

"Joe, if their job is to take us out before we see the inside of a courtroom, we might have something going down before the day's over."

"Yeah. No kidding," Joe said looking around the dining hall. "I doubt they'll try anything in here. Too many guards. But out there, we've got to keep our heads on a swivel. Keep to the common areas. The only places that don't have cameras are the showers and stairwells."

"Respect everyone, trust no one," Ramsey finished the thought.

Chapter 14

Alto, Georgia

Christy lay on the top bunk, staring at the stained concrete ceiling. She had been praying for the truth to be revealed so she could be set free along with Joe and Ramsey. She prayed for their safety as well as hers. At least breakfast had been uneventful. That was the best she could say. Between the feelings of anger, sadness, and mostly fear, Christy had had no appetite. She had followed her cellmate, Hannah, to the dining hall and back. Hannah seemed quiet and introverted. That was okay. Christy could be that way herself at times. Conversely, Christy admitted to herself that she hadn't exactly been the most congenial tablemate at breakfast. She regretted that now. There was a lot to learn if she was going to get through this ordeal, however long she might be here, and she was hoping Hannah would be willing to mentor her, for lack of a better term, in the ways of prison.

Christy rolled over and leaned over the side of her bunk to look down at Hannah. Hannah, a petite, brunette with a fair complexion, was curled up on her side, eyes shut, gently rocking back and forth. Christy watched her for a moment. She looked so young and innocent. *What could she have done to earn a sentence to this place?* Christy didn't know whether or not it was acceptable to ask. As she studied Hannah's face, something seemed off. A sheen of perspiration covered her forehead and there were intermittent expressions of pain and anguish.

"Hannah? Are you okay?"

"She's fine. Leave her alone," came a voice from the door.

Christy looked up and saw a tall twenty-something woman scowling at her. She wore khaki prison scrub pants and a matching top with the sleeves rolled up. Her hair was shaved close at the sides, spiky at the top and gelled into place. Her physique was that of one who played forward on a college basketball team, tall and solid. It was obvious she was trying to assimilate a masculine look.

"Who are you?" she asked.

"Christy."

"You Hannah's new cellie?"

"That's right. And you are?"

"Name's Miranda Winch, but everyone around here calls me Randy," she said as she eyed Christy. "Aren't you a pretty one! How long you in for, beautiful?" Randy asked as she stepped closer and placed a hand on Christy's leg.

"I'm *not* interested!" Christy said as she abruptly pulled her legs up and jumped down from her bunk.

Christy squared off facing their visitor. At five feet eleven inches tall, Christy stood a few inches taller, but Randy, carried at least thirty pounds of muscle with very little fat. Her facial features and chiseled physique led Christy to believe Randy was probably using steroids. As a former collegiate volleyball player and now an Ironman triathlete, Christy was quite toned herself, but in a slender feminine way. Christy wasn't looking for a fight, but she knew a bully when she saw one and there was only one way to handle a bully.

Randy smirked, clearly amused, as she looked Christy up and down. "First time in, babe?"

Christy simply stared back without saying a word.

"I'll take that as a yes, so ask around. I can either be your best friend or your worst nightmare. You might think your straight but, sooner or later, all you fems will end up with a stud. Everyone wants a guy to love them and protect them. Gay for the stay then straight at the gate. If you even want to go back. You'll figure that out soon enough. Until then, you can step out and leave me and little Miss Hannah to ourselves."

Christy looked down at Hannah who was now sitting on the side of her bunk staring at the floor.

"And if I refuse?" Christy asked defiantly.

Randy's eyes grew wide with rage. She puffed her chest out and opened her mouth to speak.

"No, it's okay, Randy. She'll go," Hannah spoke dryly.

Christy looked down at her cellmate. "I'm not leaving you."

"No, it's fine. I'll be fine. Please go," Hannah answered.

Christy stared back. Concern was etched on her face.

"You heard her, babe. Take a hike," Randy said.

Christy ignored her and looked down at Hannah who looked up tearfully and nodded almost pleadingly.

"You're sure?" Christy asked.

"Yes," Hannah nodded. "It's almost time for chapel anyway. You said you wanted to go. Go. I'll be fine."

"If you want play, you can stay; otherwise, just go away," Randy taunted him with a dismissive wave.

Christy took one last look at Hannah and stepped out of their cell.

*****

For a brief moment, Christy was able to let her guard down, albeit slightly, as she sat in the sparsely populated chapel service being held in the dining hall. Worship had been led by a band consisting of all inmates. They were actually quite talented and sang a mixture of hymns and contemporary worship songs which Christy was familiar with. Currently, the chaplain, a Southern Baptist minister named Don Brooks, was teaching on the Beatitudes from Matthew Chapter 5. Like the pastor from her church, Pastor Don seemed to genuinely care about what he was teaching. He didn't raise his voice or put on some showy act. He taught like a caring parent speaking to his adult children. Christy looked around and got a sense that many in attendance were very receptive to Pastor Don. She memorized the faces. It would be good to connect with some fellow Christians.

Pastor Don's teaching struck a chord with Christy. Actually, it was what Jesus had said but it struck a nerve nonetheless.

Blessed are the merciful, for they will be shown mercy.

Does that apply when confronting bullies like Randy? Christy was standing up for her cellmate. She also refused to be bullied herself. How does one show mercy in such a situation? Or was the mercy required, that which she was extending to Hannah? Protecting those who couldn't protect themselves was one of the core values of her faith. It was what Joe and his fellow SEALs were all about and one of the many reasons she loved him. Hannah had told her to go, but Christy now regretted leaving her. Even though she barely knew her, she felt like she should have stuck around and watched out for her.

Christy tried to refocus on Pastor Don before her mind drifted off to Joe. She would have plenty of time to dwell on Joe later.

Blessed are the peacemakers for the will be called sons of God.

Well, that makes sense. It wasn't like Christy was going to go around looking for a fight. However, maintaining peace, sometimes required the threat of violence. That was certainly the case in preventing wars on the world stage and it was likely going to be the case here where there was only one law. The law of the jungle.

Christy kept herself in peak physical shape. From what she had seen so far, that wasn't a priority with most of her fellow inmates. Randy being the rare exception. Additionally, she now had almost a full year of Krav Maga and Brazilian Jiu Jitsu training. At Joe's encouragement, she had enrolled the week after they had escaped their captivity with the *Los Fantasma Guerreros* cartel. It had already saved her life once. Would she need it again in here? She prayed she would be exonerated before she ever had a chance to find out.

As it was, even in chapel service, she couldn't shake the sensation that she was being watched. She kept noticing a particular woman frequently looking over in her direction. Christy snuck a glance out of the corner of her eye. There she was again looking right at her. Christy casually turned her head as if to take in that side of the dining hall. The woman quickly faced back to the front. Christy gave her a quick once over. There was a vague familiarity about her, but she couldn't place it. The woman was fairly tall, slender to the point of being nearly gaunt. She had classic African features; rich dark mahogany skin that concealed her age, high cheekbones, her natural hair pulled back. Try as she might, Christy just couldn't place her.

They stood for a final hymn and then Pastor Don closed out the service. As they began to file out, Christy saw the woman looking in her direction once again. Christy tried to make eye contact, but the woman glanced away and quickly walked out of the dining hall. Christy thought about trying to catch up with her but quickly dismissed the notion. She had no idea what that was about and was too concerned she might find herself in a bad situation. Everything here was so new and foreign to her. It was quite intimidating.

Christy followed the other women out of the dining hall. They were back outside and following a looping sidewalk that led back to their prison dorms. There were three full length basketball courts arranged within the loop with three large dormitories seated around the outside of the loop. Open fields separated this area from several other buildings. A softball diamond could be seen a couple hundred yards away. In many ways, the prison reminded her of a small college campus, except that this campus was surrounded by large fences lined with razor wire.

Christy arrived back at her assigned dorm and tried to blend in with the other inmates as they entered a common area where dozens of inmates wearing either prison khakis or white jumpsuits were milling about. Many sat around square tables, with fixed metal seats, playing cards. Others huddled in various groups while others sat on the floor leaning against the wall. Christy climbed the stairs to the second deck and entered her cell. Hannah was sprawled on her bunk with her eyes closed.

"You okay?" Christy asked.

Hannah didn't stir. Christy took a closer look and was immediately alarmed. Hannah's face was pale with the blue hue of cyanosis around her mouth. She wasn't breathing.

Chapter 15

Alto, Georgia

"Hannah! Wake up!" Christy pounced onto the bed as she made a fist and vigorously began rubbing Hannah's sternum with her knuckles in hopes that the painful sensation would stimulate a breathing response. Christy jumped to her feet and bolted out their door. She leaned over the railing and began yelling for the corrections officer's attention.

"My cellmate's not breathing! We need a medical response team and some Narcan now!"

A stern-faced black female officer looked up from whatever she was reading. She was startled at first but quickly responded by picking up her phone and speaking into it. She grabbed a small tackle box and began running toward the stairs. Satisfied that help was on the way, Christy ran back into their cell to attend to Hannah.

"Hannah! C'mon, wake up!" Christy said applying another sternal rub which elicited no response.

"Hannah! Open your eyes!"

Christy in desperation pinched Hannah's right nipple and rotated it as far as her skin would allow. This caused a response. Hannah's right hand tried to grab Christy's in effort to stop the painful stimulus.

"That's it, Hannah! Stay with me!" Christy encouraged loudly as she gave Hannah another twist.

Hannah was still pale but this time both of her hands reached up in protest. Christy pried open Hannah's eyelids revealing pinpoint pupils, confirming a likely opiate overdose. She noticed some blue residue in and around Hannah's right nostril. *Fentanyl!* Probably the same cheap garbage version many of her regular ER overdose patients were using. The drugs were shipped to the Mexican cartels from China and then transported across the southern border where they found their way into every city and small town in America. They were a cheap substitute for the more expensive prescription opiates and preferred over the stigmatic heroin but just as deadly if not more. President Galan was trying to put a stop to the trafficking. Joe and Ramsey had been directly involved with that effort. *And now we are all in prison at the hands of those who don't want it to stop.* Christy thought ironically as she kept applying sternal rubs to Hannah while waiting for help to arrive.

A crowd had gathered outside their cell. Christy could hear the corrections officer yelling at the inmates to get out of her way. The officer finally cut through the throng and burst into the room.

"Medical response team is on the way. What do we have?" she yelled excitedly.

"I just got back to the cell from chapel and found her like this. Looks like fentanyl," Christy responded. "She needs Narcan! Do you have any?"

"I've got some, but I'm not authorized to use it," the officer responded as she knelt down by the bed and opened the orange tackle box. "Only the medical team is authorized to give it."

"I'm an ER doctor, licensed in this state, hand it over! She can't wait!"

The urgency of the situation and the authority in Christy's voice made the officer pause.

"Now, please!" Christy commanded.

The officer shrugged her shoulders and shook her head as she handed Christy a small box. Christy quickly opened the box and removed a small bottle with the opiate antidote. She inserted the tip into Hannah's nose and squeezed. The medication was atomized into a fine mist which was injected up into the sinuses where it is rapidly absorbed into the blood stream and quickly reaches the opiate receptors to reverse the opiate effect. Christy kept applying a sternal rub to Hannah's chest while verbally coaching her to open her eyes.

After what seemed an eternity, Hannah began to wake up. She began with a soft moan which quickly progressed to a banshee-like wail. Her arms began to thrash about. Christy gently grabbed Hannah's wrists and spoke soothingly to her.

"Hannah, it's me, Christy, your new cellmate. You were unconscious, but you're better now."

"It hurts!" Hannah half sobbed half yelled.

"I know it does," Christy spoke calmly. "But you're gonna be alright. I'm going to help you."

"Was she trying to kill herself?" The officer asked.

"No!" Hannah nearly growled as she gritted through the pain of opiate withdrawal. "I just…I just needed to…I just wanted to stop hurting."

The medical response team burst into the room. A nurse headed up the team. She looked like she was in her late forties, well-seasoned, and knew her business. A good nurse to have during a busy shift loaded with high acuity patients. A tattoo circling her left upper arm could be seen peaking below her scrub top. The name on her ID was Judy. Christy explained to her the situation, who she was and what she had done for Hannah. The nurse looked at her skeptically.

"You say you're a doctor?" She asked eying Christy suspiciously as an EMS crew arrived and began placing Hannah into a stretcher.

"Yes," Christy replied.

"An emergency medicine doctor?"

"Yes, I work down in Duluth."

"So you're *that* doctor. The one that was arrested on the news with those Navy SEALs last night?"

"Yes," Christy said quietly.

"How did you end up here of all places and so quickly I might add?"

"I'm asking myself that same question, ma'am," Christy answered.

"Well, lucky for her, you were in the right place at the right time," she said with a shrug. "I'll take a save anyway we can get it," Judy said as she stood to follow the EMS team down the walkway.

"Thank you," the corrections officer said quietly before rising to her feet. "I'm officer Singletary, by the way."

"Christy Tabrizi."

"You mind if I just call you 'doc'?"

"That'll be fine, Officer Singletary."

"Good. I need to get back downstairs and make sure everything is in order. Meet me down there in say fifteen minutes. I'll need to fill out an incident report with you."

"Yes, ma'am." Christy replied as the officer stepped out of her cell.

Christy said a quick prayer on Hannah's behalf and then stepped over to the stainless-steel sink to splash water on her face and wash her hands. She looked for a hand towel but couldn't find one. *You're in prison, Tabrizi. You don't rate hand towels.* She found her threadbare prison issued shower towel and used it to dry her hands. The room was suddenly filled with loud expletives as Randy came barging in.

"What did you do to my Hannah?" she yelled angrily.

"What did *I* do?" Christy said squaring up. "More like what did *you* do? She nearly died a few minutes ago from a fentanyl overdose, but I'll bet you know *nothing* about that. Isn't that right?"

"You're right, sweet pea, I don't!" Randy was standing right up in Christy's face now. Spit flew from her mouth as she yelled. Her breath smelled strongly of tobacco and marijuana. "But I *do* know that somebody better start mindin' her own business. She also better start learnin' who's who around here!"

Randy emphasized her last point with a sharp jab of her index finger to Christy's chest. In a blur of motion, Christy grabbed Randy's finger and bent it back into a submission hold. Randy yelped in pain as she quickly dropped to her knees. The crowd of onlookers gawked in astonishment. Christy lowered her voice and spoke calmly as she stared directly into Randy's eyes.

"You don't scare me, you and your tough butch act. I know what you are. You're an abusive coward. Consider this your warning. From now on, you stay away from this cell, you stay away from Hannah, and you stay away from me. Try me again and I'll break every one of these fingers," Christy emphasized the last part with a sharp yank of Randy's finger.

"Make a hole!" barked officer Singletary as she stormed through the crowd and into the room. "What's going on in here?!"

"Nothing, ma'am," Christy answered, quickly letting go of Randy's finger. "We're good."

"Nothin' huh? Sure don't look like nothin'! Is she botherin' you?" Singletary asked Christy as she gestured toward Randy.

"No, ma'am," Christy answered.

"And what about you?" she asked, turning to Randy. "Is she botherin' you?"

"No, ma'am!" Randy replied sharply while giving Christy an icy glare.

"Good," Singletary pronounced. "Then inmate Tabrizi, you come with me. Inmate Winch, make yourself scarce. And I better not have to come up here and deal with the two of you again or you're both going to secure lockup. Now get!"

Randy gave one last menacing stare toward Christy before she turned and left the room.

"My desk, Tabrizi. Let's go."

Chapter 16

Grand Island, New York

The cold autumn evening was scented with a comforting aroma of dried leaves and the smoke of seasoned oak. The flames crackled in the fire pit beside the waterfront while their reflection danced atop the calm surface of the Niagara River. Maria O'Shanick clutched a thermal mug of chai tea and gazed out over the water. The usual soothing serenity of a bonfire by the water was elusive tonight. Her entire family had met for Sunday dinner, as they usually do, and now everybody was gathered around the fire; her husband, Jack, their oldest child, Jacob, and his wife, Barbara, their older daughter, Marina, and her husband, Tommy, their youngest son, Sean, and his fiancé, Abby, and their youngest, Anna. All but Joe and Christy. Maria had found a kindred spirit in Christy and had immediately adopted her as one of her own even before Christy and Joe had officially become a couple. Ramsey too. All of Joe's SEAL teammates were special. She considered them her boys, but Matthew - she preferred to call him by his first name - was Joe's closest and most loyal friend. Ever since she and Jack had watched the three of them arrested on national news last night, Maria had been in a near constant state of prayer with her friends and, tonight, with her family.

Things had been so good as of late for the O'Shanick family. Marina was completely recovered from the near fatal gunshot wound to the chest she had suffered last June when she and Christy had been abducted by the mafia. Jack had healed from his injuries suffered during the same incident. Sean and Abby were due to be married in a couple of weeks, and she hoped Joe and Christy wouldn't be too far behind them.

That was until this. This was so wrong. She knew her son. Christy and Matt Ramsey as well, for that matter. They were good people. There was no way they had committed the crimes they had been arrested for. This was the work of that crooked Senator Fowler or, more likely, those who were backing him. Maria was born and raised in the Philippines. She had helped run her family's small restaurant until the day a young Navy enlisted man named Jack O'Shanick had married her and brought her here, to his hometown. Maria's family back home had struggled to maintain their business amid corruption at many levels, whether it be local criminal elements or government officials. She knew corruption when she saw it. Fowler was a smarmy con artist and a self-serving, devious, crook.

They all sat quietly as they listened intently to Jack's end of a phone conversation with his longtime friend and lawyer, Tom Brinkworth. From what Maria could glean, it didn't sound good. A minute later, Jack ended the call and sighed as he pinched the bridge of his nose.

"What'd you find out, Dad?" Anna asked.

Anna and Marina both favored their mother physically; petite, long dark silky hair, with perfectly blended European-Asian facial features. Where they differed was personality. Marina tended to be quiet and laid back, Anna was inquisitive and outgoing. A bundle of energy, she was an ER nurse and very mama bear-like when it came to her family. That was especially true when it came to Joe. Anna adored all three of her brothers, but she and Joe had always been close, and he was her hero. She had been the first one over when the news broke last night.

"Tom reached out to a friend of his from law school who is a criminal defense attorney in Atlanta. His name is Nick Marcella. He's a senior partner with a well-known law firm and they can represent Christy and Matt as well. It took them all day to track down everyone. Apparently, the FBI wasn't giving out any information due to national security, but Marcella went after them with both guns blazing and finally got them to give up where they're being held."

"So where are they?" Jacob asked.

"Joe and Matt are being held at a Federal Penitentiary in Atlanta. Christy was moved to a women's prison northeast of Atlanta. Tom says that is not unheard of but highly unusual. He thinks they should have been in a detention center until released on bond which should have already happened but, apparently, their bond hearings have been pushed back until tomorrow. He tried to get into the prison today to meet with Joe but was turned away. I won't use the exact words Tom used but, suffice it to say, this is all highly irregular and this guy, Marcella is fit to be tied."

"So what's going to happen, Jack?" Maria asked.

"According to Tom, Marcella and his team are going to demand to meet with Joe, Matt, and Christy and have their bonds set at a hearing tomorrow. Once they post bond, they will be released. An arraignment will follow and then it will likely go before a grand jury which will likely vote in favor of a trial. If that happens, then they will begin to build their cases for a criminal trial, which he says could take months or even years."

"Will that mess up Joe's Navy career?" Sean asked.

"I don't know, son. I guess we'll have to find out. I hope not."

Chapter 17

Atlanta, Georgia

An hour past the lights out call and the cell block had quieted from the din of several hundred voices to a haphazard chorus of snoring men. The block was dimly lit. A modicum of light was necessary for the corrections officers to keep watch through the night. It was still a jungle, even when all the animals were locked in their cages.

Ramsey lay on his bed fully awake. He and Joe had managed to stick together for most of the day. Although they had picked up on many people watching them, there had been no incidents. Yet. They had gotten some time out in the yard and even managed to hit the weights and get in a thirty-minute run around the perimeter without drawing too much attention. It had helped to pass the time and time was something they had plenty of.

Ramsey and Joe spent the majority of their indoor time in Joe's cell playing Rummy and talking to Joe's cellmate, Benny. According to Benny, Ramsey's cellmate, the giant King Kong Bundy lookalike, was named Alan Myslinski. Behind his back, the other inmates called him *The Missing Link*. For a quiet, bookish sort, Benny seemed to have his ear to the ground for the goings on within the prison. After learning how Joe had handled Myslinski earlier that morning, he quickly warmed up to his new cellmate and had given Joe and Ramsey a crash course in life at "The Big A," a rundown of who's who, and a primer on the prison code among the inmates.

Word of Joe and Ramsey's confrontation with Myslinski had traveled fast, earning the pair some quick respect but, Joe was concerned this may draw the wrong kind of attention. Unfortunately, that couldn't be helped. Try as they might to keep a low profile, they couldn't avoid every situation. Doubly so with any number of hostile inmates who may be under orders to eliminate Joe and Ramsey. They would have to remain vigilant. But that was a given, hit order or no order.

Although, Myslinski had seemed to avoid Ramsey and Joe throughout the day, Joe and Ramsey both agreed that Myslinski was likely to strike out at Ramsey during the night as a form of retaliation to save face among the other inmates. Benny agreed and warned that the rudimentary weapons known as prison shanks were plentiful and that Myslinski was likely to have one. While playing cards earlier, Ramsey and Joe ran through several different possible scenarios regarding how Myslinski might attack and how to thwart off such an attack.

An hour past *lights out* and there had been no noise and very little motion from Myslinski on the bunk below. A man that large most likely had some form of sleep apnea and would be a loud snorer. Nothing. Was he someone who didn't fall asleep easily or was he actually planning something? Time to find out.

Ramsey quietly began to mimic a snoring sound of his own. He lay on his side; eyes open just enough to see as he slowly turned up volume on his snoring. Ten minutes passed with not even a hint of movement from below. Another ten minutes passed, then twenty. Maybe he really was asleep? Ramsey didn't think so. He would wait out his prey. Another half hour passed. Ramsey was beginning to ache on his left side and longed to roll over, but he embraced the discomfort. It would help keep him alert. He continued his simulated snoring as he watched and listened for movement. Finally, a slight creek sounded from below followed by the soft slap of bare feet coming into contact with the concrete floor. Ramsey tensed. Myslinski could be preparing to strike or he could simply be answering the call of nature. Ramsey would know soon enough.

A minute passed and nothing happened. No movement from below and nary a sound. Suddenly, in a blur of motion, the large man was towering over Ramsey with his right arm held overhead, poised to strike. Ramsey's right hand shot out like a rattlesnake striking at a victim. Ramsey's outstretched fingers struck Myslinski directly in his eyes while the large man's beefy arm swung in a rapid downward arc. Too late to block the strike, Ramsey remained on his left side, lest he roll in either direction and expose his chest or back to danger. The fingertips to his eyes threw off Myslinski's aim as he hollered out and grasped at his eyes with his left hand. Ramsey felt a hot searing pain as something sharp struck him in his right shoulder. He gritted his teeth as he overrode the pain and threw a sharp jab at Myslinski's throat. His strength weakened by the blade in his right deltoid, Ramsey still made contact but immediately knew the blow was not forceful enough to incapacitate his large cellmate.

Ramsey delivered a quick snap kick to Myslinski's face and the rolled up to a sitting position. His left hand swung up from the bed. In it, Ramsey held a long white sock with his prison issued padlock inside. The makeshift weapon struck Myslinski in the side of the head, further stunning the rotund behemoth. Ramsey wasted no time as he jumped off his bunk and swung the padlock in the direction of Myslinski's left knee. He scored a direct hit on the man's kneecap, connecting with a sickening crunch. With a loud bellow, Myslinski collapsed to the floor. Ramsey spotted the bloodied prison shank and kicked it toward the door. He stood over his attacker and waited. Myslinski was out of the fight. The man reached for his knee, but his expansive girth would not allow him to cradle it. He rocked back and forth moaning in pain.

Ramsey looked down at his right shoulder as the sound of running footsteps approached. Blood was expanding under his white t-shirt and running down his arm. The wound throbbed but he had been hurt worse. He checked his radial pulse. It was strong, no arterial wound. His hand functioned fine as well. All good.

"What's going on here?" Officer Trenton shouted as he came running up.

"He tried to kill me in my sleep," Ramsey said gesturing to the floor where the shank lay.

Trenton looked down at the shank and then up at Ramsey's bloody arm.

"Where all did he get you?"

"Just here in the deltoid," Ramsey showed him.

"And what about him?" Trenton nodded toward Myslinski.

"Self-defense," Ramsey answered. "He was trying to kill me. I had to defend myself. I struck him in the head and the knee with a padlock. I'll cooperate fully and answer all your questions, but he needs medical attention."

"He have any penetrating wounds, inmate Ramsey?"

"No, sir."

Trenton keyed his radio and called for backup and a medical response team.

"I need to cuff you before we enter," he said calmly. "Turn around and cut up through the chuck hole."

Ramsey turned around and extended his hands through the slot as he was ordered. Trenton applied the cuffs but not as tight as the other officers had. The medical team arrived accompanied by several other officers. Trenton instructed Ramsey to step aside as he opened the door and let the team in. Several members immediately began to attend to Myslinski.

"Inmate Ramsey," Trenton began. "Officer Maxwell here will escort you over to medical. Once released, you will be held in the Segregated Housing Unit pending an investigation. If you are found guilty of any rules infractions or crimes, you may be held longer in the SHU and you will face disciplinary measures within this institution and/or added time to your sentence. If you are found innocent, you will be returned here to general population. You will also be issued a new cellmate. Is all of that clear?"

"Yes, sir," Ramsey replied.

"Very well then," Trenton nodded. "Officer Maxwell, you may escort the inmate over to medical."

Ramsey gave one last glance over at Myslinski, who was looking at Ramsey but immediately looked away when their eyes met. He hoped Myslinski had gotten the message, but one never knew with animals like that. He hoped whatever investigation was going to be conducted would be wrapped up quickly. Being tossed in the SHU would leave Joe hung out to dry.

Chapter 18

Washington D.C.

FBI Director Snyder's office was, what he liked to call, *controlled clutter*. Snyder tended to be organized but, presiding over the premier law enforcement organization of the United States required an office that was burdened with phones, computers, flat screens, and papers. Reams of paper were stacked all over his main desk, his computer desk, credenza, and even a special desk he had installed against the wall that required him to stand when he worked. He currently stood at that working desk going through the arrest reports of Senator Fowler and Victor Tupolev.

These documents, along with the statements given by O'Shanick, Ramsey, and the others painted a significantly different picture than what was currently making its way through the media circuit. A picture that also differed from the narratives of Wickenheiser and SAIC Winkelman. Snyder had spoken to both men. Winkelman defended his actions on the premise that there was nothing to incriminate Senator Fowler other than the statements of O'Shanick and the others and he was not about to hold a sitting senator and presidential candidate under arrest without corroborating evidence. Wickenheiser backed him up. Considering the potential political ramifications, Snyder couldn't blame them. Snyder could just picture the verbal abuse Winkelman had taken from Senator Fowler before dropping the charges.

Conversely, SAIC McPherson had come to the opposite conclusion, holding Fowler under arrest and had not found any reason to charge O'Shanick and the others with any crime. Everything changed on Saturday when McPherson had been shot while out jogging and Winkelman was named the acting SAIC. A wet behind the ears detective in a small-town police force could spot that red flag. Snyder had known Agent McPherson. He was a good man with a stellar reputation and ran his field office according to the FBI motto of fidelity, bravery, and integrity. Something was off. Snyder pressed a button on his phone to reach his secretary.

"Yes, Director Snyder?"

"Marjorie, please have Deputy Director Wickenheiser come to my office and set up a conference call with Special Agents Huggins and Gomez of the Atlanta Field Office."

"Right away, sir."

Based on the arrest reports of Special Agents Huggins and Gomez as well as the sworn statements of O'Shanick and the others, McPherson had reached a different conclusion and taken a different action than Winkelman. Snyder had heard Winkelman's side of things. McPherson had been murdered. Perhaps the arresting agents could shed some light on the issue.

Deputy Director Wickenheiser knocked on Snyder's open door a minute later. "You wanted to see me, boss?"

"Yeah, Jimmy, have a seat," Snyder said as he scooped several files off the tall desk and sat down at his main desk across from his deputy director. "Have you gone through these files in detail?"

"Which files?" Wickenheiser asked. "The files from Atlanta?"

Snyder replied with a single nod.

"Yeah, what about them?"

"Did anything strike you as odd?" Snyder stared intently across his desk.

"Of course," Wickenheiser said furling his brow. "Depending on which side is telling the truth, some serious crimes have been committed. We're potentially talking about impeaching and or imprisoning a sitting president or imprisoning a senator who happens to be running for president. We're sitting on the crime of the century here and we don't even know yet what it is? On top of that, the SAIC was killed, assassination style, and we don't know whether or not it's connected.

I've delegated several teams of agents to investigate. We *have* to get this right."

"Speaking of McPherson, doesn't it strike you as odd that the day he gets whacked, his successor reverses everything? Drops all charges on Fowler and arrests the people who found him in the company of the cartel and several abducted American citizens?" Snyder probed.

"I find it highly concerning, boss, but put yourself in Winkelman's shoes. Imagine the political and potentially legal pressure that was being dropped on him the moment he takes over for his slain boss and friend. He had to act one way or the other. I think he took the path of least resistance but that doesn't shut the door on our investigating the entire matter thoroughly, sifting through the evidence and bringing the right people to justice."

A rapid two rap knock came at the door. Snyder was well familiar with his secretary's knock.

"Come in, Marjorie," he spoke loudly.

The door opened and a short, spritely older woman appeared. She had short but stylish hair that used to be dark brown but was now mostly gray. She wore a small pair of rimless eyeglasses that magnified a set of piercing blue eyes. What Marjorie Boland lacked in height, she more than made up for in spunk and energy. Snyder knew she was in her early seventies, but her youthful vigor made her seem twenty years younger. A widow going on twenty years, she had married her high school sweetheart right after graduation before he left for Parris Island. He had survived three combat tours in Vietnam only to die of cancer some thirty years later. It was believed to have been caused by Agent Orange. Vietnam had gotten him in the end. Rather than remarrying, Marjorie had married her career. The longest active employee at the Bureau, she had personally worked for six different directors and knew the inner workings of the Bureau better than anyone. Marjorie possessed a sharp mind matched by an equally sharp tongue, yet no career aspirations beyond her current position, and as a result, Snyder often confided in her when he needed some blunt wisdom.

"I'm sorry to interrupt, Director Snyder, but the Atlanta Field Office has informed me that Agents Huggins and Gomez are out of the office and cannot be reached at the moment."

"Did you let them know who was looking for them?" Snyder asked as his personal cell phone vibrated on his desk, signaling an incoming text.

"How long do you think I've been working here?" she answered feigning insult. "You think I don't know how to throw the weight of this office around?"

"Message received, Marge," Snyder said with a chuckle. "Keep pestering them and make sure they try their cellphones."

"I already told them to do just that. They're supposed to call me back as soon as they reach them," Marjorie said as she stepped back into her reception area while closing the door behind her.

"That little bitty could probably run this place without you or me around," Wickenheiser commented as he shook his head and smiled.

"She already does and will likely be here long after you and I are gone," Snyder answered as he picked up his cellphone. "On that note, I agree with you; we have got to get this Fowler situation right. Some serious crimes have been committed and the election hangs in the balance. We…"

Snyder froze as he peered intently at his cell phone. Wickenheiser looked on with concern but waited patiently, saying nothing.

"…are trying to get in touch with the arresting agents to get their version of what happened which is why I called you in here," Snyder said as he closed out of the text and placed his phone face down on his desk and looked up. "But, apparently, they can't be reached at the moment, so I'll let you get back to overseeing the McPherson case while I chase down a few leads of my own. We'll reconvene when we get ahold of Huggins and Gomez."

Snyder quickly stood signaling the meeting was over.

"Everything okay, boss?" Wickenheiser asked as he stood.

"Huh? Oh, yes! I'm good. Just a little overwhelmed at the enormity of the task before us is all, but we're up to it," Snyder blurted out in a nervous fashion.

He continued to stand as he waited for his deputy director to take his leave. Once the door was shut, Snyder opened up his phone and went into the texting app. Sweat began to bead on his forehead as he reread the message and thumbed through the message. He quickly gathered up his suit coat, along with a charcoal gray scally cap, and walked out of his office.

"I'm stepping out for a few, Marge. Back in about twenty."

Snyder didn't wait for a response. He fast walked his way to the emergency stairwell and out of the J. Edgar Hoover building.

Chapter 19

Atlanta, Georgia

The prison rumor mill was in full operational mode when morning arrived. The inmates in close proximity to Ramsey's cell fed the others with varied reports; everything from Ramsey killing *The Missing Link* to Ramsey being killed. A group of investigators was still combing through their cell. Joe had scouted it out earlier with a couple of casual walk-bys but couldn't discern anything.

Once again, Benny had been in touch with the grapevine and believed he had the real scoop. Both Ramsey and *The Missing Link* had been seen in medical. Myslinski had been transferred to a nearby hospital where his injuries would be looked at more closely. Ramsey's wound had been washed out, sewn up, and he had been put on antibiotics. He would be spending the day in the SHU.

"Will he be safe over there?" Joe asked.

"Reasonably," Benny answered without looking up from his book. "It's much more restricted over there and he'll be in a cell by himself, but the reality is, no place is perfectly safe here. If someone wants to get to you, there are always ways. He's safer there than he is in gen-pop, but most people hate it over there and can't wait to get back to gen-pop. Why?"

"What do you mean, why?" Joe replied sharply. "That's my best friend. Someone just tried to kill him, and I can't be around to look out for him."

"From what I've seen, he can take care of himself," Benny replied, briefly looking up at Joe before looking back down at his book.

"Besides, The Missing Link won't be bothering him anytime soon and nobody's gonna retaliate over what your friend did to the Link. If anything, your friend just earned himself a lot of street cred in here over that incident. You too for that matter. The whole prison knows about you nearly choking him to death yesterday."

Joe simply nodded and leaned back against the wall as he sat on the lone wall-mounted seat in their cell. If Benny was as connected with the prison's inner workings as he seemed to be, then surely he would know if there was a hit out on him and Ramsey. Either there was no hit or Benny wasn't letting on. Officer Trenton as much as told him there was a hit. Why was Benny not letting on?

"Street cred," Joe pressed his lips together into a wry expression. "Not sure how far that goes when there's a target on your back in a prison full of lifers," Joe said looking over at Benny expectantly.

"Well, steer clear of the Mexicans and you should be alright," Benny said absently without looking up from his book.

"So you know about the hit on us?" Joe asked.

"Yep."

"Why didn't you say something?"

"Because you already know," Benny replied factually, still seemingly engrossed in his book.

"How could you know that?" Joe asked astonished.

"Because you're both Navy SEALs. You're highly intelligent and well trained in situational awareness. You busted a cartel, a Russian crime syndicate, and a crooked senator, who just so happens to be running for president, and then a day later the tables are turned and you're in here. It doesn't take a genius to figure out that there is a major corrupt power play in the works and that you guys are the key to bringing it all down. If Joe Sixpack can figure out that the two of you have a target on your back, then surely you two know as well. Besides," Benny said looking up at Joe, "if they get even a hint that I said anything to you, then I'll be their next target."

"How do you know all of this?"

"You're all over the news, O'Shanick. Everyone in here knows who you guys are. You're famous," Benny shrugged nonchalantly.

"So why do you think we only have to watch out for the Mexicans? Wouldn't everyone want in on this?"

"Because the cartels run the prisons and *they* want the hit. They've put the word out for everyone else to back off. Even the Russians. But you've also got some fans."

"Fans?" Joe asked with his eyebrows raised.

"Yes, the bikers. A lot of them are military veterans. They've got their own thing going on but most of them are hard-working blue-collar patriots and they can't stand Fowler. They all cheered when he was arrested. You guys are good as long as you don't cross them. They don't get along with the cartel gangs but maintain an uneasy truce with them. They've already told the Mexicans to stay away from you two."

Joe's eyes narrowed slightly. Nothing good is free.

"Is there a catch to that?" he asked.

"Could be," Benny answered. "They may try to recruit you. I'd tread lightly on that. If you ever get out of here, you're theirs for life. Doesn't seem like the kind of life a guy like you wants to live. Conversely, if you turn them down, you might end up *persona non grata* and then you're really screwed. SEAL or not, if the bikers and the cartel are both after you, you have nowhere to run. The only thing left are the black gangs, which are not an option, and the Aryans and you don't strike me as a white supremacist."

"Not in the least," Joe agreed.

"Then you need to walk a fine line like what I've been doing."

"So do you think the cartel gangs will back off just because the bikers told them to?"

"No," Benny looked Joe dead in the eye. "They'll just plan it out better but at least you know who to watch out for."

"Great," Joe sighed.

The way out of here was going to be a very narrow and treacherous road. Not only were there some majorly powerful entities at work trying to frame him along with Ramsey, Christy, and everyone else, but as Benny just confirmed, they were trying to have them eliminated while in prison and likely before they could testify. As Navy SEALs, they were the tip of the spear, the apex predators in the world of warfare. Operating in the midst of the enemy was nothing new to them. The problem here was they weren't allowed to kill anyone despite the fact that they were being hunted. Get caught by surprise and they could be killed. React the wrong way and kill an attacker and they could have serious time added to their stay.

Stay? We shouldn't even be here!

The trick was going to be to survive long enough to make it to trial where they could prove their innocence. He was fairly confident they could do just that. They just had to get to the courtroom. What they had on Fowler should at the very least sink his presidential campaign and place *him* in prison. He thought he and Ramsey had a fighting chance, literally. It was Christy he was worried about. How was she holding up? Joe knew she was one tough lady and had excellent coping skills, but this could be overwhelming for anyone emotionally let alone having people trying to kill you.

His concern for Christy led him to start praying. Joe closed his eyes, leaned back against the wall, and began to pray. Still relatively new in his faith, Joe was still getting used to the whole idea of prayer and often struggled to find the words. Christy often told him to speak plainly from the heart. That prayer was to be a conversation, not a recited bunch of memorized words. "God already knows what's on our hearts, He just wants us to come to Him with it," she would say. Joe was learning to do that but still struggled at times. Christy empathized and told him that she sometimes experienced the same thing and, in those instances, would pray some of the Psalms aloud, thinking about the words as she prayed them.

"You don't happen to have a Bible in here, do you?" Joe asked.

Benny snorted a laugh. "Allow me to introduce myself. My name is Benjamin David *Cohen*! You can't get any more Jewish than that. No. I don't have a Bible."

"Sorry, I didn't know. Don't you guys read the Old Testament though?"

"Yes, only we call it the Tanakh. There's a copy on the shelf. Knock yourself out."

"Is there a way I can get a copy of the Bible in here?"

"You can probably buy one at the commissary, but you won't have that kind of money for at least a month or two. The other way is to get someone to mail one to you. You really believe all that stuff?"

"Didn't used to but, yes, I'm a firm believer now."

"How'd that happen?" Benny looked up from his book with a spark of interest.

"I met a real Christian," Joe began. "Not some religious nut or nominal Christian but a true follower of Christ. In all honesty, I was an agnostic at the time and didn't care to hear about it, but she was different. She never forced her faith on me. If anything, she piqued my curiosity and I started asking her questions. Over the past year, we had a lot of long discussions, but she never judged me or condemned me. She was pleasant to talk to and she encouraged me to search out the answers. I read a lot of books to challenge her; Dawkins, Harris, Hitchens but she was able to answer using logic, reason, scientific explanations, and more. She pointed me to books by Frank Turek, C.S. Lewis, and Lee Strobel and I came away convinced by the evidence."

"What evidence?"

"Where do you want to start?" Joe asked. "Evidence for God?"

"No, I believe in God. I'll even go so far as to say you and I believe in the same God since Christianity arose from Judaism. We just don't believe that Jesus is Messiah. What evidence do you have for that?"

"Well, let me ask you this; if I wanted to mail a letter to you anywhere in the world, how many lines of address would it take?"

Benny did a quick count before responding. "Three."

"So with three lines of information, I can mail a letter and it will get to you, wherever you might be?"

"Yes."

"Okay and how many Old Testament prophecies are there about Messiah?"

"I have no idea," Benny replied.

"Roughly 332," Joe answered.

"Seriously?" Benny looked back in shock.

"Yes, seriously. Now, if I can send a letter anywhere in the world using three lines of code, don't you think 332 prophecies are going to demand even higher specificity?"

"Of course, but are you really going to expect me to believe Jesus fulfilled all those prophecies?"

"Of course not," Joe answered. "Not because I told you anyway. Like I said, I didn't believe any of it. Christy challenged me to study it; read the prophecies and read the gospels. They match up. He really did fulfill them. All of them."

"Give me an example," Benny challenged.

"Alright," Joe nodded as he stood and studied the bookshelf. He found Benny's copy of the Tanakh, made a show of blowing dust off the cover and tossed it beside Benny. "How about you read Psalm 22 and Isaiah 53. Read them and then compare them to Jesus' crucifixion and what it meant."

Benny looked up at Joe, sighed, and began to search through the Tanakh.

"O'Shanick!" An officer called from the cell door. "You've got a visitor. Let's go!"

Chapter 20

Alto, Georgia

"Twenty-eight…twenty-nine…thirty!"

Christy finished a set of Spider-Man pushups and hopped back up to a standing position. She slowly paced inside her cell as she counted off a twenty second rest and then began a set of thirty jump squats. Her watch having been confiscated during processing, she had no way to time her sets, so she worked them to thirty or failure. She was ten minutes into a planned thirty minute High Intensity Interval Training (HIIT) workout and already the sweat was pouring off her face and drenching her white tank top. Her leg muscles burned in protest as she worked through her second set of jump squats. Despite having just completed an Ironman triathlon a week ago, she wondered if she would be able to complete the full thirty minutes of this workout. Christy was used to swimming, biking, and running for hours at a time. These explosive calisthenics were something she hadn't done in years, dating back to when she played volleyball for the University of Tennessee, now that she thought about it, and her body was protesting the very foreign stress. *Lots of new things to get used to here,* she thought to herself. There was plenty of room to run outdoors but swimming and biking weren't going to be happening on this side of the razor wire fence.

Over the past twenty-four hours, Christy had observed that most of her fellow inmates were overweight and out of shape. Some severely so. Likely due to a combination of ample leisure time watching

TV and all of the junk food the inmates were purchasing by the bagful at the commissary. Christy wasn't trying to be critical. No longer a collegiate volleyball player, she had once gained fifteen pounds during her first year of medical school until one her classmates, Wendy Conlan, a marathon runner, had convinced Christy to start working out with her. By her second year of medical school, Christy had toned up and slimmed back down to a very fit physique. She had maintained it ever since. She had no idea how long she would be behind bars, but she wasn't about to let her fitness slide. If there was one thing she learned as an ER physician, people who live a fit lifestyle were rarely patients. They rarely got sick, rarely suffered severe mental health disorders, and rarely developed high blood pressure, diabetes, and all the other disease processes such as coronary artery disease and strokes that much of sedentary America suffers from. *Use it or lose it,* Christy often said. The body followed the Law of Inertia; an object at rest tends to stay at rest while an object in motion tends to stay in motion.

She powered through a set of mountain climbers and then settled into a plank. She tried to focus on counting off ninety seconds, but her thoughts kept drifting back to her current situation. Although not overly prone to emotions, Christy's mind had been teeming with them in a crescendo fashion. At the forefront was anger over the great injustice of her and her friends being wrongfully arrested when all they did was rescue a dozen women out of the hands of human trafficking perverts. There was also sadness, but more increasingly, fear.

Try as she might to remain focused and trust in God, there were plenty of things to fuel that emotion. Could they really be facing these ridiculous charges? Could they actually be convicted and face considerable years of imprisonment? The answer to both was yes. They were up against an incredibly powerful and relatively unknown global entity that had unlimited resources. Christy didn't even have a lawyer yet. *Does Joe? Ramsey?* Her father was working on that but, even if she had a legal dream team, would it be enough to stand up to what they were facing? Would the judge be fair or be a part of this…*conspiracy?* Christy wasn't of the mind to be a conspiracy theorist but was that what this was? Yes, it sure seemed like it. Would she spend a good part of the rest of her life in here? Would Joe? Would they ever see each other again let alone build a life together like they had begun talking about? Or was this her new life? If she did get out of here, would she still have a job? Would she even be licensed to practice?

That thought coursed through her mind as she stood up and walked off another rest cycle before beginning a set of eight count pushups which were burpees with two pushups in the down position. By the time she had completed ten, the searing pain in her shoulders and legs matched what she was feeling emotionally. Rather than bottle her emotions up like she normally did, Christy embraced the pain and let her emotions flow. Tears flowed freely as she grunted through the painful pushups and leaps only to drop into another one. She pushed past her goal of fifteen and punished herself with another five. A menacing roar, a mixture of physical and emotional pain coupled with exhaustion, echoed off the concrete walls as she struggled through the last pushup. Christy leaped to her feet and walked off another rest, pacing her small cell like a caged tiger.

Her thoughts returned to Joe. This past year with him had been the best year of her life. They had been to the brink of death together and returned. Several times, no less. During one of those times she had, actually had, what she believed to be a brief vision of their future together. A vision of her and Joe with several young children swimming at his parent's house and playing in the snow. It had been so vivid and peaceful during the split second before what, at the time, seemed like certain death. Christy had embraced it just like she had Joe and his family who had embraced her. The thought of all that being taken from them by a corrupt political cabal, making the ultimate self-serving power play and callously destroying the lives of any who got in the way, caused a rage to well up within Christy like she had never experienced before.

Rather than transition into a set of side lunges, Christy yanked the sheets off her mattress and threw them aside. She angrily pulled the rubber mattress off her bunk and threw it up against the bare wall where she began striking it with a flurry of savage punches. A series of left jabs followed by a hard right. More lefts and another right. Christy saw the innocent faces of the girls they had rescued. Many of them bruised and beaten. Some so young they were barely into puberty. Most of them malnourished and timid with a blank stare of traumatically scarred emotions. She saw the smug defiance of Victor Tupolev, the Russian mob boss, and Senator Fowler, the presidential candidate, whom she blamed for the state the girls were found in. However, Fowler had somehow, not only been cleared of all charges, but either he or the people backing him, had managed to get Christy, Joe, and all those who rescued the girls arrested and thrown in jail. Christy's punches became harder and more furious as the indignation over this cruel injustice fueled her rage. Despite the rubber foam mattress, her knuckles began to bleed as visions of a future with Joe were displaced by the self-righteous Fowler laughing at her as people lined up to shake his hand.

She thought of the girls, the victims, the girl last week, Lindsay, who had shown up in Christy's ER after being shot while escaping Tupolev's pimps only to die from her wounds. Tears mingled with sweat and the rivulets rolled off her face and onto the floor as pent-up rage flowed out of her. She punched even harder and a guttural growl began to sound as she thought of so many promising futures being destroyed; hers, Joe's, Ramsey's, Lindsay's, Daniella, Yoana, and so many more, all at the hands of ruthless men who would stop at nothing to accumulate wealth and power.

Christy ignored the burning pain in her arms and shoulders as she punched with even greater fury as these thoughts circled around in her mind. She thought of Joe quietly telling her that he loved her while being spun toward the door by the agents who had broken into in her house. Guilt and sorrow washed over her, mixing with rage as she, once again, reminded herself that none of this would have happened had she not asked Joe and Ramsey to locate and rescue the rest of the girls whom Lindsay had told her about moments before dying. Christy's growling turned into a staccato grunt which matched the flurry of punches barely cushioned by the thin mattress as she repeatedly struck the wall. Finally, with one last heave, she struck the wall and collapsed to the floor, physically and emotionally drained. She sat against the wall, cradling her knees to her chest and briefly banged the back of her head against the wall in a tearful fit of rage before laying her head down on her arms in a heaving state of anger and despair.

Chapter 21

Atlanta, Georgia

"Inmate 1001001 for visitation," the husky corrections officer said through the thick window.

The officer behind the window checked a computer screen, nodded, and pressed a button. A loud electronic buzz sounded, and the heavy steel door opened. The officer escorted Joe into the visitation room. There were a couple dozen tables with permanent seats fixed around them. Since normal visiting hours were on Fridays through Sundays, all the tables were empty except one in the back corner. Two men sat at the table. Joe didn't recognize the first man; a dark haired, fit man who looked young but Joe guessed was in his mid-fifties. He wore a charcoal gray, tailored suit with red paisley tie and well-polished black wingtip shoes. He was also in a wheelchair, the lightweight kind used by active paraplegics. A blond man sat next to him wearing a navy blue blazer, yellow shirt with navy blue stripes, and khaki chinos. Joe instantly recognized him.

"Mr. Brinkworth!" Joe exclaimed.

Tom Brinkworth was a personal friend of the O'Shanick family. He and Joe's father had grown up together on Grand Island, played hockey together, and sailed together. Whereas Jack O'Shanick had enlisted in the Navy, Brinkworth went on to play college hockey at Cornell. A solid defenseman in front of the net, he also had an ability to move the puck and make plays. He captained the team his final two years and was drafted by the now defunct Quebec Nordiques but turned down a chance to play in the pros to attend law school at Cornell. He had been practicing criminal law for over thirty years and had actually represented Joe last June during his encounter with the mafia. Despite being in his upper fifties, Brinkworth looked several years younger with a tanned face, short but styled blond hair, and broad shoulders. Joe and his siblings always joked that Mr. Brinkworth reminded them of Fred from the Scooby Doo cartoons in looks, voice, and mannerism. That aside, he had a reputation as a fierce attorney, something Joe had witnessed personally, and he was a welcome sight.

"Joe, I'm sorry about the circumstances, but it's good to see you," he said as he stood to shake Joe's hand. "Your dad called me Saturday night and I came as quick as I could."

"I'm beyond grateful, Mr. Brinkworth," Joe said shaking the man's hand. "It's really good to see a friendly face that I know I can trust."

"That's why I'm here, Joe," Brinkworth said as he gestured toward the man in the wheelchair. "I'd like you to meet Nick Marcella. Nick and I went to law school together up at Cornell. He practices criminal law down here in Atlanta as a senior partner with Marcella, Ferraro and Krysztof, one of the top law firms around."

"Pleased to meet you, Mr. Marcella," Joe said offering his hand in greeting.

"The honor is all mine, Mr. O'Shanick," Marcella said as he shook Joe's hand. "Please call me Nick."

"Nick it is, and I'm Joe."

"Have a seat, Joe, and I'll go over the game plan," Brinkworth said as he pointed to an open seat and took his own seat. "To start, I'm not licensed in the State of Georgia, which is why I reached out to Nick. Since this is a federal case, I can come alongside as co-counsel through a legal clause known as *pro hac vice*, but Nick and his firm will need to take the lead since the charges were filed in Georgia. I'll be helping out as much as I can but, if I were sitting in your spot, I would want Nick representing me as well."

Joe nodded as he glanced over at Marcella who confidently looked back at him and nodded.

"Our firm will also be representing Mr. Ramsey, who should be on his way here to join us," Marcella said as he looked to the door which was just starting to open. Ramsey emerged escorted by another officer. "Ah, that must be him now."

Ramsey walked over to the table. Joe and Brinkworth stood and introductions were made all around.

"Mr. Ramsey, I was just telling Joe how my firm has been retained by Joe's father to represent both of you. You will each be appointed your own lead counselor for the proceedings but, in actuality, it will be a team effort which will allow us to pool evidence in discovery and workout defense strategies." Marcella looked directly at Joe, "Joe, I will be your lead counsel and, Mr. Ramsey, my partner Eddie Ferraro will be representing you. I trust him with my life. The only thing better than his trial record is his golf game and he's a scratch golfer. The prosecuting attorneys all call him 'Eddie the Rat' because he's a sneaky rat in the courtroom, always outsmarting them and one step ahead. He always finds a way to win."

"My kind of guy," Ramsey remarked.

"He is and you'll like him. Trust me. He would have been here today but he's in court all day. That's not a problem though. We have your bond hearing this afternoon and I can represent both of you. My plan is to get you released so you don't have to spend one more minute in this hell hole," Marcella said looking around. "This should never have happened. This is no way to treat a couple of decorated war heroes and I plan to fix that right away."

"Has your office, by any chance, been contacted about Dr. Christy Tabrizi?" Joe asked.

"Yes. Tom gave us her name along with the two of you. One of our junior partners, Kelley Ekland, is heading up to meet with her and handle her bond hearing today. Same scenario, Kelley will be her lead counsel as part of our team approach for all three of you. Kelley is one of our rising stars. Dr. Tabrizi is in good hands."

"Can I ask where she is?"

"She was shipped up to Lee Arrendale State Prison and hour and a half northeast of here. Same boat as the two of you, she should have been kept in the detention center locally. The fact that they saw fit to move the three of you into actual prisons raises several red flags. I won't say it's unprecedented but it's highly irregular."

"Because somebody wants us eliminated," Ramsey interjected. "We're the only eyewitnesses to what really went on down in Belize. If we testify, Fowler's campaign has a good chance of sinking fast, regardless of whether or not he goes to jail. I don't even think they care what happens to him so long as they win the White House. If they can keep us from testifying? Dead men tell no tales."

"We've considered that explanation," Marcella nodded. "If you have anything that will corroborate that, it would be helpful for the bond hearing today, not to mention building your defense."

"It's a combination of speculation on our part and scuttlebutt from the inmates but I don't think you'll get any of them to testify to it and risk becoming a snitch," Joe answered. "Rammer and I are one thing; we can take care of ourselves. It's Christy that I'm worried about. If you get only one person out today, please let it be her."

"My plan is to have all three of you released on bond, if not your own recognizance, this afternoon. The legal precedents and the law are on our side. If we *can't* get you all released, then we really are up against a nefarious movement."

Joe and Ramsey nodded solemnly.

"So, that being said," Marcella began as he removed a legal pad from a leather attaché slung over the side of his wheelchair, "why don't we begin with you recounting everything that actually happened? Let's start with how you got involved."

Chapter 22

Washington, D.C.

Director Snyder vigilantly scanned his surroundings as he walked with a purposeful stride. His objective was only a couple of blocks down E Street from the FBI headquarters, but he had spent the last fifteen minutes walking a haphazard pattern along various streets, reversing course and ducking into stores to ensure he wasn't being followed. Satisfied, he walked the final block, turned down 7th Street and entered a small coffee shop. The morning rush was over and he was able to order immediately. His simple order of a short black coffee was filled within seconds. He handed the barista a five, waited for his change, placed a dollar in the tip jar, and made his way out to an open-air courtyard. He spotted the exact bench that was described in the text, took a seat, and sipped his coffee.

After a minute, he set his coffee down and bent forward to retie his shoelace. Looking under the bench, he spotted the prepaid cellphone taped to the underside of the bench. He subtly grabbed the phone while straightening his pants leg and palmed it. He then reached inside his suit coat and pulled his hand out with the cellphone now visible. There was only one number loaded on the phone. Snyder dialed it. An Asian accented voice answered and spoke mockingly.

"You're doing well, sir. The fact that you've followed our instructions to the letter, tells us you are determined to keep your little indiscretion from destroying your family and your career,"

"What is it you want?" Snyder asked impatiently.

"Ah, a man who gets right to the point. Cut the crap, as you say? I like that," the man teased. "Then *I* will get right to the point. The wrong man is in the White House. The right man had a little indiscretion that needs to be swept under the rug, as you say. Much like your situation. Don't you think?"

Snyder paused before answering. "Yes," he muttered quietly.

"Good!" The other voice said condescendingly. "I thought you would see it our way. Now listen to me very carefully. Your underlings kept the pilot from crashing the plane but now it's up to you to land the plane. Do you understand what I mean?"

"Yes."

"Very good. Make it happen. If you do so, your dalliance will never be brought to light and you, my friend, will be aptly rewarded at the proper time. I understand you have a special meeting today?"

"Yes," Snyder responded.

"There are certain facts that are undeniable. Use them to earn his trust and then throw him off the hunt with misinformation and reasonable doubts. We will take care of the rest but know this, we will have our eye on you at all times. Now, dispose of this phone. There will be no reason for us to converse any further. If I have to get ahold of you, it will mean you did not do as we instructed. You do not want that to happen."

"Understood."

"I understand you are a good Catholic?" the voice asked.

"I try," Snyder said genuinely contrite.

"Then I suggest you go to confession at the church near your office. Seven P.M., first confessional on the left."

The line went dead in Snyder's ear. His hand shook as he pocketed the phone. Things just got real. No, that wasn't right. Things got real two days ago, the moment SAIC McPherson was murdered. *That has to be connected,* Snyder thought as he grabbed his coffee and stood.

Snyder looked around. There was no one in the courtyard but him. Still, someone had eyes on him. They knew the moment he sat down on the bench. The courtyard was surrounded by a posh extended stay hotel on one side and a trendy apartment building on the other side. There were plenty of rooms looking into the courtyard. Somebody went to great extent to send him a message when they could have sent it along with the original text. They knew he would consider that, he thought, as he began to walk out. Their way of showing they were everywhere and yet nowhere. They weren't to be taken lightly.

Therein lied the dilemma, Snyder considered as he exited onto 4th street. Whoever this was, they were clearly backing Fowler all the way the White House and were willing to kill, steal, and destroy to get him there. Although he and Fowler were of the same political party, Snyder knew enough about Fowler to know he was as self-serving as they come and would sell out the nation to the highest bidder. President Galan, on the other hand, was a true patriot. Snyder may not see eye to eye with Galan on certain issues, but in the end, they both agreed that America was indeed a special place and aimed to preserve that legacy for their children.

From what Snyder had learned so far, the Fowler incident would indeed derail his campaign if an honest investigation were conducted and the findings truthfully reported. It was equally obvious that a certain well-organized element was not going to allow that to happen. All things considered, it was obvious to Snyder what the ethical choice was; oversee an honest investigation and let the facts speak. In which case, Fowler would not only lose the race but wind up in prison. But things were no longer even. Snyder had allowed himself to fall into their trap. If that affair ever came to light, his life would be ruined. His career, his marriage and by extension his family, and perhaps even his life depended not only on fixing the investigation and the evidence but backing Fowler all the way to the White House. Whoever they were, they owned him now.

Chapter 23

Alto, Georgia

Consider the blameless, observe the upright;
there is a future for the man of peace.

But all sinners will be destroyed;
the future of the wicked will be cut off.

The salvation of the righteous comes from the LORD;
he is their stronghold in time of trouble.

The LORD helps them and delivers them;
he delivers them from the wicked and saves them,
because they take refuge in him.

Christy had read the last lines of Psalm 37 over and over, prayed it aloud several times, and now she lay on her remade bunk as it resonated through her mind. She chastised herself over her earlier breakdown. Although it had felt good on a primitive level, she had allowed herself to be overwhelmed by her circumstances and consumed by her emotions, something quite out of character for her.

When the Apostle Peter got out of the boat and walked on the water, his eyes, ergo his mind was focused on Christ. It was when he allowed himself to be distracted and frightened by the storm around him when he sank. Christy knew better. No matter how critical a patient may be or how chaotic the ER could be, she would silently pray a quick plea for wisdom and poise and God would always see her through. This should be no different. He had allowed all of this to happen. There was a purpose. She didn't know what that purpose was but as long as she put her trust in God, He would see her through it.

She prayed for Joe and Ramsey. Yes, they were Navy SEALs who had been forged in the fiery crucible of BUD/S and further honed over years of training and combat, but they had gotten ensnared in a political/legal battle, against an enemy that considered them to be expendable pawns. This was *not* something they were trained for. There was a political machine trying to bury them and they would need help beyond their special warfare skills.

After snapping out of her earlier meltdown, Christy had replaced the mattress on her bunk, made her and Hannah's beds, and straightened up their tiny cell. Putting things in order had always been a form of therapy for Christy when her thoughts were in disarray. After tidying up their cell, Christy had looked through Hannah's small collection of books and found the Bible she was currently using to pray. Reading and praying through more Psalms allowed her to have a God-centered focus rather than a self-centered focus, providing a needed reset and a welcomed peace. She soon found her eyelids growing heavy as relaxation set in and gave way to drowsiness.

Christy woke with a startle, sensing someone was in the cell. Her confrontation with Randy was still fresh in her mind. She hadn't seen the last of Randy. Christy admonished herself for falling asleep and letting her guard down. She opened her eyes a crack and gave the cell a quick scan. She didn't see anyone, but her instincts told her she was not alone. Christy quietly slid the Bible off of her chest where she had laid it before dozing off. While doing so, she sensed more than heard movement from below. She couldn't see down there without rolling over to look. There it was again. Christy formed a quick plan and tensed to move. In a blur of motion, she rolled to her right, pivoted, and swung her long legs over the side. She landed in a crouch ready to defend herself and strike. A figure lay prone on the bed, wearing khaki prison pants and a white tank top. The figure jolted in surprise when Christy landed next to her, sitting bolt upright with a gasp. It was Hannah.

"Geez!" she said, "I think you just took ten years off of my life!"

"I'm so sorry," Christy replied apologetically. "Your friend, Randy, and I had a little dust up while you were gone and I'm a bit on edge. I heard a noise and thought you were her."

Hannah looked down at her hands and sighed. "Randy's bad news. She runs this joint. You need to stay away from her. I'm serious. She'll kill you."

"I think it's a little late for that," Christy as she sat down on the small desk seat attached to the wall. "I don't know how that would be possible anyway, me staying away from her, with her coming in here to take advantage of you," Christy let her words linger as she watched Hannah for a reaction.

Hannah continued to look down at her now fidgeting hands as she sat on the side of the bed. She remained silent.

"Hannah," Christy knelt down on the floor and looked up into her pale blue eyes. "Tell me what's going on. I want to help you."

"You can't," she said barely above a whisper.

"Why do you say that?" Christy asked.

"Because I'm beyond help. I'm a lost cause."

"Why do you think that?"

"Are you kidding me?" Hannah said looking up at Christy. "Look at me! I'm an addict! I've been an addict since I was a freshman in college. I've been to rehab twice, and I keep using cuz I can't stop. I don't even care if I get high anymore; I just want to feel normal, and I'll do anything to get that!"

Tears began rolling down Hannah's cheeks. Christy placed a hand on Hannah's hands and continued to look in her eyes. There was more to her story, but Hannah had stopped talking and seemed hesitant to go there.

"Let it out, Hannah. I've seen a lot. You won't shock me. Let me help you," Christy pleaded gently. "How did it start?"

Hannah took a deep breath. "It was so stupid. I was a freshman at Georgia. I was planning on being a pharmacist. How ironic," Hannah said rolling her eyes. "I was studying hard but got myself all worked up over our first chemistry test. There was this guy. We weren't really seeing each other but we hung out, kind of. I told him how nervous I was and that I didn't think I would be able to get through the test. He gave me a Lortab to calm me down and it worked. I was so chill, and I cruised through the test and got an A. I have to admit, I loved how it felt so I asked him for another one, you know, for next time. Well, next time soon became all the time. It turned out he was one of the biggest drug dealers on campus. He was only too happy to keep me supplied as long as I slept with him. I got a 3.6 GPA fall semester but by spring semester I was taking pills by the handful. I stopped going to class. I stopped studying. I pretty much lived at his house off campus."

"Well, needless to say, I failed all my classes and my parents were fit to be tied. They knew something was up. We were an upper middle-class family in Marietta. I went from a straight-A student, soccer player, homecoming queen in high school to a college flunky in one year. I didn't want to go home that summer, but they made me and figured out real quick that I had a problem. I confessed everything and they were actually really good about it. They got me into a rehab place. I spent a few weeks there and came home clean and sober. I got a job at a nice restaurant waiting tables. The tips were great, but the staff were almost all addicts. They were getting high at work and after work. I relapsed my first week there. Before long I was right back where I was before; taking handfuls of pills several times a day."

Christy held Hannah's gaze and gave a nod of understanding and encouragement to continue.

"My tip money wasn't keeping up with my habit, so I began stealing from my parents. I would charge things to my dad's credit card and then go straight to a pawn shop and sell it for cash. My dad has everything on auto-draft and I didn't think he paid that close attention. Well, he did. I charged up over five thousand dollars in one month. Back to rehab I went; only this time, I had given up. I didn't care anymore and had no desire to get clean. I checked myself out the first week. My parents were furious and refused to let me come home. I moved in with my manager at work. It was good at first. I was back working, he treated me good and kept me high. Then one night, the owner walked in on us passed out in his office after hours. There was a bag of Roxy's on his desk. We were fired on the spot. And then…" Hannah stopped abruptly, squinting her eyes shut as the tears came harder

"Then what?" Christy gently prompted.

"Then I started stealing from the rest of my family," she said sniffling as she grabbed her prison shirt off the bed and used it to dry her eyes. "I would come by in the morning after my parents left for work and my two younger brothers were at school. I would steal some of my mom's jewelry and pawn it. My dad and my brothers are hunters. I started stealing their rifles and selling them. I even stole both of my brothers' X-boxes and pawned them. I mean, what kind of a sister does that to her little brothers!"

"Addiction is a form of slavery, Hannah. People will do unimaginable things just to get their next fix. We had an attending physician at my medical school who was everyone's favorite. He was a great teacher, funny, and a great physician. Still is. A few years ago, he went public with his opiate addiction. Very similar story to yours. One thing I will never forget; he has a wife and children and said they are his world and he would do anything for them but, when he was struggling with his addiction, his family no longer mattered. All he cared about was getting that next handful of pills just so he could feel normal again. You're not the only one."

"He's right," Hannah sniffled. "I would have cleaned my parents out had they not sent me here."

"*They* sent you here?" Christy asked incredulously.

"Yep," Hannah nodded. "They tried to get me to go back to rehab but I refused. Daddy knew what I was doing and put cameras all around the house to prove it. He pressed charges and I was sent here. I don't blame him. I would have cleaned them out. I just know I would have. That wasn't why he did it though. He told me that since I wasn't interested in getting help that he was going to put me in a place where I couldn't get in worse trouble or hurt anyone else. He also hoped that this would be my wake-up call and that maybe I would get help while I was in here."

"Have you tried to get help?" Christy asked.

"At first, I did, and I was actually motivated but then the withdrawal kicked in. I tried to fight it. I really did, but it's hard. So freaking hard. The prison offers counseling and group therapy, but that doesn't help when your body feels like it's in fire and in suffering what feels like the worst flu imaginable. I tried several times, but I couldn't do it. This place is loaded with just about every drug ever made and, knowing how to get my fix makes it too tempting every time I'm withdrawing."

"Is Randy your supplier?"

"Yes," Hannah nodded as she looked down at her feet again. "Among other things. She is the king bull in here. A real hustler. She knows the right COs to bribe; she runs the drug trade in here, the gambling, and the pimping."

"Pimping? In here?"

"Oh, yeah," Hannah nodded vigorously as she nodded at Christy. "There are hundreds of women in here, many of them young, who are bored and lonely and will do anything for a little sexual pleasure. Randy has turned that into quite a lucrative operation. She pimps out sexual favors in return for money, contraband, enforcers, and just about anything she wants."

"Is that what she's doing with you?" Christy inquired discreetly.

Hannah looked down at her fidgeting hands and didn't answer.

"Hannah?" Christy said gently laying a hand on Hannah's shoulder. "Is that what went on yesterday morning?"

Hannah nodded so slightly as to be almost imperceptible. "Yes," she whispered.

Christy lowered her head and tried to look up into Hannah's eyes. "How long has she been using you like this?"

"First week I got here," her voice was low and shaky. "Randy checks out all the new arrivals. Preys on them is more like it. She has amazing street sense and can see things in people. Especially their weaknesses and then she uses it to her advantage. She spotted me for an addict right way. Told me she could get me whatever I wanted. I tried to shrug her off the first couple of days. Told her I was done with using. She laughed. She was right. The very next day I was withdrawing so bad I was begging her for help. She made me…she made me…"

"That's alright, Hannah," Christy said as she patted her shoulder. "I can put two and two together. You don't have to say it."

"I've never done that before!" Hannah said crying. "I felt so…so…dirty that I ran back in here, stuck a finger down my throat and dry heaved. Then I brushed my teeth and washed my face, but I still couldn't get rid of that feeling. I mean, I know other women are into that but I'm not!"

"I understand," Christy soothed. "I'm not either."

"I know," Hannah replied. "By the way, that really peeved Randy when you told her as much yesterday. You need to be careful."

"Why's that?"

"Because she's sadistic. Anyone who crosses her either becomes her personal slave or ends up leaving here in a hearse."

This time, Christy was silent as she absorbed what Hannah had just told her.

"I'm serious, Christy. I've been here almost two years and I've seen a half dozen women die here."

"How can she get away with that?" Christy asked astonished.

"Lots of reasons. Nobody actually sees her do it. Even if they did, they aren't going to rat her out. Snitches fare far worse. We all *know* she does it, but no one is stupid enough to try and turn her in. It doesn't matter anyway. She's serving life without parole. This is her home for the rest of her life, and she is making it her kingdom."

"So she makes you pleasure her in exchange for drugs?" Christy asked.

"That's how it started anyway," Hannah replied. "It's grown from there."

"What do you mean?"

"Well, it started with me just having to do her twice a day. Each time, I would get an Oxy in return."

"Oxycodone?" Christy asked to clarify.

"Yes. She started me off on 20's but, with my history, they barely did the job. To get more, I had to start servicing her lieutenants and then that turned into anyone she told me to. Before long I was up to using the 60's and doing whoever she told me to. Then she swapped out the Oxys for that cheap fentanyl from Mexico. Nothing I can do. She owns me and we both know it."

"Oh, Hannah, that's terrible!"

"Life of an addict," Hannah shrugged, her eyes still watery. "It's like a suffocating darkness just like this place. If I were to dwell on it,

I'd get sick, but I've grown numb to it. I don't run in here to brush my teeth of scrub my face anymore. I just do what I have to do to get by."

Christy grabbed Hannah by both shoulders and turned her until they were face to face. "Well, *that* is going to change! I've helped many people get started on the road to a drug-free life and, if you'll let me, I can help you too."

"I don't know if I can," Hannah shook her head. "I've tried so many times before and I can't stop. I can't take the withdrawal. I just go right back."

"Hannah," Christy looked intently into her eyes and spoke evenly in a serious tone. "You were seconds away from dying yesterday. In your own words, you are allowing yourself to be pimped out just to feed your habit. Do you really want to live like this? Or die?"

"Part of me wishes I had died yesterday. Hell can't be any worse than my life is now."

"Hell is unimaginably worse and never ending. You have your whole life ahead of you. How old are you?"

"Twenty-one."

"And how much time do you have left in here?"

"One year if I make parole."

"You can be out of here in a year, clean and sober. I'll help you. I really will."

"Even if I could do that, Randy will never let that happen. She'll kill me…and you."

Chapter 24

The White House

The Galan Oval Office was decorated in equal parts scarlet and gold with navy blue trim, a throwback to his previous career as an enlisted Marine. Bronze busts of Presidents George Washington and Ronald Reagan faced the Resolute Desk from their positions along the walls behind President Galan. Two more busts faced President Galan from their positions along the walls on the opposite end of the office; those of Sir Winston Churchill and the legendary Marine Corps General, Chesty Puller. Four men who led with resolute conviction and prevailed despite overwhelming odds and adversity. Galan did not have their busts in the office because he considered himself an heir to their legacy. Far from it. Rather, the busts served as reminders to the type of men who built and protected the free world and to hold him accountable as he carried on the mission.

Manny Galan sat behind the Resolute Desk, hunched over a file that contained the latest intelligence reports regarding China's growing presence in the South China Sea. His predecessor had allowed the Chinese to expand their naval presence and man-made islands with a feint at diplomatic sanctions that did nothing to dissuade the communist nation. Everyone knew Taiwan hung in the balance. The tiny nation was the world's largest producer of semiconductors and computer chips. The Chinese had long claimed ownership of Taiwan but had little influence over the nation's production and presence in the world market. A hostile military takeover could change that, which could drastically reduce the free world's access the vital technology, virtually overnight. With that move alone, China could deal a crippling blow to the technology market and free markets in general, let alone cut off the production of all the products that depended on that technology. Everything from cell phones and appliances to cars and crucial military equipment would suddenly become unavailable as manufacturers would be unable to complete the assembly of these products without the vital computer chips. The resulting supply shortages, layoffs, and staggering inflation would create economic chaos and another depression. There was no way Galan was going to allow that to happen. Not on his watch.

This was the fifth intelligence file he had been through in the past hour. In addition to the Chinese positioning themselves to move on Taiwan, he also had Russia rattling its saber at Ukraine. If that wasn't bad enough, there was the real possibility that Ukraine was a clever fake while Russia's real objective was the reclamation of the Baltic nations of Estonia, Latvia, and Lithuania. Additionally, Iran was hard at work trying to enter the nuclear race while the Taliban was actively regressing Afghanistan back to the Stone Age. A moral crisis of humanity was playing out in that nation as women and children were ruthlessly stripped of what few rights they once had while being tortured, enslaved, raped, and killed. *And my opponents claim I'm a misogynist?* Not to be overlooked, the war against the Central and South American cartels had made tremendous headway but was far from over. The level of corruption the cartels presided over ran deep and their controlling presence was ubiquitous in those nations.

While busy enough spinning these plates, many more geopolitical hotspots demanded President Galan's attention. It was a large world to cover. He was drastically trying to build up a military, capable of covering all of these problem areas, from the bare cupboard his predecessor had left him. The resultant spending added yet another challenge as he maintained his commitment to balancing the budget. Spending had to ultimately be cut elsewhere. The monstrous domestic programs were the only real area he could go after to try and reduce spending, but decades of entitlement programs made for a people who weren't willing to give much up. His opponents in Congress and the media knew this all too well and used it to leverage their positions. Ultimately, the House of Representatives controlled the purse strings and the deficits remained while the national debt grew. Galan sighed as he closed the current file and reached for the next one. Chief of Staff Embry appeared at the open door and knocked.

"Mr. President, Director Snyder is here for his noon appointment."

Galan glanced at his watch and stood. "Thank you, JJ. Let's have him."

Galan didn't believe in playing power games by making people wait unnecessarily just to prove who was in charge. Everyone had a job with overwhelming time demands. It was well known around Washington that if one respected President Galan's time, he would respect their time.

"Mr. President," Director Snyder said by way of greeting as he entered the room.

"Frank," Galan said cordially, standing behind his desk. He may not have fired Snyder, but he was certainly going to make sure Snyder knew where he stood. "Thank you for dropping by."

"It's the least I can do, sir, all things considered. I want to apologize again for what happened this weekend. It happened on my watch, and I accept full responsibility. I'm looking forward to making sense out of this and righting any wrongs that have been committed."

"Well, Frank, it seems we have a lot of ground to cover. You've proven your worth over the years and I have no reason to doubt your loyalty. Show me you're willing to work with us, like you say, and I'm willing to put the incident behind us."

"Thank you, sir," Snyder said solemnly. "I won't let you down."

"Well now that that's squared away, let's grab some chow. The rest of the team is already assembled in the dining room," Galan said as he turned and headed for a side entrance. "Follow me."

Snyder, accompanied by Embry and two Secret Service agents, turned and followed his president out the side door through a small hallway and into the private dining room. Seated around the table were President Galan's political advisor, Aaron Sprole, Assistant Chief of Staff Martin Espinoza, Attorney General Jacobs, and White House Chief Counsel Andrew "Drew" Barlow. Galan greeted the room as he entered and waved them off as they began to stand. He took his seat at the head of the table. Embry took his seat next to the president. Galan looked at Snyder and indicated the chair at the opposite end of the table.

"Thank you all for coming," Galan began. "Lunch will be served in ten minutes. In the meantime, I'd like Director Snyder to brief us on what occurred over the weekend and then we'll discuss what to do from there. Director Snyder, if you would please."

"Thank you, Mr. President," Snyder said as he got out of his chair and stepped up to the wall where a large flatscreen hung. "I prepared a short PowerPoint presentation with what we know so far."

Snyder thumbed a small handheld remote and the large flatscreen came to life. The first slide was a picture of a beautiful young blond female.

"The best place to start is the Friday before last when this young lady, a Tracy Courtnall, was abducted from the campus of Duke University, while out for her morning jog. She was one of five young women abducted that day from various college campuses all by the same crew headed up by this man," the screen changed to the photo of a muscular, bearded man with short dark hair, a broken nose, and Slavic facial features, "Sergei Petrenko, a former Russian special forces soldier, who was running a lucrative prostitution and drug ring for Victor Tupolev," the screen changed again to show a tough-looking Russian man with thin gray hair and pale blue eyes, "the head of the Atlanta based Russian organized crime family under the same name. Tupolev is believed to have close ties to the *Los Fantasma Guerreros* cartel and controls the majority of the drug trade throughout the southeast reaching as far north as right here in DC."

Galan listened on intently, absorbing and scrutinizing everything being said and without asking a question. The screen changed again and the professional image of a well-dressed, sharp-looking man with a full head of premature gray hair appeared.

"This is Charles Courtnall, a wealthy financial investor, founding partner of Courtnall, Clark and Leeman Financial, and the father of Tracy Courtnall. A week ago today, Courtnall hired a large private investigation firm, Whitmore and Associates," the screen switched to the image of a fit, fortyish male who was mostly bald and what little sandy blond hair remained on the sides was closely shaved, "headed by this man, Clay Whitmore, to locate his daughter. Whitmore's group soon found the other girls in an online prostitution website called *The Girls of the ACC.*" Snyder knew better than to display a slide of the website full of the scantily clad girls. President Galan would not be pleased.

"They were able to use that to discover that Tracy Courtnall was being auctioned for a high price on the Dark Web. From there, they were able to trace the web posting to a computer located in Atlanta. Whitmore mobilized his team and they high-tailed it to Atlanta. Around the same time, one of the abducted girls, a Lindsay Meehan, was shot while escaping from the house of a law student who had hired her services. This has been kept out of the news but the law student in question is Clinton Williams, son of Senator Jeffrey Williams," the screen switched to the image of father and son together at a political event.

Clinton was a soft, cherub-faced young man with a shock of unruly hair. His father, the senator was a portly man with thin gray hair and a red bulbous nose who was a well-known DC fat cat, career senator. Galan was appropriately cordial with the man in public but had no respect for him whatsoever.

"Are you telling me the son of Senator Williams hired and tried to kill a prostitute?" White House Chief Counsel Barlow asked.

"Not exactly, Mr. Barlow," Snyder answered. "Yes, he did hire her services, but let's keep in mind Ms. Meehan had been abducted, raped, beaten, and forced into prostitution against her will. She had been brought to the young Mr. Williams' house where she overpowered him and escaped. One of Tupolev's pimps shot her while she was driving away in their car. She managed to drive herself to the emergency department in Duluth where she was initially treated by Dr. Christine Tabrizi," a professional photo of Christy flashed up on the screen.

"This is the same Dr. Tabrizi who was arrested?" Barlow asked.

"Correct," Snyder replied. "Ms. Meehan allegedly told Dr. Tabrizi about the prostitution ring, the names of the other girls, and where they were being held. Tracy Courtnall was one of the girls named. She also told Dr. Tabrizi that the police were in on it and begged her not to alert the authorities. Ms. Meehan succumbed to her injuries a few hours later and died. Dr. Tabrizi enlisted the help of her significant other, Lieutenant Commander Joseph O'Shanick, United States Navy Special Warfare, and his teammate and friend Master Chief Petty Officer Matthew Ramsey who voluntarily drove into Atlanta to locate and rescue the remaining girls. They found the location abandoned but, by pure happenstance, ran into Whitmore's team, learned that they were on the hunt, and offered their services. The next day, they tracked the Russians to their new location and conducted their own raid. They rescued several girls who were being prostituted but not the girls in question. They tracked them to Gwinnett County Airport shortly after, where Tupolev and Petrenko took off in a private jet with Tracy Courtnall and the other girls just as they arrived to intercept them.

"Whitmore's team tracked the plane down to Belize and Courtnall used his private jet to fly them all down there in pursuit."

The screen changed to a satellite image of a small tropical island with a small beach, a dock, a helicopter pad, and a dozen or so small tropical buildings.

"The girls were moved to this small island resort owned by a foreign shell corporation that Whitmore claims is owned by the *Los Fantasma Guerreros* cartel. Tupolev is known to have close ties with this cartel."

"It's at this point where the stories diverge," Snyder paused to take a breath before continuing. "From this point on, the principal suspects who most concern us are Senator Fowler on one side and O'Shanick, Ramsey, Whitmore, Dr. Tabrizi, Charles Courtnall, and one of Whitmore's associates, a man named Gary Lee, who was killed during the events in question. In the interest of brevity, we will refer to them as the O'Shanick group. All of their official statements match up and they coordinated their efforts to achieve their objective. The question lies in just what that objective was."

"What do you mean by that?" Chief of Staff Embry asked.

"What I mean is, we have a he said, she said situation," Snyder followed the statement looking around the table. "The facts, as we know them, are that O'Shanick and company tracked the girls to this island and conducted a military-style raid. They killed a dozen Mexican nationals..."

"Known cartel members holding kidnapped American citizens," President Galan inserted firmly.

"That seems likely, yes, Mr. President, although it has yet to be confirmed," Snyder politely countered. "Nevertheless, by O'Shanick's own statement, he and his team fired first without provocation. A firefight then ensued and, when the dust had finally cleared, there were nearly a dozen dead Mexican citizens, along with Sergei Petrenko, Ali Nazari, the deputy defense minister of Iran, and Zheng Gao, the special assistant to the president of China. All dead at the hands of O'Shanick and company. On top of all that, O'Shanick threw Senator Fowler to his death from a helicopter and tried to drown him."

"That's not how it happened," Galan stated with his arms crossed. "I've read their statements. Nazari fired his handgun at O'Shanick who fired back in self-defense. Gao tried to retrieve Nazari's gun and O'Shanick shot him in the process. The pilot put the helicopter into a spin. Fowler was kicking at O'Shanick in attempt to get him to fall off the landing skid. O'Shanick lost his footing, grabbed Fowler's shirt, who was not strapped in, and they fell out together."

"That's O'Shanick's statement, yes," Snyder nodded. "However, Senator Fowler tells it differently. He states O'Shanick killed both Nazari and Gao without provocation and then turned the gun on Fowler. Senator Fowler kicked the gun out of O'Shanick's hand and O'Shanick responded by deliberately throwing Senator Fowler out of the helicopter. He grabbed ahold of O'Shanick and they fell together. Upon landing, Senator Fowler maintains that O'Shanick then tried to drown him."

Snyder looked across the table at President Galan and was met with a stern look of skepticism.

"Mr. President," Snyder held his hands up in mock surrender, "if I may, I'm just presenting the facts as we know them so far along with the opposing statements. I'm not taking one side over the other, but I am showing the problem we face and the task we have ahead of us to get to the bottom of what actually happened."

"I follow you, Frank, but do you really believe Senator Fowler's claim? Joe O'Shanick is a trained Navy SEAL. If he had really wanted to drown Fowler, Fowler would *not* have survived to tell the tale. O'Shanick intentionally kept him alive by rescuing him so as to bring the senator home to face justice and expose a treasonous plot. He had ample opportunities to kill Fowler but chose not to. I should also remind you that the senator eluded his Secret Service detail, hopped a private jet, and flew to the cartel's private island, where he not only was consorting with known enemies of state, but was also caught in the act of attempting to rape Miss Courtnall."

"I understand sir, but…"

"He also ordered Pedro Cardenas, his host and the head of *Los Fantasma Guerreros*, to shoot Joe O'Shanick and Matt Ramsey!" Galan's voice began to raise as the Marine Gunnery Sergeant in him took over. "And for *this*, a highly-esteemed physician and two decorated Navy SEALs are behind bars! They are not out on bond, they are not in a holding cell, but in highly abnormal fashion, they have been thrown in violent prisons, while a treasonous, sexually malevolent pervert of a senator not only walks free but is strutting about on campaign rally stages while attempting to steal the election by leveling charges of murder at these brave individuals and accusing me of sending a hit squad to assassinate him!"

"I understand your frustration, Mr. President," Snyder replied with a shaky voice. "Please, keep in mind that, as stated earlier, this is a situation where it is one person's word against the other."

"I believe it is the word of one senator who was caught with has hand in the cookie jar against a half dozen brave Americans and several victimized young women," Galan countered.

"Be that as it may, sir, it is the situation at hand, and we are quickly investigating every aspect in the interest of ascertaining the truth. The facts *do* give credibility to the senator's claims. I understand your frustration, but statements aside, we have a dozen dead foreign nationals to account for and the only people who did any killing were O'Shanick and his team. The nation is well familiar of your past associations with Lieutenant Commander O'Shanick and Master Chief Ramsey. I have no choice to proceed as is."

Chapter 25

Atlanta, Georgia

Joe and Ramsey stood hunched over as they shuffled their way out of the prison transport van. A not-so-small crowd was gathered behind the news cameras flanking the walkway into the Richard B. Russell Federal Building. Someone had made sure the news would be present. Nothing painted a picture of guilt like two men in prison khakis shackled to the point they could only shuffle walk. Behind the cameras, the crowd was a mix of supporters and haters. Many held signs with varying themes from "Save the SEALs" to "Murderers" and even "Baby Killers."

Baby killers? Really? Joe thought to himself as he and Ramsey shuffled along led by their corrections officers. A few minutes later, they were led into a small meeting room. A conference table took up the majority of the room. Several people were already seated around the table, including Nick Marcella but it was another person who immediately caught Joe's eye. Seemingly unhindered by her shackles, Christy excitedly jumped up from her chair and began to shuffle towards Joe as fast as she could. Their handcuffs preventing any chance at a hug, Joe grabbed ahold of Christy's hands and pulled her in close. Their foreheads touched and Joe looked into her almond-shaped emerald green eyes.

"Are you alright?" he asked quietly.

"This whole thing is a nightmare but I'm holding up," she answered. "How are you doing?"

"Better, now that I can see you. I've been worried about you."

Christy smiled through watery eyes. "I've been worried about you too. I'm praying for you and Matt, that God will protect you and get us all out of this."

"Well, let's pray we make bond. I'd much rather deal with this back at your house than from inside prison," Joe said as he disengaged, fully aware everyone was waiting on them.

"Hey, Matt," Christy said as she gave Ramsey a quick peck on the cheek.

"Good to see you, Christy," Ramsey answered back.

They all took their seats and looked up at Marcella who sat at the head of the table. To his right, sitting across from Christy, was a tall but slender female who appeared to be in her early thirties, about the same age as Joe and Christy. She had shoulder length, straight medium-brown hair with brown eyes and a small, straight nose centered on an oval face that tapered to a narrow chin. She wore a black business suit with a white button-down blouse. On the surface, she was certainly attractive, but Joe also sensed a brooding intensity that suggested she was a hard-charging, tough woman who was not to be taken lightly. To her right was a tall, thin man who appeared to be in his fifties with classic Italian features. His thinning hair was slicked back and sat atop a narrow face with dark eyes and prominent chin. A pair of rimless reading glasses were perched on his long nose. He wore a tailored, charcoal gray double-breasted suit with a white shirt and gold cuff links. He reminded Joe of and old-fashioned mafia don who could go toe to toe bare, knuckles with anyone in the street and only to return home and bounce his grandkids on his knees. Tom Brinkworth sat to his right.

"Before we begin, gentlemen, I'd like to introduce you to Kelley Ekland. I believe I told you about her earlier, Kelly will be representing Dr. Tabrizi. Next to her is one of my other senior partners, Eddie Ferraro."

"Call me, Eddie," the dapper gentleman said as he reached across the table and shook Ramsey's hand followed by Joe's. "I'll be your lead counsel, Master Chief Ramsey."

"I appreciate it, sir," Ramsey answered with a nod.

"So, first up, we have your bond hearings," Marcella continued. "You'll be called in, one at a time, where you will appear before the district magistrate, read your charges, and informed of your bond amount. Joe, you're facing multiple charges including murder of a United States resident, Sergei Petrenko, and the attempted murder of a United States senator. Your bond could be quite high."

"How high?" Joe asked.

"As high a two million, in all honesty," Marcella said looking at him over the top of his reading glasses.

Joe swallowed hard. There was no way he could post that kind of bond. His parents would insist upon doing it for him, but they would have to put the family's construction business *and* their house up to even come close. No way would he allow them to do that. He would have to ride out the time to his trial in prison.

"Chief Ramsey, you're probably looking at upwards of a million yourself," Marcella continued.

Rammer's hosed too! Joe thought. There was no way he could make that. *God, at least let Christy have a low bond.*

"And, Dr. Tabrizi," Kelley Ekland jumped in, "you're probably looking at no more than fifty thousand dollars."

Oh, thank God! Joe thought with relief as he watched Christy stoically absorb that information. The thought of her spending any more time in prison was unbearable.

"So what you're saying is, the Chief and I are hosed," Joe commented.

"Not at all, Joe," Marcella replied cheerfully.

"Sir, with all due respect, neither the Chief nor I can afford the bonds you read off to us."

"I know that, Joe but you have several things in your favor. To begin with, the judge we have today is usually quite lenient with first time offenders and your service records should go a long way toward drastically reducing your bond."

Joe opened his mouth to speak but Marcella held up his hand.

"Hear me out a second, Joe," Marcella said with a gentle smile. "More importantly, Charles Courtnall's attorney, T. Chesterton Cooper, called me earlier today. They want to hitch wagons with us, so to speak, and compare notes, same with the attorneys for Whitmore and Associates. That's a huge pool of resources that will be a tremendous help in preparing for the upcoming trial. Before we finished our call, however, he also informed me that Mr. Courtnall insists on paying everyone's legal expenses and will post everyone's bond, regardless of the amount."

Joe's jaw dropped in disbelief. He glanced at Christy and Ramsey, both of whom were sporting surprised expressions as well. Joe quickly recovered.

"I can't let him do that for me," Joe protested.

"Me neither," Ramsey agreed.

"Same here," Christy added on, shaking her head.

"Cooper said Courtnall knew you would say that but that the issue is non-negotiable. You all volunteered to put your lives on the line to rescue his daughter and the other girls. He feels terrible that you all are being put through this and he insists on doing everything he can to make this right. He was willing to give up all of his vast wealth to get his daughter back and you got her back for him. He feels an immense debt of gratitude and insists on handling all of this. Quite frankly, we agree with him. Never have we ever seen such a selfless act of heroism," Marcella said as he glanced at Ekland and Ferraro who nodded in agreement, "nor have we ever seen such a terrible injustice, carried out at the hands of a treasonous senator who should *never* be president. This case has enormous historical consequences that will affect the free world. My partners and I all agree that we will not only fight with everything we have to see that justice is served. Mr. Courtnall also insisted on paying all legal fees for the three of you, but we turned him down. We are taking this on *pro bono*."

Chapter 26

Washington, D.C.

*F*ather Patrick smiled and nodded politely in return as people greeted him while he strolled west on H Street. It was a perfect October day. The sun shone brightly in the cloudless sky, warming his priestly garments in the slightly cool air. He wore the traditional Catholic priest's cassock; a black robe-like garment with full sleeves and a hem just above the ankles. It was cinched snugly, drawing attention to his trim waist and broad shoulders, products of years of training and competing in mixed martial arts. He still trained but he had long ago given up competing. His left shoulder had dislocated so many times that it was unstable. That was a different time, before the priesthood, in a far different place than here.

His birth name had been Jin Feng. He had grown up in a low-income, working-class family in Beijing. Like many low-income Chinese children, Jin Feng had suffered from malnutrition and was comparatively small for his age when he was a young teenager. As a result, he was often picked on and beaten by the older and larger youths. In response, his father had offered to work after hours as a janitor at a martial arts gym in exchange for Jin Feng to receive training. Jin Feng struggled at first but eventually began to thrive in *Sanshou* and boxing. What he didn't gain in height, he more than made up for in muscle and ability. Jin Feng began competing and found he had a natural talent and fighter's instinct on the mat. He soon added MMA to his training and felt like he had found his calling in life. The

MMA was just starting to become popular in China and Jin Feng was one of the nation's rising stars. He soon began to see the possibility of doors opening if he could find his way onto the world stage. A new tournament, *The Art of War Tournament,* was coming to Beijing and Jin Feng was determined to thrust himself onto the world stage by winning it.

Jin Feng never tapped out. During a sparring match with one of his instructors, Feng found himself on the wrong end of a grappling move that pinned his shoulder behind him. Rather than tap out, he endured the pain until his shoulder gave way and dislocated. It continued to dislocate over the next several months with increasing frequency. The government had not quite gotten behind the MMA, even the nation's premier fighters, and would not pay for surgery. Jin Feng would not be deterred and decided to adapt by learning to fight differently. It had worked. He competed and earned a slot in the tournament, excelling in the early rounds of the tournament without any shoulder difficulties. He had made it to the welterweight semifinals when his opponent, a Brazilian Jiu Jitsu specialist, executed a countermove that dislocated Jin Feng's shoulder and ended his title quest.

A well-dressed, high-priced gambler had taken notice of Jin Feng's gritty fighting spirit and met him in the medical room after the medical staff had reduced his shoulder. He introduced himself as Liu Fan, the son of Liu Shunyuan, the head of the Liu Dynasty. Originally one of the Chinese organized crime Triads, the Liu Dynasty had grown into a large international syndicate that thrived in many lucrative ventures, some legitimate, some not. Liu Fan was helping his father build up a reliable network of intelligence operatives and enforcers. He was looking for men like Jin Feng who could assimilate into any scenario and be able to handle themselves if the need arose. He promised good money, but Jin Feng saw something else: a ticket out of China.

Liu Fan's vision was to develop loyal soldiers of Chinese origin who would assume new identities that would not connect them to China and, more importantly, to the Liu Dynasty. He also envisioned soldiers who could be seen in nearly any professional location and not set off alarms. It was his idea to send Jin Feng to a training facility in the Philippines where he spent two years learning Tagalog, English, and Spanish in addition to spy craft, tactical and firearms training, and many other useful skills of the trade. He then obtained citizenship in the Philippines, changed his name, and enrolled in a Catholic seminary in Manila where he became Father Patrick Santos. He now served as a missionary to the United States, ministering in Chinatown and central Washington, D.C.

Father Patrick turned left onto 10th Street and walked a couple more blocks to his destination. He glanced at his watch as he entered the church, a classic Victorian Gothic Revival structure with a stone exterior. *Ave Maria* emanated from the pipe organ as he dipped his right hand in the holy water, made the sign of the cross, and genuflected before the altar. He made his way to the confessional, entered, and took his seat. This was one of his scheduled times for hearing confession, one of several duties he carried as a minister at large to the Washington area. It would likely be, what he called, a no-hitter. Monday afternoons in Washington were not exactly prime time for Catholics to make their confessions. To his surprise, he heard the door to the other side open and close, followed by the shuffling of a person settling into the chair. After a slight pause, he heard the tiny door slide open allowing the parishioner to speak through a small screen in privacy.

"Bless me, Father, for I have sinned. It has been two weeks since my last confession. I am struggling in gossip, infidelity, and double mindedness."

Father Patrick instantly recognized the coded phrase informing him that one of his agents, "John D" in particular was bringing him some valuable intelligence. "John D" was the Americanized version of *jiandie,* which was mandarin for spy. He was one of several agents Father Patrick had recruited and developed over the past several years since the Liu Dynasty had assigned him here. Father Patrick was the only one who knew John D's real identity. The man had risen to a position of importance and was a highly valued source of information for Father Patrick.

"En el nombre del Padre, del Hijo y del Espiritu Santo…"

Father Patrick answered his agent in Spanish, reciprocating the code and informing his agent that he had the correct priest and could proceed with his intelligence update.

"Bulldog is in war mode," John D began, using the Secret Service code name for President Galan. "He and the attorney general are shaking the FBI tree to see what falls out. The attorney general is conducting his own investigation into the incident, independent of the FBI and also monitoring the FBI. They suspect an inside job."

"Do they suspect anyone in particular?" Father Patrick asked.

"They're looking heavily into the Acting SAIC Winkelman but they are also suspicious of Deputy Director Wickenheiser."

"What about the director?"

"Snyder?" John D answered. "To a lesser degree, I guess. Right now, Galan smells a rat and is suspicious of everyone, but Snyder gave a briefing during lunch that actually put the president on defense a little."

"Really?" Father Patrick sat up and leaned into the metal screen that separated the two. "How's that?"

"He laid out some convincing evidence," John D responded. "There was no hit or any operation ordered on Fowler. I know that for a fact. Fowler got caught in the wrong place at the wrong time, but he's doing everything he can to wriggle off the hook and those SEALs are going to take the fall. Snyder presented the timeline of events and pieced the evidence together earlier. Even Attorney General Jacobs had to admit it won't paint a flattering picture of Galan in the court of public opinion. That *is* what you guys are going after, isn't it?"

"You don't know who *we* are, nor do you know anything about our objective!" Father Patrick admonished with a harsh whisper. "It would behoove you to concentrate on *your* objective lest you be found to be a liability."

An awkward silence followed Father Patrick's rebuke. John D knew what happened to those who were found to be a liability.

"Point taken," he answered. "But I *will* say this; if O'Shanick and his crew get to tell their side of the story, public sympathy will swing in their favor. You may want to consider seeing to it they never get a chance to get before a camera or a jury."

"Point taken," Father Patrick mocked. "We know how to handle this. However, painting a picture is not a guarantee," Father Patrick continued in a milder tone. "We need a blue dress."

"A blue dress?" John D asked.

"Before your time," Father Patrick dismissed. "We need a smoking gun. Some damning evidence. Something that shows Galan indeed ordered an attack."

"But the reality is he didn't," John D protested.

"What is it you Americans say? Perception *is* reality?" Father Patrick asked as he slid the screen open a crack and passed a white envelope through.

"Yes," John D said as he accepted his cash payment.

"Within that envelope, is a thumb-drive. It contains a Trojan Horse program that attaches to an email and embeds itself into any computer from which that email is opened. You are to see to it that it finds its way into the computer of the president's secretary"

"How am I supposed to do that?!" John D asked in alarm. "Do you have any idea how closely monitored her desk is, let alone her computer?"

"You need not worry," Father Patrick said reassuringly. "This was developed by a top rate hacker. It will breach all firewalls without tripping any alarms."

"I don't care!" John D hissed. "I'm rarely ever in the secretary's room. How do you expect me to get close enough to her computer to insert a thumb drive?"

"You weren't listening to me," Father Patrick answered. "I'm not expecting you to insert the thumb drive into her computer. Even if you could get close enough, there is too much security and the USB ports are all turned off for this exact reason. You simply need to send her an email with the program attached."

"But I rarely ever send her emails. She may suspect something."

"That's not our concern. You have your orders. You're a clever fellow, you'll figure it out. For your trouble, we have tripled your usual payment. Take a look for yourself."

John D opened the envelope and thumbed through the cash. It was all hundreds and a lot of them. The thumb drive was also in there.

"I want this done before morning. Leave your usual signal so I will know you have carried out this simple task as instructed."

"What is this for anyway?" he asked looking at the thumb drive.

"Perception," answered Father Patrick's Asian voice as he slid the divider on his side shut.

Chapter 27

Atlanta, Georgia

"United States versus Joseph James O'Shanick," the Honorable Christopher Gordon, Federal Magistrate, read from a sheet of paper.

Judge Gordon was a heavyset, grandfatherly type with a mostly bald head, thick gray eyebrows, with a matching thick gray mustache. He wore round, rimless reading glasses perched on the end of a bulbous nose.

"Mr. O'Shanick, you have been charged with two counts of attempted murder on a United States citizen, possession of a deadly weapon, assault with a deadly weapon, the unlawful detaining of a United States citizen along with the unlawful invasion of a foreign nation, and multiple counts of murder of foreign nationals during said unlawful invasion." The judge looked up from the paper he was reading and peered over the top of his reading glasses at Joe. "Do you understand these charges?"

"I do, Your Honor," Joe answered as he stood before the judge, arms and legs shackled, wearing his khaki prison uniform.

"And do you understand your rights?"

"I do, Your Honor."

"Very well," Judge Cooper glanced at his sheet and then looked back up. "You will stand trial for these counts. You may also be subject for extradition to Belize where you may stand trial for the murder and invasion charges. Do you understand this?"

"Yes, Your Honor."

"Very well. Does the prosecution wish to add anything before we determine bond?"

"Yes, Your Honor, we do," the United States Attorney, Alan Janowsky answered.

Janowsky was a stocky male in his late thirties with a full head of thick salt and pepper hair parted to the side and a matching goatee. He wore a gray wool two-piece suit with black wingtip shoes.

"The prosecution contends that the defendant does not live in the area, has no family in the area, is not employed in the area and represents a tremendous flight risk. Although, the prosecution recognizes and appreciates the defendant's military record, the prosecution would like to stress that we are not dealing with a fleet officer in this case. Mr. O'Shanick is highly trained special warfare operator. As part of this, he is trained in the art of escape and evasion. Furthermore, he possesses advanced skills in combat including, weapons, demolitions, and hand to hand combat. He is a trained killer, Your Honor. He has killed countless times in combat and now stands trial for the murder and attempted murder of many more. The prosecution contends that Mr. O'Shanick is not only a tremendous flight risk, but he is far too dangerous to be allowed to roam free, especially when the object of his attempted murder is a sitting United States Senator who is actively campaigning for president. What if he tried to finish the job? According to 18 United States Code, section 351, he is subject to imprisonment. Therefore, we strongly recommend Mr. O'Shanick be held without bond."

Judge Cooper looked over at Joe and Nick Marcella. "Would the defense like to respond?"

"Yes, Your Honor," Marcella said as he wheeled himself a little closer. "My client is a decorated officer in the United States Navy. For the past ten years he has served our country with honor and distinction and has risked his life for our nation in multiple combat tours. He has no prior criminal record, and he is gainfully employed serving as an active-duty officer in the Navy, albeit at a meagerly low salary compared to most people in the civilian world. In light of this and his distinguished service, we request Mr. O'Shanick be released on the lowest bond possible."

Judge Cooper stared at Joe in contemplation. He glanced at the U.S. Attorney before looking down at the documents in front of him. He set the papers down, removed his glasses and leaned forward, resting his elbows on the bench with his hands clasped.

"Mr. O'Shanick, I have taken into account your distinguished service record. I have also considered the fact that, up until now, you have no past criminal record," the judge paused before continuing. "However, in light of the circumstances and, considering the nature and seriousness of your charges, I must also take into account the points made by the prosecution. Your actions on the days in question, suggest a conspiracy to assassinate a sitting United States senator who happens to be a contender for the presidency. If released on bond, I have no guarantees that you will not seek out an opportunity to complete this task; therefore, it is the opinion of this court that you be held without bond until such time as a trial finds you guilty or innocent."

The rap of Judge Cooper's gavel echoed around the mostly empty interior of the courtroom. Joe stared at the judge in disbelief, but the judge avoided eye contact by keeping his head down and rifling through some documents. The bailiffs gently grabbed Joe's arms and led him back to the anteroom. Ramsey and Christy looked up at him expectantly as he entered. Joe shook his head grimly in response.

"Mr. Ramsey," the bailiff summoned.

Ramsey stood and shuffle walked around the table toward the bailiffs. "You were denied?" he asked Joe as they passed.

"Denied," Joe confirmed. "No easy day."

"No easy day," Ramsey echoed as the bailiffs escorted him out the door.

Chapter 28

Atlanta, Georgia

"Joe, are you serious?" Christy's voice was a mixture of anger and concern. "The judge really didn't let you out on bond?"

"No," Joe sighed as he dropped into the chair next to Christy.

Ferraro and Ekland were out in the courtroom with Marcella which left Joe and Christy alone at the table while a couple of federal marshals stood watch at the two doors.

"Why not?" she asked, whispering as she leaned in.

"Because he thinks I might try to finish the job on Fowler," Joe answered as he grabbed her hands with his and held them.

"You've got to be kidding me!" she exclaimed.

"I wish I was," he replied. "The U.S. Attorney painted me as trained killer gone bad, and the judge went right along with it. I'm sure Fowler and the media will have a field day with that one. I just hope they don't pull that on you. How has it been for you up there, by the way?"

Christy spent the next few minutes recounting her first two days in prison. Most of that time was focused on her cellmate, Hannah. She didn't want to worry Joe by telling him about Randy. He had enough to deal with as it was. A few minutes later, the bailiff returned with Ramsey. He looked at Joe and Christy and stoically shook his head. Both quietly shook their heads in response.

"Dr. Tabrizi?" the bailiff asked. "If you'll come with me, please."

Christy stood, looking down at Joe with concern as she stepped around her chair and walked to the open door. Joe said a silent prayer for her as he watched her walk out to learn her fate for the unknown number of months before the trial. Ramsey dropped down into the chair on Joe's left.

"Frickin' government attorney convinced the judge that I'm an assassin who poses a risk to the government," he said with disdain. "I mean what the actual…how in the world can we put our lives on the line for our country, serve with distinction and, all of the sudden I'm freaking Lee Harvey Oswald and you're John Wilkes Booth! Are they even looking at what actually went down?"

"No clue," Joe said gently shaking his head. "The real evidence hasn't even been presented yet. The truth is on our side though. This isn't over."

"Maybe not," Ramsey said while glaring at the floor before looking up. "But, meanwhile, you and I will be spending God knows how long looking over our shoulders inside a prison while that lowlife rapist, Fowler, is out on the campaign trail, spewing lies and getting closer to the White House, where he will really begin to screw this country over! It's not right, Joe. It's not right."

"I hear you, brother," Joe nodded, "but you and I have been through far worse than this in Iraq, Afghanistan, Central America. We'll get through this as well."

Ramsey snorted. "At least in those hellholes, we were carrying rifles and *we* were the predators. Now we're the hunted and everyone else is hunting us, including our own government."

"Only if we let ourselves be the hunted," Joe countered.

"What do you mean?" Ramsey quietly asked through furled eyebrows.

"What did we do when the Gulf Cartel was chasing us back to our extraction point when we blew up their warehouse in Matamoros?"

"We set up an ambush and killed every last one of them."

"Exactly," Joe said pounding a handcuffed fist on Ramsey's thigh for emphasis. "We became the hunters and fought them on *our* terms. We'll just have to do it again."

"You got a plan there, Joe?"

"I'm working on it."

"You always say that."

"True, but we always figure something out," Joe said holding up a fist. "Never out of the fight."

Ramsey bumped Joe's fist with his own. "Never out of the fight."

The door to the courtroom opened and Christy appeared accompanied by the bailiff as well as their attorneys. Joe looked at her expectantly but the look on Christy's face told him everything he needed to know.

"They denied you bond as well?" he asked in astonishment as Christy sat down next to him.

She looked at him and responded with a quiet nod.

"It's going to be appealed," Marcella said as he wheeled himself to the head of the table. "You should all be out on bond, but the government is seeing fit to railroad you and they've got the magistrate in their favor. The district judge will be a different story, especially for Dr. Tabrizi."

"They have very little legal precedent to stand on," Kelley Ekland added. "The law is on our side on this one. We'll fix it."

"What do we do in the meantime?" Joe asked.

"In the meantime, we start building our defense," Eddie Ferraro chimed in from the far end of the table. "We gather as much evidence as we can, and we take it to the district judge when we appeal your bond. I'd like to cram so much evidence down his throat that he dismisses the charges."

"To that end, Joe," Marcella said as he opened his bag. "I got the prison to hand over your cellphone. I charged it this afternoon. Why don't you pull up the video you were telling me about?" Marcella asked as he slid the phone down to Joe.

Chapter 29

Atlanta, Georgia

"What video?" Ramsey asked.

"I filmed the beach assault," Joe said as he picked up his phone.

"You did?" Ramsey asked astonished.

"Yes. If you remember, I had my phone mounted on my chest plate carrier vest. Right before we initiated the assault, I thought how nice it would have been if we could have the drone feed sent to our phones in live time to get a quick bird's eye view. For some strange reason, I got the notion to record the events, so I activated the video camera."

"You serious?" Ramsey asked. "How much did you film?"

"It cut off when we took fire on the beach after getting Clay and the girls on the RHIB," Joe said as he worked his phone, "but I got everything in the bungalow with Fowler."

"Holy crow!" Ramsey exclaimed. "He basically admitted to everything he was doing! Total freaking treason! And then *he* ordered Cardenas to kill us! You've got all that?"

"Sure do," Joe grinned slyly as he continued to work his phone.

"Shouldn't that be enough to get us off?" Ramsey asked, looking up at Marcella.

Marcella folded his hands on the table and looked over at Ramsey. "No telling how far the prosecution will be willing to go. They could still raise a fuss over you guys firing the first shots and initiating the attack, but if Fowler's admissions on that video are as self-incriminating as they sound and he really ordered the cartel boss to kill you boys, then, if we play our cards right, we should be able to get you off, if not getting this whole case dropped. And we *certainly* should be able to get you released on bond."

Ramsey and Christy exchanged hopeful glances while Joe worked his phone. Could this ordeal possibly have a happy ending sooner than they expected?

"It's not here," Joe muttered aloud.

"What?" Christy asked in surprise.

"It's not here," Joe said a little louder.

"What do you mean, it's not there?" Ramsey spoke. "No way you would have deleted it."

"I didn't delete it, but it's not here!" Joe said clearly upset. "Somebody must have gotten into my phone and deleted it. Not all is lost, though. I backed it up. I just find it highly alarming that someone could have gotten into my phone and deleted it. It raises the question of what else they can get to."

"How could they do that, Joe?" Ramsey asked. "You're a stickler for security. I know you had that password protected."

"Maybe somebody used the Face ID to unlock it while you were sleeping?" Ekland offered.

"No," Joe shook his head. "I never set that up. Six-digit passcode only."

"Who else knows your code, son?" Ferraro asked.

"Just these two," Joe said glancing at his two closest friends, "but I know it wasn't them. I'd trust them with my life. Nobody else."

"Did either one of you have someone approach you regarding his code?" Ferraro asked.

"Negative," Ramsey answered shaking his head with Christy doing the same.

"Did any of you ever write it down anywhere?" Ekland asked.

"No," they all answered.

"Hmm," Ekland said squinting her eyes in thought. "Those are supposed to be nearly impossible to hack into, but it has been done. Rare though. I'm talking government intelligence agency rare and, even then, only on very few occasions. If somebody or some agency successfully hacked into your phone, this is one serious entity we are up against."

"Yeah, like a presidential candidate, his party, their bureaucrats, the cartels, the Chinese, the Iranians, and God knows who else backing him," Joe responded. "Where do you want to start?"

"Whoever it is, they're all in on Fowler. They must have searched through your phone to find out if you had anything on him, found the video and deleted it," Marcella commented.

"Like I said, that's cause for alarm but, in the meantime, we will have to get ahold of the backup."

"Any chance it could still be backed up on the cloud?" Christy asked.

"I doubt it," Joe answered. "When you delete a photo or video, it usually gets deleted from the cloud as well."

"But it's worth a try," Ekland said as she pulled her laptop out of her leather legal attaché, opened it up, typed in her password and passed it over to Joe.

"Oh dear God *please* let it still be on there," Christy spoke out loud as Joe fumbled over the keys with handcuffed hands.

A minute later, they had their answer. "Nothing, it's gone."

Christy's shoulders collapsed as Ramsey blurted out an expletive.

"Hold on now, guys," Joe said calmly. "As soon as Fowler went on TV and talked up this farce, I figured there was a major fix going on and that this video may be our only evidence to pin this back on him."

"So you're saying you made other backups?" Ramsey asked. "Please say yes."

"I most certainly did."

"Is that what you were working on right before we were arrested?" Christy asked.

"Yes."

"Where is it, Joe?" Marcella asked.

"I made two actually," Joe answered. "One is saved onto my laptop at Christy's house and the other I emailed to our commanding officer, Lieutenant Commander Harrison."

"One is none," Ramsey began.

"And two is one," Joe said finishing an old SEAL mantra.

"Is your house nearby?" Ferraro asked.

"No," Christy shook her head, "It's up on Lake Lanier."

"Is there a way we could get into your house and get that laptop?"

"Yes, I have a friend who could stop by and get it."

"Stacy?" Joe asked.

"Yes."

"Call her," Joe said handing over his phone. "I've got her stored in my contacts."

Christy dialed the number. Stacy picked up quickly. Everyone listened in awkward silence as Christy reassured her close friend that she was ok but didn't have time to go into detail. A couple of minutes later, she hung up.

"Stacy will head over as soon as she finishes her afternoon clinic," she said looking at Joe and then looked up at Ekland and Marcella. "She's an OB/GYN."

"That's great," Marcella answered. "The sooner we get that video, the sooner we can work on an appeal and our defense."

"If it's what Lieutenant Commander O'Shanick says it is, we should show it to the U.S. Attorney and see if he is willing to drop or at least reduce the charges," Ekland commented.

"If it's what he says it is, we should show it to the world and sink Fowler's campaign!" Ferraro added. "Stick it right back in his face and put *him* in a federal prison, the mutt!"

"Let's get these good people cleared of their charges first," Marcella spoke from the head of the table. "Joe, can you get ahold of your commanding officer and see if he can email his copy right now?"

"Sure," Joe said opening the phone while Marcella slid over a business card with his email address and contact information. A few minutes later, he ended the call.

"Lieutenant Commander Harrison says he has it on his personal computer at home. He'll try to wrap things up at the base and head straight home to get it but said it will probably still be two hours."

"That's alright," Marcella nodded thoughtfully. "As soon as we get that video, we'll begin working on your appeal and see if we can go even farther in regard to having some or all of the charges dropped.

I'm sorry we couldn't get you out on bond today. We'll try again as soon as we have what we need. Is there anything you all need from us that we can address while we are all here?"

Joe, Christy, and Ramsey all shook their heads.

"Alright then. We will be in contact with each of you as soon as we know anything."

Everyone stood. The attorneys quickly gathered their documents and filed them into their attaché's. Ramsey made for the door to give Joe and Christy a moment alone. They quietly looked at each other, eyes locked in silent communication. Christy's normally serene face was etched with concern. Joe gazed into Christy's emerald green eyes and longed to hold her. He moved his hands up to cradle her face, but they were abruptly stopped short by his handcuffs shackled to his waist.

"For Pete's sake, I just want to hold you," he said frustrated.

Christy smiled as she gently took his hands and pulled him in. She rested her head on his shoulder. It was the closest they could get to an actual embrace. The warmth of her closeness soothed Joe as he inhaled deeply, savoring the faint scent of lavender in her hair. Just two nights ago, this was a regular thing. Now, he wondered if he would ever see her again. It was clear now that there was a high-stakes power play at hand. A power play in which he, Christy, and Ramsey were merely pawns. If the powerbrokers were willing to take out an FBI agent in charge and if they were able to hack into phones, they were more than willing and able to take out Christy or all of them for that matter.

"Christy, promise me you'll be careful. We're up against something sinister here. I'm talking pure, dark evil. Whoever is involved is all in. They'll stop at nothing to get Fowler over the finish line."

"I will, Joe. I promise."

"I'm serious. I've got plans for you. For us. I've even seen us with our…" Joe hesitated.

Christy took her head off Joe's shoulder and looked directly at him, her eyes piercing into his with an intense curiosity. "Our what? What did you see?"

Joe gazed back, at a loss for words.

"Joe? What did you see?"

"It's crazy," he said shaking his head. "It's just something that happened to me when we were in Belize. It was just for a second, but it seemed so real."

"What?" Christy asked her eyes boring into his. "What was it?"

"It was just something I saw. Right when Cardenas tried to shoot me. It all happened in less than a second. I was lunging for his rifle, and everything slowed down into this super slow-motion. I fully expected to die, only I clearly saw, I don't know, a vision? Some kind of dream? I'm not sure exactly but I clearly saw you and me with our… our…"

"Our children?" Christy asked, her eyes still pouring into his.

"Yes!" Joe answered in shock. "How did you know?"

"Two little girls with long dark hair like mine and a little dark-haired boy like you?" she continued breathlessly.

"Yes! But, how do you…"

"Were we swimming with them off your parents dock?!" Christy interrupted excitedly.

"Yes!" Joe answered, his voice registering total shock. "And also playing in the snow, but how do you know this?"

"I saw it too!" she answered.

"You did? Really?"

Christy's perfectly straight white teeth beamed as she nodded enthusiastically, her eyes misting up.

"When?" Joe asked, still shocked.

Christy's eyes dimmed. "When the mafia guys shot your sister, Marina, and I was about to be next. I had the same vision. That guy was pulling the trigger when you shot him. I saw it all in slow motion just like you and I had that vision at the same time. It was so surreal. I see that picture of us with our future children all the time. Joe, we *have* to get out of this! I want that family with you! I want us!"

"Then we have to survive this, Christy. You have to watch your six every minute! Twenty-four seven. I can't be there to protect you, but I'll be praying for you. Promise me you'll be careful."

"I will and you do the same," Christy answered gently. "I pray for you all the time. You know that."

"Yes," Joe said as he kissed her. "I do."

They kissed again but this time more lingering until a muscular red-headed corrections officer interrupted them.

"O'Shanick, let's go!" he ordered.

"You too, Tabrizi!" A black female corrections officer ordered as she entered the room.

The male corrections officer grabbed Joe by the arm and turned him away from Christy. Joe looked longingly over his shoulder as he was led away. He prayed and vowed they would see each other again but also knew this could be the last time he ever saw her. There were untold forces aligned against them. Anything could happen. Joe was determined to soak in one last look. Christy's long dark hair was pulled back into a loose ponytail. She wore no makeup, but Joe didn't think she needed it anyway. She was clad in handcuffs, shackles, and ill-fitting prison khakis, completely concealing her lithe, athletic figure. She never looked more beautiful.

Chapter 30

Buford, Georgia

The late afternoon sun lit up Buford Dam Road as Dr. Stacy Morgan drove her late model Honda CRV with the widows and sunroof open. The oppressing heat of summer had given way to more pleasant temperatures while the foliage remained green. As she turned onto Christy's street, Stacy was reminded that this was one of their running nights. Just two nights ago, at this time, she and Christy were in the company of Joe and Ramsey enjoying a dinner Joe had prepared for them. And *what* a dinner! Joe was an amazing cook. Taught by his Filipino mother, whom Christy absolutely adored. Joe was the real deal, and they had such a bright future together. Or at least she hoped they did. Stacy had never seen her friend so happy. What was being done to them was beyond cruel and a major injustice.

Ramsey too. He was an honorable man. A true gentleman around Stacy and Christy but one could tell he, like Joe, could flip a switch and become the type of warrior nobody wanted to tangle with. They didn't talk about what they did, and they never acted like they were trying to impress anyone. They were humble, gentle, humorous, and kind. Despite all of that, they carried themselves with a natural confidence and grace that gave others a glimpse of the caged lion that lurked within. Stacy found it alluring. He had completed his twenty years in the Navy and was planning on moving out here with Joe in a few months to start a new business. She found the thought of something more than a friendship with Matt intriguing to say the least. That was two days ago. Now? Now, she had no idea what the future held for her three friends.

She pulled into Christy's driveway and turned off her engine. Two nights ago, the driveway and street were awash with flashing lights, law enforcement, and media. Had all that really been necessary? Stacy exited her SUV and walked up to the front door. She pulled out the key Christy had given her and let herself in. What she saw caused her to stop in her tracks.

The entire house looked like the aftermath of a major earthquake. Stacy held her hand over chest, overcome with horror as she walked through her friend's once beautiful house to find every room had been wantonly ransacked and destroyed. Debris was everywhere. Furniture was flipped, cushions carved up, artwork pulled off the walls and vases smashed to the floor. Every cupboard and drawer in the kitchen had been emptied out onto the floor. The appliances pulled away from the walls. A flood of emotions raged through Stacy; fear and sadness at first but, as she surmised what had happened, those emotions gave way to rage.

Standing at the back of the house, she looked out the sliding glass door to the lanai and Christy's neighbor Tom Crittendon sitting on the end of his dock. She slid open the door and ran out.

"Tom!" she called as she ran toward his dock.

Crittendon, looked over his shoulder. Stacy could see he was fishing. He smiled when he saw her and stood up. He was in his early fifties, a retired Army NCO from the 82nd Airborne. He sported a fresh short haircut with a salt and pepper goatee. Tall and barrel chested, his forearms looked like they could snap someone's neck with little effort.

"Well, hey there, pretty lady!" But he immediately registered the concern in Stacy's countenance, reeled in his line, and set his pole down. "Stacy, what's wrong?"

"Somebody broke into Christy's house and trashed it!"

"What?!" He said with a mixture of anger and surprise. "I've been keepin' and eye on the place but I ain't noticed nobody comin' around!"

"Tom, it's a mess inside. I came over to find Joe's laptop. Would you mind helping me? It's very important."

"Of course I will," he said in his thick Georgian drawl as he and Stacy began walking back to the house. "How are they doing, anyway?"

"I'm not sure. I've only gotten to talk to Christy this afternoon and only for a couple of minutes. Most of what I know is what the news is reporting."

"Which is nothing but a bunch of Bravo Sierra," Crittendon growled. "They ought to be giving those three a medal but instead they're getting tarred and feathered while the real criminals run free."

"You're right," Stacy said as they walked up onto Christy's lanai. "But Joe has something on his laptop that could help their case, so we have to find it."

"What the…" Crittendon remarked as he surveyed the damage and debris throughout Christy's house.

"It's terrible!" Stacy remarked as she walked into the kitchen and began sifting through the debris. "She said Joe left it on the kitchen counter. I remember him using it right before the FBI stormed the house."

"They stormed the house?"

"Yes! You'd have thought we were a bunch of terrorists or something."

"Did they arrest you too?" Crittendon asked as he rummaged through the debris in the adjacent great room.

"No, they didn't have a warrant for my arrest, but they've sent agents to interview me twice so far. It's like they're on a witch hunt or something." Stacy said as she moved over to the counter against the back wall. "Has anyone talked to you?"

"Not yet," he said absently as he searched through the built-in shelves and cabinets. "Probably will as soon as they figure out Joe and Rammer been bunkin' at my place. You havin' any luck over there?"

"No," Stacy answered. "I'm gonna check Christy's bedroom."

Twenty minutes later, a thorough search of the house had failed to locate either Joe or Christy's laptops.

"Nothing," Crittendon commented. "I know Joe and Christy both had iPads as well, but they ain't here either. They left her TV and Blu-Ray player so I doubt it was a robbery. Whoever it was seemed to be after anything they thought might be incriminating. They tossed this place like pros and I'm ashamed to admit that I never heard a thing. I should have. That's on me. Christy's like a little sister to me. I've always watched out for her. I'm sick over this. What did Joe have on his laptop anyway?"

"I don't know. Christy just asked me to find it and run it up to their attorney's office as soon as I found it. She said it was really important. Shoot! Now what?"

"Call their attorney and tell them what you found," Crittendon answered with a sigh. "Meanwhile, I'll call the police. After that, I'm takin' pictures. Someone is going to pay for this."

Chapter 31

Virginia Beach, Virginia

Lieutenant Commander Patrick Harrison slid out of his black GMC pickup truck. Per his routine, he had changed out of his working uniform and into his civies which, today, consisted of khaki cargo shorts, 5.11 desert sand boots, and a black well-worn Pink Floyd *Dark Side of the Moon* t-shirt. Even with his trim athletic build and his sandy blond hair cut into a short regulation haircut, he looked more like a landscaper than a special warfare officer. That was his desired effect. He reached across the seat, grabbed his backpack, and slipped it on. He shut the door to his old truck and marched purposefully toward the twelve-story condominium building overlooking Virginia Beach.

Harrison walked up to one of the pillars on the outside of the building's parking deck, grabbed a handhold, and effortlessly scaled it up to the balcony of a second-floor condo. He pulled himself up by the railing until he had a foot on the railing and leaped up to the third-floor balcony's ledge. He, once again, pulled himself up to the railing.

"Evening, Pat," a pudgy seventy-ish balding man greeted him. He was sitting in his customary balcony chair reading the newspaper, completely unfazed by Harrison's sudden appearance. "Join me for a cold one?"

"Can't today, Mr. Nelson, I've got something I have to get to right away," Harrison said as he leaped up to the fourth-floor balcony.

His neighbors were used to his rather freakish method of ascending to his tenth-floor condo. Less than a minute later, he vaulted the railing for his balcony. He had timed it both ways and he could reach his condo faster this way than if he took the elevator which he only used when carrying items that wouldn't fit in his backpack. Even then, he usually took the stairs. As the Task Force Commander over four platoons, his operating days were essentially over, save for very rare occasions; nevertheless, as long as he still wore the Trident, he was bound and determined to be able to match the men under his command, mile for mile and skill for skill. Stairs and balcony climbs were just part of it.

Harrison fished out his key and unlocked the sliding glass door to his condo. Normally, a large two-bedroom condo overlooking the ocean would be way out of his officer's salary price range. Early in his career, he had married a local socialite who was the only daughter of a wealthy blue blood family. For a wedding present, her parents had given them this beautiful ocean front condominium. Harrison had returned early from a six-month deployment to Iraq and thought he would surprise his young bride. It was he who was surprised when, like tonight, he vaulted their railing only to look through the sliding glass door to find her with another man in an extremely compromised state on their living room couch. In a fit of rage, Harrison gathered up the man's clothes and hurled them off the balcony. He then grabbed the man by the neck and threw him out into the hall. During the ensuing divorce, her parents offered him a cash settlement to keep their princess's indiscretions quiet, but he demanded the condo, to which they quickly acceded.

Harrison pulled a beer out of the refrigerator, shrugged off his backpack, and sat down at his dining room table. He opened up his laptop and took a swig of beer as he waited for it to boot up. He thought about the mess O'Shanick and Ramsey were in. It made him sick. Those were good men. Exceptional men. Two of the best he had ever had the honor to command. It made him doubly sick when he watched the video Joe had sent him. The wrong people were being charged. Fowler should be executed just for his role in blowing half of Echo platoon out of the sky last year. This video would right that wrong, but the fact that O'Shanick had been concerned enough to send a backup and now *needed* that backup spoke volumes as to how this whole SNAFU was being rigged.

Harrison entered his password to open the computer and took another swig. He froze suddenly. His froggy sense was tingling. Someone was standing behind him. One swift move, Harrison pivoted off his chair and dropped to one knee while reaching behind him to retrieve his subcompact Glock 43. He never got the chance.

Chapter 32

The White House

The White House quietly glowed in the floodlights of the pre-dawn hour. From the outside, a faint light could be seen in the windows of the third floor on the northeast corner; inside was the president's private gym. The room had previously been used as a bedroom and even a sitting room but it had been converted into a fitness room during the Clinton Administration. President Galan and First Lady Maria, both fitness enthusiasts since their days in the Marine Corps, had upgraded the gym to accommodate their various workout routines. Due to Manny's demanding schedule, their early morning workouts were one of the few times in the day they had time alone together with few interruptions.

Manny Galan preferred to hit the weights in the morning and run the White House grounds with some of his staff members and occasional visitors before lunch, when his schedule allowed. That wouldn't be happening today. He had a full schedule this morning and then he and Maria would be boarding Air Force One for campaign rallies in Denver and Phoenix. He would have to get both weights and a run in before he met CIA Director Spratt for his morning intelligence brief.

Manny was finishing a set of seated military press on his Powertec gym while Maria was effortlessly following along with an online Pilates workout. She wore black leggings and a white tank top tied at the waist with her long dark hair tied back in a ponytail. There were several flatscreens tuned to various news outlets hanging around the room, but Manny's eyes were glued to his age-defying wife as she performed her workout. Looking into the large wall mirror, Maria caught her husband looking her over and smiled.

"Shouldn't the leader of the free world be paying attention to the news?" she asked with a playful smile.

"The news has nothing on you, mi amor," he smiled at her through the mirror as he set the bar down after his last rep. "And everyone knows it! Even the Secret Service. They didn't assign you the code name *Bonita* for nothing."

"Manny," she clucked, "you know as well as I do that they give all family members a code name beginning with the same letter. Since they named you *Bulldog,* they had to give me something with a B. I suppose it could have been worse."

"Well, I think they nailed it," Manny said as he walked over and gave his wife an appreciative smack on her rear end. "I should be done with my run a little early," he said suggestively.

"Is that a promise or a warning?" Maria teased.

"Both!" Manny said as he stepped onto the treadmill and inserted his earbuds.

"Married over thirty-five years, two children, and he still wants the goods," Maria playfully voiced.

"You know it!" Galan replied.

"Manny, you need to see this!" Maria called out.

"What is it?" he asked as he turned around.

Maria was pointing toward one of the flatscreens. The newsfeed was giving a breaking report. The caption at the bottom of the screen read:

NAVY SEAL JUMPS TO DEATH IN APPARENT SUICIDE

"Oh, dear God, no," Manny muttered as he hopped of and found the remote. A grim-faced male reporter was standing outside of a high-rise building speaking to the camera. Galan turned up the volume and listened to the report.

"…the body of Navy SEAL, Lieutenant Commander Patrick Harrison was found on the ground below his tenth floor Virginia Beach condominium. Although there were no witnesses, local authorities report Lieutenant Commander Harrison left a suicide note on his computer. Although we cannot confirm this at this time, our sources tell us that, in this note, Harrison confesses to his involvement in the raging scandal in which President Galan is alleged to have ordered the attempted assassination of his rival, presidential candidate, Senator Robert Fowler. We reported live three nights ago when Lieutenant Commander Joseph O'Shanick and Master Chief Petty Officer Matthew Ramsey were arrested for their involvement in the attempted assassination of Senator Fowler," and the screen changed to show official military photos of Joe and Ramsey followed by video of their arrest the other night. "Both men are under the command of Lieutenant Commander Harrison." The reporter paused, waiting for his counterpart in the studio to comment.

"Jonathan," the studio reporter began, "do we know, specifically, what was written in this suicide note?"

"No, Chuck, at this point we don't. All we know is that Lieutenant Commander Harrison confessed to his involvement; however, the exact words and details have not been disclosed, as of yet."

"Well, Jonathan, this certainly lends credence to Senator Fowler's claim that President Galan dispatched a kill squad of Navy SEALs to assassinate him. If this is proven true, this would be perhaps the be biggest scandal in the history of the presidency…"

"Manny! What is going on?!" Maria exclaimed in shock.

"Something diabolical," President Galan replied as he muted the volume. "Did you see how quickly they glossed over Lieutenant Commander Harrison's death and went directly to their fake narrative? We can't even mourn the tragic death of a special warfare officer! No such order ever came from me. And no way did that Navy SEAL commit suicide. This has gone from allegation to framing and there are good people getting killed in the process."

"What are you going to do?" She asked.

"Get tactical and fix this thing."

Chapter 33

Virginia Beach, Virginia

"Here he comes."

Chief Mark St. John, police chief of the Virginia Beach Police Department, looked out to the parking lot and saw a convoy of police cars and dark late model SUV's pulling up. The doors opened and several dark suit wearing men stepped out.

"Tell me again why we had to stand down until this guy got here," the department's detective bureau commanding officer asked his boss.

"Because he said so," St. John answered dryly. "The deceased was the commanding officer of the two SEALs accused of trying to assassinate Senator Fowler. That makes this a matter of FBI interest. We're just the small-town constables getting in his way as far as he's concerned. Now put on your smiley face and behave."

"Chief St. John?"

"Yes, sir!" St. John came to attention before offering his hand.

"Frank Snyder, FBI. My apologies for stepping all over you boys at the last minute, but as I'm sure you're aware, this falls within the purview of a top-priority investigation. Has everything been sealed off?"

"Yes, sir, my men stopped what they were doing within minutes of your call. The computer was left on, presumably by the deceased, with the suicide note pulled up. Apparently, he disabled the passcode so all you have to do is press a key and it will open right up. His cell phone was left unlocked as well. Odd, but maybe he was making it easy for those who would have to come in behind him and take care of his affairs. It's all been dusted but if you want your team to go over it again it's all yours. Your agents are up there now."

"I see, and where's the body?"

"Lieutenant Commander Harrison remains have been properly bagged and are ready to transport back to D.C. with you, sir."

"Very good. Then let's head up to his condo."

"Right this way, sir," Chief St. John said as he began walking in the direction of the building.

A minute later they arrived out front of LCDR Harrison's tenth floor condominium. Two of Snyder's agents, from the local field office, were posted out front. Upon sighting the director, they dutifully stood aside to allow him to enter along with two of his Washington-based agents while the rest of the investigations team waited outside for the go ahead. Before entering, Snyder and his men donned shoe covers and gloves to protect the integrity of the scene. They entered the unit and Snyder immediately saw the table where Harrison's laptop and cellphone lay.

"Why don't each of you pick a bedroom and give it the once-over." Snyder said with a nod to the adjacent bedrooms. "I want to take a look at his laptop."

The two agents disappeared, each to one of the two bedrooms, while Snyder struck a key on the computer bringing the screen to life. He picked up the cellphone which also opened up without requiring a security code. Quite convenient. His tech experts could have gotten into it, but it would have required time and questionable legality. Whatever team whacked this guy was professional enough to wait on their mark to have opened his electronics before they offed him and disabled the security before they timed out.

Snyder opened the phone function and scrolled through the recent calls. He found the call he was told to look for and deleted it. He checked the other calls the texts and saw nothing else of concern and then quickly returned the phone to its place on the table. He leaned over as if studying the suicide note on the laptop's screen and waited for his agents to emerge from the bedrooms. He addressed them when they did.

"Anything of note?"

"No, we're good, sir," one of the agents answered.

"Good, then it looks like we are ready to get started. Bring the team in and go over this place with a fine-toothed comb. It was most likely a suicide, but there's a lot riding on us getting this right so it's up to us to make sure it wasn't something more. I have to get back to Washington. I'll take Harrison's body back with me so our examiners can get right on it. Call me when you're close to finishing up and I'll have another plane sent down to pick you all up," Snyder said before turning for the door and stripping off his gloves while he walked out.

Chapter 34

Atlanta, Georgia

"Here you go, Ben," Joe said, tossing a new soft leather-bound Bible on his cellmate's bunk.

"What's this?"

"A little follow through," Joe answered. "You read Psalm 23 and Isaiah 53, right?"

"Yeah, so?"

"So, I told you they were prophetic writings about the crucifixion. Read it for yourself and tell me what you think. I bookmarked Matthew 27 for you." Joe took a seat on the wall mounted seat across from Ben.

"You've barely been here three days, Joe. How did you get this?"

"They're from my mom. She probably used Amazon Prime is my guess."

"She would have had to have done that the minute she knew where you were," Ben postulated.

"That'd be my mom. Now read."

Ben spent a few minutes combing through the text. His face a scowl of interest mixed with skepticism. He looked up at Joe and shrugged.

"Okay, I can see the similarities," he said.

"Did you in verse 46 where Jesus was on the cross and he quoted Psalm 23?" Joe asked. "A lot of people read over that without making the connection."

Ben looked back down and reread the part. "Yeah, I see it."

"Keep in mind, that Psalm was written through David one *thousand* years before the crucifixion. In fact, crucifixion hadn't even been invented at that time."

"What's not to say that whoever wrote the gospels didn't just make it all up to fit the narrative?" Ben asked.

"Good question; why would they do that?"

"What do mean; why would they do that? For personal gain or to control people," he shrugged. "I don't know."

"Okay," Joe continued, "What did they gain? What did Matthew gain?"

"No clue," Ben shrugged.

"How about death?" Joe suggested.

"Really?" Ben looked up.

"Yes," Joe answered. "In fact, ten of the twelve original apostles were killed for their faith. Most people do things out of motive for sex, money, or power. Think about it. What are most of the people in here for? It's almost always sex, money, or power. If the gospel writers were out for personal gain, it sure backfired on them. Instead of sex, money, or power, they got persecution, poverty, and death. Would you endure that for something if you knew it was a lie?"

"Doubt it."

"Yet every one of them went the distance. Martyred. Not one of them tried to save himself by recanting.

"Who's recanting?" Ramsey asked as he entered the cell. "We gettin' out of here, Joe?"

"Shoot. I wish. No, we were just having a little Bible discussion. Speaking of which, my mom sent you a present," Joe said handing an identical Bible to his friend.

Ramsey looked down at the Bible with a bit of apprehension. "Joe, I love your mom and all, but, uh, is she expecting me to read all this?"

"Oh, you better believe it!" Joe grinned maliciously. "There will be a quiz this Friday."

"I might have to call in sick, but do thank her for me, Joe."

"So they sprung you from the SHU?" Joe asked.

"Yeah, just walked over."

"Is it as bad as they say?"

"If I had a good book to read it wouldn't be so bad. I imagine it would get pretty old after a couple of weeks though," Ramsey said casually.

"O'Shanick. Ramsey," came a grizzled voice.

Joe looked up and saw a very tall, wiry man with dark brown eyes, long medium brown hair, and a receding hairline. He reminded Joe of the Hall of Fame Baseball Pitcher Randy Johnson.

"That's us," Joe answered.

"You might want to head to the day room. There's something on the news you'll want to see."

Joe glanced a questioning look at Ramsey who shrugged his shoulders in response. Joe stood and they stepped out of the cell. Joe stuck out his hand.

"I'm Joe."

"Jim," he said shaking Joe's hand with a crushing grip. "But everyone calls me *Condor*," he said as he turned to Ramsey.

"Matt," Ramsey said shaking his hand as they walked side by side. "So what is it we are going to see?"

"Nothing you want to see but something you'll want to know," Condor monotoned as they reached the day room at the end of the common area.

There were two flatscreen televisions on each side of the day-room, each with several benches facing them. Condor led them to the side where about two dozen mostly middle-aged or older white inmates sat. Most had long hair and various states of facial hair. Joe presumed they were mostly bikers. The other side was mostly middle-aged or older black men. Integration didn't seem to be a priority in here. The TV was showing the end of a commercial advertising a reverse mortgage. A morning news show resumed and the headline immediately grabbed Joe and Ramsey's attention. Each sported a grim look as they listened to the news anchor report on Lieutenant Commander Harrison's supposed suicide. Joe's anger burned as he watched the false narrative unfold before him. He felt several pairs of eyes upon him and Ramsey. Whether or not they were hostile or sympathetic, he couldn't tell. He didn't care. He was preoccupied with the tragic death of his commanding officer. More than that, his friend. A brother in arms. Harrison had taught Joe a great deal in the art of leading special warfare operators both outside the wire and inside the wire. His loss would be a big blow to their task force.

"What do you think, Joe?" Ramsey asked.

"I think it's a bunch of bravo sierra is what I think," Joe said through gritted teeth as he turned to face his friend and leaned in close. "No way did PH ghost himself! Somebody had him killed and made it look like a suicide. And that suicide note? Did you hear what the news said? It was typed into his computer. Not handwritten. Anyone could have put that there. You and I both know there was no order. This is a total setup!"

Joe looked around and saw that they had drawn a crowd. Condor and a half dozen of his grim-faced biker friends had gathered around the two of them. Joe stood up straight and faced them.

Condor spoke first. "We might be a bunch of outlaw bikers, but most of us served and some of us have the shrapnel to prove it. Be that as it may, we don't care much for a bunch of traitors screwin' with our country, so you got one chance to give us the straight scoop on what y'all two are involved in. We have our own sources so if we find out you lied to us, we'll turn you into eunuchs and then personally hand what's left of you over to the cartel boys."

"You believe everything the news reports?" Joe asked.

"Other than the football scores, not much," Condor answered.

"Well then, we're on the same page," Joe replied. "So let me tell you what really happened…"

Chapter 35

Washington D.C

Jin Feng aka "Father Patrick" ducked down an alley that ran behind several businesses. He stepped through an open doorway into the kitchen of an upscale Chinese restaurant. A small room for private gatherings was just off the kitchen to his left. He glanced at his watch and confirmed that he was precisely on time as ordered. He entered the room and greeted his real boss, Liu Fan, in the appropriate manner of respect. Jin professionally hid his surprise when he immediately recognized the short, dark-haired, muscular man seated next to his boss, smoking a cigar. For a powerful man, Salvatore La Rosa was not well known, and he liked it that way. Jin assumed it would not go well were he to express any semblance of recognition. The fact that Feng did not introduce him confirmed that notion. La Rosa was originally from Brooklyn where he had built his credentials as a street soldier and later a crew leader or *Caporegime* with one of the mafia families that ran New York City. La Rosa had specialized in union relations, narcotics trafficking, and racketeering before he went "legit" and began working behind the scenes for his chosen political party. He had brought his trade skills and contacts to work cutting deals between the party and labor unions, but it went far beyond that. La Rosa also served as the liaison between the party and the cartels, Russian mafia, and his own La Cosa Nostra. He worked out of the party chair's office as an unofficial assistant to the chair. In mafia parlance, if the party chair was the don, La Rosa was the underboss, much like Liu Fan was to his father's organization. La Rosa didn't answer to Liu and Liu didn't answer to La Rosa. They represented powerful entities that had formed an "unholy alliance" sharing mutual goals. As an operative for the Liu Dynasty, Jin wasn't supposed to know all of this, but he made it his business to have commanding knowledge of all players in this worldwide chess match.

"Ah, Father Patrick, right on time," Liu said. "Let's hear your report."

Jin hesitated as he glanced wearily at La Rosa.

"I appreciate your concern for compartmentalization Father Patrick, but Mr. La Rosa is a friend of ours and he is very interested in what you have to say."

Jin masked his emotions. He did not expect La Rosa to let himself be seen by Liu's underlings, let alone spoken of so freely. Either Jin had majorly screwed up and was not going to leave the restaurant alive or he had just been promoted to a much higher level of trust. He consciously touched his rosary. He may be an ordained priest but that was just his cover. He had no idea if any god actually existed and normally wouldn't care, but if there was a god, he would gladly accept a little divine favor right now.

"Our mole in The White House has, once again, proven to be a valuable asset," Jin paused not sure how much Liu wanted him to divulge in front of their guest. Liu nodded and motioned for him to continue.

"He reported back to me that FBI Director Snyder has carried out our directive to move the investigation from Senator Fowler to President Galan."

"Snyder's a Boy Scout," La Rosa interjected. "How can you be sure of this?"

"We applied leverage," Jin replied.

"Leverage, huh?" La Rosa responded. "We've got a lot riding on this horse, Father. I need to know just how sure this is before we proceed. What kind of leverage are we talking here?"

"I hired a trusted Russian asset. She's extremely professional and very effective. She's also difficult to trace back to us. She lured Director Snyder into an, shall we say, indiscretion and provided us with plenty of incriminating photographs. I have shown these to Snyder along with pictures of his children at school for insurance. He will do as he is told. I gave him strict instructions regarding how to brief the president yesterday. Our White House asset was present at that meeting and reported back to me. Snyder is on board."

"Good," La Rosa nodded. "That's a big piece of machinery to have online. I might sweeten the pot a little by having Fowler dangle a carrot in front of him along the lines of a higher position in the DOJ if he delivers for us. That's good work, Liu," La Rosa said to his counterpart at the table.

"There's more, my friend," Liu said looking at La Rosa as he nodded for Jin to continue.

"Yes. We are planting evidence of an order among key members of the chain of command that will support the narrative that Galan ordered the hit on Senator Fowler."

"Would that have anything to do with that SEAL officer who took a leap off his balcony?"

"Correct," Jin answered succinctly, not wanting to reveal his methods or more information than was necessary.

The fact was, the Liu Dynasty had nearly two dozen operatives, some naturalized citizens, some documented immigrants, all of whom had official covers posing as business owners or operating businesses owned by the Liu Dynasty, whom Jin could dispatch to take care of problems using less than legal but highly professional and effective means. To handle the SEAL commander, he had dispatched two former members of the Jiaolong Assault Team, better known as The Sea Dragons, the Chinese Navy's version of naval special warfare. Initially, Jin had sent them to eliminate Harrison and remove all traces of the video one of La Rosa's plants had learned of during O'Shanick's bond hearing at the Atlanta courthouse yesterday. La Rosa had sent a team of his own to toss the doctor's house, but he had no assets near Virginia Beach; therefore, he reached out to Liu Fan who, in turn, put Jin on the case. Jin dispatched the two agents from nearby Alexandria. Jin had also spotted an opportunity and quickly altered the Trojan Horse he had given John D, their White House mole. He had it emailed to the agents as they raced down I-95. It placed an operational order into Harrison's hard drive linking him to O'Shanick and could be traced all the way up to the White House. Jin's operatives had managed to arrive at Harrison's condominium only minutes before he made his usual climb up to his balcony. Despite getting the jump, it required every skill and a lot of trauma for Jin's agents to subdue the very physically adept Harrison. They originally planned to make it look like he shot himself with his handgun; however, due to the number of traumatic injuries they were forced to inflict, they decided to mask them by tossing him off his balcony while semi-conscious. They thought well on the fly.

La Rosa stared at Jin expectantly before speaking. "So that's it? You're not gonna tell me what yuz did?"

Jin summoned every nerve he had to keep a straight face. This was not some street punk he was facing down. Adding to that, he had no idea what Liu Fan was expecting of him. Jin stuck to his instincts and slowly nodded in acknowledgment. La Rosa studied him another moment before speaking.

"Good. I like a guy who knows how to keep his mouth shut." He nodded approvingly and then turned to Liu. "You run a good shop here, Liu. You get us the results we need, help us pin Galan and get Fowler elected and we'll deliver what you need. Favorable trade deals and an open border for the Mexicans to move your meth and fentanyl."

Liu stared back with a blank expression.

"Yeah, we'll give you Taiwan too. Fowler will have to rattle his saber, threaten some economic sanctions, and put on a good show for the voters, but we won't take it any farther than that. The press will convince the voters that we don't need another conflict. Matter of fact, time your invasion for when this whole Galan thing goes to trial. The news will have something else to focus on. But ya gotta deliver," La Rosa stabbed the air with his cigar to emphasize the point.

Liu looked across the table at Jin. "Has your White House asset completed his assignment?"

Jin had strolled by the White House less than an hour ago. John D's car was parked in its usual spot with the tires turned slightly to the left. He nodded and said, "Yes."

"Then we are ready for the next step. Have Director Snyder use the evidence obtained from the SEAL's computer to seek out a warrant to examine the computers of the Secretary of Defense, the president's personal secretary, and Chief of Staff Embry. Justice Scarborough will be accommodating. Mr. La Rosa will see to it this information is leaked to the press." Liu waved his hand signaling to Jin that he was dismissed.

Chapter 36

Alto, Georgia

"O'Brien!"

"That's you, Hannah. C'mon," Christy stood and helped her petite cellmate stand.

Together, they walked to where a black female nurse, in light blue scrubs, stood holding open the door into the prison infirmity's examination area. The nurse gave a Christy a quizzical look.

"I'm her cellmate and I'm also a physician," Christy said by way of explanation. "I'm just trying to get her some help."

"I'm sorry, but inmates cannot be accompanied by other inmates," the nurse responded as she began to close the door, "You'll have to wait out here."

Christy returned to the seating area and began looking for a seat among the dozen or so other inmates. Several talked amongst themselves in a familiar manner while others simply sat alone. Christy didn't know anyone and had a lot on her mind, so she opted for a corner chair against the far wall. She leaned her head against the wall, closed her eyes and began to pray for Hannah. It had been a rough morning. Hannah had woken up early with severe pain and abdominal distress from opiate withdrawal. Christy had wanted to get her in with the prison medical staff yesterday but, by the time she returned from Atlanta, the infirmary had already closed. The Suboxone the hospital had given Hannah yesterday would only last twenty-four hours at best. The proof of which became evident this morning when the withdrawal had set in causing Hannah to feel like she had contracted an unimaginable and very painful bout of the flu.

Suboxone, if the medical staff were willing to treat Hannah with it, would suppress the worst of the withdrawal symptoms and prevent Hannah from craving more opiates. Despite a common misconception, it was not substituting one addiction for another, like those who go on methadone. The Buprenorphine component of Suboxone binds itself to the brain's opiate receptors in a way that suppresses the addiction and allows addicts a pathway to eventual recovery where they can stop using medications altogether. Christy was hoping the prison's medical staff would have a similar objective. If Hannah could free herself from her addiction, she could free herself from Randy's control and begin working toward a sober life which she would desperately need if she wanted any chance of restoring her life when she was released from prison.

Hannah would need more than just medical therapy. She would also need cognitive therapy, coping skills, and a new lifestyle. Christy had plans for that as well. She had helped many patients and acquaintances toward a recovered life and hoped Hannah would be receptive to this as well. One step at a time.

Christy's thoughts were disrupted by an uneasy feeling like she was being watched. She subtly scanned the room with her eyes, quite cognizant that, like Joe and Ramsey, she too could be a target for elimination. She saw no malevolent eyes looking her way but how could she know for sure? Everyone in this room was a convict, some of them likely violent offenders. *Trust no one!* Joe had impressed upon her.

Across the room, a face triggered Christy's memory. The tall slender woman with the rich dark skin she had noticed in chapel two days ago. Even then, she had seemed vaguely familiar to Christy. She wasn't looking at Christy now, but Christy was sure she just had been just like she had been in chapel the other day. Christy wasn't sure what to think. The woman *had* been in chapel after all. Perhaps Christy was misreading things and the woman was not a threat. On the other hand, Christy was certain the woman kept studying her and it left her with an uneasy feeling. She take the initiative and go talk to her? Perhaps they had met before? Or perhaps she had been commissioned to take Christy out?

Christy's decision was put to rest when the door opened and Hannah came out. Christy stood and met her cellmate. Together they walked past the woman and exited the infirmary. Christy sensed the woman watching her leave but suppressed her urge to look back.

"So how did it go?" Christy asked.

"Good, I guess," Hannah answered uneasily. "They're starting me on Suboxone like you wanted. I hope it works. They just gave me some, but I still feel like I was run over by a truck."

"It will kick in within the hour," Christy encouraged. "This is a good thing, Hannah. It's a big step for you but a crucial one. We've got a lot of work to do but we *will* get you better!"

"We?" Hannah asked as they pushed open the doors and stepped outside.

"Yes, we," Christy replied. "I told you I would help you. This is part of what I do for a living."

"You're really interested in helping me?" Hannah asked. "I've been a failure all my life. I've failed every time I've tried to get sober, and I've hurt every person I love along the way. Why would you want to be a part of that?"

"Because God loves you," Christy replied plainly.

Hannah didn't respond. They walked along in silence. Christy looked around the prison yard while giving Hannah time to digest what she had told her. It was cloudy but warm. Dozens of khaki clad inmates milled about the grounds. A basketball game was in play on one of the courts in front of their dormitory. Christy looked around for Randy but didn't see her. If there really was a price on her head, Randy would not be the only threat. She was just the only recognizable threat. Finally, Hannah spoke.

"I doubt that. I think God gave up on me a long time ago."

"Why do you believe that?" Christy asked as she pulled open the door to their dorm.

"Because look at me," Hannah explained. "I'm a druggie who's in prison for stealing from her own family. I hocked my little brother's game set and stole thousands from my parents. I'm a total failure. A screw up. How could God love me, Christy?"

"Because He always has. Ever since He created you, you have always been special to Him."

"Maybe that once was, but I've screwed up too many times. I just can't believe He would still care about someone like me," Hannah stated as they climbed the stairs.

"Well, He does. Remarkably, He loves all of His creation, no matter how bad we've screwed up," Christy said as they reached their floor.

"What makes you so sure?"

"Follow me," Christy said as she led Hannah to their cell.

She walked in and pulled Hannah's bible off the shelf. Christy opened it and worked through the pages until she found what she was looking for. She handed it over to Hannah.

"Read Romans 5:8 and tell me what it says."

Hannah sat down on her bed. She looked up at Christy and then back down and read. "But God demonstrates His own love for us in this: while we were still sinners, Christ died for us."

"So there you have it, and there are many more scriptures and parables declaring the same thing," Christy declared.

"But I've done so many bad things," Hannah replied, her eyes watering.

"It doesn't matter," Christy said shaking her head. "Look at who God wrote that through. Do you know anything about Paul?"

"Just that he was one of the apostles."

"Are you aware that he wasn't always the Apostle Paul? That he was formerly Saul of Tarsus, a devout Jewish leader who persecuted and helped *kill* the early first century Christians?"

"No, I wasn't aware of that," Hannah answered looking up at Christy.

"Well, he was, and he did way worse things than you or just about anybody else in this prison, yet God still loved him, forgave him, and called him to become perhaps His greatest apostle and messenger. You can read all about it in the Book of Acts. If He can do that with Paul, He can and will do that with you, Hannah O'Brien."

"Okay," Hannah began skeptically, "even if that were true, why would *you* want to help me?"

"Like I said, because God loves you," Christy said locking eyes with Hannah.

Suddenly, their door was kicked in. Christy and Hannah both jumped in response.

"I thought I told you to stay away from property!" Randy snarled as she entered the room with two of her minions in tow.

Chapter 37

Alto, Georgia

"And I thought I told you to stay away from this cell!" Christy replied as she stood and faced Randy.

A fight was coming. Christy knew that much for certain. She began to prepare herself mentally. Randy had brought two of her toughs along and they blocked the only way out. Was this just about Randy trying to reclaim Hannah as well as her pride or was this something more? Something like a move to silence her as Joe had warned the people backing Senator Fowler would do?

"Let me tell you somethin' you prissy stork," Randy said with gritted teeth as she stepped forward and grabbed Christy's prison shirt in her fists. "I'm top dog around here and nobody tells me…"

In a flash of motion, Christy's hands shot up between Randy's arms and swept out breaking her grip. Christy then followed through with simultaneous cupped hand slaps to Randy's ears stunning her instantly. She then pulled Randy toward her, kneeing her in the groin several times before pulling Randy's head down and delivering several knees to her face.

Christy threw Randy to the side and turned her attention to Randy's sidekicks. One was a stocky Hispanic woman with a high and tight haircut who looked like she was taking steroids; the other, a heavy-set Black woman with 70's style Afro. Both advanced on Christy at the same time. Christy set up in a fighting stance she had learned in her Krav Maga training. She held her hands up in front of her face and watched her opponents. The Hispanic woman made the first move, striking forward with fast right jab. Christy, reflexively pivoted on her left leg and used her left forearm to deflect the punch. She then pulled down on the woman's arm and delivered punch of her own to the woman's face followed by a second and then a third. Momentarily distracted, Christy felt her head yank back as the other woman had moved in, grabbed Christy's ponytail, and pulled hard.

Christy lost her balance and fell backwards to the floor with a sharp yell. The large Black woman pounced on Christy's chest and poised to strike. Using her legs, Christy drove forward in a squirming motion while repeatedly poking at the woman's eyes. Hannah suddenly jumped in behind the woman and applied a hammer choke which was short lived when the Hispanic woman pulled her off by the hair leaving Christy to fend for herself. Christy continued to wriggle forward and was able to clear her right leg just as her head slid into the wall. No room to maneuver, the large woman leaned forward and tried to smother Christy with her weight. Christy knew she had to get out from under the big woman and fast. Christy wrapped her left leg around the woman's right leg locking it in while she pushed off with her freed right leg. The woman's hefty bulk seemed insurmountable, but Christy summoned her strength and overcame the weight and the two rolled to Christy's left. Gaining the better position, Christy began to deliver forearm strikes to the woman's face and throat, causing the woman to let go in a feeble attempt to protect her pudgy face.

A sharp blow struck Christy's exposed right flank as the Hispanic woman stomped down with her heel. Stunned and winded, Christy turned her head and saw the hirsute woman's raised heel come down a second time, this time crashing into Christy's ribs. As she raised her heel to strike again, Christy rolled into her, grabbed her planted leg, and continued to roll as the woman's heel came down again. Off balance by Christy's move, her heel struck harmlessly into Christy's hip before she fell back into the concrete wall and toppled on top of the still sprawled Randy. Christy quickly pulled herself up onto her knees, grabbed the woman's lower leg and ground her knee into the exposed shin. The woman shrieked in pain but was too incapacitated to fight back. Christy did not relent. Out of fury and anger she continued to apply pressure, eliciting a banshee wail from her attacker.

"STOP!" Came the commanding voice of Officer Singletary as she flew into the room. "Get off her, Tabrizi! What's going on here?!"

"They attacked us!" Christy said breathlessly as she rolled into a sitting position and cradled her knees while trying to catch her breath.

"Is that so?" Officer Singletary said looking at the sprawled forms crowding the tiny cell. "It looks to me like you attacked them."

"These three goons come into my cell, and you think I attacked them?" Christy asked, exasperated. "Really?"

Singletary said nothing as she continued to survey the scene. Hannah lay near the door, curled up in the fetal position crying.

"Look what they did to Hannah," Christy said pointing to her petite cellmate. "You don't think they were the aggressors? What was I supposed to do?"

"You were supposed to call for help is what you were supposed to do," Singletary said as several large officers arrived as reinforcements. "You're all going to the SHU until we sort this one out."

"She can stay," Singletary said pointing down at Hannah. "But for the rest of them, get them outta my sight!"

Several officers entered the room and began shouting commands. Christy obediently assumed a prone position and allowed the officers to apply a set of handcuffs. As they helped her to her feet, she saw the large Black woman screaming as she resisted the officers.

"No!" She screamed and cussed as she continued to writhe around in resistance. "I ain't going to the hole! I can't do it no more! Nooooo!"

Two officers led Christy out of the building and down the walkway to the main building where the Special Housing Unit - the SHU - was located. They entered the building and led her through a series of security stops before entering a dark hallway lined with heavy steel doors. They stopped in front of one such door where one of the officers produced a key and unlocked the door. Christy was led in, and the door was shut behind her. A small slide was opened, and she was instructed to slide her cuffed hands into the slot where they unlocked her cuffs. The slot slid shut. A small strip of frosted glass allowed the only light into the small, dank cell. Christy sat down on the solitary bunk and laid down. She took a deep breath, slowly exhaled, and closed her eyes.

Chapter 38

Atlanta, Georgia

The heavy steel door buzzed as the lock opened and allowed Joe and Ramsey to enter the visitor's area. A couple of tables were in use this afternoon. From the back, their attorney, Nick Marcella waved. He was seated with an older gentleman whom neither Joe nor Ramsey recognized. The older man stood as they approached. He was tall, slender, and well dressed; dapper might be a better description, wearing a pinstriped charcoal gray tailored suit with a burgundy silk tie, perfectly knotted with a gold tie bar. He had thinning gray hair, parted to the side, and a confident grin. His nose looked as if it had been broken a time or two.

"Gentlemen," Marcella began, "I'd like you to meet one of our founding partners. This is Chester Krysztof. Chet, this is Joe O'Shanick and Matt Ramsey."

"Hey, it's good to meet ya," Krysztof said as he offered his hand.

"Nice to meet you too, sir," Joe said shaking the man's hand.

Joe immediately noticed the callused hands and scared knuckles along with Krysztof's firm grip. Along with his broken nose and confident poise, Joe immediately surmised this man had spent his formative years as a street brawler before becoming an attorney. He liked what he saw. They were going to need some fighters on their side if they were ever going to get out of this mess.

"Have a seat, boys, we've got a few weighty matters to discuss," Marcella said gesturing for them all to take a seat.

"I'm sure you've already learned of the untimely demise of your commanding officer, Lieutenant Commander Harrison. My condolences."

Joe and Ramsey nodded their appreciation.

"That's one of our concerns, Mr. Marcella," Joe started. "There is no way he killed himself. Somebody got to him."

"Someone good," Ramsey added. "Harrison was one solid operator. There aren't many people who could take him on and live to talk about it."

"That was our consensus as well, but we wanted to get your thoughts on it," Marcella responded. "So that leads us to believe that someone knew he had that video as there is no trace of it on his laptop. There *is* the typed suicide note and confession but, if as we believe, he didn't kill himself, the note was planted and the video removed."

"Which makes me think we have a leak," Joe interjected. "He wouldn't have told anyone he had that video; *furthermore,* he was killed just a few hours after I called home asking him to send us the video."

"That's what we figured," Marcella nodded looking over at Krysztof. "But we wanted to confirm that with you. Now there *is* the possibility that someone could have tracked your email of the file to Harrison, but here's why we don't think that's the case. Dr. Tabrizi's house was expertly tossed, and your laptop was nowhere to be found."

"It's gone?" Joe asked.

"I'm afraid so, Joe," Marcella nodded grimly. We think it happened yesterday afternoon around shortly after our meeting at the courthouse. Which means we likely have a leak. Now please don't get offended, but I have to ask this; did either of you discuss any part of our meeting with anyone?"

"No," Joe spoke as he and Ramsey both shook their heads.

"I didn't think so. Is there any chance Dr. Tabrizi may have said something?"

"I highly doubt it," Joe answered. "Christy is one squared away lady. She knows better than to talk about something like that."

"Then that leaves me, Kelley Ekland, Eddie Ferraro, and the two bailiffs who were in the room. I'll vouch for my partners and assure you it wasn't them. I have the names of the bailiffs and I'm gonna have Mr. Krysztof here look into it."

Joe looked over at Krysztof. "How do you plan to do that?"

"I wasn't always an attorney," Krysztof replied with a confident grin. "I know some people."

He didn't say much but Joe got the message. The fact that he didn't say much gave Joe confidence.

"I'm good with that," Joe replied before turning back to Marcella. "My bigger concern, however, is the fact that, without that video, we have nothing to go on other than our testimonies."

"That's true, but if we can establish that one," Marcella held up his index finger, "the bailiffs leaked confidential information, two, who they leaked it to and, three, that the leaks resulted in the destruction of evidence and the murder of a Navy SEAL officer, we have a very good chance at establishing a conspiracy to commit, which lends support to your testimony and could be enough to drop your charges."

"I get that," Joe nodded, "but there is much more at stake here than just us. If no charges are brought on Fowler, he may very well be elected next month, and this entire country is screwed along with much of the free world. We *have* to find that video!"

"I understand, Joe, I really do," Marcella said sympathetically, "but I can only present what I have before a jury. We'll keep looking for it and there are several investigative teams looking into it, including NCIS, so hopefully something will turn up but, in the meantime, we have to begin building your defense with what we have."

"I get it, Nick," Joe exhaled as he leaned back deep in thought. "There just has to be another option we haven't considered."

"Hey, wait a minute," Joe sat back up and looked at Ramsey. "What is it we tell our men about staying off social media?"

"Because once something is posted online, it's there for all to see and it can never be completely erased," Ramsey answered. "Are you thinking what I'm thinking?"

"Yes!" Joe answered and looked across at Marcella and Krysztof. "I saved that video to my cloud."

"Right but when you tried to find it, it was no longer there," Marcella answered.

"True, but there should still be a digital footprint of it somewhere. If we can get someone to piece it back together, we might not only expose who did this, but we might even be able to recover the video."

"I confess, I know a lot less about the internet than likely either of you," Marcella answered, "but I'm one who keeps his options open. It's certainly worth exploring. It would seem to me, however, that we would need someone with a great deal of computer savvy but also someone we can trust."

Joe looked at Ramsey then back at Marcella. "We know just the guy."

Chapter 39

Charlotte, North Carolina

The offices of Whitmore Investigative Services looked nothing like the seedy offices often depicted in Hollywood. Instead of the squeaky wooden chairs, gunmetal desks, and file cabinets cluttered with papers, Whitmore Investigative resembled an upscale financial corporation with well-lit rooms, carpeting, modern workspaces with commanding views of downtown Charlotte and tasteful decor.

Deep within the offices of Whitmore Investigative was a large windowless room that was soundproof and electronically protected. A large, C-shaped desk took up a large portion of the room, which resembled NASA's Mission Control with a number of computer screens arrayed around the desk and even on the wall. Seated behind the desk was a young, thin Black man with a shaved head and a rich mahogany skin tone. He was stylishly dressed wearing a black tailored suit with a starched white button-down shirt, a red paisley tie with matching pocket square, and gold cuff links. Roderick Boulware was anything but pretentious. He was the consummate professional in everything he did whether it was how he dressed, how he competed in basketball and tennis, or how he performed at his job. And it showed. Boulware excelled at everything he put his effort into.

Boulware had grown up, the oldest of five children in a working-class family in inner city Philadelphia. His father worked two jobs so their mother could stay home. Both parents had stressed the importance of education, something that a young Roderick had shown a keen aptitude for in math, science and, especially, computers. He earned an academic scholarship to Carnegie Mellon in Pittsburgh and graduated Summa Cum Laude in Computer Engineering. When looking to establish a computer investigative team, Clay Whitmore reached out to a trusted friend who happened to be the chair of computer engineering at Carnegie Mellon and he recommended Boulware straight out. Boulware had truly found his niche applying his immense skills in helping Whitmore Investigative Services bring just a little bit of justice to the world. Last week's accomplishment, helping the team locate and rescue the daughter of Charles Courtnall and several other abducted girls, had been one of the most satisfying victories yet.

That was why Whitmore's subsequent arrest along with Chuck Springer, the company's executive officer, was so enraging. They had done a good deed, scored one for the good guys and exposed some really bad players, and then it had all been turned on its head. As a result, Boulware had doubled his efforts trying to find and piece together every bit of evidence there was to be had to not only spring his boss but the rest of those involved while, hopefully, hanging the guilty. He had been able to find plenty on the Tupolev organization and their sex trafficking ring, but he was having a much more difficult time linking everything to the key figure, Senator Fowler. His research had shown a lot of supposed and questionable association regarding the senator but nothing concrete as of yet. Fowler was one slick politician surrounded by a huge army of well-funded political operatives. Getting to him would be one of the biggest challenges Boulware had ever faced. That was just how he liked it, he thought to himself, as he glanced up at a framed picture of Vince Lombardi his father had given him when he went away to college. In it was one of the legendary coach's famous quotes:

> *"The difficult we do right away. The impossible will take us a little longer."*

A chirp sounded in Boulware's ear, a signal from his AirPod that he had an incoming call. He looked down at his phone, which was perched on the desk, and saw the call was from Whitmore's lead counsel, A.C. Turnbull. Boulware tapped his AirPod to answer the call.

"Boulware," he answered in his rich baritone voice.

"Hey, Rod," came Whitmore's voice.

"Clay! It's good to hear your voice, brother! How are you holding up?"

"Chuck and I are managing,"

"I'm glad to hear that, boss man, but I'd much rather see you back here, running your ship as a free man. We're all working hard here to make that happen."

"I have no doubt you are, Rod and that's why we're calling. We need your help."

"Of course, Clay, anything," Boulware answered.

"You're patched into a conference call with me, Chuck, A.C., Mr. Courtnall's attorneys, and the O'Shanick's attorneys. I'm going to have Joe's attorney explain what's going on."

"Okay, I'm listening," Boulware asked.

"Mr. Boulware, my name is Nick Marcella. I'm lead counsel for the group representing O'Shanick, Ramsey, and Dr. Tabrizi. Joe used his iPhone to film the rescue mission when it first began and has video evidence that we think would not only incriminate Senator Fowler but, more importantly, exonerate everyone involved on this side."

"That's outstanding," Boulware replied cautiously, "but if you're asking for my help, I'm anticipating that there is a SNAFU somewhere; otherwise, you wouldn't be calling me.

"You're right, Mr. Boulware, there's a problem. The video is missing. Stolen would be a better term. It was erased from his phone and his cloud. He emailed a backup to his commanding officer…"

"Who, if I might take a guess, is the gentleman headlining the news who is reported to have taken his life by jumping from his balcony."

"Sadly, you are correct, Mr. Boulware. Joe also had it on his laptop but, like everything else, it too was stolen."

"With all that has transpired over the last few days, I guess I shouldn't be surprised," Boulware sighed. "And since it was on his iPhone, you're hoping the video might be recoverable?"

"Indeed we are, Mr. Boulware. My client and your boss tell me that you're extremely talented in this area and if anyone can pull this off, it will be you."

"I appreciate the vote of confidence," Boulware replied. "Let me state up front that recovering such a video is theoretically possible; however, if the people behind this have any degree of capability, it will be extremely difficult."

"Are you saying you can't do this?" Marcella asked through the phone.

"No, sir. I said it would be extremely difficult, but if you can forward me Joe's log-in ID and password for his cloud, I'll get started on it right away," Boulware said as he looked over at the Vince Lombardi quote.

Chapter 40

Air Force One

The majority of Air Force One's passengers were peering out the windows to get a glimpse of the Grand Canyon as it slowly passed below. At President Galan's insistence, the late Charlie Daniels recitation of *My Beautiful America* played overhead as the passengers reverently took in one of the nation's most breathtaking landmarks. Prior to takeoff, the pilot had informed President Galan that the clear skies and late afternoon sun would provide a spectacular view of the geological wonder and offered to perform a slow climb to the north after taking off from Phoenix. How could anyone say no to that?

Up front, in the presidential suite, the president and first lady knelt together on one of their couches as they stared in awe at the kaleidoscope of colors on display below them. The reverential words of Charlie Daniels playing overhead were not lost on Manny. It had been his extreme honor to serve, first as a Marine and now as Commander in Chief, over this great nation. As he looked out the window, a pit began to grow in his gut at the thought of a traitor like Senator Fowler using this nation, its people, and national treasures like this magnificent landmark as a bargaining chip to serve his own lust for power. The burning rage that began to form ruined what should have been a surreal moment for Manny and his wife.

The Phoenix rally had gone well enough. The die-hard supporters had come out in full force. They didn't place much trust in the press and there was no love lost for Senator Fowler; therefore, Fowler and the media's false narrative was not gaining traction among Galan's supporters. The opposition clung to the narrative, taking it at face value. That was to be expected and Manny knew there was nothing he could do about that. The issue as always lay with the swing voters. No telling how this would end up until the dust cleared. Manny knew what the truth was, but would the truth be presented before the American people in a fair and honest manner or would the false narrative carry the day? As the Grand Canyon faded behind them, Manny glanced at his watch. It was time to go work on getting the truth out. As if in confirmation, the VC-25A aircraft, currently designated as Air Force One since it carried the president, began a banking turn to the east as it headed to Galan's next rally in Denver. Galan gave Maria an appreciative pat on her attractively curvaceous hip and stood up.

"No!" she playfully whined. "Skip your meeting and stay in here with me. Can't somebody take notes for you?"

"Well, it's kind of like, I have to be there," Galan said as he slipped back into his suit coat. "What are you going to do?"

"I'm going to relive my youth and play Super Mario Brothers," Maria deadpanned.

"What?" Galan asked in surprise.

"I'm kidding," she replied as she held up a Karen Kingsbury novel. "I'm going to read and pretend you're sitting next to me by a cozy fire up at Camp David. Do you think you'll be long?"

"What do you think?" Galan asked dryly as he straightened his tie and checked his appearance in a mirror.

"I think the next time I see you we'll be landing," Maria said as she stood and kissed her husband. "But I hope you will be telling me that this whole fiasco in Belize has been exposed for the lie that it is, and that Fowler has resigned in shame and we won't have to even think about this election anymore."

"If that's the case then we'll cancel all the rallies for the week, head straight to Camp David, and curl up by that fire," Galan said as he kissed his wife and turned for the main cabin.

The conference room was already filled with Galan's staff when he walked in and took his seat at the head of the table.

"Did everyone like that flyover?" he asked, wanting to start what was likely to be an unpleasant meeting on a pleasant note.

"Yes, Mr. President," his campaign chairman, Kim Pritchard, answered. "But I've never heard that monologue before. Was that Charlie Daniels?"

"The one and only," Galan nodded. "He was a great American. He truly loved this country and spent a lot of time oversees entertaining our armed forces. I had the pleasure of meeting him a couple of times. Gosh, he was a true gentleman and such an entertainer. We need more like him," Galan smiled in appreciation.

"Well, may I suggest we obtain permission to play that monologue right before you take the stage at the upcoming rallies? I can't think of any more patriotic means in which to lead in to your taking the stage."

"I like it," Galan nodded. "In fact, there is a beautiful video that accompanies that. You could play that as well. You can find it on YouTube. Yeah, find out who owns the rights to it and see if they'll let us use it. Good thinking, Kim."

"Alright," Galan said, sitting up straighter and looking up at one of the flat screens, "Frank, where are we on this whole Fowler debacle?"

"Good afternoon, Mr. President," Snyder began. "May I assume you're well briefed on the situation involving Lieutenant Commander Harrison?"

Galan nodded.

"I flew down to Virginia Beach this morning to personally to meet with the local law enforcement officials who were first on the scene as well as to ensure that the investigation is being handled flawlessly and by the book."

"Thank you, Frank," Galan said acknowledging his FBI director. "What have we learned?"

"Beginning with what we know, there definitely was a suicide note left open on Lieutenant Commander Harrison's laptop. My analysts say it was typed in at around the time of his death. I'm having it added to the screen so you can read it for yourself," Snyder's video was replaced with a still image of a typed letter. "I sent copies to

Attorney General Jacobs and your chief of staff, but this is the original you are looking at on your screen. If I could draw your attention to the highlighted area, you will see that Lieutenant Commander Harrison did confess to his involvement with an ordered raid on Isla Esmeralda and a personal attack on Senator Fowler. The preliminary medical exam is consistent with death due to massive blunt trauma sustained secondary to a fall from a significant height."

"Frank, does his note say who gave the order?"

"No, sir, it does not."

President Galan nodded slightly without uttering a word. Attorney General Jacobs did the same. After a brief pause, Snyder picked up the hint and continued.

"Moving on, we have some new findings which you will find of particular concern. My team just cracked Harrison's email program and there are several emails in there that also show there was an order to attack Isla Esmeralda and Senator Fowler is actually named as a target."

"Repeat your last," President Galan said, stoically breaking his silence.

"There were several emails found on Harrison's laptop that indicate that, not only was there an order to attack the island in question but targeted Senator Fowler specifically."

"Frank, I'm going to need you to elaborate on that one," Galan replied.

"Of course, Mr. President," Snyder said in a sympathetic tone. "There were several emails back and forth between Lieutenant Commander Harrison and O'Shanick. They are cryptic but appear to be discussing a mission in which O'Shanick and Ramsey, under the cover of being on leave, are heading to the Caribbean to enjoy a couple of days of "R and R" at a resort. I'm posting the first one to your screen now."

The screen changed to an image of an email sent by LCDR Harrison to LCDR O'Shanick.

"This one was sent on Wednesday, the day before O'Shanick and Ramsey hopped aboard Charles Courtnall's private jet. It wishes them luck but warns O'Shanick not to collect any "souvenirs." We interpret that to mean there are to be no survivors."

"That's quite a leap, Frank," Galan commented skeptically. "What led you to *that* conclusion?"

"Context, Mr. President. There are subsequent emails that clarify the picture. If I may?"

Galan signaled for Snyder to proceed. The screen changed to another email sent from LCDR Harrison.

"This was sent late Thursday night around the time Courtnall's plane landed in Belize with O'Shanick and Ramsey onboard along with Clay Whitmore and several of his associates. As you can see, Lieutenant Commander Harrison informs O'Shanick that there will be an HVT - a High Value Target - at the resort but not to linger and, this time in bold face letters, stresses no souvenirs. He then recommends trying a drink called *Sol Diablo de Muerte.*"

"Sun devil of death," Galan translated out loud.

"Correct, sir," Snyder replied. "The team mascot for Arizona State University. Senator Fowler's home state. Based on the timing and circumstances, we believe this is a kill order for Senator Fowler."

"While I will concede one could be led to this conclusion, Frank. I happen to know O'Shanick and Ramsey. Both have impeccable service records and reputations. I find it highly unlikely that either man would go along with something like this. I don't know Lieutenant Commander Harrison personally, but his service record and reputation are equally impeccable."

"That's our assessment as well, Mr. President, but the emails we obtained suggest that either these three were acting on orders or all three went rogue. We tend to doubt the latter. The fact is, a mission did occur and all but Senator Fowler and the Russian crime boss, Victor Tupolev *were* killed, sir. Our working theory is the order came from higher up," Snyder said letting his last statement hang in the air.

"What are you suggesting, Frank?" Galan asked.

The screen returned to Snyder's video feed.

"Sir, I'm merely stating that the order originated somewhere. It either came from up the standard chain of command or Harrison, O'Shanick, and Ramsey were sheep-dipped by Joint Special Operations Command into a CIA operation. NCIS is conducting this part of the investigation with our oversight. We have spoken to SEAL Team

Four's commanding officer Commander Jerome Moslander and he denies any knowledge of any such order or operation. He is cooperating fully and has handed over all of his personal and official electronic devices for investigation. I haven't heard back from NCIS yet, but I suspect this will turn up empty although we will continue to pursue this all the way up to the chain of command including the Chief of Naval Operations and even the Secretary of Defense."

The last statement caused President Galan to look up at the bank of wall monitors. A look of shock registered on Secretary of Defense Carl Abernathy's face while the CNO, Admiral James Houston, remained his usual stoic self.

"Frank," President Galan began in a firm tone. "I will say right here and now, for the record, that I gave no such order and, furthermore, no such order ever originated from this administration. We are either dealing with a rogue commander, of which I highly doubt, or this is an elaborately designed framing effort and those emails were planted. I might be an old Marine Corps grunt, but I'm certainly not ignorant to the fact that your computer analysts are more than capable of conducting a forensic examination of these emails for point of origin and actual time stamps to see where these emails actually originated. Please tell me that such an examination is being conducted as we speak."

"We are indeed, sir," Snyder answered. "But, in the meantime, we are obligated to investigate every possibility which includes the possibility that such an order was given. This *does* mean we will have to issue subpoenas for computers, tablets, and cellphones all the way up the chain of command, including the West Wing."

"I'm well aware of what needs to be done, Frank, and you'll have my administration's full cooperation. I have nothing to hide and there is an election coming up which requires the record be set straight ASAP. It goes without saying that I expect you to sit on this latest development until the truth is ascertained. I don't want any leaks of this Bravo Sierra to the press. The media will latch on to this and run with it and we will really be up against it."

"Mr. President, there are many people involved with this investigation and several agencies. I cannot promise you there will be no leaks, but I *can* promise you they won't come from my office," Snyder replied earnestly.

"Fair enough, Frank," Galan responded. "Be ready with an update tomorrow. I'll talk to you then."

Snyder's monitor briefly went blank and then switched to a silenced news feed. Galan looked around the table.

"Thoughts?" He asked.

"If even an iota of this gets out in the press, we're screwed," Kim Pritchard, Galan's campaign manager, blurted out.

"This is Washington," Galan's Chief Political Advisor Aaron Sprole replied. "Odds are it will be headlining tomorrow's news. We have to accept that fact and come up with a strategy to handle it and fast."

"You're both right," Galan answered. "So, Aaron, Kim, let's have you two take your staff out and come up with a strategic response for when this hits the news." Looking up at the screens, he added, "I'd like the AG, SecDef, CNO, and NSA to stay online with us and Chief Counsel Barlow along with Embry and Espinoza to remain in here, please. The rest of you are dismissed for now. Thank you, everyone."

Chapter 41

Air Force One

The appropriate screens went blank before returning to various news feeds while the majority of the personnel stood up and filed out of the Air Force One conference room. Galan took a sip of coffee as he waited silently for the room to clear. In less than a moment, the door was shut. Galan calmly rested his elbows on the polished oak table, folded his hands together, and looked up at the bank of screens.

"Everyone in this meeting knows that no such order ever originated from this administration. That leaves us with two possible scenarios; either we have a rogue actor within our ranks or we're being set up. Thoughts?"

Despite the collective power and intelligence gathered, no one ventured to comment.

"This *is* the interactive portion of the program, gentlemen," Galan spoke interjecting a bit of humor, which caused a few chuckles and lightened the tension. Attorney General Jacobs spoke first.

"The initial statements of O'Shanick and Ramsey are consistent with those of Dr. Tabrizi, Charles Courtnall, Clay Whitmore, and the rest of his staff not to mention Courtnall's daughter and the other young women who were abducted and sold into the sex slave industry who just happened to be on that island. The Courtnall girl testified that Fowler beat her and was seconds away from raping her had O'Shanick not shown up. Prior to Lieutenant Commander Harrison's alleged suicide letter and these emails, all of the evidence we had supports what their testimonies state happened. I can't say for certain that those emails aren't real but without them, Fowler's narrative falls back in on him."

"Director Snyder seems to think they're real," Galan challenged as he took another sip of coffee.

"He's better than that," AG Jacobs replied dryly. "Let's look at the facts. First, a highly-esteemed and decorated Navy SEAL jumps to his death after an alleged guilt trip for his involvement in a highly unlikely conspiracy that was supposedly ordered from this administration? I find that hard to believe on many accounts not the least of which being guys like that have the skills and connections to disappear and go underground. If he truly was involved, which I doubt, he'd be a ghost not a corpse. Second, Harrison and O'Shanick openly communicate this by email using unsecured email accounts? I also find that hard to believe. Perhaps a couple of lower-ranked enlisted soldiers but not special warfare operators and certainly not seasoned officers with high security clearances. The simple fact that both his computer and phone were not secured with a passcode is highly irregular let alone that incriminating emails were saved rather than deleted. None of this adds up, yet Snyder seems to buy into it. I've known Frank for a long time, he's far better than this. Rather than jump to conclusions, he should wait until after those devices were torn apart and a thorough forensic analysis of the evidence was conducted. With your permission, Mr. President, I'd like to step in and have my own team of investigators conduct our own examination of these devices to determine the actual origination and time stamps of these emails. Then I'd like to compare them with Frank's results and see how they match up."

"Granted," Galan answered.

"Mr. President, if I may throw in a word of caution?" Chief of Staff Embry spoke up.

"Yes, JJ?"

"If the press gets ahold of this, which we can assume they will, they will absolutely crucify you for having the Attorney General step in and take over a crucial part of the investigation. You'll be accused of having your Attorney General obstruct justice."

"With no evidence, JJ," Galan countered. "I *do* see your point but, at this point, we have to discern whether or not this evidence is real. The press is already crucifying us, and they'll continue to do so unless we find something to disprove their false narrative. The way I see it, we don't have a choice if we want any hopes of salvaging this race before the election; furthermore, we must also consider the fact that there are several good people who are currently incarcerated over this incident. Based on what we know, they should be commended for what they did in rescuing those young women; instead, they are behind bars. If this conspiracy is as nefarious as we believe, and Saturday's assassination of SAIC McPherson suggests it is, then there is a very real possibility that O'Shanick and the others could all be targets. If nothing else, we owe it to them to rectify this situation ASAP."

"Mr. President," Assistant Chief of Staff Espinoza chimed in, "perhaps we should at least appoint an independent counsel to conduct the investigation. That would play better in front of the American people."

"Normally, I would agree, Martin," Galan replied, "but we don't have the time for that, and in this case, I don't think the press is going to cut us any slack regarding this matter anyway. Preston," Galan said looking back up at the screen, "get it done. Fast."

"Yes, sir."

"CNO Houston," Galan said addressing the Chief of Naval Operations on another screen.

"Yes, Mr. President?" The young four-star admiral answered peering into the camera.

"Contact your NCIS commanding officer and have him put his best team on this matter. A different team than that which is working with the FBI. They are to cooperate fully with the Attorney General's investigators on this. They are to have full access to any pertinent emails or communications, personal computers or official, beginning with Lieutenant Commander O'Shanick and all the way up the chain of command including your office."

Galan noted the concern register on Admiral Houston's face.

"Admiral, I have no reason whatsoever to suspect you of going rogue on me. I'm simply trying to quickly get to the bottom of this. I will be ordering a similar investigation of the entire West Wing including my personal devices. Only investigators with top-level clearance will have access. You know what Fowler's plans are for the armed forces. If we don't solve this problem in time to have a prayer of winning a second term, Fowler will have your subs tracking whale mating rituals in the arctic circle and your surface fleet will be replaced with sailboats crewed by social workers."

"Aye, Mr. President," Admiral Houston acknowledged with a half smile. "And if may be so bold as to say that I concur with Attorney General Jacobs. I spoke with Captain James Bennett earlier today, whom I believe you know is the Naval Special Warfare Task Unit Commander over the SEALs in question. He knows all three of them personally. Captain Bennett told me there is no way any of his special warfare operators would engage in such an operation, particularly Harrison, O'Shanick, and Ramsey, and they certainly wouldn't be careless enough to communicate in such a reckless manner. In his and my opinion, this is a setup, Mr. President; furthermore, we both believe Lieutenant Commander Harrison, one of *our* officers, was killed and his death was made to look like a suicide. I sincerely hope the medical examiner conducts a very thorough investigation of Lieutenant Commander Harrison and looks for signs of injuries that suggest there was a fight before he was thrown off that balcony. There's no way an operator of Harrison's caliber went down without a fight. Quite frankly, sir, I'm outraged. I've lost a highly trained operator, and a very fine officer at that, with two more of my finest behind bars, framed for a crime I don't for one minute believe they committed. In short, sir, I'll do whatever it takes to clear my men's records, as I will yours, sir."

"Thank you, Admiral. I have no doubt you will," Galan replied, once again, very pleased he nominated Admiral Houston for CNO last year.

"Andrew," Galan said turning his attention down the table to the White House Chief Counsel. "I want you to assign a team to fly down to Atlanta and interview Lieutenant Commander O'Shanick, Chief Ramsey, Dr. Tabrizi and then head up to Charlotte to interview Whitmore, Charles Courtnall, his daughter Tracy, and the other young ladies who were rescued from that island. I'll get SecState Priestley to arrange for interviews with all of the foreign nationals that O'Shanick and Ramsey rescued as well. The truth is on our side and one way or another, we are going to bring it to light in an undeniable way."

"Mr. President," Assistant Chief of Staff Espinoza spoke up, "I don't mean to speak out of turn, but we better get to it fast. Take a look at the newsfeed, sir."

Everyone's attention turned to the bank of flat screens on the wall. A breaking news headline was plastered across the various news stations:

Emails indicate SEALs were ordered to assassinate Senator Fowler.

Chapter 42

Washington, D.C.

On the south side of Chinatown's H Street, a Vietnamese restaurant sat wedged between a sushi bar and several Chinese restaurants. It was known for its Pho among other Vietnamese dishes. The main room was long and narrow, lined with dark wooden chairs and tables. Only a third of the tables were occupied which was not unusual for a Tuesday evening in October. A solitary flatscreen was mounted on the brick wall behind the bar. The bar was currently devoid of patrons. A middle-aged Asian man stood sideways behind the bar, watching the news while washing glasses. The six o'clock anchor signed off and the screen changed to the intro for the seven o'clock host, Chelsea McMann. A breaking news caption dominated the screen prompting the Asian man to turn up the volume.

"Good evening, I'm Chelsea McMann," the young female host began. "We have breaking news out of Washington tonight. Sources close to the investigation into the assassination attempt on presidential candidate Senator Robert Fowler have told us that incriminating emails were discovered on deceased Navy SEAL, Lieutenant Commander Patrick Harrison's, laptop. Our sources tell us that these emails reveal that he not only ordered fellow Navy SEALS Lieutenant Joseph O'Shanick and Master Chief Matthew Ramsey to carry out the mission but to kill everyone on the resort island and to leave no survivors. Emails further indicate the order originated from further up the chain of command, possibly as high as the White House."

"We reported earlier this morning on Lieutenant Commander Harrison's gruesome suicide in which he left a note on his laptop confessing to his involvement in the Fowler assassination attempt. The discovery of these emails appears to corroborate the accusations against the two Navy SEALs under his command, Lieutenant Joseph O'Shanick and Master Chief Matthew Ramsey. For more on this, joining us tonight from Columbus, Ohio, where he is out on the campaign trail, is the intended victim of the attack, Senator Robert Fowler with his comments."

The screen switched to a grim-faced Fowler, wearing a gray suit with a white shirt and scarlet red tie, seated before a green screen image of Ohio's capital city.

"Senator Fowler, thank you for taking time out of your busy schedule tonight to join us."

"You're quite welcome, Chelsea."

"Senator, what are your thoughts regarding these latest developments?"

"Quite frankly, Chelsea, I'm outraged as I'm sure every other American citizen is as well. This is an attack on the sacred foundations of our nation which we hold dear. I may have been the intended victim, but it's the American people who are the real victims. This was an attack on our electoral process, on the freedom of Americans to choose who they would like to lead them. Make no mistake about it, when the dust has cleared on this matter, we will find that there were dozens of people involved in this attack on our nation and I firmly believe Jorge Galan will be at the top of that list!"

"Senator, I know you have believed that to be the case since this started, but how can you be so sure Jorge Galan is behind all of this?" McMann asked

"I'm glad you asked that, Chelsea," Fowler pressed his lips together with a grim nod before continuing. "Men like O'Shanick and Ramsey are caged animals. They don't act until their handlers release them. They obviously had intelligence to know where I was meeting with several foreign officials. A meeting to establish a working relationship for future peace agreements and non-violent solutions once I become president, by the way. Not only were they briefed ahead of time, but they were well equipped with assault rifles and other military grade equipment with the intent, like the emails indicate, of killing every last one of us in cold blood. A well-planned and equipped mission of this sort can only originate from higher up. Now as a ranking member of the Senate Armed Forces Committee, I am well acquainted with the fine people who run our armed forces and I am also privy to their operations. This is highly irregular, not to mention illegal and, indeed, treasonous. No one that I know in the Pentagon would ever take part in such a mission unless directly ordered from above. Even then, I would expect our top military leaders to blow the whistle on such an order.

"No, Chelsea," Fowler said shaking his head in disapproval, "if I had to guess, I would venture that Galan did an end around and sent this one through the CIA. We all know the CIA has long been suspected of getting its hands dirty in many of the blunders and illegal acts that have indelibly tarnished the integrity of our great nation. The Bay of Pigs disaster, the Kennedy assassinations, Vietnam, the Iran Hostage crisis, Iran Contra, Panama, failure to prevent the attack on 9/11, the war in Iraq, and Saddam's fictitious weapons of mass destruction; I could go on and on. If, as I suspect, this turns out to be a CIA operation ordered by Galan, then when I'm president, I will personally see to it that the CIA is cleaned out, if not dismantled, while Galan and his goon squad led by Joe O'Shanick rot in prison for the rest of their lives.

"And that brings up another matter," Fowler continued. "We spend millions of dollars per person each year to train up our special forces' soldiers - Navy SEALs, Green Berets, and others like them - but what do we get in return? Yes, it was members of SEAL Team Six who rescued Captain Phillips and who killed Osama Bin Laden, but for every success story, we hear ten times the number of abuses and criminal acts carried out by special forces personnel.

"Last year, Galan led us into his personal war on select cartels in Central America, carried out mostly by special forces. As a member of the Senate Armed Forces Committee, I can tell you this war has cost the taxpayers hundreds of billions of dollars and what do we have to show for it? Thousands of innocent deaths, a propped-up cartel, and a thriving drug trade and at the cost of taxpayer money that could have been better served fixing Social Security, Medicare, and our education system.

"I went down to Belize to begin the process of bringing an end to all of this madness and was nearly killed by Galan's rogue hit squad. Enough I say. When I'm president, heads will roll and I will see to it that the entire military gets an overhaul, beginning with a drastic reduction of the special forces if not their elimination altogether. We've evolved past the need for barbaric warfare. We have some of the most sophisticated smart weapons in the world. It's time to reimagine our military as a smaller, more efficient, carbon-neutral, peace-keeping force made up of a diverse people from all walks of life who truly represent America and will convey our peaceful mission to the global community," Fowler said, concluding his statement with a determined stare.

"Senator Fowler, thank you for your time," McMann spoke.

"Thank you, Chelsea," Fowler said breaking into a smile.

"When we return," McMann continued as Fowler's image disappeared, "we will have more commentary from our experts. Stay with us…"

The newsfeed cut to a commercial and the bartender returned to washing glasses. The restaurant patrons continued eating their dinners having not paid the news any attention. All except for a young, athletic Asian male who was sitting alone at a nearby table. He had short dark hair, brooding dark eyes, and the stubbly beginnings of a goatee. He looked down from the television and pushed away his half-eaten bowl of Pho. He stood, dropped a twenty and a ten on the table, and walked out.

Chapter 43

Washington, D.C.

FBI Director Snyder walked up the church steps and entered the vestibule where he dipped his right hand in the holy water font and blessed himself with the sign of the cross. He entered the church sanctuary and turned left toward the confessional booth. He took a seat and slid open the small door exposing a decorative bronze screened partition.

"Bless me father for I have sinned. It's been two weeks since my last confession," Snyder opened with the traditional phrase.

"Indeed you have, my son," an Asian voice emanated from the screen. "Perhaps you have brought an offering for your adulterous sin committed at the school of our holy mother?"

Not only was this guy confirming to Snyder that he was speaking to the right person, but he was reminding him of what was being held over his head. Snyder hesitated. He was about to break the law. Violate his sworn oath. *Maybe I should just confess to Lynn and weather the storm,* he thought. *The divorce would be costly and sheer misery but isn't that preferable to this? I haven't broken any laws yet?* That wasn't true. He had already tampered with and erased evidence earlier that day with Harrison's phone. Snyder then remembered the images of his family that appeared on his phone. Would they really harm his family? He knew the answer to that. He wrung his hands and broke into a sweat, chastising himself for getting drunk and stupid Saturday night. He fell right into the oldest trap in the world. The Honey Trap.

There was only one way out. His honor was gone but, hopefully, his family would survive even though he likely wouldn't. Snyder steadied his clammy hands and took a deep breath.

"I personally visited the crime scene this morning. There was an incoming call from O'Shanick yesterday. I deleted it."

"Had anyone seen the phone before you?" the voice asked.

"It had been checked for prints, but no one opened it before me," Snyder answered.

"You know this for certain?" the voice asked in an accusing manner.

"Yes," Snyder sounded more confident than he felt.

"There will still be records," the voice stated. "You will see to it that those records are erased."

"I'm not the NSA!" Snyder whispered nervously. "I have no access to something like that. I don't even have the authority to tell his cell carrier what to do. Even if I did, doing so would raise a lot of flags. I risked a lot just doing what I did!"

"Very well," the voice said dismissively. "What else do you have?"

Snyder had hoped he had given whoever was on the other side of the screen enough to satisfy him, but that wasn't to be. No turning back now.

"Someone has been probing into O'Shanick's virtual cloud."

"Continue," the voice prompted.

"My expert has a program monitoring O'Shanick's cloud. Ostensibly, he believes he is watching for the presence of a criminal element as part of the investigation. In reality, it's to tip us off for anyone looking into what happened to the missing video. There has been activity there this afternoon. He thinks someone is inside the cloud trying to recreate the video."

"Is that possible?"

"Theoretically, yes," Snyder answered. "But my expert tells me it is extremely difficult."

"But possible?"

"Yes," Snyder conceded.

"Has your expert been able to determine who it is?"

"To a certain degree, yes. It's someone inside Whitmore Investigative. As I am sure you know, they are the investigative firm that was involved in this matter. Clay Whitmore and some of his associates are currently being held in a Charlotte jail."

"So O'Shanick has been in touch with them, and they know about the video. They then put one of their men on to finding it," the voice speculated out loud. "You must see to it that does not happen. Do you have anything else for me?"

"Yes. An investigation of Harrison's laptop revealed your people deleted the video, but we found evidence that Harrison emailed a copy to someone."

Chapter 44

Atlanta, Georgia

The warm humid day had cooled into the mid-seventies while the setting sun painted the cloud speckled sky with an array of dazzling pink, orange, and magenta colors. The prison yard was empty save for Joe and Ramsey who were trotting out the third of four laps around the track. They were completing the final mile of a *Murph* workout. Named in honor of Lieutenant Michael Murphy, a fellow SEAL who won the Congressional Medal of Honor sacrificing his life to save his men during a compromised mission in Afghanistan, a *Murph* workout consists of a mile run followed by 100 pull-ups, 200 push-ups and 300 squats followed by another mile run, all while wearing a twenty-pound vest. Joe and Ramsey didn't have access to the vests, but the workout was still grueling even without the vests. Sweat glistened on their shirtless bodies as their arms and legs pumped in a display of well-trained efficiency and strength. They ran side by side at a rapid clip as they rounded the turn into the final lap. Ramsey began to pull ahead as he lengthened his stride.

"No way, old man!" Joe said in synch with his breathing as he increased his speed to match that of his best friend and trusted chief petty officer.

Ramsey responded by flipping Joe the bird and increasing his speed even more. Despite pushing forty and holding several years over Joe, he could still outrun just about anyone in the platoon. All but Joe. As the platoon's commanding officer, Joe took it upon himself to lead by example and outwork everyone under his command. It was an example his lacrosse coach had set back in high school on Grand Island, and it had served Joe well during his lacrosse years at the Naval Academy and all his years with the teams. Ramsey might edge him out in a sprint but there was no way Joe would let him win this mile. Of course, Ramsey was probably thinking the same thing about Joe.

Joe dug deep and found enough speed to pull even. They still had a good 300 meters to go. An all-out sprint, at this point, would cause him to bonk before they got there. Still, Ramsey seemed to be steadily increasing his speed as if he had no limit. Breathing much harder now, Joe summoned his reserves to match speed. Together they charged on in a seemingly dead even race. Joe's lungs burned matching his arms and legs. They rounded the final turn and Ramsey turned on the afterburners only to find Joe had done the same and had pulled ahead by a nose. They crossed the makeshift finish line, marked by their shirts, and slowed to a brisk walk cool down. It took both a quarter of a lap before they had recovered enough to speak,

"Care for a rematch?" Ramsey joked.

"You like getting beat by an officer, don't you?"

"Just the opposite cake-eater," Ramsey quipped. "I had that one."

"Right up until the end. Second place is still first loser," Joe returned the barb. "Yeah, I'll do a rematch."

"Good," Ramsey replied. "But tomorrow."

"Oh, God bless you!" Joe exhaled with a sigh of relief followed by a laugh.

They finished the lap, collected their white t-shirts, and took a seat on a set of aging wooden bleachers. They sat in silence, savoring the refreshing breeze as the last remaining rays of sunlight ceded to the dark.

"We better head in," Joe broke the silence. "Not supposed to be out here this late."

"Five minutes. I like it out here," Ramsey replied. "I feel like a caged animal in there."

"I copy, Rammer, but we're still caged out here as well," Joe said looking at the nearly forty-foot-tall concrete wall surrounding the athletic fields in "The Yard." Several armed guard towers could be seen lining the top of the imposing structure.

"True, Joe, but as long as I can see the sky, I know there's still a world where I can be free."

"We'll be out there soon enough," Joe commented.

"You sure about that?" Ramsey challenged.

"Absolutely."

"Forgive me if I don't share your optimism, Joe."

"Have faith, my friend. The truth is on our side."

"I'd like to believe that, but whoever is behind this is seeing to it the truth never sees the light of day. They just killed our CO and my first platoon leader for crying out loud!" Ramsey said, the anger clear in his voice.

"I know, Rammer! Believe me, I know. Paddy's death is on me. I sent him that video. Had I not done that, he would still be alive. It's killing me."

"I wasn't blaming you, Joe," Ramsey said a little less abrasively. "You did the right thing. No one could have foreseen that. I'm just saying that unless Boulware can find that video, we are frickin' hosed. The only people who know the truth have all been tossed in prison; meanwhile, the scumbags behind this are planting false evidence against us and the media is shaping public opinion with their false narrative. No way we'll get a fair trial or an impartial jury. And that's if any of us live long enough to make it to a trial. We're going to have to come up with a contingency plan,"

"Like what?" Joe asked.

"Like figuring a way out of here."

"Are saying what I think you're saying, Rammer?"

"Daggum right, I am, Joe. If we don't get out of here soon, we'll never get out. I'm not living the rest of my life in here looking over my shoulder. Sooner or later someone's gonna catch us with our guard down. I'm not living that way. Not when we know we did the right thing. Screw that. Our only way out of here is going to be going over that wall. Or under it. Or through it; however we do it, we need to ghost this place, and soon."

"And then what?" Joe asked.

"What do you mean, then *then what*?" Ramsey replied in kind. "We'll go underground. We know how to do that. And we'll find the guys that tossed Paddy off his balcony and do the same to them. Then we'll go after Fowler and every last fat cat politician who have screwed honest working-class patriots like us over and put the screws to them for once. Now that I think about it, I wish you *had* drowned Fowler. Had you not saved that little dipwad, we wouldn't be here right now, his smug face wouldn't be all over the news. and Paddy would still be alive."

Joe looked back at his friend without reply.

"I'm *not* blaming you, Joe," Ramsey said. "I already told you that and I mean it. I'm just stating the facts. No good deed goes unpunished. This entire incident is a terrible injustice and I'm about ready to visit them with a little justice of my own!"

"I get it, Rammer. I really do," Joe replied. "But let's say we did make it out of here. Yes, you and I could go underground but we would still spend the rest of our lives looking over our shoulders. And what about Christy? She'll still be locked up. Clay, Courtnall, all of them. How does that help them?"

"I already thought about that, Joe. We bust them out as well."

Joe cocked his head in disbelief. "Have you lost your ever-loving mind?"

"Maybe," Ramsey shrugged, "but, the way I see it, I'd rather go out swinging than to spend the rest of our lives in here. Same for Christy and all of them. If we stay in here, they aren't going anywhere either. I'd rather bust out of here and try to bust them out. They deserve it and nobody else is going to do it. We owe it to them. I'd rather die doing that than wait for some cartel scumbag to shank me when I'm not looking."

"In times of war or uncertainty there is a special breed of warrior ready to answer our Nation's call. A common man with uncommon desire to succeed. Forged by adversity, he stands alongside America's finest special operations forces to serve his country, the American people, and protect their way of life. I am that man," Ramsey said, reciting the first section of the Navy SEAL Creed. "This is a war on our country and it's definitely a time of uncertainty, Joe. We aren't serving our country nor are we defending those who cannot defend themselves if we sit back and accept our fate. We *have* to do something, brother."

"Never out of the fight," Joe replied.

"Never out of the fight," Ramsey nodded.

"Alright, if it comes down to it, I'm with you, but hear me out, Rammer. Let's start working on a plan but, if in the meantime, Boulware can salvage that video, let's see where that leads. I'd much rather we all walk free than to spend the rest of our lives running as fugitives. I can't imagine Christy living like that, let alone Courtnall and his family. We need to give this a chance."

"I hear ya, Joe, but if it doesn't work out, I'd rather die with my boots on."

Chapter 45

Washington, D.C.

Less than a block up H Street from the Vietnamese restaurant, the Asian man sat at a small desk in his furnished loft apartment. A flat screen television was tuned to a cable news station which was rehashing the latest development in this latest election scandal. He paid scant attention to the news as he worked furiously on his laptop computer. The veins bulged on his muscular forearms as his hands danced over the keyboard, intermittently typing and clicking. Every now and then, he would stop to jot down notes on a pad of engineering graph paper. In just one hour, he had filled nearly two pages. His lean chiseled face and dark Asian eyes were an emotionless mask as he methodically worked through his inquiry.

His Garmin GPS watch vibrated with an alert. A small motion-detecting camera he had mounted above his door was alerting him that someone was climbing the stairs leading to his apartment. His loft was on the top floor - the third floor - of the small building. There was only one other apartment on his floor, and it was currently vacant. The building was old and in need of being torn down in favor of a trendy high-rise condominium complex. He chose it for this reason. He valued the privacy. Anyone coming up the stairs was looking for him. That wasn't good. Nobody should know where to find him.

He picked up his cellphone and opened up the security app. Two Asian men appeared, slowly ascending the stairs. Both had athletic builds and wore black turtlenecks with matching black jeans and dark sunglasses. They moved with cat-like grace, keeping their feet to the outside of the stair treads so as to minimize any chance the old wooden steps would creek unintentionally announcing their presence. They weren't coming for a social visit. He briefly considered waiting for them to come through his door and jumping them. He quickly dismissed the thought. He might have had the element of surprise, but there were two of them and, if they knew who he was, they were likely armed. He decided on a different plan. He captured their faces with a quick screen shot and, wasting no time, sprung into action. He pocketed his phone and quickly gathered up his laptop. He threw it, along with the pad of notes, into a backpack full of essentials he kept as a go bag and strapped it onto his back. A solitary window opened to an alley behind the small apartment building. He opened it and climbed out. A small ledge allowed his feet just enough purchase that he could stand and quietly close the window. Once closed, he sidestepped to a drainpipe he knew was there and quickly climbed down. Striking the ground, he ran down the alley and around the adjacent building until he was back out by H Street. He remained close to the building's front where he was relatively concealed by a set of railed steps that led up to a Chinese restaurant. From there, he could monitor the main entrance to his small apartment building. The main floor held a Chinese deli and bubble tea bar that has already closed. His vigilance was rewarded when, after a few minutes, the men in black emerged from his apartment entrance and immediately got into a dark-tinted Toyota Camry. As soon as they were inside, the waiting driver immediately took off.

The Asian man memorized the vehicle's license plate and ran over to his motorcycle, a bright green and black Kawasaki Ninja H2. He unhooked his helmet from a strap on his backpack, placed on his head, and climbed onto his bike. The engine emitted a high-pitched roar as it revved to life. He nudged it into gear with his foot and took off in pursuit. Having gotten a head start, the Toyota was already several blocks away. He worked his way up through the gears and sped up the street, weaving around several cars until he got close enough to regain visual sight of the black Toyota. He was just in time to see it turn left down Ninth Street. He leaned into the turn, the sporty bike handling it easily and sped up to get a closer look at the car. Once he was able to see the license plate and confirm he had the right car, he slowed and allowed the car to pull ahead. He wanted to remain relatively out of sight while still able to track the car. The car continued down Ninth Street, crossing Pennsylvania Avenue followed by the National Mall and on down until it turned right, taking the on-ramp that merged onto I-395 South.

A minute later, they crossed the Potomac River and exited onto the southbound lane of the George Washington Memorial Parkway. He increased the throttle to keep up with the speeding Toyota as they passed the concrete and glass structures of Crystal City on their right and Ronald Reagan National Airport on their left. Even in the evening hour, there was still a fair amount of traffic necessitating he weave around the cars in order to keep up. He tried to stay far enough behind so as not to be noticed by the Toyota's occupants.

Three minutes later they entered Old Town Alexandria. Shortly after, the Toyota turned left onto Madison Street and made its way down four blocks before taking another left into a parking deck. The Asian man stopped a block short and parked his motorcycle. He proceeded on foot to the parking deck where he found the front lined with hedges, offering him some concealment. The lower level was nearly empty, and he had no trouble spotting the three men as the exited the black Camry. All three were Asians, like him. While waiting for them to enter the adjacent office building, he unslung his backpack and retrieved a small electronic device about the size of a deck of cards. Once they were inside, he assumed the natural aura of someone who was supposed to be there and casually walked through the parking deck. He quickly scanned the area taking note of every security camera. He removed his cellphone from his pocket and pretended to be thumbing in a text when he "dropped" it on the ground right behind the Toyota. He dropped to a knee to pick it up and, with his back to the only camera within view, he quickly attached the magnetic tracking device inside the Toyota's rear bumper. He stood and continued on his way walking up the ramp to the next level and followed the deck to where it let back out on the next street over. He began to loop back around to where he had parked his motorcycle while considering his options along the way.

He had a license plate, a tracker, a photo of two of the men, and a possible office location. That was a good start. He needed a place to hole up and get to work on finding out who was after him, and why. He couldn't return to his loft in Washington. Whoever had come looking for him would likely try again. He looked at the street signs and sighed. She was only a few blocks away. It would be awkward, but it was the best option. He mounted his motorcycle, started it up, and did a quick U-turn. He took the next left onto North Pitt Street and passed by a group of trendy townhouses a few blocks later. The light was on in the front room she used as an office. Not surprising. She usually kept late hours. Would she be alone? He hoped so he thought as he drove another block before parking his bike. He secured his Ninja H2 and quickly walked back up the block to her door and knocked.

"Identify yourself," her familiar voice spoke through her Ring camera doorbell.

"It's Tran," he answered.

"Tran?" she asked, sounding incredulous.

"Yes, Jade, it's me, Tran Van Truk," he answered. "I'm sorry to drop in unannounced, but I need your help."

Chapter 46

Alexandria, Virginia

The door opened revealing a petite Vietnamese female with long silky dark hair, wearing black leggings and a concert t-shirt from U2's 2017 Joshua Tree Tour. Her name was Tien Vinh Nguyen. She went by her American name of "Jade." She had grown up in Boston, Massachusetts where her childhood friends nicknamed her "Winnie" based on the proper pronunciation of her family name which sounds like "win." A musical prodigy on the piano, she turned down a full scholarship to Juilliard to major in computer science and engineering at MIT. She had earned her doctorate degree by the age of twenty-four and, despite being heavily recruited by many tech corporations offering sizable compensation packages, she chose to go into the employment of the Central Intelligence Agency. Although her main job was probing the CIA's cyber defenses for holes, she had shown a unique ability for analyzing digital data and banking activity and was often "borrowed" by the Directorate of Analysis to assist with analyzing intelligence and designing cyber-attacks to assist with operations. In her spare time, she designed computer applications and software for medical industries. It was this venture that had made her a multi-millionaire and allowed her to spend the bulk of her time serving the nation that provided her family a life of freedom after her paternal grandparents fled South Vietnam in 1978.

"Why, Tran Van Truk, I don't know whether to slam the door on you or slap you."

"Please, Jade," Tran said instantly exasperated, "I really need your help."

"Of course you do;" she said accusingly, "otherwise, you wouldn't be here."

"That's not fair," he answered with a quick glance up and down the street. "Can you please just let me in?"

Jade stood shaking her head with a hand on her hip. She let out a sigh and stepped back, allowing Tran to enter. She closed the door and turned to face him, surveying him with a disapproving scowl and her hands on her hips. Tran waited nervously for the dressing down he was about to receive. To his shock, Jade broke into a smile and leapt up into his arms clinging to him like a koala bear in a fierce hug.

"Oh, Tran! I was so terrible to you last spring in Virginia Beach! The things I said to you, refusing to take your calls and then I heard you were in a coma after being shot and nearly killed by the mafia up in Niagara Falls! I thought I'd never see you again!"

"Well, I'm still here," Tran said awkwardly as he tried to process the sudden swing in Jade's behavior. "And, for what it's worth, I'm sorry I took off on you like that."

"Your friends needed you, I get that now," she said leaning back so she could look Tran in the face. "I was too busy being self-centered and disappointed to see that. I expected too much of you. It wasn't right. And I should have come to see you, but I was afraid. I never even called to check in on you. I'm sorry, Tran. Will you forgive me?"

"Of course, but I did take off on you the first week we were together after my deployment. I understand your anger."

"Tran," Jade said holding his face in her hands. "You're a SEAL. You had a teammate in trouble, and you answered the call. It's what you do. I knew that but my mind just wouldn't process it. I'm different now."

"I don't think there is much your mind can't process," Tran replied skeptically.

"You forget, I'm an Aspie, I'm not always the most socially adept. Now let me down," Jade said as she loosened her legs and slid her petite frame down to a standing position.

Tran had met Jade at Little Creek - the name of their Virginia Beach amphibious warfare base - while she was temporarily assigned there as an analyst and cyber-warfare specialist. In addition to her natural attractiveness, Tran was immediately drawn to her quirky personality and highly intelligent yet unassuming witty sense of humor. As they got to know one another better, Tran began to notice some subtle personality traits. Having had a close friend with Asperger's Syndrome while growing up, Tran quickly picked up on Jade's status on the autism spectrum. She was highly functional, well-adjusted and, surprisingly, quite open about her condition. Shortly before she turned three, her parents, both internal medicine physicians, recognized her remarkable intelligence seemed to be lacking the social interaction and verbal skills expected of a young girl her age. She was quickly assessed and presumed to be on the autism spectrum. Fortunately, they had been of financial means to get Jade into an early interventional program where she received cognitive therapy and applied behavioral analysis. As a result, Jade had been able to assimilate socially and developed many close friendships. She was able to function at a level that allowed her to accelerate ahead of her peers and enter college early. Jade had been fortunate. Many people on the autism spectrum are not diagnosed in time or do not come from families with the financial means or access to intervention programs. Others are simply further along on the spectrum and have lower probability of successful intervention. Tran's childhood friend was one such case and would likely always be dependent on his family. Jade functioned at such a high level, that Tran, had he not been familiar with Asperger's Syndrome, likely would have just thought her to be a highly intelligent person with a quirky and occasionally feisty personality.

Tran was well known in the teams for his exceptional sense of humor delivered in a dry, nearly emotionless manner that kept his teammates thoroughly entertained. He could also perform impeccable impressions of cartoon characters, celebrities and, perhaps most humorous to his teammates, their commanding officers. A self-aware and also highly intelligent man, Tran was well aware that he was in many ways himself unique and even odd in some ways. Jade had proven to be a good match and he had quickly developed an interest.

As much as they enjoyed each other's company, some issues had arisen. Jade could be a very spirited and passionate person, but sometimes this led to a level of attachment that battled with an underlying insecurity. That had become an issue in their relationship. Tran's life as a Navy SEAL often required being deployed or sent out of town for weeks if not months at a time. They were sometimes called up with minimal notice. Additionally, his training schedule was erratic and subject to last minute changes. As someone who's internal wiring preferred, if not demanded, order in her life, Jade did not respond well to this. She loved Tran but had become increasingly clingy and emotionally volatile regarding his frequent departures. It reached critical mass several months ago when, shortly after returning from deployment in Central America, Tran's platoon had been given a week's leave. Jade had not done well while Tran had been gone for months on a combat deployment. Upon his return, Jade had seemed cold and distant at first, a response she was honest enough to say had been a defense mechanism to cope with his absence. After talking through it, she warmed back up and became more like her energetic and passionate self. Tran promised her they would spend the entire week together when his leave began, and she had been absolutely elated. A few days into his leave, Tran had taken Jade to the beach on Joint Base Camp Pendleton to teach her how to surf. They had had several great days together and Jade had been back to her smiling self, until Tran had gotten a call from his platoon chief, Master Chief Ramsey, who had informed him that their platoon leader and close friend, Lieutenant Commander Joe O'Shanick, had narrowly escaped death after plunging over Niagara Falls followed by another incident where someone tried to kill him in the hospital. Within the hour, Tran and another teammate, Jamie Mueller, were in Ramsey's truck heading to Niagara Falls to look after their friend. Jade had not responded well to yet another one of Tran's sudden departures. She had become quite irate and had been unable to see Tran's side of things. He knew she wasn't being selfish as much as her mental wiring just did not provide adequate coping skills for dealing with Tran's frequent and often unforeseen departures. During the ride back to her apartment, Jade had given Tran an ultimatum; if Tran left with his teammates, they were through. Tran tried to reason with her, but she wouldn't budge. His level of commitment to his teammates was unmatched and there was no way he would not go with them.

Tran had been shot and severely injured during an attack on Joe's family. The trauma surgeons had had saved him, but it was several weeks before he recovered enough to return to Virginia Beach. When he did eventually return, he learned that Jade had put in for a transfer the day he left, and the CIA jumped at the opportunity to have her back in Langley. She was unaware of Tran's near fatal injuries. Tran had tracked her down and actually drove up to try and work things out but, as he was pulling up to her townhouse, he saw her walk out with another man. He kept on driving and didn't stop until he was back in Virginia Beach. As much as he liked her and had felt a connection, Tran had eventually gotten over it, consoling himself with the fact that her inability to cope with his lifestyle as a SPECWAR operator would have caused bigger problems down the road and they were better off apart. As a result, he had really dreaded this reunion, anticipating a particularly uncomfortable level of awkwardness. Never in a million years had he expected this warm reception, let alone Jade apologizing.

"So," she said as she stood looking up at him with a twinkle in her eye, "you said you need my help. What is it that made you get on your motorcycle and drive all the way up here from Virginia Beach for me to help you with?"

Gone was the cold indifference, the calculated monotone she had used four months ago to tell him they were through. He looked down and saw the playful smile and youthful curiosity of the Jade he had been drawn to.

Uh-oh, Tran thought as he chose his next words very carefully.

"Have you been watching the news?" he asked, probing to see her initial reaction.

"Ah, yes, Joe and Ramsey," Jade said knowingly. "Everyone is saying President Galan sent them to kill Senator Fowler. I should have known that's why you came. Team business."

"That's just it, Jade," Tran said. "They would never do something like that, and President Galan would never give such and order. This entire thing *has* to be a setup. Our Task Force Commander, Joe's superior officer, Lieutenant Commander Harrison was killed this morning and I'll bet it has everything to do with this."

"I saw that," she responded in a serious tone, the smile now gone from her face. "He didn't jump, did he?"

"No way did he jump and no way was he involved passing on an order like that. They're trying to hang Joe and Rammer…"

"And get Fowler elected," Jade said completing the sentence. "I know, Tran. I've been following this. And I know you know that I know Joe and Ramsey. They're good men. As are you. I don't believe any of this."

"Then you know I have to help them."

"I wouldn't expect anything less of you, Tran. So how can I help?"

"It's a big ask, Jade," Tran spoke seriously. "I wouldn't ask you if the lives of some very fine people weren't at stake."

Jade held up her hands, palms up, and made an expectant facial expression urging Tran to get to the point.

"I'm in need of your hacking skills. Two guys tried to jump me at my apartment. I evaded them and followed them down here to an office building a few blocks away. I need to find out who they're working for and what they're after."

"They came after you?"

"Yes."

"This way," Jade turned and began walking up the stylish wooden staircase.

Chapter 47

Alexandria, Virginia

Tran followed Jade up to the second floor on which there was a bedroom at each end of the narrow townhouse. She led him into the front room which she had made into her home office. There were several computers and even more monitors. A large map of the world took up one wall while a large map of North America hung on the opposing wall. They were connected by a wall with several large television screens. She sat down in a comfy leather office chair that seemed to swallow her petite frame and then struck her keyboard which caused two large screens to light up. She looked up at Tran expectantly. Tran looked back nervously, still caught off guard by her warm reception.

"You gonna give me something to go with?" She asked.

"Huh?" He responded awkwardly.

"I need some intel, frogman! Something I can work with to conduct a search."

"Oh!" Tran replied shaking his head at himself as he unslung his backpack and knelt down beside her. "Yes, I've got pictures of the car make and model, license plate, the address of the building they entered and pictures of their faces," he said opening his cell phone to the pictures app and handing it over.

"This is a good start," Jade said as her fingers began to dance across the keyboard. "Why didn't you just get in touch with your inner ninja, tie them up, and sweat the information out of them?"

"Because D.C. isn't a combat zone, I'm technically not legally allowed to carry a firearm in D.C., I had no idea if they were feds, and even though I only saw two of them, there could have been more."

"Yeah. Good call," she said with a sideways glance and a humorous smile. "I would have done the same thing."

Tran snorted a slight laugh. He marveled at her ability to carry on a conversation while her fingers typed at superhuman speed.

"Wait!" She said as she continued to type and click the mouse. "You said you followed them *down* here? That would not make sense if you were in Virginia Beach. You would have followed them *up* here. And then you said D.C.! So where are you staying?"

"I'm renting an old flat in Chinatown."

"Oh no," Jade said with genuine sympathy, "You were medically discharged from the Navy because of your injuries."

"Not exactly," Tran answered. "They're holding my billet pending my passing the physical standards. I'm up here at George Washington University Hospital on a training rotation with the trauma service and EMS while I get back in shape."

"And how's that going?" she asked. "Oh, send the facial pictures to my phone. I'll enter them into a facial recognition program. That can run while I'm searching for your friends' car."

"Is this legal?" he asked as he texted the pictures.

"Should be," she murmured. "I'm allowed to access it for official government business. I'd say this qualifies. So why didn't you look me up sooner?"

"Really?" he asked.

"Yes, really," she responded while working the mouse with her right hand and thumbing her phone with her left hand.

"I didn't think you would want to hear from me," he answered quietly.

"I did leave you with that impression, I suppose," Jade replied passively with her eyes still focused on the task before her. "I'm better now. New Jade. Two point zero."

"I *did* drive up here in August, but I saw you walk out with another man, and I just kept on going."

"A man?" she asked, sounding surprised. "There hasn't been a man since you, Tran. Wait a minute. Was he Vietnamese?"

"Yes."

Jade began to laugh. "That was my older brother, Huy, you amphibious halfwit!"

"Really?"

"Yes, ding-a-ling! He came to visit me. No other guy has been here."

"Well, don't I feel like a complete…"

"Gotcha!" Jade exclaimed, staring intently at one of the screens.

"What do have?" Tran said as he stood to look over her shoulder.

"Hold on," Jade said while typing. "There! Have a look."

Tran leaned in to get a closer look. "Jasmine Pacific Global?"

"Yes. That's who the car is registered to. Kind of."

"What's that mean?" Tran asked as he stood back up.

"It's actually registered to a shell corporation, but Jasmine Pacific is the conglomerate it belongs to. Guess who heads it up?"

"No clue," Tran answered. Jade loved guessing games.

"Liu Shunyuan," she stated matter of factly.

"Help me out here, Tien," Tran said shrugging. "I'm just a sailor."

"Liu Shunyuan is the head of the Liu Dynasty. He's kind of the George Soros of the Far East. His net worth is unknown but estimated to rival that of Elon Musk and Jeff Bezos. They have their hands in everything; global trade, rare earth mining, fossil fuels, and that's just scratching the surface. They're believed to oversee China's drug manufacturing and exportation, human trafficking, and nuclear arms technology. His son, Liu Fan, resides here in Washington where it's rumored he oversees all the American operations of the Liu Dynasty and wields great influence with the Washington insiders. He's the president and CEO of Jasmine Pacific Global."

"So they're a Triad," Tran said knowingly.

"More like a mega Triad," Jade corrected. "They're way bigger and far more widespread than any of the other Triads. They have a lot of legitimate enterprises and government influence which allows their criminal enterprises to thrive under the radar, so to speak."

"So the guys in the car work for him?"

"That would be a good guess. You said they went into that building," Jade said as her fingers resumed their dance across the keyboard. "The building is owned by Jasmine Development, a commercial real estate company that is also part of Jasmine Pacific. They have an office on the top floor but there is also a wealth management company named Golden Sun Financial, which is also a sub corporation of Jasmine Pacific only through another shell corporation."

"So you're saying that this Jasmine Pacific owns the building and two of the businesses within it?" Tran asked.

"Yes. I need to check on a couple of the other businesses listed but these two for sure are part of Jasmine Pacific which is the strong arm of the Liu Dynasty."

"Is the Liu Dynasty known for using strong arm tactics like sending those two goons after me tonight?"

"Definitely," Jade spoke into the screen as she continued to work her computer like a concert pianist. "They are glorified organized crime, Tran. Well-funded, well-connected, and their presence is everywhere, especially in governments around the world, including ours. They are rivaled only by the cartels in power but have far less enemies."

"So do the cartels answer to them?" Tran asked.

"Not really. They have a working relationship that works to both of their benefit. Other than using the cartels to smuggle drugs and people into the United States, the Liu Dynasty works in different areas. They each have their own turf, in a manner of speaking."

"Roger that," Tran nodded in understanding. "But none of this explains why they are interested in me."

"Guilt by association?" Jasmine offered. "You *are* a member of their platoon. If they *did* kill Lieutenant Commander Harrison, maybe they are trying to take everyone out not knowing who knows what."

"That seems a stretch," Tran replied. "But plausible. I should warn everyone."

Tran picked his cellphone off Jade's desk and fired off a group text. His thumb hovered over the send button when a dire thought occurred to him.

"Jade, could they have found me by tracking my cell phone?"

"Yes!" she said with sudden alarm in her voice, her fingers hovering over the keyboard. "If they have a halfway decent hacker, it's child-play!"

"Shoot!" Tran exclaimed as he began packing up his backpack. "I can't believe I didn't think of that sooner! We've gotta get out of here! Grab what you need and let's di di mau!"

"I have a lot of sensitive data here, Tran! I've got to secure it!"

"They could already be here!" he hissed. "Make it fast!"

Jade leapt to her feet and quickly went about removing hard drives from her processors and gathering up all sensitive thumb drives and discs. She stuffed them all into a backpack while Tran opened a side panel in his backpack and retrieved his handgun, a Smith and Wesson M&P Shield Plus 9mm. There was already a round chambered. He flipped off the safety and took up watch at the door. A minute later, Jade moved up behind him, visibly shaken.

"Wait for my signal," he said as he quietly crept down the hall, keeping to the wall.

He quickly cleared Jade's bedroom and shared bath before he took up position at the head of the stairs and waved her on. Jade nervously fast-stepped up the hall. The contents of her backpack making a metallic clank as she walked. Tran held his finger to his lips and signaled for her to slow her pace. She arrived at his side, and he signaled for her to wait as he slowly began to work his way down the stairs. He kept to the edges in hopes that the polished oak steps wouldn't emit a telltale sound. Fortunately, it was a new townhouse development, and the boards were well fit and had not warped yet. He made it down without a sound, clearing the open foyer as he went. He signaled Jade to wait and then turned to clear the downstairs which consisted of a half bath/utility room and then an open kitchen area and great room. All was clear.

As he walked back to the stairs, the sudden sound of breaking glass came from upstairs followed by the sound of Jade screaming. Tran rushed back to the stairs. His handgun at the high ready position, he charged up the stairs only to be met by Jade rushing down. Her normally light tan complexion was a white as a ghost.

"Tran! Somebody just launched Molotov cocktails through the windows!"

Tran looked around the ninety-degree bend in the stairwell and saw the glowing shimmer of flames reflecting off the hallway walls. Both bedrooms were on fire.

"We've gotta get out of here!" Jade yelled as she pushed passed Tran.

Tran followed her down and grabbed ahold of her backpack just before she reached the front door. He pulled her to the ground and held her down with his hand over her mouth. Jade looked up with panic and confusion in her eyes.

"Running out that door is exactly what they want us to do," he said calmly as he removed his hand from her mouth. "They torched the upstairs to force us to run down and out for safety. They'll be waiting by the front and back doors."

"How do you know this?" Jade asked.

"What do you think I do for a living?" he asked.

Jade began to speak but he shushed her. "That was a rhetorical question. Is your car in the garage?"

Jade nodded.

"Good. Where are the keys?"

"On the table, by the door," she answered as a loud crash sounded upstairs.

Tran could see flames beginning to appear at the stairwell's turn. Another minute of two and the downstairs would be on fire as well. Fortunately, the smoke was still contained upstairs. He snuck a glance down the hall and saw the windows of her great room. He didn't see anyone looking through them, but it was dark outside and he couldn't be sure. He looked up and saw the switch for the hallway light. Switching it off would announce they were downstairs, but with a fire raging upstairs, where else *would* they be? He reached up and switched it off. Automatic gunfire immediately erupted from the back with the sound of shattering glass. Tran recognized the sound of an AK-47. He pulled Jade into the stairway alcove as the 7.62-millimeter rounds struck the front door. He only heard the one rifle which gave him an idea.

"Jade, listen to me," he said as he stood and pulled her to her feet. "When I say the word, I want you to dash across the hall and into the garage. Leave the door open. You got it?"

Jade nervously nodded her understanding. Tran could feel the heat as tongues of fire were now reaching to them just a few feet over their heads. Tran waited as the gunfire kept coming. The gunman was holding his finger on the trigger and blindly spraying into the townhouse. *Forcing us down and then out the front door,* Tran assessed. He waited. The heat nearly unbearable as the smoke began to engulf them. The gunfire paused.

"Go, Jade! Now!" Tran yelled as he gave her a shove toward the door to the garage.

Jade ripped open the door and stepped into the garage. Tran followed right behind her, grabbing her keys off the table as he leapt into the garage. The gunfire opened up again, splintering the door as it hung on its hinges swinging in the hallway. Jade had been wise enough to leave the garage light off, thus not giving away their position.

"Get in!" he whispered forcefully as he turned toward the vehicle. Even in the dark, he was thankful to see Jade had a Toyota 4Runner and had wisely backed it into the garage, one of many personal safety tips he had instilled in her. He opened the back door and tossed in his backpack as Jade did the same from the passenger side. They jumped in front. Tran held his handgun in his right hand as he pushed the start button. The 4.0 Liter V-6 engine came to life. He held his foot on the brake as he shifted the SUV into gear. He silently hoped the contractor skimped on the garage door as he quickly moved his foot to the accelerator and pressed down hard. The 4Runner lurched forward and crashed through the aluminum paneled garage door. A loud screeching sound encompassed the 4Runner as the garage door scraped the roof while he drove through it. For a second, the panels obscured his sight but were pulled away as the garage held onto its door like a lady trying to prevent a thief from snatching her purse. Automatic gunfire erupted as they charged out Jade's short driveway and into the street.

"Get down on the floor!" Tran yelled as numerous rounds struck the driver's side door and shattered the windows.

Behind him, Tran saw a flurry of sparks as the computer room they had just been in minutes before came crashing down into the garage, engulfed in flames. Flashes of gunfire could be seen in the rearview mirror as he stomped on the gas pedal, putting as much distance between them and the danger behind them. He took the first left to get out of the line of fire. As he rounded the corner the sickening sound of shredded rubber emanated up through the floorboards and the SUV began to feel sluggish. Tran cursed out loud as the vibrating steering wheel informed him they had more than one tire out and the vehicle was quickly becoming inoperable.

"Jade! Get up and get ready to run!"

"What?" A shocked Jade asked. "Why?"

"They shot out the tires! If we keep going, they'll catch us in no time. We're gonna have to exfil by foot."

"How's that any better!?" She asked as she sat back up in the seat, nervously looking around.

"Because, in this thing, we are sitting ducks!" Tran said as he took another left. "But I've got an idea that might buy us a little time."

Chapter 48

Alexandria, Virginia

Tran inched the limping SUV over to the curb.

"Grab your bag and let's go!" He said as he turned around and retrieved their backpacks.

They climbed out of the 4Runner, shut the doors, and ducked through a service alley behind another block of townhouses. A pair of headlights swept across the alley as they rounded the corner. Tran quickly glanced over his shoulder and saw the same late model Toyota he had seen earlier.

That figures, he thought to himself as he motioned for Jade to keep moving. Tran grabbed her hand and quickly led her down the alley, trying not to make any noise. He desperately hoped they had not been seen. If they could put a couple of blocks between them and their attackers, he was confident they could evade them.

"*Ting xia!*" a male voice yelled from behind.

Recognizing the Mandarin word for stop, Tran tugged Jade's arm as he broke into a full sprint. They turned down another street as automatic gunfire erupted behind them. Bullets whizzed by Tran's ears and slammed into a brick wall across the street as he led Jade around the corner.

"Tran! They're shooting at us!" Jade yelled; the fear evident in her voice.

"Shh! Just stay close to me!" he whispered loudly trying to encourage her.

Up ahead, he spotted a low brick wall topped by a wrought iron fence separating a row of floodlit trees from the sidewalk.

"On me!" he said as he leapt onto the four-foot-high wall.

Tran turned to help Jade up but saw she had already climbed up on her own. He helped her carefully cross over the spiked wrought iron fence and before scaling it himself. As they jumped down. Tran quickly looked around and saw the trees did not provide as much cover as he had hoped.

"Jade! Listen to me! Lay down as close against this wall as you can and don't move until I tell you. You got it!"

Tran saw her quietly nod as she dropped to the ground and flattened herself tight against the brick wall. There were two floodlights planted into the ground, illuminating the trees. He quickly turned each one until their bright light was pointing out at the fence and away from the trees. As expected, he heard footsteps rapidly approaching and wasted no time disappearing deeper into the trees where he took up position behind a large cherry tree. He peered through the trunk where it split into separate limbs, took aim with his handgun and waited. He saw the two darkly-clad Chinese thugs race by and breathed a slight sight of relief as their footsteps began to fade. He willed them to continue up the street, hoping they wouldn't deem this copse of trees worth searching. He glanced down at Jade. Her petite form remained pressed up against the wall, but he could see her shaking in fear. To her credit, she remained silent. Unless their pursuers climbed the fence, there would be no way they could see her let alone shoot her.

Suddenly, she jumped up screaming that a spider was crawling on her as she frantically began to run in place while trying to brush herself off. Jade was terrified of spiders.

"Jade! Jade!" Tran hissed. "Pipe down and get down! A spider can't hurt you!"

"Yes, it can!" she shot back in a near phobia fueled panic.

Tran dashed out and grabbed her. He clamped his left hand over her mouth while keeping his right arm extended with his Smith and Wesson. He half dragged his visibly shaken friend into the trees as he kept vigil for their pursuers. Surely, they had heard the commotion and would be back to investigate. They reached the cherry tree and he watched the fence as he tried to settle Jade down.

"We're gonna have company now, for sure," he whispered in her ear. "I'm gonna let go, but you have *got* to stay quiet and stay down behind me, Jade. Can I count on you?"

Jade nodded and Tran unclasped her mouth. "Good, now stay down and don't move!"

Tran took up his previous position peering through the split cherry tree trunk as he scanned the fence. The floodlights may have ruined his night vision but at least he had a slight advantage with them now shining out through the fence. *If* they appeared at the fence. Tran wouldn't approach that way. It was too obvious and too easily defended. If these guys had any decent training, they would come at him from a different angle. Something less expected.

Great, Tran thought to himself as he quickly looked around. The lot was on a corner. It appeared to be a small park, of some sort, bordered on the front two sides by the wall and, behind him, by two brick townhouse buildings that angled away from each other. A lot of points to cover and he was by himself with a handgun facing at least two men with AK-47's. To make matters worse, he could now hear several police sirens rapidly approaching. *No easy day, Tran.* He knelt down beside Jade, keeping his eyes on the wall.

"Jade," he whispered as he gently tapped her shoulder. "I need you to do me a favor."

"What?" she nervously whispered a little too loudly.

"I want you to watch that wall for me," Tran said as he pointed toward the wall they had climbed over. "Pay attention for motion of any kind. Use your peripheral vision. It spots motion better at night than looking straight on. If you see anything, *don't* make a noise! Just give my leg two quick taps. I'll be right here next to you watching the other wall."

"G-got it!" Jade stammered.

Tran hugged her tight with his left arm to reassure her. "I've got you, Jade. I won't let anything happen to you."

"I know," she whispered a little more calmly.

Tran stood back up and melded himself with the tree. He was grateful that he was still wearing black fatigue pants, black boots, and a black turtleneck, which he had warn as part of his paramedic uniform. Thankfully, he had removed the light blue uniform shirt earlier. A brief thought flashed over him. The last time he had wielded his handgun in a defensive posture, was up in Joe's hometown where he had been shot multiple times and nearly killed by a bunch of mafia thugs. He quickly ignored the thought. Dwelling on it wouldn't do him or Jade any good here.

What he *did* wish he could fix was the lighting along the other wall. Like the wall they had just traversed, it also had two floodlights but they were still focused inward. A trained pair of eyes might be able to pick out Tran and Jade. Fortunately she was similarly dressed in black leggings and her U2 shirt, but he would really prefer the lights shine outward. He quickly thought it over. If they had heard Jade's screaming, they already knew he and Jade were in here. Moving the lights wouldn't change that, but it might improve his tactical situation just a bit.

"Jade," he said kneeling back down. "I need to turn the other lights around so they can't see in here. Stay right here. I'll be right back."

Tran heard her weakly acknowledge him as he kept low and quickly set out to reposition the other two floodlights. He arrived at the front corner without incident and spun the light out toward the street. He doubled back, using the trees to conceal his movement and worked his way around to the light at the far end of the wall, near one of the townhouses. Tran was careful to approach it from the side and avoid looking directly at the light so as to preserve as much of his vision as possible. It was a good thing he had.

Just as he arrived at the light. He saw two dark figures jump down inside the wall. Tran, instinctively, spun the light so it glared right in their eyes and fired two shots in their direction before beating a hasty retreat back toward Jade. They were too far out of range for a single arm shot with a small handgun, but it had forced them to drop them to the ground while he got out of the area. Both men opened up on full auto, firing at the spot Tran had just been. They got to their knees and Tran fired three more shots at them as he ran past them concealed behind the glare of the floodlights. They reflexively dropped back down.

Tran knew they wouldn't stay down. They would soon realize they had the tactical advantage and need only move out of the light and the odds would be heavily in their favor.

Tran dropped to his belly and slithered up behind a tree trunk directly in front of his two attackers. Tran peered around the trunk and took aim as the two men popped back up. He fired three quick bursts dropping the closer of the two. He switched his aim to the second man and fired his last two rounds. His handgun's slide locked open as the other man began to return fire. Tran crouched behind the tree trunk. He deftly released the empty magazine from his gun while he fished a fresh magazine out of a neoprene holster wrapped around his waist. He slammed it home and released the slide. He waited. The shots stopped. Tran peered around the tree trunk and fired two quick shots. The gunman opened fire and Tran ducked back behind the tree. The gunfire rapidly stopped again. Tran was close enough to hear the sound of his attacker reloading. Now was his chance. Tran sprung to his feet, leaned around the tree and froze. His attacker wasn't there. Out of the corner of his eye, Tran saw the man dash behind the light and disappear behind a tree. *Not good!*

The sirens were getting louder. Tran had to make several decisions and fast. What little tactical advantage Tran had possessed was now gone. He hastily worked his way away from the attacker and to Jade.

"Jade, listen to me," he said as he pulled her to the other side of the cherry tree. "There's one man left. I'm going to stay here and provide cover. When I say the word, I want you to get over that wall as fast as possible. I parked my bike a block south of your townhouse. Wait for me there. If I'm not there in ten minutes, then get somewhere safe," he said fishing his keys out of his pocket and handing them to her.

"Tran, I'm scared. I'm not leaving without you!" Jade protested.

"Jade, if I'm not there within ten minutes, I've either been arrested or I'm dead. Either way, you need to get somewhere safe. Now! There's no time to argue. Head for the wall now! Go!"

Jade took off in a sprint and was up and over within seconds while Tran watched for movement or gunfire. Neither happened; instead, the black Toyota appeared out of nowhere on the opposite street. The other gunman sprinted out of the tree line, scooped up his fallen comrade, tossed him over his shoulder, and made for the wall. Tran was tempted to go after them but quickly dismissed the thought. The police would be here any second. Considering Joe and Ramsey's predicament, he didn't want to risk being caught by the authorities, especially after having just shot someone. It was time to bolt. He watched the man climb up onto the brick wall while the driver exited the vehicle and climbed up the other side of the wall. They exchanged the body over the wrought iron and then the gunmen followed by climbing to the other side and leaping down to the ground. The driver handed the body down to the gunman and the two proceeded to toss the gunman's body into the car's trunk. They got into the car and took off.

Tran could only speculate that the attackers didn't want to be anywhere around when the police arrive which, by the proximity of their sirens, was imminent. Tran decided a quick exfil before the police arrived would be the smart move. He turned and ran for the wall, navigating it easily as if it were just another evolution on the obstacle course. He jumped down to the sidewalk, fished out his cellphone, and began walking a normal pace with his head down. With his backpack slung, he looked the part of a student walking home. He was nearly a block away when several police cars came racing up the street and sped right on by him, paying no mind to the young Asian walking down the street looking at his cellphone.

Chapter 49

McLean, Virginia

For much of the twentieth century, senators and congressmen alike spent most of their time in the Washington, D.C. area. Their busy schedules and five-day work weeks demanded it. That changed significantly when in 1995, then Speaker of the House Newt Gingrich, decreased the congressional workweek from five days to three days. As a result, a majority of congress head for the airports to board the first flight home where they can devote more time to their constituents and, in many cases, fundraising. Some maintain a small apartment or row house for when they are in Washington. Some simply have a fold out couch in their office allowing them to sleep and shower rent free. A few, usually those who have amassed considerable years and power in the nation's capital, maintain more substantial residences in and around the Washington area.

In a secluded neighborhood of McLean, Virginia, Senator Robert Fowler owned a "modest" six-thousand-square-foot colonial-style mansion tucked away on a two-acre plot surrounded by a large stone facade wall. His wife, Cassandra, the former football cheerleader turned socialite, had spent upwards of two million dollars decorating the interior and installing a state-of-the-art gym in the large, finished walk-out basement. In addition to the various weight machines, cardio machines, and Pilates studio, the gym was complete with a sauna, steam room, massage area, a bar, and a large circular hot tub built into the heated white tile floor.

Theron Belknap sat at the bar, hunched over his laptop, working to propel his boss's campaign forward while trying to ignore the senator who was entertaining his guests in the hot tub. The only guest of importance was Senator Jeffrey Williams, the senior senator from Georgia, who had looked ridiculous when he waddled out from the changing room in a flowered pair of board shorts that seemingly defied the law of gravity clinging to his pasty and quite rotund figure. The two senators sat in the hot tub, each flanked by a pair of young, high-priced escorts wearing G-strings and fake smiles. At Fowler's request, Belknap had procured the escorts during the flight back from Columbus and put out the invite to Senator Williams. Fowler's wife, Cassandra, had taken a direct flight back to Phoenix after the Columbus rally and was likely entertaining her own guests in their Scottsdale mansion's hot tub.

"Robert, I dare say that when you are the president and I'm senate majority leader, it would behoove us to conduct our weekly meetings in a manner such as we currently find ourselves," Senator Williams pronounced with the beginnings of a bourbon induced slur.

"I think you're on to something, my friend," Fowler leaned forward to clink his colleague's glass before they both downed the remains of their tumblers. "My first executive order will be to install a hot tub into the White House basement."

"Ah! Good thinking!" Williams said as he held his tumbler up while a stately appearing butler refilled it. "That's where the Marilyn Monroe door is located."

"I'm told that's an urban myth," Fowler said referring to the underground tunnel that led from the White House to the Treasury Building through which former President John F. Kennedy was rumored to have had his Secret Service agents sneak the late bombshell into and out of the White House.

"Well, I propose we find out for ourselves once you take up residence," Williams said holding up his index finger in proclamation, to his own amusement.

"Indeed!" Fowler said with a well-practiced laugh for Williams' benefit.

Belknap, seated at the bar behind Williams, caught Fowler's eye and held up his hand showing five fingers. Fowler acknowledged his chief of staff with his eyes. He set his drink down on the tiled floor behind him and stood up, pulling both of the young women up with him.

"Well, Jeffrey, I think you have things well at hand here. These two ladies and I are going to head into the steam room for a bit. Sweat out our iniquities, if you will. We'll leave you to it here, my friend," Fowler said as he and his two escorts stepped up out of the hot tub.

"Don't do anything I wouldn't do, Mr. President!" Williams called out jokingly behind them before turning his attention to the two escorts who remained with him.

Both women, took their cues and began to earn their pay. After a few minutes, Williams was fully engaged in the task at hand when a familiar voice materialized.

"Sorry to barge in at such a time, Jeffrey, but we have rather urgent matters to discuss," the voice said curtly.

Williams opened his eyes and looked up. Salvatore La Rosa, the unofficial vice-chairman of their party, stood at the edge of the hot tub. He was dressed in a black pinstriped suit with a starched white shirt, red tie with matching pocket square, and handcrafted black leather Bontoni shoes. The shoes alone were worth over two thousand dollars. He stood scowling down at the senator.

"Girls, the senator and I have a few things to discuss. Go powder your noses," he said with a subtle toss of his head.

Williams sighed disappointedly as the two escorts stood, grabbed what could be called their swimsuits, and climbed out. He watched longingly until they disappeared into one of the changing rooms. The door shut behind them. Belknap and Fowler's house staff seemed to have also left the gym, leaving just him and the sinister looking La Rosa. Williams leaned forward to retrieve his rather large swim trunks that were floating atop the turbulent water.

"Don't bother," La Rosa said. "I really don't care to stand here while you try to squeeze your bloated carcass into those things."

Williams sat back, apparently winded by the effort. "What is it you want, Sal?"

"I want you to understand your place!" La Rosa snapped. "You might be a fat cat senior senator, but you answer to and dance to the party. That means you answer to me, and you *will* address me with the appropriate measure of respect! Is that clear, *Jeffrey*?"

"Fine," Williams answered with a slight roll of his beady eyes, the bourbon dulling his inhibitions. "What do you want, *Mister* La Rosa?"

In a flash, La Rosa leaped into the hot tub, causing a stunned reaction by Williams. La Rosa grabbed the senator's shaggy hair on the back of his head and forced him forward and under the water. Williams' arms flailed as he tried to resist but he was too flabby and weak compared to the stout party enforcer. La Rosa waited until the senator seemed to weaken and then pulled his head back slamming it into the tiled deck behind him. Williams appeared to have sobered up significantly.

"I think you need a little reminder of the power structure in this town, you pompous water buffalo," La Rosa snarled. "You exist at the party's pleasure, which means you exist at *my* pleasure! I could kill your right now, walk out of here like I own the joint and *nothing* will happen to me! Fowler will only be president and you will only be senate majority leader if we say so. That means you *will* serve at our bidding if you want to keep your place at the trough. Is that clear enough for you, Jeffrey?"

A wide-eyed Williams nodded vigorously.

"Good!" La Rosa answered while still pinning the senator's head to the back of the hot tub. "Then answer me this; why are those two SEALs and that doctor babe still alive?"

"W-what? What are you talking about?" Williams asked, his voice trembling.

La Rosa thrust Williams' head forward and back under the hot and turbulent water before he had time to take a breath. La Rosa counted to twenty and pulled Williams up and back into the pool's edge.

"Does that refresh your memory?"

Williams gasped for breath while nodding vigorously. Panic beginning to set in.

"I thought it might," La Rosa said icily. "Now answer the question."

"I, I don't know!" he stammered.

"Wrong answer!" La Rosa snapped as he forced Williams forward and back under the water.

He didn't have to wait as long this time. Williams was already out of breath and thoroughly panicked. He pulled the senator up and back into the hot tub's edge. Out of patience, he didn't allow the senator a chance to speak.

"I'm gonna make this so clear that even a pickled tub of lard like you can understand. O'Shanick and his two friends are a problem for us. You assured us you could make that problem go away. It's been two days and no results. I don't like that. It doesn't reassure me that you have what it takes to be senator let alone the leader of the Senate. If they're not gone by this time tomorrow, you and I are gonna go for another swim. Is that clear enough, Jeffrey?"

Williams nodded fearfully.

"That's better," La Rosa said as he let the senator go and stood up. "Make it happen then."

La Rosa turned and stepped up and out of the hot tub. Williams stared after him while remaining motionless in the hot tub. La Rosa calmly began to walk out as he straightened his soaking wet tie and jacket.

"You owe me a new suit," he announced over his shoulder. "I'm sending a bill to your office."

Chapter 50

Alexandria, Virginia

Tran scouted the surroundings for Jade as he approached his motorcycle. He had walked a circuitous route making sure he wasn't being followed. Jade was nowhere to be seen. Had she been intercepted? She was extremely intelligent, gifted in fact, but she did not possess the same level of street smarts and situational awareness Tran had. He began to second guess himself as he searched the surroundings more intensely. He made a sound tactical decision under dire circumstances. Second guessing himself would not be productive. He pulled out his phone, dialed her number and hoped she answered.

"Hello?" she answered on the second ring.

"Where are you?" Tran asked urgently.

"I'm watching my house burn down," she answered plainly.

"Are you kidding me?" he responded in frustration. "Someone might see you! We have to get out of here!"

"Well excuse me, Tran! An hour ago, I was sipping a chai tea and working through some satellite photos without a care in the world. Next thing I know, you show up and we're being shot at and my house and everything I own is up in flames. I had to go back and see it. There's a crowd of people here anyway. No one knows who I am."

"I get that, Jade, but we've got people after us. I'm two blocks over. Hurry!" Tran said as he hung up.

As he mounted his bike, he realized his helmet was back at Jade's, likely a melted blob of foam and plastic at this point. He didn't like to ride without a helmet and especially didn't want Jade not wearing a helmet but there was nothing he could do about that now. What he *could* do was disable his phone. They had likely used his cell signal to track him to Jade's townhouse. Things had moved to quickly for him to fix that, but it was something he needed to take care of immediately. He unslung his backpack, opened up a side pocket, and retrieved a small safety pin which he used to remove the SIM card from his iPhone. He placed the safety pin and SIM card in his backpack and mounted the iPhone on a cellphone mount situated on his motorcycle's console. Jade came running up. She handed him the keys and mounted the seat behind him. The engine roared to life as Tran turned the key.

Tran put the bike in gear and made a quick U-turn. While he was executing the turn, a car came screeching around the corner. The same late model Toyota from earlier.

"Hold on tight!" he yelled as he hit the throttle.

Jade wrapped her arms tightly around Tran as the Ninja's supercharged 998cc engine accelerated them down North Pitt Street like a rocket. The black Toyota accelerated in kind but not as quickly as the sleek motorcycle. He took the next right onto King Street, leaning hard into the fast turn and thankful there were no cars around.

"What's the quickest way to the beltway?" Tran yelled over his shoulder.

"Stay on this for about five blocks until we get to South Henry! Then take a left!" Jade yelled back. "How did they find us?"

Tran didn't answer immediately as he concentrated on weaving in and around traffic in the narrow street. The restaurants and shops had all recently closed leaving scant traffic. What few cars there were, Tran worked his way around thus providing a buffer between them and their pursuers. Hopefully, they wouldn't attempt to shoot with cars in between them. The traffic light ahead turned yellow. Tran gunned the throttle and shot through the intersection as it changed to red. That ought to help.

"They're tracking my cellphone. Maybe yours too, by now," he yelled. "We need to ditch them when we cross the Potomac!"

Tran drove with one eye on the rearview mirror and one eye on the road ahead. He saw the Toyota swerve into the oncoming lane to get around a car stopped at the light. The Toyota raced through the light narrowly missing a collision as it kept up the chase. Tran thought for sure there would be at least one police car giving chase but nothing so far. Between Jade's townhome and the incident in the park, they were probably preoccupied. It was just as well. He'd prefer to lose their attackers and regroup without taking his chances with law enforcement.

Tran increased their speed and weaved the bike around a few more cars, hoping to increase the distance. His eyes began to tear up with the additional speed, making it difficult to see. He had never ridden without his helmet before. The helmet's visor made the wind a non-issue. Once they got onto the interstate, it would be next to impossible to ride at speed.

"Jade," he yelled over his shoulder. "In the top pocket of my backpack is a pair of sunglasses. Can you get them out for me?"

"I'll try!" she yelled back.

Tran kept the bike steady, knowing Jade would have no way to hold on while she was working his backpack. She carefully opened the pocket and found the pair of tactical sunglasses. She reached under his arm and handed them up. Tran grabbed them and slipped them on. A noticeable difference. South Henry Street loomed up ahead.

"This is us!" Jade said as she wrapped her small arms tightly around Tran.

The light was yellow and would be turning red before they got to the intersection. Tran slowed slightly as he approached looking for cars.

"It's a one-way street. You're clear if you hurry!" Jade yelled.

Tran leaned them into the turn and accelerated through it onto South Henry. It was three lanes wide and all one-way, allowing him to open it up. They raced down the street weaving around the few cars they encountered. In the rearview mirror, Tran could see a pair of headlights weaving around cars behind them and assumed it was their attackers but could no longer make out the car. The light ahead turned yellow, but he flew though it just as it turned red. He didn't look back to see if the Toyota would pass through the red light. He was sure they would, and he had a plan in mind. South Henry Street merged with South Patrick Street forming a large parkway. Signs for I-95 and I-495 began to appear. Tran had the motorcycle racing along at over 100mph, hoping he could put enough distance between them and their attackers that they wouldn't be able to see which on-ramp he used. If they knew who he was and didn't see which way he went, he hoped they would assume he was heading back to Virginia Beach and would take I-95 South. For this reason, Tran took the on-ramp for I-95 North.

He slowed slightly as they whipped around the clover leaf and merged onto the interstate. There were more cars here, even at this later hour, but Tran kept to the right-hand lane and stayed behind a minivan as they approached the Woodrow Wilson Bridge.

"Is your phone backed up?" he yelled.

"What?" Jade yelled back.

"Is your phone backed up?" Tran yelled louder.

"Yes! Always!"

"Good! Take my phone and launch both mine and yours into the Potomac as we cross!"

Jade didn't argue. She knew just how easily they could be tracked using their cellphone signals. Tran retrieved his phone from its holder on the console and placed it in her hand. Jade flung it over the bridge railing into the darkened waters of the Potomac River below. She then did the same with hers.

"Done!" she yelled, as she tapped Tran's shoulder and then leaned in to grab ahold of him.

Tran maneuvered around the minivan and hit the throttle. The Ninja surged ahead, rocketing across the bridge at breakneck speed. Casting a glance into the rearview mirror, he couldn't make out the Toyota or any other vehicle pursuing them. It didn't matter. They were after him for something and it was likely connected with what was happening to Joe and Master Chief Ramsey. They would be back. It was time to change things up.

Chapter 51

Alto, Georgia

The screaming wouldn't stop, and the sleep wouldn't come. Christy lay on the concrete slab, in the predawn hours, cold, sore, and exhausted. Sore from the bruises she sustained in her fight with Randy and her minions yesterday. Sore from laying on a concrete slab with no mattress, pillow, or even a blanket. There was absolutely no comfortable position she could find.

The cell was dark, save for a sliver of light peeking through the door slot. It was cold and forbidding with a stale, musty air. She could barely see the damp concrete walls in the darkness, but their intimidating proximity would be suffocating to a claustrophobic.

The cavernous hall outside her room echoed with the panicked shrieking and screaming of another inmate that had persisted since lights out. Occasionally, another inmate would yell for her to shut up but that just seemed to intensify the screaming all the more. Christy had prayed for her earlier, but the woman shrieked on. Unable to sleep, Christy had spent several hours praying for Joe, Ramsey, Clay Whitmore, Charles Courtnall, Tracy Courtnall, Hannah, her own family, Joe's family, President Galan, and nearly everyone she could think of.

She had always been a pretty good sleeper. The lengthy hours of residency and medical school had only served to improve that vital skill. *Sleep when you can and eat when you can* had been the motto. She was naturally a night owl and preferred working the night shifts because she had no trouble sleeping during daylight and they paid more, allowing her to be nearly finished paying off her student loans; however, she occasionally found herself unable to sleep during nights when she wasn't working. When that happened, she would spend some time in prayer, which usually resulted in her falling asleep. Other times she would read a novel. As a physician, she spent considerable time reading journal articles or taking test modules. A good fiction adventure was always a welcome escape where she could let her mind relax as she immersed herself into the story.

There were no books in this cold, tiny cell in solitary confinement. Just a cold slab of concrete, the screams of a mentally ill inmate, and a darkness that was as much from a lack of light as it was a lack of anything good.

Tired and sore from laying on her back, she rolled to her left side. Her shoulder and hip immediately began to ache as they took the brunt of the pressure pressed against the hard slab. Her head angled awkwardly down, placing an uncomfortable strain on her neck with nothing to support it. She didn't know much about prisons, but she recalled hearing that inmates in solitary confinement spent twenty-three hours a day in their cells and were only allowed out for one hour each day. *What an encouraging thought,* Christy thought to herself as she gave up on her side and rolled back supine.

Even just something to place under her head would make this far more tolerable. Earlier, she had considered removing her prison jumpsuit and rolling that up for a pillow, but the cell was too cold and she would lose what little body heat she still had. A fleeting thought made her wonder if this was what Hell is like: suffocating darkness, loneliness, and misery. Why would anyone willingly choose that? She quickly dismissed that thought. This side of eternity, even the worst of the worst still experienced some of God's presence and goodness. Hell would be a complete removal of God and His goodness. The absence of which would be pure darkness and evil. That would be infinitely worse.

Christy prayed some more. She thanked God for His forgiveness and grace. After all, she reminded herself, we are all sinful and all deserving of Hell. Only His Son was truly good. Christ was innocent of any sin, yet He willingly paid the penalty for our sins in our place. Only through Him can we escape the eternal torment we deserve.

Her thoughts were interrupted when a key sounded in the door. The door opened and the dimly lit corridor silhouetted a rather stout corrections officer. Christy sat up, startled, as she wondered what the early morning visit was about.

"Tabrizi, you've been sprung," the woman spoke from the door with a voice that sounded as if she needed to clear her throat.

"Sprung?" Christy said hopefully as she pivoted and set her feet on the floor.

"Yes, tall, dark, and shapely, you're outta here, babe. Now you gonna come with me or do you wanna stay in this rat hole?"

"I'm coming!" Christy said excitedly. "This is really happening?"

"Yeah, babe," the officer responded as they stepped into the corridor.

She had short brown hair, cut into a fine fade around the sides and back. She matched Christy's height but was at least twice if not three times Christy's weight. Whereas Christy was trim and athletically toned, the officer was a mound of muscle wrapped in a significant layer of fat.

"No cuffs?" Christy asked glancing at the officer's badge. "Officer Baker?"

"No cuffs," Baker answered cheerfully as they were buzzed through a large steel door. "You look like you played some ball in your day. Did you play in college?"

"Yes, at Tennessee," Christy answered pleasantly.

"Dang, girl! You played basketball for Tennessee? I played for 'Bama! What years did you play?"

"No, I played volleyball," Christy replied. "I'm sorry."

"Volleyball?! Are you kidding me?" Officer Baker said sizing Christy up as they waited for another door to open. "What a waste of talent," she said shaking her head.

"We all have our faults, I guess," Christy shrugged jokingly with a smile as they stepped outside.

She took the officer's ribbing happily. This was the first lighthearted moment she had had since being dragged from her house four nights ago. It seemed like an eternity and now she felt like a huge weight was being lifted off her back. Did this mean Joe and Ramsey were getting out too? Did the judge reconsider and they made bond? Were their charges shown to be false and were now dropped? She could only hope.

They entered Christy's dorm. Officer Baker nodded to the night officer of the desk as they passed by. As Christy headed for the stairs leading to her cell where she would gather what few items she had, her thoughts turned to Hannah. She felt a twinge of remorse leaving Hannah to fend for herself. She prayed Hannah would be able to use the Suboxone to stay off the fentanyl while she took advantage of the prison's addiction program. Hopefully, Randy would leave her alone. Doubtful.

"This way first, Tabrizi," Officer Baker said grabbing Christy's arm just as she was about to begin walking up the steps.

Slightly confused, Christy followed the officer to another heavy steel door which the other officer electronically buzzed open on their arrival. They walked down a short corridor passing by what looked like a break room and several offices before entering a locker room.

"You're required to take a shower," Officer baker said pointing to a tiled shower area with multiple shower heads.

There was an anteroom with several clothing hooks and a solitary bench against the wall that held a stack of white towels. With a groan, Officer Baker plopped her heavy frame into a metal folding chair on the opposite wall. Christy looked at the officer uneasily and was met with a slight shrug of the shoulders.

"Prison policy," Officer Baker said nonchalantly. "I'm not allowed to let you out of my sight."

Christy shrugged and began to disrobe. She was modest but, after years of playing sports and being a physician, she was not uncomfortable showering around other women. She stepped into the shower area and turned on one of the showers. Within a minute, the water was steaming hot. She stepped into it and let the hot water cascade down her back. The pressure was like that of a firehouse. After numerous hours in the cold cell of solitary confinement, the hot water was a welcome soothing massage. She spent a minute stretching her sore muscles and then began to feel uneasy. Perhaps it was her imagination, but Christy sensed that Officer Baker was watching her with an odd interest. Now feeling uncomfortable, Christy turned away and grabbed some body wash out of the wall dispenser. She quickly soaped up her body, lathered her hair, and then rinsed off. She leaned back and allowed the steaming hot water to push her long dark hair behind her head before turning around and shutting off the shower. When she turned to walk out of the shower bay, Officer Baker was standing in the way.

"What's your rush, sugar?" she asked suggestively.

"I'm done. I just want to dry off and get dressed," Christy answered trying to act aloof to the developing situation.

"There's no hurry. I know you must be sore from laying on that concrete slab. Everyone gets sore from that. How 'bout we stand under that hot water and I'll give you a massage?"

"No, thank you," Christy spoke curtly as she tried to step past the officer.

Baker produced a metal baton and held it out to block the exit. Christy stepped back. A sudden chill washed over her that had nothing to do with the fact that she was standing there naked while dripping wet. Her senses were on full alert.

"I'm not getting out today, am I?" she asked as she began running several scenarios through her head.

"You're a smart chick," Baker said sneering.

"Then what do you want from me?" Christy asked.

"You know what I want," Baker answered, eyeing Christy up and down lasciviously before nodding to the showers behind her.

"Please don't," Christy pleaded. "I'm not that way."

"Well, sweetheart," Baker began, "You're in prison now and, from what I understand, you're gonna be here a long, long time, so you may as well learn. Now, you might decide to bunk up with that little cutie in your cell or you might become Randy's new fem but I can help you out in here."

Christy's eyebrows furled as she looked back at Officer Baker.

"That's right, gorgeous," Baker nodded slyly. "For a little honey time with you each week, I can get you all the meds you want to run your own little practice in here. I can get you the choice pick of jobs and just about anything you want, and I can keep Randy off your back."

Christy furled her brow even tighter.

"You heard me. Randy runs this joint on the inside because I let her run it. But if you play ball with me, I'll let you be the new queen."

Christy fought to keep a straight face as a flood of emotions raced through her mind. She was in shock after believing she was getting out of this prison only to find out it was all a ruse. She was disgusted at what Officer Baker was trying to coerce her to do, which was made worse by Baker's ogling while standing before her without a stitch of clothing. She was distraught over the prospect of remaining in this prison for years to come. And she was scared. She silently prayed for wisdom.

"Please don't do this," Christy pleaded quietly. "I just want to do my time and get out of here. I don't want any trouble."

"You're in the big leagues now, sweetie. It doesn't work like that here," Baker shook her head while eyeing Christy appreciatively. "A fem as pretty as you and a body like that? You have no chance. Randy ain't the only dude lookin' at you. Someone's gonna claim you, right quick. At least with me, you'll have it good in here. You might even like it."

Christy knew she was at a crossroads here. She might have been able to fend off Randy but how long could she keep it up? Even now, Officer Baker stood before her waving her baton in a menacing fashion. Running afoul of an officer would bring down far too much bad attention. Something she definitely did not need. It was unlikely she could get by her without a fight and, even if she did, she couldn't begin to imagine the long-term consequences. She hung her head in resignation, sighed, and turned back to the showers.

Christy turned the water back on and stood under it, waiting. Officer Baker looked at her knowingly and nodded. She removed her duty belt and set it down on the bench as she sat down and began to unlace her boots. She stood up and quickly removed the rest of her uniform, carelessly tossing it all on the bench. Baker shuffle stepped into the shower, being careful not to slip under her top-heavy weight. Her large belly hung down enough to cover her genitalia, much to Christy's disgust. As she approached, Christy nervously turned toward her.

"Oh, you *are* a dish!" Baker said excitedly as she neared, causing Christy to take a cautious step back.

"Oh no, darlin'!" Baker smiled as she lunged forward. "Don't you back away from me, now!"

With a blur of motion, Christy sidestepped and pivoted around Baker. She fired a palm strike to the back of Baker's head, taking advantage of her forward momentum to slam her face first into the cinder block wall. Baker screamed out in shock and pain as she turned her bloody face toward Christy. Christy wasted no time, delivering a heel strike to the large woman's solar plexus, knocking the wind out of her and causing her to drop to her knees and vomit. Christy then delivered a series of kicks to the woman's side before using her heel to upend Officer Baker's significant bulk into the corner.

"I said *please,*" Christy spoke calmly before turning and walking out of the shower.

Chapter 52

Charlotte, North Carolina

The dimly lit halls of Whitmore Investigative Services echoed with the sounds of rubber soled boots as Deon Johnson made his hourly rounds. Johnson, a married forty-two-year-old father of three, was the owner and chief operator of Deon Tactical, a security firm that provided private property security and personal protection services. A former Marine, Deon had served in Clay Whitmore's platoon as an NCO. After leaving the FBI and forming Whitmore Investigative, Whitmore had reached out to Deon about starting a security team for his office and helped him get it off the ground. Deon Tactical had expanded over the years, providing a nice income for Deon and his family. Deon Tactical's main office was in the same building, occupying the floor below Whitmore Investigative. Deon normally ran the firm during the day but one of his night officers had a wife who had to have an emergency c-section due to preeclampsia. Deon could have delegated the shifts to some of the other officers, but he preferred to lead by example and stepped up to work tonight and tomorrow night. It was one of many reasons he was well revered by his staff and by Clay Whitmore.

Despite being forty-two, Deon kept in top shape and could run and shoot with the best of his officers. One look at his tall frame with wide shoulders and narrow waist as he strode down the hall with an athletic grace left little doubt of his fitness in anyone's mind. He demanded the same of his officers and they were well paid for their dedication and skill.

Arriving at the door to the Information Technology anteroom, he saw the light was still on. He knew Roderick Boulware had been working late on something and decided to check in on him. He pushed the door open and walked to the back of the room where a secure door stood guarding Boulware's nerve center. Deon knocked as he unlocked the door and entered. He found Boulware just as he had left him two hours ago; sitting up with perfect posture in his favorite ergonomic work chair, working his computers while impeccably dressed. The only difference was Boulware had actually removed his suit coat.

"I've heard of burning the midnight oil, but the sun is due to come up soon and you've got a full day ahead of you, Rod. What gives?"

"Sometimes we have to press in, Deon, and this is one of those times. I'm close to extracting some evidence that could exonerate Clay and Chuck and time is of the essence."

"What is it?" Deon asked as he folded his arms and leaned against the door frame.

"A video that Navy SEAL, O'Shanick shot during their raid on the cartel last week. I'm told it would not only get our bosses off but bring down Fowler in the process. Some very powerful people have gone to great lengths to ensure that video is lost into oblivion."

"For real?" Deon asked hopefully. "You think you can find it?"

"Oh, I've found it," Boulware answered calmly in his baritone voice. "I just need to finish recreating it."

"What's that mean?"

"Whoever is covering for Fowler hired some very skilled people to, in a computer sense, smash that video into smithereens and disperse the pieces around the internet. It was very difficult to find but I've just about managed to complete recreating the video. They're skilled but so am I and I brought my A-game tonight, Deon."

"And this video will get Clay and Chuck's charges dropped?"

"One can only hope," Boulware said looking up at Deon who suddenly put a hand to his radio earpiece and cocked his head slightly.

"Tac Seven to Tac One," came the voice of Reggie Reed through Deon's earpiece. Reggie was the other officer on this evening. He was down in Command Central keeping watch on the dozens of security camera monitors.

Deon keyed his microphone. "Go ahead Seven."

"Sir, we have an early morning visitor out front. Someone just pulled up in a truck. Some chair and party rental outfit."

"Gotta run. Take em' down, Rod!" Deon said with a wave to Boulware as he walked out into the hall. "Tac Seven, I don't remember seeing anything on the schedule for today. Did I miss something?" Deon asked as he headed for the emergency stairwell.

"Negative, sir. It's probably Simmer, Dionne and Taylor," Reed said referring to the injury law firm on the main floor. "You know how they hold events in the parking lot all the time and never bother to inform us."

"Roger that," Deon replied as he hustled down the stairs. "I'll check it out. Stand by."

Deon reached the main level and pushed through a metal door into the building's opulent lobby. The front entrance was locked at this hour. Employees entered through a back door using their ID badges. Deon peered through the glass doors. Out beyond the covered drive through entrance was a large straight truck with the words *A Night to Remember Party Rental* painted on the side. The cabin light turned on for a few seconds before it went dark again.

"Tac One, be advised, one male just exited the driver's side."

"Copy, Seven," Deon replied as he extracted the key for the front doors.

The truck was parked with the passenger side facing the building making it difficult for Deon to see the driver's side. Still, he didn't see anyone walk around the front or to the back of the truck as he unlocked the door and stepped out into the cool predawn air.

Deon's well-honed senses were signaling warnings that something was off. He unsnapped the restraint on his duty holster with his right hand while holding his flashlight in his left hand. As he approached the truck, he saw a darkly clad figure walking out towards the street. Deon called after him, but the figure never turned. He just kept walking at a brisk pace. Deon started after him but stopped. Why would he park a truck and leave it like that? *Oh, NO!*

Deon turned and sprinted back toward the building. He keyed his radio mike as he raced through the doors.

"Tac Seven! Tac Seven! Activate the fire alarm and get yourself clear! That truck might be rigged!"

"What about Rod?" Reggie's animated voice came through his earpiece.

"I got him," Deon replied as he raced up the stairs, two at a time. "Just get as far away from here as possible, now!"

The fire alarm was blaring as Deon reached the fourth floor and raced down the hall which was now illuminated by emergency flood lights. The white strobe lights of the fire alarms added to the direness of the situation as he reached the IT suite. He unlocked the door and burst into the computer room where he found Boulware looking up at him with a startled look.

"C'mon, Rod! We gotta bolt!"

"I can't, Deon! I'm just about finished here. I have to do this! A lot is riding on it!"

"There's a truck parked out front that just might be rigged to explode!" Deon said as he yanked Boulware up out of his chair

"Oh, sh…"

"That's right!" Deon said as he rushed Boulware out into the hall. "Head for the back stairwell! Double time it! Let's go!"

They reached the stairs and began rapidly descending them. Boulware's stylish leather wingtip shoes made it challenging, but he kept going, nearly tumbling down the stairs out of control. The alarm kept blaring as they raced to the bottom. They leapt down the last half flight of stairs and blasted through the metal door out into the rear parking lot. Suddenly, the world exploded around them in a blinding flash of fire and vaporizing heat.

Chapter 53

Washington, D.C.

Tran awoke to the dawn's early light. His eyes opened, revealing the water-stained ceiling above him. He turned his head to the left and saw Jade was still sound asleep in the adjacent twin bed. After losing their pursuers, Tran had raced their way around the Washington Beltway and driven them back into the city from the north side. He found them a room in a hostel near Chinatown. The night manager accepted Tran's generous cash offer without raising an eye. It would have to be cash only for a while. Any use of a credit card or even an ATM withdrawal would be sure to draw attention from whoever was after them. Tran always kept $300 cash in his go-bag along with a bag full of silver coins and a handful of Walmart gift cards his mother liked to give him for Christmas and birthdays. Jade possessed a paranoia of electronic transactions, partly from her immense knowledge of computers and the cyber world and partly a mild OCD trait from her underlying Asperger's disorder. As a result, between her purse and her own go-bag, she had a couple thousand dollars cash on her. Tran hoped they wouldn't need it.

Trying not to wake Jade, Tran quietly rolled to his side, pivoted up to sitting, and placed his bare feet to the wood floor. He stood up from his bed and stretched. After working the stiffness out of his neck, he picked a grey t-shirt out of his backpack and put it on along with a navy blue pair of gym shorts. He stealthily made his way to the door, quietly unlocked it, and slipped out into the hallway. He headed downstairs to a common room where there was a small kitchenette and the promise of coffee.

A young Asian couple sat at one of two small tables, sipping tea as they watched a cable network's morning news. The images of a demolished building engulfed in flames caught Tran's eye as he selected a Columbian dark roast and placed it in the Keurig machine. The headline on the lower third of the large screen caught Tran's attention:

Truck explosion may be linked to President Galan

Tran walked over and sat down at the adjacent table to listen. The screen changed to a live feed with an on-scene reporter, a blond female, wearing a mauve, sleeveless form-fitting dress, standing before a smoldering pile of concrete and steel.

"…we can now confirm that one of the occupants of the building was Whitmore Investigative Services. Whitmore Investigative is headed up by Clay Whitmore who is one of several people currently being held in custody for their involvement on the assassination attempt of presidential candidate Senator Robert Fowler that many believe to have been ordered by President Galan."

The screen changed revealing a well-coiffed male studio anchor with the female reporter on a screen behind him.

"Madeleine, do we know if the building was occupied at the time of the explosion?"

"Peter, that's unknown at this time. Fire personnel are still working to ensure that all fires are out before giving the all-clear for rescue personnel. We can tell you that a male, wearing the security uniform of a company based in this building, was found unconscious in a nearby parking lot. He has been rushed to Carolinas Medical Center where we are told he is in critical condition."

"Madeleine, considering the fact the Whitmore Investigative is involved and given the timing of the explosion and this new information, do your sources on the ground suspect this could have been an attempt to destroy evidence?"

"Peter, sources on the ground tell me that it is too early to speculate but that this appears to have been a well-planned and well-executed bombing. The fact that it occurred during the predawn hours suggests it was not a terrorist attack or even an attempt to kill anyone since it was likely nobody other than security was in the building at the time. That certainly leaves open the possibility that this was conducted to destroy evidence. Just what evidence that was, remains to be seen."

"Madeleine, thank you," the anchor said as the screen behind him changed to a video of President Galan and the first lady stepping off Marine One during the night. "In a related story, President Galan has much to answer for with incriminating emails revealed yesterday connected with the suicide death of Navy SEAL Lieutenant Commander Patrick Harrison who confessed to his involvement in the planned assassination…"

Tran stood up in disgust. There was no way there was any truth to any of this, nor did LCDR Harrison kill himself. This was an elaborate ruse and, whoever was behind it, was killing anyone that could expose it while leaving false evidence behind. Of that much, he was sure. But why had they come after him? Tran mulled that over as he fixed a second coffee for Jade. She was a night owl who loved to sleep in, but they had a lot to do if they were going to figure out why they were being hunted and how this all fit together.

To his surprise, she was already up and had made both beds when he arrived back at their simple room. She was still wearing her black leggings and U2 t-shirt. She stood before the dresser mirror, brushing her long dark hair when he entered the room and set her coffee down before her.

"You read my mind," she said glancing at him through the mirror.

"I'm actually surprised to find you up," he said.

"Yeah, well I've never had people try to kill me before. It might be no big deal to you, but I find it just a bit unnerving and I didn't sleep well," Jade answered curtly.

"You're right, I'm sorry," Tran apologized. "In no way did I ever intend to put you in harm's way. This is all on me, but I promise you I will do everything I can to get us out of it."

"And just how do you plan to do that?" Jade asked while she tied her hair back into a ponytail.

"Couple of ways," he answered. "I'd like to hunt down our friends from last night and see who they're working for. Follow them up the chain of command. I need to find out how I became a target. I was up here when Joe and Rammer conducted that op last week. I had no knowledge of it whatsoever and was a thousand miles away. Why come after me? It makes no sense."

"They went after Lieutenant Commander Harrison," Jade offered.

"True, but he's up the chain of command. They planted evidence on his computer to further incriminate Joe and Master Chief…"

"And they kill him by staging a suicide so he can't talk," Jade said completing the sentence. "These are some scary people, Tran. Are you sure you want to take this on?"

"I can't run from it, Jade. My teammates need me," Tran said as he picked up the TV remote and clicked on the TV. "But it's even worse than you think. Watch."

The TV opened up on the same news station Tran had watched downstairs. They were recapping the story. Jade watched in stunned silence as she absorbed the information.

"Tran? Do you think these are the same people?" Jade asked with her eyes wide.

"Yes," he answered. "I don't believe in coincidences."

"But why blow up a building with no one in it?" she asked.

"I think the reporter nailed it," Tran said pointing to the images of the building reduced to rubble. "To destroy evidence that would incriminate Senator Fowler or to further incriminate President Galan. Or both…wait! That's it!"

"What's it?" Jade asked.

"If they're going to great lengths such as this," Tran said with his thumb toward the screen, "then it must be some pretty damnable evidence."

"Brilliant deduction, Sherlock," Jade commented.

Tran looked at her in a mix of annoyance and amusement.

"I'm sorry," she apologized. "New Jade. Jade two point zero."

"Anyways," he went on, ignoring her quirky awkwardness, "if we can figure out what they're after and bring it to light that might just turn the tables and get all of us out of this mess."

Jade looked at Tran curiously. "So you *think* Lieutenant Commander O'Shanick and Chief Ramsey were the good guys and happened to catch Senator Fowler on some cartel-owned Epstein Island with his hand in the cookie jar. You *think* they killed off most of the cartel and brought Fowler back to face justice only to have it all turned around on them and *they* wind up in jail instead. You *think* there is some kind of evidence, evidence you have no knowledge of but is so damning that this mystery group is killing people and blowing up buildings to ensure the truth never comes out and somehow *you*, Tran Van Truk, are not only going to figure out what this evidence is, but actually find it, get ahold of it, and bring it to light to get Joe and Ramsey out of jail along with everyone else *and* put the real people behind bars?"

"I know it sounds crazy, but yes," Tran answered.

"You are crazy, Tran," Jade said as she began packing her belongings into her backpack. "Your band is playing different tunes. I'm talking dark side of the moon."

Tran exhaled in frustration as he watched Jade finish packing her things and zip up her backpack. She slung it onto her back and walked up to Tran until she stood toe to toe with him. She looked up at him with an expectant look on her face.

"What?" Tran asked perplexed.

"What do you mean, what?" Jade asked back.

"Aren't you leaving?"

"Yes, but not without you," she answered. "C'mon, pack your gear and let's go."

"Where are we going?" Tran asked, completely off balance.

"To find your evidence," she answered succinctly.

"I thought you just said I was crazy?"

"You are crazy, Tran. But I'm not exactly playing with a full deck either," Jade said with a crooked smile and a mischievous look in her eyes. "Besides, I like Joe and Ramsey…and you, so let's go."

Chapter 54

Alto, Georgia

Christy awoke from a brief sleep to the sounds of inmates chattering as they congregated in the hallway before morning chow. It was a welcome sound. Christy had fully expected to be dragged back to solitary confinement by now. After her run-in with Officer Baker, Christy calmly walked out of the officers' locker room as if nothing had happened. In full view of the night watch officer, she walked right up the stairs and into her cell. She had quietly crawled into her bed, so as not to wake Hannah, and had lain there expecting the officers to barge into the cell, cuff her, and march her back to "The Hole." At some point she had drifted off to sleep. Mercifully. The thin mattress in this cell felt like a cloud compared to the slab she spent the past night on.

The cell door was closed, which muted the commotion outside. This allowed Christy to hear the sound of thin pages rustling from Hannah's bed below. She sat up, pivoted her long legs over the side of the top bunk and hopped down. Hannah immediately hopped up and embraced Christy in a tight hug.

"I'm so glad you're back and that you're okay!" Hannah said tearfully. "I'm so sorry you got caught up in my mess and went to the SHU for it. That place is terrible. Are you okay?"

"I'm fine, Hannah," Christy soothed as she held her sobbing cellmate. "What about you? Are you okay?"

"Just a little banged up, but nothing major," Hannah replied after gaining control of herself. "They could have killed you, you know. That was Randy's goon squad. They're all lifers. Anyone who crosses them doesn't live long. You're going to have to be real careful, Christy."

"I'm kind of figuring that out," Christy replied with a grim nod as she sat down on the lone chair while Hannah sat down on her lower bunk.

"I'm serious, Christy, we're probably both marked but you especially. Please be careful. Do *not* go into any unmonitored areas."

"I'll be careful," Christy promised. "But I want to know how you're holding up. Is the Suboxone helping?"

"So far I guess," Hannah nodded solemnly. "I guess I just think the other shoe is going to drop and I'm going to go back into withdrawal again but so far so good."

"No, it's working, Hannah. You would definitely be experiencing withdrawal by now. Stick with it and we'll be able to keep you sober but you need to start getting some serious addiction counseling. I can help you to some degree but you need more. A lot more and it will also help for you to start attending the Celebrate Recovery meetings the prison holds."

"Celebrate Recovery?"

"Yes, they hold meetings here. They're an excellent source of help in addiction recovery and can help you get ready to transition off Suboxone and never relapse again. I'd really like to get you into an Adult and Teen Challenge program when you get out of here, but we'll cross that bridge when we get there."

"I've heard of them. That's one of the places my mom wanted me to go to. Isn't that like an eighteen-month long program?"

"Yes," Christy nodded. "Which is a drop in the bucket if it gets you your life back."

"Good point," Hannah said as she stood. "We'd better get to morning chow. It's getting late. You can tell me why I would want to go to that program on the way."

"Because it works," Christy stood and walked out of their cell with Hannah. "Eighty percent of those who complete the program live addiction free the rest of their life…"

*****

"So how did you get out of the SHU so quickly?" Hannah asked as she took a bite of scrambled eggs.

"I'm not sure I'm supposed to be out," Christy said as she used her plastic spoon to slice her banana into a bowl of oatmeal.

"What's that supposed to mean?" Hannah responded with a confused look.

"One of the guards…"

"CO's," Hannah corrected. "It's okay to call them guards or bulls among the inmates but don't ever let them hear you say it. They like officers, corrections officers, or COs for short, but don't say guards. You don't want that kind of attention. Believe me."

"Thank you," Christy said in acknowledgment. "Anyway, one of the COs, brought me over here in the middle of the night. She said I was being released, but it was all just a ruse. She watched me take a shower and then tried to force me to have sex with her."

"And did you?"

"No! Of course not!"

"Then how did you get out of it?"

"Let's just say, I made her regret coming on to me," Christy said as she took a spoonful of oatmeal.

Hannah leaned in close across the table and whispered. "You gave a CO the smack down?!"

Christy nodded.

"Which one?"

"Baker," Christy said quietly.

"Baker?!" Hannah whispered incredulously. "Are you kidding me?"

"Why? How bad is that?" Christy asked, suddenly getting the feeling she was being watched.

"Umm, bad. Major bad," Hannah answered succinctly. "She is one of the most sadistic of all the COs in this joint. She's so evil, even Randy is afraid of her."

"She told me Randy works for her," Christy countered as she began to scan the chow hall out of the corner of her eyes.

"She does, and Baker calls the shots. Believe me," Hannah said putting a spoon full of eggs into her mouth and chewing thoughtfully.

"But I'll say this, when word gets around you put a beating onto Baker, you'll have more respect around here than you already have after what you did to Randy and her goon squad."

"Will that help?" Christy asked with hope while still unable to shake the feeling she was being watched.

"It won't hurt, but it won't remove the target that is definitely on your back. Between Baker and Randy, you're marked. Me too."

"You are, aren't you?" Christy nodded. "I'm sorry. I should have thought of what this might mean for you."

"I wasn't trying to put that on you. You're trying to help me. You went to the SHU for standing up for me. Nobody has ever done something like that for me," Hannah said fighting back tears. "I'm not mad at you. I'm grateful, Christy. I'd rather die than go back to being Randy's sex slave, doing tricks for fentanyl."

"Do you really think we are going to be killed?" Christy asked, the feeling she was being watched even more stronger now.

Hannah responded by pursing her lips, looking down with raised eyebrows and shrugging her shoulders resignedly. A chill came over Christy. Joe had warned her they could all be marked for death. Rather than keep a low profile, she had gone and poked not one but two bears: Randy and Baker. Neither of which were in the room but someone else was. She could feel it. Christy stood.

"I'm ready to get out of here," she said. "Are you finished?"

Hannah nodded and stood. They collected their trays and walked out of the chow hall, depositing their trays as they went. Many heads turned and watched the two walk out but one person in particular watched intently. The tall, slender woman with rich mahogany skin stood with her tray and followed Christy out, watching from a distance.

Chapter 55

Grand Island, New York

"O'Shanick Construction, this is Marina speaking. How may I help you?"

"Marina! This is Tran Van Truk! It's so good to hear your voice!"

"Hey, Tran!" Marina said into the phone excitedly as she motioned for her mother to come out to the reception area from her office. "How are you?"

"A few scars, but otherwise I'm as good as new. How about you?"

Tran and Marina had both been near fatally injured on the same day a few months back when an organized crime family attacked them during a bike ride around the island. Tran had been struck by a van and shot several times while trying to defend Christy, Marina, and Joe's unconscious father. The mafia soldiers had made off with Christy and Marina, and Marina had been shot in the chest while trying to escape a few hours later. It was Christy, along with Dr. Tony Alendretti, a lifelong friend of Joe's who happened to be working a nearby emergency room that day who had stabilized Marina enough to get her to the operating room.

"Same here. A few scars but I'm fully recovered. Gosh, this is the first time you and I have talked since…well, you know. I'm glad to hear you're okay." Marina paused as the reality struck her. "Thank you…for what you did that day," her voice croaked.

"Unfortunately, it wasn't enough," Tran said solemnly. "Total mission failure on my part. I'm sorry."

"Tran," Marina said earnestly, "greater love has no man than this, that he lay his life down for his friends. You nearly died trying to protect us and we will always be in your debt."

Marina saw her mother walk into the reception area and placed Tran on speaker phone.

"Tran, there's someone here who would like to say hello…"

"Hello, Tran!" Maria O'Shanick said excitedly.

"Hello, Mrs. O'Shanick," Tran spoke cordially, "I wish I was calling under better circumstances."

"What's wrong?" Maria said with sudden concern. "Did something happen to Joe in that prison?"

"No, ma'am. I'm sorry," Tran said quickly. "I was just referring to this entire situation. There is something extremely sinister going on and I know how hard it must be affecting you all up there."

"Oh…yes," Maria said recovering. "I'm sorry, Tran. I thought you were about to spring some bad news on us. You have to be careful with me, I'm getting old and jumpy."

"Oh please, Mrs. O'Shanick…"

"Ina, Tran! Mrs. O'Shanick is too formal for my boys," Maria playfully scolded. She was very fond of Joe's teammates, Ramsey and Tran in particular.

"Ina. Yes, ma'am," Tran answered. "What I was gonna say is, you don't look a day over thirty. You and Marina could pass for sisters."

To an outsider, Maria and Marina *could* pass as sisters. Marina inherited some of her father's height, but they otherwise matched with their long dark hair, slender build, and soft Filipino facial features. Marina smiled listening to Tran compliment her mother.

"You're too kind, Tran, but thank you. So please tell me you are calling with some good news about, Joe, Christy, and Matthew."

"I wish I was, ma'am. Truth is, I'm as in the dark about all of this as you. I'm trying to make some sense of it, and I would really like to be able to get ahold of Joe. I tried calling the prison but got nowhere. I was hoping you might know of a way I can get ahold of him?"

"We've had the same problem, Tran. They won't let us talk to him. In fact, we've only talked to him once and that was when he was meeting with his attorney. We would like to go down to Atlanta, but his attorney tells us the prison isn't allowing visitors other than legal counsel. He said he is fighting that, but it's only been a few days. We *did* get to FaceTime with him and Matthew for a few minutes."

"Oh, really? How are they doing?"

"Oh, you know how they are, they act like nothing phases them and this is just a temporary setback."

"True, but at least you got to talk to them, Mrs. O, I mean, Ina. Maybe I could try getting in touch with them that way. Would you be willing to give me his attorney's name and number?" Tran asked.

"Of course I will give it to you," Maria said while pulling her iPhone out of the side pocket of her black leggings. "I'll text it to you right now."

"Actually, Ina, I'm calling from a pay phone. I don't have my cell with me right now. If you could just read it off to me, I'll write it down." Tran didn't want to alarm Joe's mother any more than he already had.

"Will you call me back as soon as you learn anything new?" Maria asked after reading off the number.

"Absolutely, ma'am. I'm gonna call right now. This is nothing but pure evil. I'm so sorry you all are going through this. I'm hurting for my team too. If I can do anything to help right this wrong, I will."

"I know you will, Tran. Joe thinks very highly of you, as do all of us. Please be careful."

Chapter 56

The White House

"Mr. President?" Assistant Chief of Staff Espinoza spoke while standing just inside the doorway. "We're ready when you are."

President Galan set his pen down and took a deep breath. *Half the world waits, while half gets on with it anyway,* the old lyric played in his head. The building explosion had set off numerous secondary explosions throughout the media. Understandably so, yet the media seemed to gloss over the known facts in favor of rumors, half-truths and outright lies. All morning long, so-called *experts* had pontificated on various news outlets, building the narrative that this was just another "egregious act" by a power mad, rogue president desperate to swing the election. Nothing could be farther from the truth, but how can the truth prevail against a narrative being propagated by the purveyors of information? The only answer was to go to the public. Live without a net.

"Let's get on with it then, Martin," Galan said as he rose from behind the desk in his private study adjacent to the Oval Office.

Two of the president's personal Secret Service agents joined them as he stepped into the hall and began the short walk to the White House Press Briefing Room. Various staffers stood in the hall as he passed. He felt like a death row inmate on his way to his execution. Not an altogether inaccurate comparison.

"Josh, I hope the Secret Service has a policy against throwing spears in the press room," Galan said to the agent on his right, Special Agent Josh Peters.

"Only the physical ones, Mr. President. Can't do a thing about the verbal spears."

Normally, Special Agent Peters would have laughed at his boss's light-hearted comment, but the heaviness of the situation overrode his sense of humor. Peters had worked for three different presidents. President Galan was, by every measure, superior to the previous two presidents by a huge margin. Regardless of what one thought of his policies, President Galan treated all the staff, from the servers to the Cabinet members, like they were part of his family. He knew them all by name and genuinely cared about them and their families. As part of President Galan's personal protection detail, Peters had stood in many a room and witnessed what his president was like behind the scenes. If integrity is defined as doing the right thing even when nobody will know, then President Galan's picture should appear next to the word in every dictionary.

Hence the reason Peters felt so morosely perplexed. There was no way Jorge Galan was in any way guilty of all the press and his opponents were accusing him of. Peters knew the man was not capable of such acts; furthermore, as one who stood against the wall during private meetings, Peters had never witnessed any conversation or policy that would cause him to even consider that his president was behind these acts. Behind his stoic face, Peters was a mix of raging emotions. Sadness and concern for a man he revered. A godly man and patriot who genuinely cared about the nation and its people and, by extension, the people outside this nation of whom his policies affected. Even stronger was a brooding anger towards those who were committing these heinous acts while placing the blame on President Galan and imprisoning innocents like Lieutenant Commander O'Shanick and Master Chief Ramsey, both of whom Peters had met when President Galan had honored them in a Rose Garden ceremony.

They reached the Press Briefing Room. President Galan wasted no time. Without waiting to be introduced, he charged up onto the platform to begin the previously announced noon press conference. He ignored the sudden flurry of questions and immediately began to speak.

"Good afternoon," he said as he gripped the lectern with both hands. "I'll take your questions in a moment after I've made a brief statement."

President Galan had no notes and no teleprompter. The White House emblem stood out behind him as he stood on the blue carpeted platform. He looked directly into the cameras at the back of the room and spoke from his heart.

"As you all know, an office building in uptown Charlotte was decimated early this morning when a truck, packed with explosives, was parked in front of the building and detonated. Rescue workers recently discovered the remains of two victims, whose identities are known but will not be released until their families have first been notified. Please honor these victims by not pursuing these details until such a time as appropriate. Efforts continue, as we speak, to search for any other survivors and or victims. The only known survivor at this time, remains in critical condition at Carolinas Medical Center in Charlotte. I would ask all Americans to join me in praying for the victims and their families."

"With preliminary reports, we have a good idea as to how this heinous act was pulled off, what we do not know yet is who is behind this or why it was conducted. We *can* confirm that one of the occupants of the office building was Whitmore Investigative Services, the same firm that was involved in an incident that occurred last week involving the rescue of several abducted American woman from an island owned by the *Los Fantasma Guerreros* cartel in which my opponent, Senator Robert Fowler, was a guest at the time. Whether or not this was a coincidence or Whitmore Investigative was the target of the attack has yet to be determined."

President Galan paused before continuing. He gripped the podium even tighter and took a deep breath to quell the anger rising from within. It was time to take the gloves off.

"I *am* well aware of the rumors and speculation circulating as to my involvement in this alleged conspiracy and I am here to tell you, the American people, that I had no knowledge of or any involvement with the attack in Charlotte this morning or the events that transpired last week in Belize. I am well aware of the allegations that have been leveled against me and the evidence that has been presented through the media. I will tell you, unequivocally, that no such orders originated from me or from my administration; furthermore, I believe that, based on preliminary interviews conducted by the Department of Justice, along with the known character and integrity of the men and women involved, that there was no such order given anywhere within the chain of command. The facts and statements provided indicate that a rescue operation was conducted by a small group of brave men and woman, voluntarily responding to the desperate plea for help from a father, to rescue several American women who were abducted by an organized crime group and sold into the sex slave industry. Several of the women rescued have provided statements in which they describe being snatched off the street, savagely beaten on several occasions, including lashed with an automobile fan belt, injected with heroin, and forced to have sex with dozens of men each day. The only people refuting this are Victor Tupolev, the head of the Russian criminal organization that performed the abductions and enslaved these women, and Senator Fowler who not only happened to be a guest of the cartel, but according to one woman's statement, struck the woman and was in the process of forcing himself on her sexually when Lieutenant Commander O'Shanick entered the room and stopped him."

The press erupted in voices of skepticism and anger, shouting questions at President Galan.

"I haven't finished my statement yet!" He spoke forcefully over the noise, his commanding demeanor from his days as a Marine Corps Sergeant Major shocking the press into silence. "It seems as though your minds are already made up as your reporting this week has shown. I told you I would take your questions when I'm done, but for right now, I'd like to address the American people, if that's alright with you," he spoke, his tone indicating an admonishment rather than a request.

"Thank you," he continued. "Now, if I may, I'd like to ask my fellow Americans a question. Particularly those who are parents. What would you do? What would you do, if your daughter was suddenly missing and the facts pointed to her having been abducted and likely sold into the sex slave industry? What would you do if you went to the authorities and they couldn't help you? I have a daughter as do many of you. I would search the ends of the Earth until I found her and God help anyone who stood in my way. I think if you will objectively look at the facts and the evidence, you will see that is what happened in this case. If it *does* pan out that way, then Senator Fowler has a lot of explaining to do. My administration has cooperated fully in this investigation and will continue to do so because we know the truth is on our side. We had nothing to do with this; furthermore, I believe a great injustice is being carried out. Many innocent people have been inexplicably incarcerated without bond while several others have been killed. For that reason alone, I want an honest and thorough investigation so that we can get to the bottom of this and see that the victims get justice, the innocent go free, and the guilty are held accountable. Now I will take your questions."

A cacophony of voices immediately began to clamor for the president's attention.

"Yes, Monica," President Galan said pointing to a reporter from CNN.

"Mr. President, are you actually accusing your opponent, Senator Robert Fowler, of attempted rape?"

"I'm saying one of the women rescued from the cartel's island submitted a statement in which she states Senator Fowler was forcing himself on her sexually but was stopped by Lieutenant Commander O'Shanick who, himself, gave a sworn statement corroborating the woman's statement. I'll leave it to you to draw your own conclusion. Next? Yes, Bradford," Galan said pointing to a reporter from MSNBC.

"Mr. President, a minute ago you claimed not to have any involvement with the attack on the island last week, yet you also sound as if you approve of what was carried out. How are the American people to infer that you support a violent attack by armed mercenaries that resulted in the deaths of dozens of foreign nationals and an attempt on the life of your opponent while claiming you had no involvement despite evidence to the contrary?"

"Bradford, I will repeat my earlier statement. I did not give any order that had anything to do with the rescue mission of last week, nor did I have any knowledge of it. Now that we have, once again, established that fact, let us examine your choice of words used in your question. You chose to employ the term *foreign nationals* rather than what they actually were which was cartel soldiers who were holding a number of women captive for the purpose of sexual exploitation. You also described the rescuers as mercenaries. A mercenary is a professional warrior paid to engage in combat for a foreign army. All those involved, including Lieutenant Commander O'Shanick and Master Chief Ramsey state they went voluntarily with no expectations of compensation."

"Excuse me, sir, but don't you find that just a little hard to believe?" Bradford asked with a smirk.

"Find what hard to believe, Bradford?"

"That anyone would volunteer for such a mission without expecting some sort of compensation. Why would anyone do that?"

"Because it's the right thing to do, Bradford," President Galan stated factually while looking critically at the well-coifed and manicured reporter. "Because there are still honorable people who do honorable things without expecting compensation or seeking any attention. Maybe you have never met anyone like that in your line of work, but I have been privileged to serve alongside thousands of honorable men and women just like that, and now I am honored to be their Commander in Chief. And to your statement, had that been my daughter on that island, held at the hands of ruthless criminals who had been routinely beating and sexually exploiting her, I would personally owe those men and women a debt of honor I could never repay. Think about it had been your daughter. Next question. Yes, Sasha," he said pointing to the CBS correspondent in the third row.

"Mr. President, despite your denial of any involvement, between the accusations leveled against you by Senator Fowler, the incriminating emails found on the laptop of deceased Navy SEAL Lieutenant Commander Harrison, and the tragic event earlier this morning involving a key player in this attack on Senator Fowler, there is a sequential trail of strong evidence that all points to you. Do you really expect the American people to take you at your word?"

"Sasha, I have full confidence that the American people are capable of examining the facts of the incident, weighing the evidence, applying critical thought and reasoning, and coming to a conclusion of their own. It is *our* job, yours and mine, Sasha, to present the American people with the most accurate representation of the facts in an unbiased manner. I've opened my entire administration to investigation because I am willing to do that. Are you willing to report the news and facts in an unbiased manner?"

Sasha did not reply but simply stared back with a look of astonishment.

"No reply?" Galan asked. "Interesting. Okay, next. Yes, Christopher," Galan said pointing to a reporter from ABC.

"Mr. President, Senator Fowler along with many of your critics have speculated that your war on the cartels is actually a bid to prop up the Gulf Cartel by taking down all of its competing cartels. This could lead one to believe that you are working for or with the Gulf Cartel. We have just learned that surveillance footage of the truck bomb explosion this morning showed a man exiting the truck who had several tattoos on his arms that are consistent with those seen worn by members of the Gulf Cartel. In light of this and the speculation that you are allied with the Gulf Cartel, would you care to comment on this?"

Where did THAT come from? Galan asked himself. *They sure aren't backing down from their narrative, are they?*

"Christopher, the information you just shared is news to me. Regardless of whether or not it is true, let me say, unequivocally, that I am not in the employ of or a partner to or in any way cooperating with *any* criminal organization, not the least of which would include the drug cartels. Can I make myself any more clear?"

"Your stated position is clear, yes, Mr. President," the ABC reporter said in a knowing manner in front of the cameras. "And since you are being clear with the American people, perhaps you wouldn't mind being clear on something else. Earlier, you said that the actions of Lieutenant Commander O'Shanick were, in your words, *honorable.* Senator Fowler alleges that Mr. O'Shanick threw him to his death from a helicopter. Is that your definition of honorable…sir?"

Chapter 57

Atlanta, Georgia

"So according to my cellmate, Benny, people *do* escape this place frequently," Joe said quietly as he dealt out the next hand of Rummy.

They were playing cards at one of the common area tables. Other than their cells, it was one of the safest areas in the prison. The area was under constant camera surveillance and there was always at least one corrections officer present; furthermore, the bikers maintained a presence in the area and Condor had assured Joe that he and Ramsey were safe in their midst.

"But here's the crazy part," Joe continued. "They only go out for a few hours and then they sneak back in."

Ramsey looked up from his cards, a confused look on his face. "Say again your last?"

Joe chuckled. "I kid you not, Rammer. From what I've learned, they sneak out to have sex, buy drugs, or get things like cell phones, and then sneak it all back in. They like it that way. They get three hots and a cot, make some money, and get a little taste of the free world while they serve out their sentence without going fugitive."

"All the power to them," Ramsey shrugged as he sorted and arranged his hand. "They don't have targets on their backs. You and I do. If we don't beat these charges, we're going to spend the rest of our lives in here looking over our shoulders. So how do they get out?"

"Apparently, there are several breaches in the fence."

"That's great, only problem is there's a thick concrete wall the size of Fenway's Green Monster between this rat hole and the fence. How do they navigate the wall?"

"They don't. The stay in a separate part of the prison known as *The Camp.*" It's for lighter sentences and guys gettin out soon. It's on the other side of the wall."

"Well, the problem, as I see it Joey-O, is we are on the wrong side of the wall. Has anybody tried to breach the wall from this side?" Ramsey said as he drew a card from the deck.

"Not that I know of but hear me out; those drugs and contraband make their way to this part of the prison. There has to be a connection. We figure out what that is and we may find a way to the camp. It's one step closer anyway. If they come and go as frequently as Benny tells me, then it's lightly patrolled and should be something you and I can pull off. We've infiltrated much more difficult targets than a fence."

"Roger that," Ramsey said as he dropped a card on the discard pile. "So what we have to figure out is how to get over to the camp without drawing attention. Maybe find our way onto a work detail that goes over there? Laundry? Kitchen police?"

"That's what I was thinking. When Condor gets back from his work detail…"

"O'Shanick! Ramsey!" A beefy CO with thick forearms called as he walked up to the table with a taller but just as thick officer. "Your lawyer's here."

Joe and Ramsey got up from the table and allowed the officers to cuff them before being led out to the administration building where Nick Marcella and Chester Krysztof were waiting for them. After having their cuffs removed, they sat down at the table.

"You guys holding up alright?" Krysztof asked, once again impeccably dressed in a black two-piece suit with a black button-down shirt and a burgundy red silk tie with matching pocket square.

"Heads on a swivel," Joe answered. "Have you found out who the leak is?" Joe said in reference to his missing laptop and Lieutenant Commander Harrison's staged suicide death.

"They've been questioned but so far they ain't sayin' nothin'," Krysztof answered. "But we got someone watching them. Don't worry."

"I'm assuming you gentlemen are aware of the truck bomb explosion from this morning?" Marcella asked, leaning forward in his wheelchair with his hands clasped on the table in front of him. He wore a charcoal gray two-piece suit with white shirt and red paisley tie.

"Yes, sir," Joe and Ramsey nodded together.

"I'm not stupid, gentlemen," Marcella continued. "With us having a leak the other day and now this, I wouldn't blame you for leveling your suspicions on one of us, but I can assure you it wasn't us."

"The thought crossed our minds," Joe said, "but your firm is in the national spotlight and will have a reputation riding on this one, so we ruled it out."

"Okay, I just wanted to clear that up before we proceed," Marcella said as he opened a leather folder and picked up a pen.

"I am afraid I have some disturbing news to share," Marcella began with a serious tone. "The authorities have not released this yet, but Clay Whitmore's attorney passed on to us that Roderick Boulware was one of the casualties along with the owner of the security firm that contracts with Whitmore. Did you know Mr. Boulware?"

"No, sir, not personally," Joe s said shaking his head. "I know Clay thought very highly of him and he was the one who was able to lead us to each place where those girls were being held. Do you think this had anything to do with his trying to reclaim our video?"

"A number of reasons come to mind, Joe, but that is chief among them, yes."

The affirmation made Joe shudder. It was bad enough being unfairly arrested and thrown into prison, but guys like Boulware and Harrison had nothing to do with this. They were innocent.

"Did he leave behind a wife and family?" Joe asked.

"No, thank God," Marcella answered. "He was single. No kids."

"That's a relief," Joe sighed. "It doesn't make it any easier to take, knowing he was killed because of what he was doing for us though. Please tell me this is being investigated by good people."

"There's no way to know," Krysztof spoke up. "There's so many crooked people wrapped up in this that we can't trust no one."

Joe looked at Krysztof and Marcella. He was speechless. Without the video, they had no hard evidence. Just their testimonies and, judging from President Galan's press conference earlier, the press was bent on propping up Fowler's narrative. Everything President Galan said was dead on and true, yet the press seemed to ignore it completely and continue on with their ridiculous questions. How would any jury not be biased? How would they stand a chance without any solid evidence?

As if he read Joe's mind, Marcella answered the question. "We're working on finding another computer expert who can reclaim that video for us."

"Mr. Marcella, as much as we need it, I don't know that we can or should."

"Why is that, Joe?"

"Look what just happened to Roderick Boulware," Joe replied. "Anyone who is remotely connected to us in the way of corroborating statements or evidence gets schwacked. We can't expose more people like this. We have to find another way."

"I understand that, Joe, but what else can we do? We need that video. But you just reminded me; one of your teammates contacted me earlier this morning," Marcella said as he retrieved a thin laptop out of his leather attaché.

"Who?" Joe asked leaning in with curiosity.

"A Tran Van Truk."

"Tran!" Joe and Ramsey said in unison.

"He said he needs to talk with you most urgently regarding this case. Says he had an incident last night and thinks it might have something to do with all of this. He said he may have some information that might help."

"Really?" Joe wondered aloud.

"Yes. I pressed him on it, but he said he would only talk on a secure line and only when you were present. I told him we would be meeting with you two and would contact him on a secure video chat. Bear with me a moment while I set it up."

Joe and Ramsey exchanged hopeful glances while Marcella went about setting up the video chat. Joe looked over at Krystof, his attire, as tasteful as it was, did little to conceal the scarred knuckles, calloused hands, and a nose that had been broken on at least one occasion. He was also intrigued by Krysztof's tough-sounding northern accent.

"Mr. Krysztof, do you mind if I ask where you're from originally?"

"Course I don't mind. I'm from Buffalo."

"I thought you were from up my way. I grew up on Grand Island."

"Yeah, I knew that," Krysztof answered. "It's in your file but I also met your dad's attorney, Brinkworth. I actually played football at University at Buffalo with his old man back in the day."

"Small world," Joe acknowledged. "What part of Buffalo are you from?"

"Lovejoy," Krysztof said proudly.

That explained the scarred and callused knuckles. Lovejoy was a mostly Italian working-class neighborhood on the east side of Buffalo. It was nicknamed the "Iron Island" since it was surrounded by railroad tracks. Joe knew that back in Krystof's youth Buffalo was divided up into various ethnic neighborhoods: Italian, Polish, Irish, Puerto Rican, Black, Slavic and more. In those days, few people had cars. As a result, families were tight and so were the neighborhoods. It led to a lot of turf wars between neighborhoods. That's just how things were. Now the city was much more blended. Krystof might have gone on to be an attorney but didn't get those knuckles from playing the piano. *Good,* Joe thought. *If we want any chance of getting out of here in an honest fashion, we're gonna need some brawlers on our side.*

"Okay, gentleman. Tran just texted back and said he's ready," Marcella announced as he pressed a few keys and turned the laptop so all could see.

Tran's face materialized on the screen. "Joe! Rammer! Whiskey Tango Foxtrot?!"

"Hey, Tran!" Joe and Ramsey greeted him simultaneously.

"How did you get wrapped up in all of this?" Ramsey asked. "Aren't you still up at George Washington for some medical training?"

"Correct, Master Chief, I am but, for some reason, some people are after me and now I'm laying low. I got their plate and had Jade run it. It traces up to the Liu Dynasty. Have you ever heard of them?"

"No," Ramsey said.

"Me neither," Joe added.

"I have," Krysztof spoke up. "They're the biggest Chinese crime outfit over here. They're everywhere actually. They have a piece of action in every corner of the globe. You really traced those plates to them, son?"

"Excuse me, but who are you, sir?" Tran asked.

"Chester Krysztof, co-counsel."

"Okay, thank you. Yes, we tracked their plates to a company owned by the Liu Dynasty. I got facials of two of the guys who tried to pay me a visit and Jade matched them to former Chinese special forces, Sea Dragons no less."

"What are Sea Dragons?" Marcella asked.

"Basically China's version of Navy SEALs," Joe answered. "Tran? Do you think they are working for this Liu Dynasty?"

"Correct, Joe. They're here on official visas. They're cover is financial analysts for Golden Sun Financial in Alexandria, but their records show they fly all over the country for business meetings, ostensibly to recruit new high-priced clients. Hidden in all that is a huge money laundering scheme according to Jade, but the bottom line is they came after me last night and it actually went kinetic," Tran said using a term that described a firefight.

"Mother of God, they're going after the entire platoon!" Joe exclaimed.

"That's what I'm thinking too, Joe. They tracked me on my iPhone to Jade's townhouse last night, so I ditched our phones and any means of tracing us. Going underground, you know. I bought some burner phones and the first thing I did was contact the other guys to warn them. So far, other than Lieutenant Commander Harrison, I'm the only other one."

"I don't get that though," Joe replied. "You haven't been operating with us since…"

"Since our little run in with your mafia friends back home," Tran said completing the sentence. "I know. I'm the last person they should be coming after. Not that I want them to go after anyone else, but it does strike me as odd."

"Well, Harrison makes sense," Joe postulated. "He's *my* commanding officer and they used his computer to plant that fake suicide note in which they make it out to look like he confessed to relaying an order to kill Fowler; however, you were nowhere near any of this. *That* I don't get. Where were you when they first found you?"

"I was in my flat. I had just finished a twenty-four-hour EMS shift. I was eating dinner at a nearby restaurant when I learned about Lieutenant Commander Harrison's death. I immediately knew something was up and then that dipwad, Fowler, comes on and spews his BS. I went back to my flat but was so furious I couldn't sleep so I got online and started trying to piece together the facts. My Ring doorbell notified me there was motion. I gave them the slip and followed them down to Alexandria. I enlisted Jade's help and then they attacked us there. They literally torched her house, guys. They mean business; they came after me in a car and on foot with full auto AK-47's."

"Geez, Tran, I'm sorry," Joe said astonished. "How'd you get away?"

"By being a slippery, sneaky frogman, sir," Tran smiled lightly.

"Hooyah!" Joe and Ramsey said quietly.

"Is Jade with you now?" Joe asked.

In response, Jade slowly leaned into the camera's field. She held a humorous face with her eyes wide open in an intense penetrating glare with her lips pursed. Her quirky humor, even under difficult circumstances, was well known and gave both Joe and Ramsey a needed chuckle.

"Hi, Jade," Joe said still laughing as she disappeared off the side of the screen. "So you guys have tracked this group up to a Chinese criminal organization?"

"More like an international conglomerate with criminal roots, but yes," Tran answered.

"Could they be working with Fowler's backers on this mess and it's all related?"

"Yes, Jade said they have major ties globally including the Russians, the cartels, Iran, and have been heavily involved with our government behind the scenes. In fact, they suspect that the party chairman, J. Paul Jeffries, has a…" Jade's elbow shot in from offscreen and connected with Tran's ribs, eliciting a grunt from Tran.

"Umm, the answer is yes," Tran concluded.

Joe surmised Jade's elbow was to keep Tran from revealing anything even close to classified over the internet, regardless of how secure the connection. It was no great secret that J. Paul Jeffries, the chairman of Fowler's political party, had a son who was a bagman for his father, securing deals with foreign entities trading influence for cash. Having a party trading influence to foreign nations, several of them sworn enemies of the United States, was highly concerning to anyone who cared but, not surprisingly, it was constantly swept under the rug by the party and dismissed as "Russian disinformation" by the media and talking heads. That certainly would explain why a Chinese criminal organization would be pulling out all the stops to derail President Galan's campaign in effort to put a known traitor like Fowler in the White House.

"Good copy, Tran," Joe said assuring his friend and teammate that he understood the relationship Tran was hinting at.

Marcella looked on with interest. In preparation for this case, he had familiarized himself with his clients as well as their profession in Naval Special Warfare. He was intrigued to learn that the prototypical Naval Special Warfare Operator would be a championship wrestler with a high IQ. Listening in on the conversation, he got the sense that that was exactly the type of men he was dealing with.

Meanwhile, Joe felt the opposite. He didn't believe the Liu operatives had gone after Tran simply because he was a member of Joe's platoon. Yes, it was possible, but Joe suspected that was low hanging fruit and that the real answer was within reach but he just couldn't grasp it. There had to be another reason. Other than Tran being a part of Echo Platoon, what other reason would they have had to connect just Tran and Harrison? At least for now, that is.

"Tran, did you and Lieutenant Commander Harrison ever communicate by phone, text, or email?" Joe asked.

Even within the Naval Special Warfare community where BUD/S and shared combat experiences broke down a lot of the formality between officers and enlisted rates, it would still be a bit unusual for an officer higher up the chain of command to have informal interaction with an enlisted man under his command.

"Affirmative, Joe. We played each other online in an ongoing chess match. I know it's not exactly sat but we both love to play, and he was actually quite good."

"Did he do this with anyone else that you know of?"

"No clue, Joe. Why? What are you thinking?"

"I'm just wondering if they used his computer or his phone to find who he's been communicating with. Like you said, you haven't been around Virginia Beach or training with Echo so why would they want to come after you? Did you talk to him at all in the past couple of weeks other than your chess matches?"

"Not by phone. We occasionally trade emails about music related things since we're both musicians. Why?"

Joe paused as he carefully considered his response. Clay Whitmore had sworn up and down that Roderick Boulware could match up with many of the world's top computer experts, but Jade was on another level altogether. If anyone could find that missing video, she could. It was also possible that Tran's interaction with Harrison by computer may allow her a back door into his hard drive and memory cloud which could be another means of access. This could be their best shot at recovering the video and exonerating themselves. On the other hand, Joe was extremely reluctant to involve them. Whoever was behind this nefariousness had shown they were more than willing to kill, and if this morning's bombing of Whitmore's building proved anything, they were willing to do so at terrorist levels without giving a flying flip about collateral damage.

Tran had nearly been killed after having been ran over by a truck and shot several times while riding shotgun on a bike ride with Christy, Marina, and Joe's dad. Joe couldn't imagine asking Tran to expose himself, along with Jade no less, to search for evidence that might no longer exist; however, Joe reasoned, it wasn't just him that needed this video for a chance at exoneration. There was Ramsey, Charles Courtnall, Clay Whitmore, Chuck Springer, and Christy. How many lives did Christy touch in a positive way each year as an emergency medicine physician? How many people trusted Courtnall with their retirements and finances? Whitmore and Springer and the people they helped as investigators? Not to mention those men all had families. It was an extremely difficult decision. But Joe had spent the last decade being trained in how to make those decisions and actually making them on the battlefield. He looked at his friend's image on the computer screen. Tran was more than a friend; he was a brother. Joe made his decision, took a deep breath, and spoke.

Chapter 58

Washington, D.C.

The dark clad figure strode purposefully down 10th street. There were fewer stores and restaurants on this street which meant fewer people. Those who were present seemed to sense the danger in his presence and quickly moved out of the way. He was no threat to any of them, but he was dangerous. Quite dangerous, in fact.

His name was Jian Chang, "Johnny Chang" to his American acquaintances and clients. He was a wealth manager with Gold Sun Financial but that was his cover. Although he actually did manage wealth and investments for numerous Gold Sun clients and had accumulated a sizable portfolio for himself and his benefactors along the way, his main job was something quite different. Johnny Chang had acquired many lucrative "skills" before moving here from China. Many of them acquired during his eight years of service with China's Jiaolong Assault Team, an elite special forces unit of the People's Liberation Army also known as the Sea Dragons. He was a trained killer. A master of small arms, small unit tactics, covert reconnaissance, demolitions, hand to hand combat and long-range sniper skills, Johnny could kill in any number of ways from a distance or, as he preferred, by hand.

His skills had been brought to the attention of the Liu Dynasty by his unit's commanding officer who was handsomely paid to funnel talent toward the criminal organization. Chang had been lured away by the promise of wealth and, more importantly, the ability to apply his skills on a worldwide stage. He hadn't been disappointed. Although he had dutifully married and had two children as part of his cover, Chang traveled the world on assignments. He racked up numerous wealthy clients, established laundering schemes, bedded beautiful and exotic women around the world, and killed, to date, 137 people in various parts of the world. Not that the number mattered to him, Chang simply kept running tallies of nearly every personal experience in his head. He knew his net worth, his investment yields, the number of women he had slept with and, accordingly, the number of people he had killed. He could even break that down to those killed by long range rifle, those killed at short range, those killed by a knife and those killed by hand. It didn't affect his conscience in the least. In fact, he had no conscience. Chang was an atheist and had long ago reasoned that, since there was no god, man was just a material being; therefore, an immaterial conscience was not possible, so morality was a social construct at best but more of a matter of personal opinion. In the truest material sense, Chang reasoned, there was no such thing as morality and, therefore, life was survival of the fittest as any true Darwinian would have to acknowledge. Chang was an apex predator. He would not only survive, but he would also rule. He simply needed to continue to work, more aptly claw and kill, his way to the head of the pack.

Chang currently ran a small unit of similarly skilled men for the Liu Dynasty. They all had covers but their main responsibility was to serve as enforcers for the Dynasty. They were one of several crews overseen by Jin Fang, better known as Father Patrick. That was where Chang was heading now. It was time to report in. He quickly ascended the steps leading into the cathedral. He dipped his right hand in the holy water and blessed himself as he entered the sanctuary. A handful of people sat by themselves scattered amongst the pews. The confessional light indicated the booth was open. Chang entered, sat down, and opened the small sliding window in the partition. He prayed in Mandarin.

"Bless me, Father, for I have sinned. It has been one week since my last confession and in that time, I have been covetous, haughty, and deceitful," Chang spoke the required phrase which let Father Patrick know who he was speaking to through the partition.

"Have you been adulterous, deceitful, or a gossip?" Father Patrick spoke the coded response informing Chang that he had the correct priest and was free to speak.

"Yes, yes, and no," Chang responded, completing the code.

"You've had some difficulty," Father Patrick began by letting Chang know he failed in his assignment to eliminate Tran Van Truk.

"He is highly skilled. We will…"

"Did I ask for your excuses?" Father Patrick interrupted.

"No," Chang answered simply.

"Correct. I did not. And now you have two people to take care of, don't you?"

"Yes."

"Tonight. No excuses," Father Patrick said simply.

"Yes, sir," Chang answered with the appropriate amount of deference.

"And what of Xi?" Father Patrick asked in reference to Chang's man who had been shot during the firefight with Tran Van Truk.

"He went for the ride with Tommy," Chang answered.

Tommy was Chang's younger brother who had detonated the truck down in Charlotte. He had stolen it earlier from a nearby rental company's return lot. He and several others loaded it with eighteen barrels consisting of ammonium nitrate, nitromethane and acetylene tanks at a warehouse outside of Alexandria that was owned by Liu Fan through a shell corporation. They had placed Xi Zhang's body in the back with the barrels. It had been vaporized in the explosion.

"The news is reporting that the driver was linked to the Gulf Cartel," Father Patrick commented. "Well done."

"It was a simple matter of applying a few temporary tattoos that resemble Gulf Cartel symbols on his arms and making sure the security camera across the street saw them," Chang said modestly.

"Without exposing his face?"

"He wore a bandana on his face and a cap cholo-style. There was only a narrow slit for his eyes, and it was still dark. He also made himself look heavier by placing padding under baggy clothes and walking hunched over to disguise his height. The authorities will never think to look for a wiry Asian man."

"I see," Father Patrick said quietly. "Very good. You have only to finish off the SEAL and his girlfriend tonight. No new assignments for now but that could change. Check your Twitter account hourly."

The screen partition slid open a slightly and an envelope containing cash was handed through. Chang took the envelope and pocketed it. He knew better than to look through it in front of his superiors.

"You'll get the other half when the job is done," Father Patrick said.

The sliding window shut on Father Patrick's side, signaling the meeting was over. Chang rose and exited the confessional booth. He quickly left the church and turned left heading down toward the Mall on Capitol Hill where one of his men picked him up on Pennsylvania Avenue. Chang got into the late model Toyota sedan, closed the door, and they sped off.

Chapter 59

Washington, D.C.

Tran remained motionless so as not to draw attention from Johnny Chang while he walked out of the church. He was leaning forward with his arms on the wooden pew in front of him, resting his head down on his arms while looking down at his iPhone screen hidden form the view of others. He and Jade had purchased a couple of small cameras that could be monitored through an app on their newly purchased phones. Tran had positioned the camera in one of his backpack's MOLLE straps in such a manner so as to allow him to monitor the confessional booth, behind him just off the main entrance. His tracker was still operational which allowed him to follow the Toyota. It had remained parked at the Gold Sun Financial office until late this afternoon when it made the drive up to Washington. Tran decided to see if he could follow behind from a distance using his motorcycle. They actually came almost directly to him as they drove into Chinatown, which allowed Tran to pick up their trail easily enough. When he saw Johnny Chang exit the Toyota and make his way down Tenth Street on foot, Tran parked his bike and followed from a discreet distance until he saw him enter the church. Earlier that day, Jade had run Tran's pictures of their attackers through a facial recognition database and had matched the two men with Johnny Chang and Xi Zhang, both Chinese nationals working in finance, an obvious cover based on the events of last night. Tran was wearing a wig and a cheap pair of sunglasses under a beanie cap, giving him enough confidence to follow Chang into the church. He had entered in just enough time to see Chang slip into the confessional.

Tran suppressed the urge to follow after Chang when he left. He could always find him again. In fact, he could continue tracking him, using his phone, right here while he waited. His instincts told him to wait and see who came out of that confessional booth as that person was likely higher up the chain of command. Tran highly doubted Chang was here for religious reasons.

A full thirty minutes passed by with no activity. Tran could clearly see the twin doors leading to each side of the confessional. Could there be an unseen door in the back for the priest to use? The thought unsettled Tran nearly as much as the thought that perhaps he should have resumed his trail of Chang, who was now all the way back down in Alexandria. Too late for that now.

The sound of leather-soled shoes clicking on the polished floor caught his attention. Tran studied his phone's screen and watched a dark-haired, thirty-something male in professional business attire walking toward the same confessional booth. He checked to make sure the phone showed the camera was recording. The man entered the confessional and, like Chang earlier, emerged a few minutes later. Tran had no urge to follow after him. He could be a player in whatever scheme was occurring or he could simply be a parishioner here for his confession. Tran would have Jade run his face later but remained intent on finding out who was behind the confessional door.

Tran reviewed his options while he patiently waited. Chang and his partner were obviously heavy hitters, but they were still the hired help. It was likely that they had limited knowledge of the Liu Dynasty and its involvement in this political conspiracy. That's what it was, wasn't it? Tran didn't think of himself as conspiracy minded but, considering the predicament Joe and Ramsey were in, not to mention real bullets had been flying in his direction last night, that's exactly what this was. *Certainly a conspiracy to commit murder!* Nevertheless, if whoever was in the confessional revealed himself, Tran would get a picture and send it to Jade for facial recognition. Meanwhile he would trail the man to see where he led. If that trail became a dead end, Tran would fall back and pick up his trail on Chang. Sooner or later, *someone* would lead him up the chain of command and he would see just how far this went. If he could expose the corruption, and he was certain there was a significant amount, perhaps he could spring his teammates from prison while he pulled the plug on Chang's operation to kill him and Jade. It was a long shot but that was better than sitting around waiting for more bullets to fly in his direction. Tran preferred to be the hunter, not the hunted. Waiting around for someone to kill you usually resulted in just that.

Tran noticed some motion on his camera and watched as a physically fit male with dark brown hair, who seemed about fifty years old, appeared in the entrance and quickly made his way to the confessional. There was something familiar about the man, but his image was too small to make out his face clearly. Tran snapped a screen shot and caught a side profile just as the man was stepping into the confessional. He enlarged the image and studied the man's face. His eyes narrowed as he struggled to match the face with a name he knew he had within the archives of his mind. *Wait a minute...Holy...!*

Tran was looking at the face of FBI Director Francis Snyder. Tran immediately felt like the first tumbler on a safe combination lock had just fallen into place getting him a little closer to cracking the safe open to find out what's inside. Could Director Snyder really be involved or was he truly just here for confession. Although Snyder was an Irish Catholic, Tran believed he was here to talk to whoever was behind door number one, only it wasn't to offer up his confession. Now Tran was torn. Did he follow Director Snyder out of here when he left or did he stay to find out who this mystery person is? If Snyder was involved, he could be paramount in busting this case wide open and might be worth pursuing when he left. On the other hand, Snyder had come here rather than have the mystery man go to him. Did that indicate that even FBI Director Snyder was answering to a higher power other than the One this church represented? Tran was on the fence about that; however, his curiosity for the unknown won out and he decided to let Snyder leave while Tran would hang around to find out who was behind that door.

A few minutes later, Director Snyder emerged from the confessional booth and hastily retreated back out of the church. The pull to follow one of the top law enforcement officials in the land was strong but Tran fought it off. Snyder had likely conducted his business and was on his way back to his office or probably even home. Either way, Tran felt certain he was doing the right thing by staying. Whoever this was would hopefully lead him to someone or something bigger than the FBI.

Ten minutes later, the other confessional door opened and an Asian man in priestly vestments stepped out and looked out over the church allowing Tran a good look. Tran immediately spotted a fellow warrior. The priest was short but muscular and walked with an athletic grace. He had a flattened nose and a cauliflower ear but a square jaw and dark piercing eyes. His short-cropped jet-black hair had the beginnings of some gray hair on the sides. He might be a priest, but he hadn't always been one. He might serve God, but he was working for someone who considered himself a god. Tran waited for the priest to exit the church before he stood and began to follow him. The little voice in his head told him he had made the right call.

Chapter 60

Alto, Georgia

"Mmmm, I needed that," Officer Baker said contentedly.

"You're quite welcome, ma'am," Randy said as she sat up. "If you turn over, I'll give you a massage."

"How can I say no to that?" Baker grunted as she rotated her heft into a prone position on the break room couch.

"Karen! What the flip happened?!" Randy exclaimed as she noticed the extensive bruising on Baker's left flank and back.

"Your friend, Tabrizi, sucker punched me last night."

"How did *that* happen?"

"I tried to flip her in the shower last night. She let on like she was game and caught me off guard is all. Won't happen again," Baker spoke nonchalantly.

"Did you throw her back in the hole?" Randy asked as she straddled Baker's backside and began to gently massage her bare back.

"No."

"No?" Randy asked surprised. "Why not?"

"Because there would have to be a reason and the wrong people might start asking her questions; besides, I thought you might want another crack at her."

"Yeah, you're right. Tabrizi and I have some unfinished business," Randy said as she kneaded Baker's triceps.

"You need to handle her soon…and decisively," Baker said as a subtle suggestion. "The other cons know what went down. If you don't fix things, you'll lose their respect and I'll be looking for another stud to run this barn."

"I'll handle it!" Randy said defensively. "By this time tomorrow, she'll be leaving this place for good."

"She better be," Baker admonished. "Mmmm…" she moaned thoughtfully.

"Mmmm?" Randy pronounced it as a question. "Feels good?"

"It does," Baker said dreamily, "but that's not what I was thinking."

"What were you thinking then?" Randy asked as she kept massaging.

"I was just thinking it's a shame we gotta waste her. There aren't many tall, fit fems in this barn that look like her. None actually."

"True but she won't tame," Randy remarked. "She's gotta go."

Baker looked at her watch. "Speaking of which, it's time for you to be going to. It's almost bed check."

"So I'm back in my dorm?" Randy said as she slid off Baker and began to gather her clothes.

"Of course you are, babe," Baker said with a grunt as she pushed herself up to a sitting position. She then leaned forward and snatched her undergarments off the floor. "Just make sure you handle Miss tall, dark, and lovely discreetly so you don't end up back in the hole."

"Have I screwed one up yet, Karen?"

"No, babe, you haven't," Karen said while buttoning her uniform shirt. "Just be careful is all. She's dangerous. You and I have a good thing going here running the action in this place. Don't screw it up."

"I won't. I swear I won't," Randy said as she pulled her shirt back on. "I like what we got goin' here too."

"Good," Baker said as she pulled her uniform pants on. "Once Tabrizi is gone, you should have no trouble with the cute little cellmate of hers."

"I hear that. She's a sweet little thing. My little money maker," Randy nodded with a sly grin.

"Oh, one more thing, babe," Karen said as she picked up a large mesh laundry bag loaded with ramen noodles, boxes of crackers, peanut butter, and packages of cookies. Randy knew several of the items would all contain cleverly concealed packages of various drugs: weed, cocaine, meth, fentanyl and Ecstasy. "Now give Momma some sugar."

Chapter 61

Atlanta, Georgia

"So how much of a hurt did you guys put on the Gulf Cartel?" Condor asked as he stood watch while Joe and Ramsey showered.

"Quite a bit," Ramsey answered. "Our Task Force operated on the gulf side. That's mostly Los Fantasma Guerreros, Los Zetas, and the Gulf Cartel," Ramsey answered.

"So what the news and Fowler are saying about the president propping up the Gulf Cartel by taking out their competition is BS?"

"Absolutely," Joe answered as he rinsed off.

"Total BS," Ramsey added. "They were all targets. Galan's fighting a righteous war trying to rid Central America of those plagues."

"Well, have you seen what the news is reporting?" Condor asked in his deep voice. "They say it was the Gulf Cartel that blew up that building in Charlotte. Fowler was on the news blaming Galan. Said the Gulf Cartel did it for him to get rid of incriminating evidence at the investigator's firm."

"And that's even more BS," Joe said as he shut off the water and grabbed a threadbare white towel. "I told you, Galan had nothing to do with that mission. It was all Whitmore and us working for a good man whose daughter was abducted."

"Did you really throw Fowler out of a helicopter?" Condor asked.

"More like I grabbed ahold of him as I was falling off the skid. He wasn't strapped in and he fell with me. I wasn't trying to kill him. In fact, I made sure he didn't drown and pulled him to safety."

"That's not the way he tells it," Condor teased.

"Consider the source," Joe shrugged as he toweled off.

"They were at least eighty feet up in the air," Ramsey commented. "I thought they were both dead when I saw them fall."

"That wasn't falling, Rammer. That was landing with style," Joe said in a gesture akin to Buzz Lightyear.

"Whatever you say, Joe," Ramsey said as he finished dressing. "You about ready? Even with Condor's boys watching out for us, I don't want to be in here any longer than we have to."

"Yeah," Joe said as he pulled his prison shirt on and stepped into a pair of prison issue flip flops. "Let's go."

Together with Condor, they walked out of the communal shower. Joe and Ramsey exchanged fist bumps with Condor and some of the other bikers as they bid each other a good night.

"How's your new cellmate?" Joe asked as they headed toward their cells.

"Better than The Missing Link and about a third the size as well. I think someone told him what I did to Myslinski. He's been tiptoeing around me all day."

"Good. Maybe he'll let you sleep tonight," Joe teased as they arrived at Ramsey's cell.

"I don't care who it is. I sleep with one eye open in this place. I'll see you in the morning, brother," Ramsey said as he gave Joe a fist bump.

"Night, Rammer."

Joe hurried on to his cell. With targets on their backs, he was not thrilled to be without his swim buddy. From the first days of BUD/S, SEAL recruits had it beaten into them to never leave their swim buddy. Their survival depended on it. As strange as it seemed, Joe knew he would feel better once he was locked in his cell.

Joe walked into the cell and immediately noticed Benny wasn't there. Benny was usually laying on his bunk reading during the evening hours leading up to bed check. Despite being somewhat of a loner, Benny somehow always had good intel on what was going on within their cell block. Perhaps he was out gathering the latest intel.

Joe was about to grab his toothbrush when his senses alerted him to the presence of danger. He turned and saw a thin Hispanic male of about twenty stepping towards him with his right arm extended brandishing a crudely made prison shank. Joe immediately held his hands up in front of him, fingers spread, in a Krav Maga defensive posture that was meant to appear non-threatening.

"Think this through, man," Joe warned. "You don't want to do this. I'm no threat to you."

The young Hispanic male kept coming. Joe was nearly backed up to the wall in the small confines of his cell.

"I'm serious, dude. Get out of here!"

The man lunged toward Joe. In a blur of motion, Joe's left arm swung down and out, parrying his attacker's knife arm away while his right hand simultaneously delivered a palm strike to the attacker's nose, resulting in a sickening crunch of cartilage. Joe's left arm followed through the initial parry by wrapping the attacker's stabbing arm and pulling it into his shoulder while using his right arm to grab the attacker's right shoulder. Joe then rotated his left shoulder forward, using it to bend his attacker's wrist into a weak position which allowed Joe to grab the man's fist with his right hand and bend it into his forearm while rotating the man's arm back and down which forced his head down as he bent over. While controlling the shanking arm, Joe delivered two quick kicks to the man's face and then easily removed the shank from the man's hand as he collapsed to the floor. Joe pounced onto him, pinning his attacker down with a knee to his back and holding his head to the floor. Joe put the tip of the shank into the young man's ear canal.

"I warned you!" Joe said angrily through gritted teeth. "I told you not to mess with me! I could kill you right now! Right now!" Joe said shoving the back of young man's head and shoving the shank further into his ear canal for emphasis.

"NO!" his attacker pleaded. *"Lo siento! Lo siento!"*

"English!" Joe demanded with another menacing shove.

"I'm sorry, man!" The young man pleaded in heavily accented English. "I'm sorry! I was told to do it!"

"Who told you?" Joe demanded.

The young man didn't answer.

"I asked you a question!" Joe wiggled the shank inside the young man's ear canal. "Who sent you?"

"They'll kill me!"

"*I* could kill you!" Joe said still gritting his teeth. He didn't want to get loud and draw attention. He shoved the shank further into the young man's ear. "Now tell me!"

"La Gran Familia," the young man said as he went limp in surrender.

"La Gran Familia? Who's that?" Joe asked barely above a whisper without letting the man up.

"They're the organization down here. They run all the Latino gangs on the streets and in the prisons. They tell me I have to kill you or they don't protect me."

"Why?" Joe asked.

"They don't tell. They just say kill and you go and kill."

"Do they work for a cartel?"

"Yes. They all do. It's just the way."

"And what's your name?" Joe asked in a slightly less aggressive tone.

"Reni. Reni Mendoza," he answered sounding completely defeated.

"Okay, Reni, what will they do to you when they find out you didn't kill me?"

"They'll kill me and then you. You're marked for death. They won't stop until they kill you…and your friend."

Rammer!

Joe threw the shank under Benny's bunk where it wouldn't be immediately seen, jumped up to his feet and pulled Reni up with him. "Reni, if you want to live, you come with me right now. You try anything and I'll snap your neck; otherwise, you can go back and tell your buddies you failed and take your chances."

Joe dashed out of his cell and down to Ramsey's cell where a similar situation had unfolded. A young Hispanic male lay on the floor, writhing in pain with a badly deformed right elbow. Ramsey stood over him looking down.

"You alright, Rammer?" Joe asked.

"I'm fine. He's not though."

Reni had entered the cell with Joe. He looked down at the man on the floor with horror.

"*Madre de Dios. Estamos muertos,*" he said quietly.

"No, you're not going to die," Joe said as he reached under the other man's shoulders and pulled him to a standing position. "Get your friend up to the officer's desk. You both need to go to the ER. Tell the officer the *truth* about what happened. You'll spend some time in solitary, but you'll be safe. If you do that, then I'll know you're sorry and that I can trust you. When you get back, stick by us and we'll look out for you."

"*Vamos, Rico,*" Reni said as he led the other man out of the cell.

"Are you freaking kidding me, Joe?" Ramsey asked angered. "That punk just tried to kill me!"

"I know, the other one did the same to me," Joe acknowledged with a nod. "They were ordered to it by the Mexican gang."

"And that gives them a pass? They'll just do it again."

"Maybe, maybe not," Joe replied, squinting in thought. "They're not in the gang and maybe we can keep them out of it."

"How do you know that?" Ramsey challenged.

"Because they were ordered to do it and promised protection only if they killed us. If they failed, *they* would be killed."

"And you believe that?"

"Yeah, Rammer, I had his shank inside his ear. I saw the fight deflate right out of him."

"He could change his mind," Ramsey countered.

"I doubt they will," Joe replied. "He said they'll be marked for death."

"And I won't lose any sleep over that," Ramsey answered. "Dude just tried to shank me for crying out loud!"

"I hear you, Rammer, loud and clear. I really do, and I nearly rammed that shank into his skull, but you and I have dedicated our lives to protecting people who can't protect themselves. Those two are just caught in the middle of a way of life you and I have never had to face. Those guys can one day get out of here and live a good life. If we can turn them away to something better, then we did a little bit of good in here. Just give them a chance."

"You going soft on me, Joe? You're one of the most ruthless gunslingers I've ever been outside the wire with."

"And I still am. I'll still put more rounds on target and do so happily next time we go down range and encounter some bad guys. This is different. I'm just extending the same mercy that has been extended to me."

"You sound like Christy…" Ramsey said catching Joe's glare, "…who is not a bad person to emulate."

"Hooyah," Joe said as the final call for inmates to be in their cells sounded. "Alright, I'd better be getting back. Glad to see you're okay, brother. We'll figure out our next move in the morning."

Joe gave Ramsey a fist bump and walked back to his cell, with his head on a swivel, hoping he had done the right thing.

Chapter 62

Washington, D.C.

This guy is no priest! Tran thought to himself as he followed the priest on foot. The "priest" had spent considerable time walking a circuitous route, doubling back, lingering in store front windows to see if anyone stood out in the reflection, all the things an operator or agent with good field craft would do to ensure he wasn't being followed. Tran had to conjure up every bit of his training and skills to avoid being spotted and had nearly lost the man on a couple of occasions.

In addition to informing Tran he was dealing with a pro, it also let him know the man was heading somewhere important. He had made the right call in choosing to follow him. All the more reason not to lose him. *If only I could replace one of his rosary beads with a tracking device!*

The priest eventually turned down an alley in Chinatown. Using a small mirror on a thin telescoping handle, Tran was able to spot the priest as he entered the back of a Chinese restaurant. Tran waited several minutes to see if it was another move to expose a tail, but the priest did not come back out. That left one of two options; either this was his destination or he had walked out the front door and given Tran the slip. Only one way to find out.

Tran removed his hat and wig, replacing them with a beanie and yellow night tactical glasses. He pulled a gray and blue windbreaker out of his backpack and pulled it on. He walked around to the front entrance and entered the restaurant. Tran casually scanned the dining room as he waited to be seated. The priest was nowhere to be seen. *Shoot!* Tran thought about running out the door in an attempt to pick up the trail, but the priest could have gotten anywhere, even picked up a taxi or Uber and be miles away by now. He gave the sparsely-filled dining room one last scan to no avail. *Wait. Could there be a private room?* Many restaurants had them and if the priest was associated with some bad actors, a private dining room would be the better option for a meet. A sign indicating restrooms stood off to one side which lead to a small hallway. Tran walked through the dining area and down the hallway that led straight back. He passed a couple of small but clean restrooms as he headed toward a door leading out back. Just before the rear entrance, there were doors on each side of the hall. Both were open. On his left was a storeroom separating the hall from the kitchen where he saw a young Chinese male washing dishes. In the room on the right was a private dining room. The priest was standing before a table where two well-dressed men were seated. One was a fit, thirty-something Asian man in a navy blue blazer with an open collared white shirt and khaki trousers. The other was a stout, middle-aged man with brown slicked back hair, a tanned face, and wearing a gray silk suit with red tie and matching pocket square. Tran immediately turned left into the storeroom acting like he meant to be there.

    He pulled out his cell phone and acted like he was studying it as he approached the kitchen. He began to speak in Vietnamese which got the dishwasher's confused attention. Tran switched to a heavily accented broken English.

    "Where Union Station?" he asked in a loud voice.

    The dishwasher tried to give directions, but Tran feigned confusion. The dishwasher gave up and decided to show him. Tran activated his phone's video camera as he followed the dishwasher to the back door. He pretended to be looking at his phone as if looking at a map while he zoomed the camera and got a few seconds of video of the two businessmen and the priest. Once out in the alley, he nodded understanding to the dishwasher and headed off. He walked down the alley and found a spot where he could discreetly monitor the restaurant's rear entrance. Tran removed the windbreaker and changed back into his wig and hat. He then settled in to wait.

Once he was situated, he opened up his phone and went through each video he had shot until he found good images of each person of interest between the church and the restaurant. He took screen shots of each and texted them to Jade. She answered back immediately.

It might take a while. I've only got our two laptops and the coffee shop's Wi-Fi is slow. I don't know who the priest is but that's Liu Fan sitting at the table. I've seen the other guy but can't place him. Director Snyder is obvious. Not sure who the cute guy in the suit is. The last one is your friend from last night. I have more information on him. His name is Johnny Chang. A Chinese national who works for Liu as an enforcer. Oh, you already know that.

Tran typed a quick response while keeping a watchful eye on the alley.

So we have our confirmation that Liu is involved. We need to figure out who the other guy at the table is. Priest is probably the Lieutenant under Liu who runs the enforcers. The other guy is the priority. After him should be the young guy in the suit.

Jade responded with a thumbs up emoji.

How's the other project going? Tran texted.

Slow, she answered. *Like this Wi-Fi___33!*

You need to move to another location anyway, Tran typed. *I know you have a VPN running but we are up against pros. There's a 24hr Starbuck's over at GWU.*

Too far and I'm too busy, Jade wrote back. *Can't stop now. I'll be fine. I have a tripwire set up. If anyone tries to penetrate VPN, I'll know. Now let me work!*

The back door opened, and the priest walked out. Tran turned off his phone and tried to blend in amongst the darkness of the trash bags he was nestled between. He had even placed one on his legs for better concealment. The cleanest one he could find. Tran watched as the priest quickly disappeared around the corner. He had already determined that following after him would be less fruitful than the two bigger fish still inside. Of the two, the unknown man in the silk suit was the one he was interested in. Jade had identified Liu Fan. If the mystery man could establish a provable link between Liu Fan and Fowler's party, then they had something they could work on. The reality was that the guy could simply be an organized crime VIP or even just a drinking buddy of Liu Fan's; however, if he was a political player, then he was the one Tran needed to have a chat with, which gave Tran an idea.

Two vehicles were parked in tandem just down the alley from the restaurant. One was a black Mercedes D-class SUV and the other a royal blue late model Corvette Stingray. He had no way of knowing for certain whether or not the vehicles belonged to Liu Fan and his dapper friend, but they certainly didn't belong to the kitchen staff. He looked around. It didn't appear that anyone was around. Tran reached into a side pocket on his backpack and pulled out two tracking chips of which he had glued on magnets. He stood, slung on his backpack, and casually walked toward the cars like he was simply on his way home and cutting through the alley. He passed the Mercedes first, glanced around and quickly bent down and stuck a chip to the frame underneath the luxury SUV. He did the same thing with the Corvette, making sure to note which chip he had placed on each vehicle. He snapped pictures of each car's license plate and then hurried back to the pile of trash bags where he resumed his position of concealment. He sent the license plate pictures to Jade and also informed her which car each chip was on. The hunted was now the hunter.

Chapter 63

The White House

"Did the game start yet?" First Lady Maria Galan asked from their bedroom.

"No, mi amor," President Galan answered from the adjacent sitting room, "but it's about to. The Padres just took the field."

The San Diego Padres were hosting the Colorado Rockies for the final regular season game. A little over a month ago, they had been five games out of first, but a late season surge had brought them to even with the Arizona Diamondbacks. The Diamondbacks had already beaten the Dodgers in an afternoon game in Los Angeles. If the Padres won tonight, it would force a playoff game with the Diamondbacks. If they lost, well that would put the exclamation point on what had been a lousy day for the president.

The media had erupted in a firestorm after his noon press conference. That was to be expected. The weight of the explosion still hung heavy over him. Despite the allegations, he had had nothing to do with it and he certainly had no relations with the Gulf Cartel, or any cartel for that matter. The simple fact was someone was behind all of this, and the goal was the complete dismantling of Galan's presidency during the final weeks leading up to the election. Real people were being killed. Families were experiencing the pain of their lives being turned upside down and all to make Galan look bad. To make matters worse, it seemed as if no forward progress had been made in the investigations. True, it had only been five days since this incident began and investigations of this magnitude could take years; however, the election was now only a month away and, barring a miracle, his presidency would not see a second term.

Unlike most politicians, Galan wasn't after a second term for the sake of political legacy. He would be just as happy to retire back to San Diego and live a quiet life away from politics in a modest home near the beach on Coronado. The problem was, he couldn't bear the thought of handing the presidency over to the likes of Senator Fowler. The Galan administration had done some real good in its first term. Manny had long held to Ronald Reagan's professed secret of success; "Surround yourself with good people." Manny's cabinet and advisors had far surpassed all his expectations. The economy was chugging along nicely, America was back to being a net energy exporter, the work force participation rate was at an all-time high, home ownership was up, median salaries were up, the GDP was up, and inflation was low. Additionally, despite the claims of Fowler and his cronies, the war on the cartels was making real progress. The South American cartels had literally run to the hills only to watch their coca fields get plowed under and divided up amongst the locals to grow more legitimate crops. The Central American cartels were being systemically hunted down while their South American imports dried up. The Chinese kept supplying them with fentanyl and methamphetamines, but he was working on that.

If Fowler were to take over, his stated policies would reverse every gain America had made. The only things that would go up would be crime, unemployment, inflation, the national debt, and the misery index. Galan thought that should be painfully obvious, but it was extremely difficult to speak over a media that controlled the discourse while hurling one accusation after another his way; the latest being that he had sent the Gulf Cartel to blow up that building to destroy evidence.

Galan looked up as Maria entered the sitting room. She had let down her long dark hair and brushed it out. It hung over one shoulder in a manner Galan found extremely appealing. She had changed into a pair of black leggings and a Padres baseball jersey, a gift from the team that even had a number one on the back along with her name. She was just as avid a fan as her husband.

"Who's pitching?" she asked, glancing at the screen as she sat down next to her husband.

"Weathers," Galan responded as he draped his arm over her, and she snuggled in and laid her head in his lap.

"Yes!" Maria said excitedly. "I love him! He's really come into his own this season. Ninety-seven mile an hour fastball, great slider, and his change-up is deceptive. Is Lamm catching?"

"Yep," Galan smiled appreciating, not for the first time, that Maria knew the team better than he did.

"Good! I hope it's a no-hitter," she answered.

"I'll settle for a win any way we can get it. Just so long as we get to face off against the Diamondbacks tomorrow."

"Manny? Do you realize that would put your team against Fowler's team?"

"Yeah, I know," Galan said acidly. "The thing is, I don't even think he's a fan."

"I don't think so either," Maria agreed. "But you watch, if he thinks it will score him some political points, he'll suddenly become their biggest fan. I can just see him now putting on a brand-new baseball hat while wearing a suit and looking like the political dork he is, trying to relate to constituents he uses like pawns."

"Why Maria! Do I sense a bit of hostility?"

"If I wasn't a refined Christian woman, you'd hear a lot worse out of me. That man gets me so riled up, my inner Marine wants to come out. I can't stand listening to him go on about how terrible you supposedly are and watching his smug weasel face. It makes me want to reach through the screen and slap him."

Galan looked down at his wife and smiled contentedly. He caressed her hip as he thanked God for this spirited woman He had placed in his life. Maria could dazzle heads of state in a formal gown, captivate children as she read to them in her soothing voice and take his mind off the presidency just by being herself. *I definitely married up!*

Galan breathed a contented sigh and settled in for a few needed hours of pleasant diversion. The kids were both away at college; Lydia now a junior at Liberty and Tommy a freshman on the golf team at

Georgia Tech. Both seemed very content where they were and the media had, so far, been decent enough to leave them out of the spotlight, for the most part. It was strange getting used to the empty nest, which was a relative term considering their address was 1600 Pennsylvania Avenue, but it was nice just the same to have time alone with Maria.

The Rockies' lead off hitter stepped into the box and the umpire signaled for the game to begin. The big left-handed Weathers delivered his first pitch, a slider that started of outside and broke in over the plate for a called strike.

"Yes!" Maria exclaimed to Galan's amusement. "Did you see that slider!" she said with a playful punch to his thigh.

A knock came from the door leading out into the hall. Galan winced.

"No!" Maria said in exacerbation. "The game just started, Manny. Is nothing sacred?"

"Not here, Maria," Galan answered before turning toward the door and addressing their intruder in a louder voice. "Come in!"

Chief of Staff Embry opened the door and leaned his head in with an apologetic look on his face.

"Mr. President, I'm sorry to interrupt you both like this but Attorney General Jacobs is here and needs to speak with you urgently. I have him and Chief Counsel Barlow waiting in the Treaty Room."

Maria sat up. She knew Embry wouldn't interrupt her husband for a minor issue. If the Attorney General was here, her husband would have to attend to the matter.

"Very well, J.J.," Galan said. "Make your way to the Treaty Room and I'll join you in one minute."

Embry closed the door behind him as he left. Maria glanced at the door and then made a sad pouty face at her husband. Galan cupped her face gently in his hands and kissed her.

"I can only guess what this is about, but I'll try to make it quick. Hold my spot for me," Galan said as he rose to leave.

"I'll be right here," Maria said as she pulled a blanket down from the back of the sofa and curled up to watch the game.

The batter swung at a fastball that was low and away and turned to walk back to the dugout. Galan sighed. He was in bare feet, wearing a pair of gym shorts, and red Marine Corps t-shirt, the chest and sleeves taught over his still muscled physique. *Screw it,* he thought as he dismissed the thought of changing into more suitable attire.

Galan entered the Treaty Room and sat down behind the large table that functioned as a desk. Gathered around the other side were his chief of staff and attorney general. Additionally gathered were, Assistant Chief of Staff Martin Espinoza and White House Chief Counsel Drew Barlow. The president looked around as he sat down. He was met with several somber looks. He didn't chastise anyone for interrupting this late. He trusted his staff and appreciated the fact they were very respectful of his time. This had to be something that couldn't wait.

"Alright, whatever it is, let's hear it," he began. "Preston?"

"Mr. President, as you know, we've had a team of experts going through all the White House computers since yesterday," Jacobs began.

"And?" Galan prompted.

"Well, sir, an email was found on your secretary's computer. It was deleted but easily recovered," Jacobs hesitated. "Sir, it's not good."

"By all means, Preston, just tell me what it is," Galan with his hand gesturing for the attorney general to continue.

"Sir, it's an email which indicates an order was given from your office. An order directing CIA Director Langway to, and I quote, "sheep-dip" Lieutenant Commander Harrison, Lieutenant Commander O'Shanick and Master Chief Petty Officer Ramsey for a special mission to be run directly from the White House."

"Bravo Sierra!" Galan responded angrily. "No email like that exists because no such order was ever given. No such operation was ever conducted out of this office by me or anyone else within this administration."

"Sir, I know you," Jacobs continued. "I cannot believe any such order would ever come from you. It would be completely out of character for you."

"Thank you, Preston," Galan nodded solemnly.

"However, sir, it is my duty, as attorney general, to look into this matter and consider all evidence fairly and without bias. So please understand when I tell you I have to investigate this further."

Preston paused briefly as he saw the stern look Galan was giving him.

"We have claims by a sitting United States senator, we have corroborating emails, and we have the facts from what happened in Belize. I cannot overlook any of it and I must proceed according to the oath I swore to my office. I mean no disrespect personally or professionally, but I am forced to proceed with the premise that this may have actually happened and investigate further."

"Preston, let me ask you this; is it being taken into consideration that the email could have been planted similarly to the one found on Lieutenant Commander Harrison's laptop?"

"Yes, Mr. President, it is. Just as the possibility that you actually gave the order, and this actually happened. We have to consider all possibilities and follow the evidence to where it leads."

"I understand," Galan said resignedly. "Has anyone talked to Director Langway about this?"

"No, sir, not yet," Jacobs responded. "I wanted you to hear about it from me first. Obviously, this necessitates an expansion of the investigation, and we are seeking subpoenas to that end as we speak, but we won't speak to Director Langway until tomorrow at the earliest."

"Who else knows about this?"

"Other than the people in this room, just two of my investigators, sir."

"Good," Galan said looking around the room, "Okay, everyone, let's see to it this doesn't find its way to the press until we know, for certain, what happened. If they get so much as a whiff of this, they'll report it in such a way that, no matter how much evidence we have to the contrary, people will have already been convinced that I gave this fictitious order."

"Aye, sir," Jacobs answered.

"Have we learned anything new on the truck explosion?" Galan asked.

"We've got a team of agents on it," Jacobs replied. "The preliminary findings are the driver is suspected of having ties with the Gulf Cartel but we're a bit skeptical."

Galan's eyebrows raised with curiosity. "How's that?"

"Well, sir, for starters, we know the Gulf Cartel had nothing to do with the girls who were abducted. That was all LFG. What would they possibly have to gain unless the press narrative being circulated is true? Now I told you we are obligated to investigate that, but I don't personally believe the narrative, so we'll set that aside as a theory for the moment. Next," Jacobs pressed a remote causing a large screen display to light up with a night image of the truck's driver, "we have the driver who took great care to conceal his facial features but allowed his arms to be seen with tell-tale tattoos? That seems too easy. Either he was incredibly careless, or this was a deliberate attempt to throw us off the scent. One of the tattoos, the Santa Muerta," the screen changed to a closeup image of the driver's left forearm, "is clearly seen on his forearm here, but, if you look closely, either the ink smeared or the artist was sloppy. Those artists know they won't live long if they do shoddy work; furthermore, this particular tattoo is most commonly found on the upper arm with the grim reaper head on the deltoid. Additionally, the driver walked directly close to the surveillance camera across the street before turning up the street when a diagonal route would have been shorter. It's almost as if he knew where the camera was and made sure the tattoos were seen. All of this leads us to believe that this was a temporary tattoo intended as a false flag."

"So who is the driver and who is he working for then?" Galan asked.

"That we don't know yet, sir."

"Is there anything else we *do* know?"

"Yes, Mr. President," Jacobs hit the remote and the screen changed to a night video of the same truck and driver. "This footage was obtained from the surveillance camera of a rental company's return lot in Alexandria. As you can see, this is the same driver. The time stamp puts this within the timeframe of when it would have arrived at the building in Charlotte plus one hour."

"Which means, they loaded the thing somewhere between Alexandria and Charlotte without going too far off the beaten path," Galan surmised.

"Precisely, sir," Jacobs nodded. "It also means, that the explosives had already been premixed in their barrels and ready to load.

We checked around, there were no recent purchases of the materials needed to create the explosive agent which means the people in question have likely been sitting on it for a while in a warehouse or barn somewhere."

"I would agree, but the possibilities are nearly endless between Alexandria and Charlotte," Galan commented.

"That's true, sir, but we caught a break," Jacobs said as he advanced the display showing a map of I-95 with an exit circled. "Traffic camera caught the truck in question heading west on Courthouse Road. Less than an hour later, another camera caught him getting back on the interstate," Jacobs clicked the remote showing the truck approaching the traffic camera followed by another image of the truck heading down the on-ramp. "The time of this photo was approximately five and a half hours before the time of the explosion, sir. We are certain this is the area they loaded up the truck."

"Do we have any idea where exactly this may have occurred?"

"We have a few ideas, sir," Jacobs answered. "Fortunately, the radius the truck had to work within does not contain many industrial facilities or warehouses; a few storage units but those are highly unlikely for this kind of operation. There are several farms within the area of which they could have used to store, mix, and load the explosives. We ran through the county records of ownership, and one stands out."

Jacobs changed the images to a satellite view of a large farm with several large fields surrounding a large pond. The farm was set well back from the road and surrounded by dense woods on all sides. A large metal barn sat in the center of the property.

"This is a ninety-acre apple and peach orchard, one of many owned by Quisenberry Farms, a commercial produce corporation. About eight years ago, they were acquired by Pacific Jasmine Imports, a subsidiary company of a shell corporation known to belong to Liu Shunyuan and his son Liu Fan."

"The Liu Dynasty," Galan noted. Embry could see the wheels turning inside his bosses head as the dots were connecting.

"Indeed, sir," Jacobs nodded.

"Well, that would make sense. Just about every major mobster and crook in this country is in bed with that outfit, including our opposition party and the cartels. Talk about an unholy alliance. So you think the Liu's are behind the truck bombing?"

"It's an educated guess at this time, sir, but we certainly have a strong suspicion."

"Is there any chance our driver got off at that exit to throw us another false flag to make us look in the wrong place?"

"That's certainly a possibility, sir, but the known timestamps make it reasonably unlikely."

"Then it sounds like somebody needs to go down there and conduct a search of the grounds," Galan said phrasing his order in the form of a suggestion.

"I have two attorneys seeking a late-night warrant as we speak, sir," Jacobs answered with a slight grin.

"If we can firm this up and connect Liu with the truck bombing, then the question becomes, who were they working for and why," Galan thought aloud to the assembled group.

"I have to keep an open mind for the purpose of this investigation, Mr. President, but based on known associations, I think that answer is obvious," Jacobs responded.

"I'm assuming, Snyder's agents will be the principal investigators on this one?" Galan asked.

"Yes, sir, it falls within their purview."

"Understood, but I want you to send some people you trust down there to observe the investigation and do a little poking around of their own. We can't afford to be outflanked on this one, Preston."

"Aye, sir."

"Outstanding, Preston. This might just be the break we need to crack this nut. J.J.?" Galan said to his chief of staff. "Set up a time for Preston to meet with us in the morning for an update."

"Yes, sir," Embry nodded as he turned to his iPad to schedule a time.

"Drew, I'll need you in there as well."

"Of course, sir," Barlow answered.

"Is there anything else we need to discuss tonight?" Galan asked looking around the room. He was met with a series of shaking heads.

"Very well," Galan said as he rose from his chair. "If you'll excuse me, I have a baseball game to get back to. Good night, all, and thank you."

A chorus of good nights echoed behind him as President Galan headed for the door. He walked a little lighter than when he had entered a half hour ago. Now if his Padres could just pull off the win.

Just as he reached the door, he heard Chief of Staff Embry mutter a curse aloud.

"Mr. President, you're going to want to see this."

The concern in Embry's voice caused Galan to pause in the doorway. He hesitated before turning around. The meeting had ended on a good note. All he wanted to do was relax with Maria in private while they watched the ballgame. Was that too much to ask? Galan sighed, his right leg drew a letter J behind his left leg, and he conducted a perfectly executed about face.

"What is it, J.J.?" He asked.

"We've had another leak, sir," Embry said pointing to his phone.

He grabbed a remote off the table and turned on a flatscreen TV. It came on immediately to one of the major news networks. The bold letters at the bottom of the screen said it all.

New email reveals President Galan ordered CIA to use Navy SEALs to hunt down Senator Fowler.

It never ends, Galan thought to himself as he walked back in.

Chapter 64

McLean, Virginia

As a special warfare operator, Tran was well trained in waiting for hours if not days while conducting a recon or waiting to ambush an enemy. A little trick he learned to keep himself mentally focused was to play mental games while studying the objective. While watching the Mercedes D-class SUV and the Corvette, Tran performed a mental workout to predict who owned each vehicle. He ended up going with the Corvette for the middle-aged man, whom Jade had just texted him was, Sal La Rosa, the former mafia underboss and now shadowy assistant to his party's director. La Rosa was the kind of guy who liked power, money, and women in that order; however, Tran theorized, La Rosa was likely experiencing his mid-life crisis and, as such, attempted to assuage his age insecurities with younger women. In order to do so, he would have decided that fancy jewelry and sports cars would be the way to go.

Tran's theorizing had proven correct. When La Rosa left the restaurant, he wedged himself into the sleek sports car and sped off through the alley. The tracking chip did its job and allowed Tran to trail him from a distance. The trail led to a secluded neighborhood in McLean, Virginia that not only had a gated entrance but two Secret Service Suburbans out front with agents and bomb sniffing canines. Jade, who was following along, informed him it was Senator Fowler's neighborhood. There was no way he was going to tip his hat by trying to follow La Rosa in there, so Tran motored on down the road and found his way out to a main drag. He topped off his fuel at a gas station, got a large coffee, and kept a watch on La Rosa's tracker while he sat at an indoor table and charged his phone. His phone vibrated an incoming text from Jade.

Got a match on the priest. Father Patrick Santos. Ordained Catholic priest who did his seminary in the Philippines. He really is a priest but he's in the CIA data base for having suspected ties to the Liu Dynasty. Word is he recruits agents through blackmail and cash while running a group of enforcers. His face matches a former MMA fighter from China by the name of Jin Feng but this has never been confirmed.

Tran knew immediately that Father Patrick was also Jin Feng. The priest he had seen was a warrior and had the battle scars and cauliflower ear of someone who had spent significant time in the octagon. He was most definitely a person of interest. He would know who the traitors were and where the bodies were buried. Tran debated whether or not to break off La Rosa's trail and go after Jin Feng. He quickly decided against it for now. La Rosa could be the key link between Fowler and the Liu Dynasty. The question was, what were they doing and how could they prove it?

Can you send me his address? Can you track his cell phone? Tran typed and hit the send button.

Are priests allowed to have cellphones? LOL! I'll get on it. Was Jade's reply.

Tran checked and saw La Rosa was still at Fowler's residence. There would be no getting in there. Maybe he could get La Rosa home alone but that would be risky. La Rosa was a former underboss for *La Cosa Nostra.* Not exactly special warfare but he was no pushover either. A guy like that was street tough and would have no problem putting a bullet in someone's head and disposing of the body. Hitting him in his home should be at least a two-man job and not without breaking several serious laws. Tran sent off another text.

While you're at it, I also need La Rosa's address and who all lives with him.

As Tran waited for Jade's reply, he realized how much he missed his team. In many ways, he was an introvert, but there was a connection with his fellow special warfare operators that transcended that.

Being a vital part of even an eight-man squad and the synergy of the combined parts led them to accomplish amazing things and pull off highly complex and dangerous operations. He could sure use some of that now.

The priest is staying in the rectory at the church in Chinatown. La Rosa apparently lives alone on a golf course near Tysons, Virginia. I'm pinging you the addresses.

Tran looked at the addresses on his phone's map app using the satellite view mode. La Rosa lived in a modest home on a shaded lot with a swimming pool and hot tub. A row of hedges separated his back yard from the golf course. Looking at the layout, Tran got an idea.

Chapter 65

Tysons, Virginia

"This town is an alright town,
For an uptight town like a-this town.
This town, it's a use you town,
An abuse you town until you're downtown."

La Rosa sang along happily to Sinatra's big band hit as he sped the late-model Corvette down his quiet residential street. He kept time with the band by tapping his diamond pinky ring on the gear shift. He was in a good mood. Liu Fan had destroyed the last bit of evidence against Fowler while pinning the explosion on Galan. Their White House mole had succeeded in planting evidence on the Galan's secretary's computer, the polls were now heavily in Fowler's favor, and Galan was in full retreat. At this point, Galan wouldn't stand a chance even if the election were completely fair and honest, which it wouldn't be. They had a well-funded army of non-profits working overtime to pack the voter rolls and stuff the ballot boxes. With the amount of money he stood to make by masterminding Fowler's victory, La Rosa would be able to retire to any corner of the globe and live quite comfortably with a different shade of blond each night. He had demanded a tripling of his fee if he could successfully resurrect Fowler's campaign after the impulsive fool's colossal blunder in Belize. Less than a week later, all the pieces were in place. Truth be told, La Rosa knew he wasn't going to retire just yet. As alluring as the money and promised hedonistic adventures were, he was addicted to power. Being a mafia underboss had nothing on the type of power he now wielded on the worldwide stage. Even Fowler, the philandering sot, was scared of him and knew he owed his freedom and impending presidency to La Rosa. J. Paul Jeffries was the titular head of their party, but La Rosa was running the show and that would soon include the presidency. Life was good.

His house suddenly appeared, and he abruptly cranked the wheel, turning into his driveway at a high speed. He quickly braked to a stop and found himself at an angle too awkward to pull into the car's garage bay. *Screw it,* he thought as he shut the car off and opened the door. He had capped off the productive day with a little "recreation" at Fowler's palatial estate. Fowler had learned his lesson and, rather than travel to feed his sexual urges, was having women provided for him every night his wife was out of town, which was becoming more frequent as of late.

Cassandra was still eye candy for the male voters, and she played the part of adoring wife quite well publicly, even to the point of charming all the daytime TV talk show hosts, but behind closed doors, she and Fowler detested each other. Their marriage had been a sham from the beginning. Cassandra was a classic gold digger and the widowed Fowler had fallen for her supermodel looks and tight cheerleader body. Even a twice-divorced man like La Rosa knew it was not a marriage that stood a chance.

La Rosa struggled to get out of the low to the ground Corvette. His aging knees burned in protest as he tried to push himself up to a standing position. The seven extra dry Bombay Sapphire martinis he had consumed this evening weren't helping. He conceded to his inability and rolled out onto his hands and knees. Using the door and the seat he managed to push himself up to a shaky stand. He steadied himself as best he could, closed the door, and staggered toward his front door. After fumbling with his keys, he pushed the door open, and entered the foyer to the beeping of his alarm system. It took him two tries to push the buttons correctly to disarm and then rearm the system. Using the walls for support, La Rosa made his way to his master bedroom which, thankfully, was on the main floor. He tossed his jacket onto a chaise lounge chair, pulled off his tie and, with difficulty, unbuttoned and removed his shirt. He had to sit down on the bed to keep from falling over as he removed his shoes and trousers. Thoroughly exhausted from the task, he crawled onto his bed, collapsed face down, and was asleep within a minute.

Tran sat in a dark corner of La Rosa's nearby study and waited. La Rosa was already loudly snoring, but Tran gave him a few more minutes to ensure he was fully asleep. Satisfied, Tran cautiously crept towards the bedroom while holding his handgun at the high ready position. As he neared the door, he saw La Rosa, clad in white boxer shorts and matching t-shirt, sprawled face down on his king-sized bed. Tran snuck up and carefully worked a large zip tie around La Rosa's ankles, being careful not to wake him as he slowly pulled it tight. He then gently pulled the stout man's wrists behind his back and quickly cinched them tight with another zip tie.

La Rosa's arms tensed as he woke up and, in a state of alarmed confusion, let out a string of expletives. Tran straddled La Rosa's thighs rendering him unable to effectively move in his prone state while he continued to alternate curses and threats at his unknown assailant. Tran reached into a cargo pocket on his black tactical pants and removed a syringe full of Lorazepam he had purchased from a street dealer before riding over to La Rosa's house. He pulled the waist band of La Rosa's boxer shorts down, pulled the cap off the syringe with his teeth, jabbed the needle into La Rosa's buttocks and injected the sedative.

"Who are you?!" La Rosa angrily yelled as he tried to pick his head up and look behind him. "I will kill you! Do you hear me? I will gouge out your eyes and kill you, you mother…"

Tran struck the top of La Rosa's head with the butt of his gun. It wasn't enough to seriously harm him, but it was enough to stun him into a brief silence.

"Shut your mouth and listen," Tran said effecting a Vietnamese accent that was familiar to him.

A guy like La Rosa wouldn't be able to distinguish a Vietnamese accent from that of someone who spoke Mandarin. Tran also wore a pair of tactical gloves and a balaclava to protect his identity. He could tell La Rosa was inebriated by how he stumbled into the house. Between the alcohol and the Lorazepam, his inhibitions would soon be sufficiently low enough that Tran would likely be able to get him to talk without using too much persuasion. Before that time, Tran wanted to ensure La Rosa's only recollection would be of an angry Chinese national grilling him for information about the Liu Dynasty.

"I know about your association with Liu Fan. Tell me what was discussed at your meeting tonight," Tran said in a calm voice.

"I'm not telling you sh…"

La Rosa was again interrupted with another sharp rap to his head from Tran's gun.

"We're going to try this again, Sal. What were you discussing with Liu fan this evening?"

"And I'm gonna tell you again, you chooch, I'm not telling you sh…"

Tran pounced onto La Rosa's back and applied a rear choke hold until La Rosa went unconscious. Tran then dragged the former mobster turned political bag man into his opulent bathroom where he hefted him into the large jacuzzi tub, closed the drain, and turned on the water. Tran turned La Rosa onto his stomach and then kneeled on his back, holding the man's head up as the water began to fill the tub. La Rosa came to while the water was running. He tried to struggle but couldn't amount any strength with his hands and ankles secured. Tran waited until the water reached La Rosa's chin and shut off the faucet.

"You awake, Sally?" Tran asked. "Good! How would you like to, how does Clemenza say it in *The Godfather*, 'sleep with the fishes?' Do you understand what I mean?"

La Rosa, slightly more somnolent now, simply nodded.

"Yes, you know what I mean, don't you? I like that movie. I learn to speak English watching American movies. That's one of my favorites although you Italians know nothing about real gangsters. But you know that now, don't you, Sal? Yeah, that's why you left *La Cosa Nostra* to play in the big leagues. Isn't that right, Sal? The Triads, yes? You friends with Liu Fan now? Well Liu Fan is a hun dan who will soon sleep with the fishes himself. Now, I'm a reasonable guy so I'm gonna make you an offer you can't refuse. You tell me what your relationship is with Liu Fan and I let you live. If not, I make you sleep with the fishes. Okay, Sal? That's all I ask for.

With his eyes closed, La Rosa gave a barely perceptible nod.

"That's better," Tran said still using a heavy Vietnamese accent. "Now tell me what you were discussing with Liu Fan tonight."

"We were just talking about the explosion in Charlotte is all," La Rosa replied.

"I don't believe you!" Tran said as he shoved La Rosa's head down into the water.

With his arms bound behind him, La Rosa had no leverage to put up any kind of a struggle. Tran counted off thirty seconds and pulled his head up by his hair.

"Now try again!" Tran ordered.

"That was it!" La Rosa said breathlessly but awake. "We was talking about the explosion and the election. I swear!"

"Not only do I not believe you, but I don't care!" Tran said plunging the man's head back under the water. After another thirty seconds, he pulled him back up. "I don't care about the election. I don't care about Galan. I know you fix election. I don't care. I know you work for party and for Fowler. I want to know what arrangement you make with Liu Triad."

"Arrangement? What are you…"

Tran immediately shoved La Rosa back under the water. He was determined to convince La Rosa that the information he was looking for had nothing to do with the election and everything to do with getting an edge on the Liu Dynasty. When La Rosa woke up the next morning he would vaguely remember being grilled by a member of an opposing Chinese triad but have no recollection that he had given out vital information on the operation he and Liu Fan were conducting to get Fowler elected. Tran would first break him into talking about the Liu Dynasty and, only later, extract the information he was really after. Tran pulled La Rosa back out of the water. La Rosa coughed and gagged for a solid minute before he was able to catch his breath.

"Alright! Alright! What do you want to know?" he gasped.

"Start with what favors the Fowler administration is going to arrange for Liu Dynasty. I know they allow drug shipments. What ports?

How do they arrive? How do they get through inspections? Let's start with that, Sal."

An hour later, Tran left La Rosa lying in his now empty jacuzzi, arms unbound and snoring. He climbed up into the attic and pulled the ceiling door up behind him. Tran carefully stepped across the exposed floor joists and pulled himself up to the open area in the gable and climbed out. He pulled himself up onto the roof and then leaned over to replace the vinyl gable vent he had pried out earlier. There was no way to secure it, but it would pass inspection for the time being. Tran then grabbed ahold of the tree limb growing over the roof and climbed down to the ground.

You really need to do something about those limbs, Sal, Tran thought to himself as he began to jog down the cart path with a head full of useful information.

Chapter 66

Washington, D.C.

It was late. The coffee shop was nearly deserted. A young couple sat up front engrossed in their studies, with open laptops and open books, while Jade sat towards the back, close to the restrooms and the back door. Tran had insisted on her having an escape plan for any place she conducted her work.

"If anyone looks at you twice or with too much interest, pack your gear and slip out the back door," he had told her several times.

Jade had both laptops open and connected to the shop's Wi-Fi via secure VPN's. The VPN's offered her anonymity even while using a public system. They weren't foolproof but it was the best she could do under the circumstances. Only the most talented hackers would be able to defeat a VPN to locate her. Jade was typing furiously when her new iPhone vibrated.

Mission accomplished. On my way back.

Jade selected a thumbs up emoji and sent it. She passively wondered what all Tran had done to get the information out of La Rosa while she continued to type. A guy like him wouldn't just volunteer that kind of information. Tran was a kind and gentle man. He was very patient and caring with her, which was no easy task. Jade knew she had personality quirks and even some OCD traits - she was working on them, but it remained a struggle - but Tran seemed to take it all in stride as part of the package. He was a protector and would never lift a hand toward an innocent person; however, Jade knew there was also a dangerous side to Tran. Just like his teammates, he was highly intelligent, physically gifted and well trained. He could flip a switch and become a ruthless and lethal special warfare operator who could rain down death and destruction on any enemy regardless of the circumstances or odds against him. *Find a way to win.* Jade heard that spoken many times by Tran and his teammates. She knew that enduring attitude had been drilled into them relentlessly throughout BUD/S and was nearly a mantra throughout the teams. Tran would find a way to win. She would too. A lot was riding on her computer skills.

Jade glanced at Joe's laptop where a program was running facial recognition of "the cute guy" through a suspected terrorist database. The criminal database had come up empty. The man was well dressed and had facial features and skin tone that appeared Mediterranean or Middle Eastern prompting her to run him through the terrorist database. The screen was showing no matches. She changed the database to look through federal background checks. If he worked in Washington or had access to anyone of importance, he would likely have had to pass some kind of background check. It was worth a shot. Jade loaded the parameters and clicked on the icon to begin the search.

She took a sip of her lukewarm coffee and resumed her main project. If there was such a thing as a cyber shredding machine, Joe's video had been run through it to the point of being tiny pieces of code scattered throughout the realm of cyberspace. Whoever erased it did not want it found, ever; nevertheless, Jade had modified one of her programs to locate even the tiniest bits of information that contained code unique to Joe's video. Her nickname for the program was "Bloodhound" as it functioned similarly to giving the popular tracking dogs a piece of a suspect's clothing to get a scent and then turning them loose to follow the trail. As the bits of code returned, Jade would link the code together similar to a jigsaw puzzle. A highly complex 3D jigsaw puzzle with no box top to refer to, but that didn't matter. Jade's mind was capable of scanning through megabytes of code and spotting the trends which allowed her to link the pieces of code up with their respective mates. Now that she knew Tran was safe and, on his way back, she was able to concentrate more on this Herculean effort, which she was actually enjoying. She was nearly done, basically down to that last piece that completed the puzzle.

And there it is! Jade excitedly formatted the video and opened it in a video player. She watched in silence as the events Tran had relayed to her unfolded before her. The video was still playing after ten minutes but Jade, uncharacteristically shocked from what she had seen, was convinced she had everything they would need to bring to light what actually occurred down in Belize, and much more. Fowler had done some bragging. What this video contained was downright damning.

Her next order of business was to make backups. Somebody went to great lengths to eliminate this video. They weren't about to let it get out now. Jade sent copies to a couple of clouds and then inserted a thumb drive and burned a copy on that. While waiting for the transfer to complete, she glanced over at Tran's laptop and was surprised to see her search had already generated a hit. She clicked on the link. The photos were a perfect match and her software agreed with 98% certainty. As Jade removed the thumb drive, her jaw dropped when she read the man's biographical data.

"Excuse me, please?"

Jade looked up to see the smiling face of a slender young Asian woman standing in front of her. She had long lustrous hair pulled back loosely behind her. She was wearing black leggings and a gray Georgetown Hoyas sweatshirt. Jade recognized her as one of the students from the table at the front of the shop.

"Yes?" Jade asked.

"Coffee shop close. Where another shop open?" the student asked in broken English.

"I'm not sure," Jade replied with shake of her head.

The woman's face changed to a look of disappointment and her shoulders sagged in response.

Jade fought an urge of compassion. She needed to stay on task, but she couldn't ignore the person in front of her. She had a few minutes before Tran would arrive. She wrestled with her thoughts and reminded herself she was working on Jade 2.0. She minimized the screens she was working on and opened up a search engine.

"But let's see if we can find one," Jade said with a gentle smile.

"Oh, thank you!" The young woman said with her face lighting up. "We still learn area. Much study to do. Thank you!"

"I'm happy to help," Jade responded. "I know what it's like."

"Bai!" The woman called to her male friend and waved him over.

The young Asian male walked over and the couple stood behind Jade as she pulled up a list of open coffee shops within walking distance. Suddenly, the barrel of a gun pressed into the back of her neck. Jade's eyes went wide in response. She desperately looked around the shop but there was no one else in sight.

Chapter 67

Washington, D.C.

Tran looked through the large glass windows into the empty coffee shop. The lights were out, save for the dim glow of an exit sign by the restrooms. He tried the door anyway, but it was locked. He immediately sensed something was wrong. It wasn't like Jade not to tell him where she was going. He immediately turned and headed across the street and around the corner. Tran changed out his sweatshirt and donned the wig and hat as he worked his way to an alley that led back to the street the now closed coffee shop was on. He took up position at the alley's entrance which allowed him to monitor the front of the coffee shop. If someone had snatched Jade, they would likely have gone through her cellphone and seen he was heading back. They might be waiting to ambush him. It was a long shot. They likely would have made their move when Tran had first show up. Regardless, Tran needed to plan his next move and he may as well do it here where he might be able to pick up a trail or, better yet, someone else he could question.

He pulled out his phone and opened up his tracking app. Jade's cellphone was rapidly moving south towards Alexandria, confirming she had been snatched. La Rosa's Corvette was still at his home. Not that it mattered. Tran had gotten what he needed from him. Liu Fan's tracker was stationary in Georgetown while Chang's Toyota appeared to also be heading back down towards Alexandria paired up with Jade's cellphone; however, Tran had had Jade place another tracking chip in her brassiere and *that one* was just few blocks away and not moving. They very well could have stripped her making it a dead end, but it was the best place to look first.

Tran powered off his phone and removed the SIM card. The element of surprise was about his only ally right now and he wasn't about to give that up if they were using Jade's phone to track him. He rose and began to pick his way through the shadows until he was standing across the street and down the road from a grey townhouse on O Street, just north of Logan Circle. A couple of bored-looking young Asian men stood guarding the main entrance to the townhouse. Somebody or something important was inside. He hoped it was Jade. He was certain he could get close enough to those guys and, using the element of surprise, take them both out but, there was no way he would be able to get through the front door without waking up the entire neighborhood and bringing the police down on them.

Tran memorized the cars parked in the street and walked down to the corner of O and 13th streets. He looked up at the last townhouse's brick exterior and, seeing plenty of handholds, began to climb. Within a minute, he reached the top of the three-story structure and swung himself over the roof parapet. All of the buildings were connected on this block, making for an easy traverse back to the townhouse where he hoped Jade was being held. He took his time, staying low and keeping to the edge of the building where the parapets provided some cover. Counting off the townhouses, he was certain he was one building away from his target. Tran carefully peered over the edge and spotted the cars he memorized to confirm his position. He looked to the roof of his target and didn't see anyone up top keeping watch; nevertheless, he approached cautiously, just in case. As he neared, a slight orange glow caught his eye. It briefly intensified for a few seconds and then dulled. It appeared to be the glow from a cigarette from the far side of the roof access door, but Tran was at the wrong angle to see for sure. He heard no talking and hoped that meant only one person was up on the roof. Tran crept slowly along the parapet separating the two buildings until he had enough angle to see the poorly-disciplined individual who was careless enough to be smoking while keeping watch. It was a single male. It was too dark to see his facial features or whether or not he was armed. Tran crept back the way he had come until the access-way, once again, stood between him and the watch-stander.

Tran hunkered down behind the parapet and removed his backpack. He traded out his wig and hat for a balaclava and a handful of zip ties. He stuffed the zip ties in his pocket, donned the balaclava, and slipped his backpack back on. He vaulted the parapet and, with his 9mm Smith and Wesson at the ready, began to stealthily approach the access-way. He reached the access-way and quietly turned the corner with his gun aimed. Tran's motion caught the young Asian male's attention causing him to curse in Mandarin. At least Tran assumed it was a curse. Tran held his finger to his lips, while pointing his gun at the young man's head, who quickly got the message and clammed up. Tran had no intention of pulling the trigger and compromising this op but the young male in front of him didn't know that. Tran hoped the man would confuse him with a rival gang member who was as likely to shoot him as he would toss him off the building.

"On the ground, hands behind your back," Tran ordered using his heavily accented voice once again.

The man complied and Tran quickly secured him with zip ties. He searched him and found a Glock 19 handgun in the man's waistband. Tran quickly field stripped it and tossed the barrel off the roof. He then cut off a length of the man's shirt and shoved it into his mouth. As a final measure of security, Tran rolled him onto a nearby wood pallet and secured him to the boards with another zip tie. That was the easy part. Now Tran would have to enter the building and secure each floor while he looked for Jade. The layout of the building was unknown, the number of armed combatants was unknown, and Jade's location was unknown. *The only easy day was yesterday.*

Chapter 68

Washington, D.C.

The top floor had turned out to be empty. There were two rooms that appeared to be used for cutting and packaging drugs but there was no sign of any person when Tran had cleared them. Similarly, the middle floor had two rooms with unmade beds but no one around. Both rooms were littered with discarded condoms and used syringes overflowing out of trash cans. Tran quietly worked his way down to the main level. Muffled voices could be heard but Tran was pretty sure they were coming up from the basement. First, he had to clear the main floor which was quiet. Too quiet. Tran focused, listening for even the slightest sound that suggested human presence. Nothing. He mentally visualized what he suspected the main floor layout would be like. The townhouse was similar to Jade's in that it was long and narrow, but it lacked a garage. That meant there were likely rooms fore and aft with a kitchen in the middle. He could tell the stairs ended amidship, likely by the kitchen. The wall opened up on the lower half of the stairs which would leave him exposed if anyone was watching.

Tran cautiously leaned down peering through the wall opening. He could see into the kitchen and the narrow hall running fore and aft but didn't see a soul. He quietly moved to the bottom of the stairs, his handgun out and aimed. He turned toward the back and snuck upon the wall until the room opened up. Tran sprung around the corner; weapon aimed looking for a target. Nothing. He turned and crept down the hall toward the front room. Using the same technique, he hooked left around the corner, weapon up, ready to engage. This time there were two targets, both young Asian males clad in black jeans and hooded sweatshirts looking at their smartphones. Both sat on a couch facing the front and instantly reacted when Tran entered the room. The larger male immediately grabbed his handgun laying on the coffee table before him.

"Don't do it!" Tran warned.

The man continued, bringing his gun up toward Tran who reflexively fired two rounds into the man's forehead. He shifted his aim to the smaller man who had reached behind him and was bringing a handgun forward towards Tran. Tran fired another double tap, dropping the second man with a spray of pink brain matter.

It's on now, Tran thought as took up position behind a well-worn recliner and ducked down, aiming for the door. The two sentries, who were posted outside, burst through the door, brandishing handguns.

"Drop your weapons!" Tran ordered keeping his Vietnamese accent.

The first one through the door fired several times quickly in Tran's direction. The shots went high but Tran returned fire, striking the man in the chest center mass with two shots followed by one to the head. He collapsed at his stunned partner's feet.

"Drop it or you're next!" Tran yelled.

The man complied, dropping his handgun and raising his hands.

"On the floor! Face first, hands behind your head!" Tran commanded.

The man got down as ordered. Tran kneeled on his back and quickly secured his hands behind his back with a zip tie.

"Where's the girl?" Tran asked.

"What girl?" the young man asked with a mandarin accent.

"Wrong answer!" Tran said smashing the butt of his handgun down on the man's jaw.

The crunch of bone and teeth caused the man to emit a guttural scream of pain. Tran changed out magazines and then jammed his gun into the back of the man's knee.

"One last chance and the next shot goes through your knee," he said calmly. "Where's the girl?"

331

"Basement," the man grunted.

"How many are with her?"

"Just one," he answered painfully.

"I hope for your sake you're telling the truth," Tran said grabbing the man by the back of his shirt and yanking him up onto his feet. "Cuz we're about to find out."

Tran twisted the man's clasped hands into a painful position and forced him to walk while he held him closely with the barrel of the gun pressed between his shoulder blades.

"You so much as twitch wrong and you'll join your friends in Diyu," Tran warned using the mandarin word for hell.

He marched him to the basement door and down the stairs, keeping himself shielded by the man in front of him. They were greeted by an older Asian man who was pointing a handgun at them.

"Why, Mr. Truk! How good of you to join us!"

Tran looked and saw Father Patrick at the far end of the basement. No longer in his priestly garments, he wore black denim jeans with black boots and a black turtleneck. He grinned maliciously, holding a grilling fork and blow torch as he stood over Jade who was strapped to an armchair with duct tape. Jade's t-shirt had been removed. She was clad only in her leggings and brassiere. She was sobbing and hyperventilating in abject fear.

"Let her go!" Tran said forcefully. "What kind of priest are you?!

"Ah, so you know who I am! Well, that shouldn't surprise me. I'm told you SEALs are smart. I should have known you were too smart to follow your girlfriend's cellphone away from here but once I found the tracking chip you planted on her, I knew you wouldn't be long. But you can't be that smart if you really think I'll let this little flower go."

"Let her go and your friend here lives and you can have me," Tran said just as forcefully.

Father Patrick laughed. "I already have you and as for him..." Father Patrick shrugged and looked at the older man who still had his gun pointed at Tran.

"Hu," Father Patrick nodded.

The man named Hu squeezed the trigger and the man Tran was holding collapsed to the floor with the opposite side of his head missing. Hu adjusted his aim toward Tran's head and stared at him with a blank expression. Tran sized him up. Hu stood close enough that he couldn't miss if he shot but far enough away that Tran didn't stand a chance of disarming him. Tran had no play.

"Well, I guess that fixes that," Father Patrick said jovially. "No more Fu. I guess we could call him FUBAR, eh Truk?" he asked with a malicious laugh.

"Now drop your gun and sit down against the pole," Father Patrick said pointing to a metal pole near jade that supported a floor joist.

Tran looked at Hu. The man didn't flinch. Tran reluctantly placed his gun on the ground and walked over to the pole and sat down.

"Place your hands together behind the pole," Father Patrick instructed.

Tran did as he was told. Father Patrick stepped behind Tran and wrapped his wrists together with duct tape. He then walked around front and pulled a large folding knife out of his pocket. With a flick of his wrist, the knife opened and he cut Tran's backpack off his shoulders. He then cut Tran's sweatshirt down the middle followed by the t-shirt underneath, exposing Tran's bare chest. Father Patrick carried the backpack over to a nearby workbench, opened it and poured all the contents out. He reassembled Tran's smart phone and turned it on.

"What is your passcode?" he asked.

Speaking in Tagalog, Tran told him what he could do with the passcode. Father Patrick calmly nodded and then picked up the blow torch and grilling fork. He lit the blow torch and began heating up the grilling fork. Meanwhile, Tran began to wiggle as if under mental anguish but was actually sliding his hips over enough where he was able to reach his belt with his bound hands. Inside his nylon belt, he had sewn in a small pouch where he kept a handcuff key and a razor blade that was wrapped in tape. Master Chief Ramsey had insisted all his SEALs prepare their tactical belts in such a manner. Tran worked the razor blade out of the pouch and began to peel the tape off one side.

"That's okay, Mr. Truk. I didn't think you would be that easy."

The sharp tines heated up to a bright orange when Father Patrick slowly walked over and stood in front of Tran. Tran prepared himself mentally. BUD/S and, later SERE training - Survival Evasion Resistance and Escape - had taught him just how much pain and suffering he could endure. Everyone broke eventually but Tran was holding out as long as he could in hopes the police would show up. Surely someone had heard the gunshots and had called the police. They couldn't be far away. The police weren't the best option considering all that had happened over the past several days but, at this point, being found tied up in a house full of dead bodies would have to work in his favor. At least Tran hoped it would.

"One more chance," Father Patrick waved the glowing hot fork just inches from Tran's face.

Tran looked back stoically and shook his head. Father Patrick smiled sadistically as he jabbed the glowing fork into the center of Tran's chest. The sharp tines penetrated into his sternum resulting in an intense level of pain beyond anything Tran had ever experienced. Tran gritted his teeth and grunted, unable to breathe due to the near paralyzing pain. His skin sizzled and the smell of burning flesh was nauseating. After what seemed like an eternity, Father Patrick removed the fork.

"Have you rethought your answer yet, Mr. Truk?" Father Patrick asked as he reheated the fork in front of Tran's face.

Tran summoned up all the saliva in his mouth and spit in the sadistic priest's face. Father Patrick didn't even flinch. He simply nodded knowingly as he finished heating the fork and then calmly jabbed it back into Tran's chest. Rivulets of sweat ran down Tran's face as he fought to endure the searing pain being inflicted upon him. His jaw was clenched as a primal roar began to erupt from within. The agony persisted for at least half a minute before Father Patrick pulled the fork back out. He looked at Tran, sniffed the aroma of burnt flesh, and made a disgusted face.

"I never did care for Vietnamese barbecue," he said with a menacing laugh. "All I want is that code, Mr. Truk," he said as he began to reheat the grilling fork.

Tran looked back defiantly. There really wasn't much on the phone that would amount to anything. That wasn't the point. The police had to be just around the corner. Meanwhile, Tran began to work the razor blade back and forth across the several layers of duct tape.

If he could just keep the priest distracted a little longer, he they might escape this or at least be taken into custody where they would be able to take what La Rosa had divulged to the proper authorities. Of course, it could just as easily circle back into the wrong people but, at this point, if he couldn't get out of the duct tape and somehow overpower Father Patrick and his henchman, he had no other options. The pain was beyond anything he had ever endured but he resolved himself to hold out as long as it took. He continued to work the razor blade while Father Patrick finished heating up the grilling fork and held it just inches in front of Tran's eyes. He could feel the heat radiating off the red-hot glowing metal.

"How about now, Mr. Truk? Surely you've had enough."

Tran responded with another defiant gaze. His mouth was too dry to spit; otherwise, he would have. Tran gripped the razor blade tightly so he wouldn't drop it when the pain struck. He gritted his teeth in preparation for another go around only to watch Father Patrick turn and jab the fork into Jade's bare shoulder. Tran watched with horror as Jade writhed in pain. Her mouth opened into a breathless silent scream that lasted at least a dozen seconds before her breathing resumed and she led out a painful scream. Tears rolled down her face causing Tran to be overcome with shame.

"Enough!" Tran yelled. "You can have the code, just leave her alone!"

Father Patrick removed the fork and flashed an amused look at Tran.

"Aha! Chivalry is not dead!" He said while holding the fork up mockingly as if it were a sword. "The knight arrives to rescue the fair maiden as it were. Very well, Sir Truk, what beist thine code?"

"No, Tran!" Jade forced out while trying to recover. "Don't do it!"

Tran gave Jade a long look while he continued to saw through the duct tape. It was slow going and awkward, but he was making progress. He looked back at Father Patrick and sighed defeatedly.

"It's 2112."

"Tran! What are you doing?!" Jade pleaded.

Father Patrick walked over to the workbench and punched in the code. He leaned over the bench as he began to work through the phone. Tran continued to carefully work the razor blade while under the watchful eye of Hu.

"Aha!" Father Patrick exclaimed. "Got it!"

"Got what?" Tran asked.

"The video!" Father Patrick answered. "Hu, get us ready to leave, we have it!"

"What video?" Tran asked sounding genuinely confused.

"Don't play dumb with me, you bamboo monkey," Father Patrick said contemptuously. "The video your commanding officer shot of Senator Fowler. You know the video. It was emailed to you by Lieutenant Commander Harrison minutes before my men threw him off his balcony."

Tran glared back at Father Patrick. He continued to work the razor blade while, out of the corner of his eye, he saw Hu splashing a can of gasoline around and pouring it into a large garbage can full of scrap wood.

"That's right, Petty Officer Truk. He was no match for my Sea Dragons. None of you were. We tracked the email to your computer and couldn't believe our luck when you popped up over there in Chinatown. You *did* manage to elude and later kill one of my men last night. I had to dispose of him in the explosion this morning. It should have been you. I wish I could strap you to a barrel full of the same explosives and vaporize you like we had to do with our man, but alas, it is not to be. At any rate, now I have your phone, I have all the copies. You made it easy for me. Your girlfriend emailed the video to you right before we found her. I thought we were going to have to find you, but you came to us. That was very considerate of you Mr. Truk."

Tran glanced up at Jade with a confused look.

"The video was on the email you use for gaming. I sent a copy to your phone. If he hadn't been able to open it, he couldn't destroy it. That's why you shouldn't have said anything."

"Oh, I won't destroy it," Father Patrick sang out. "I'll keep it for leverage. Yes, as long as soon to be President Fowler dances to the strings of the Liu Dynasty, it will forever remain hidden from the public. You and your commanding officer have helped us out quite nicely, Mr. Truk. For that I thank you."

"So what now?" Tran asked trying to stall for time as he continued to work his razor blade through the duct tape.

"Now? Now, I'm afraid we must be on our way," Father Patrick said as he gathered several items up and put them in the backpack. "Hu, go empty the safe. I'll be right behind you."

Hu nodded and dragged himself up the stairs. Father Patrick picked up the blow torch and casually used it to light a cigarette. He took a couple of deep puffs and smiled at Tran.

"Are you even an ordained priest?" Tran asked.

"Of course I am," he proclaimed smiling. "Why would you doubt such a thing?"

"I dunno," Tran shrugged, "Maybe it has something to do with you running a kill squad, torturing people, drug running, and working for an organized crime outfit."

"We're all sinners," he said with a shrug as he turned and walked to the other side of the basement. "Some of us will go to heaven…"

Father Patrick took one last drag on his cigarette and tossed it into the garbage can full of kerosine and wood. It immediately erupted in flames that reached the ceiling. He returned to the worktable, grabbed the backpack by its handle, and casually began to walk to the stairs.

"…and some will burn in Hell," he said with his sadistic smile.

Chapter 69

Washington, D.C.

Tran stood and began to lunge forward in attempt to tear open the rest of the duct tape. Father Patrick gave him one last look, laughed, and began to climb the stairs. The room was already filling up with smoke. Tran's eyes were burning from the smoke and growing heat. He and Jade were already coughing. The flames began to spread across the ceiling as Tran desperately tried to break free. He gave a desperate lunge followed by another and another and…he tumbled forward as he finally broke free. The smoke was so thick that it began to dim the light in the basement. Tran rolled to his feet and searched the workshop table until he found a utility knife. He went to work on Jade's bound wrists and then her ankles. The heat was oppressing and nearly unbearable. He grabbed Jade's wrist and pulled her down onto the floor.

"Stay low and follow me!" he said as he led her through the smoke toward the stairs.

Along the way, he found his gun still lying on the floor where he had been forced to drop it. Tran grabbed it in his gloved hand and kept moving. The flames were already consuming the wall separating the stairwell from the basement. The smoke was channeling up the stairs and so thick he couldn't see the top, but it appeared to be free of flames for the moment.

"Jade," Tran said grabbing her wrist and shouting into her ear, "we need to take a breath and move up those stairs now! Are you ready?"

Jade took a breath and immediately began to cough. She gulped a little more air and forced herself to hold her breath. She looked at Tran and nodded. Together they rose and began to run up the stairs. The rising smoke and heat engulfed them as they raced up through the stairwell which was a gauntlet of heat and smoke. Flames began to bend around the wall and into the stairwell. Tran leaned into the far wall and kept going with Jade right behind him.

They burst onto the main floor and turned for the front entrance only to see the floor in front of them collapse into the basement. The sudden access to new oxygen caused the flames to shoot up in front of them, reaching to the ceiling. Tran pivoted a one-eighty and, shifting from Jade's wrist to her upper arm, began leading her toward the back door, when a dark figure leapt at him from the stairs leading to the second floor. The two collapsed to the hallway floor, bodies intertwined and tumbling. Tran's gun skittered across the floor and out of reach. He wrapped his legs around his assailant's midsection and began to squeeze while he worked his way up into a choke hold. The assailant delivered a forearm to Tran's face and then grabbed Tran's head and violently twisted it in a counter maneuver that resulted in a reverse in position. Tran now found himself laying on his back looking up into the menacing face of Father Patrick. He still had his legs wrapped tightly around the priest, allowing him enough leverage to slap his left ear with a cupped hand, grab the back of his head, and pull him into a vicious head-butt. Father Patrick's nose began to gush blood in response to yet another fracture. He responded by trying to get his thumbs into Tran's eyes, but Tran countered by delivering a series of headbutts before grabbing the priest's throat with his right hand and clamping down hard on his trachea. Father Patrick began to grunt, his teeth bared and dark eyes bulging as he tried to overcome Tran's chokehold with a desperate thumb to Tran's eye, but Tran pulled him in close thereby not allowing the priest to succeed. Had Tran not been completely engaged in this life and death struggle, he would have jumped in a startled state when a nearby gun fired four times. A loud thud occurred just as Tran tossed Father Patrick off to his side, gasping for breath.

Tran rolled to where his gun had slid only to see Jade standing there holding his gun in an outstretched position. He looked to where it was pointed and saw Hu's body collapsed on the floor in an expanding puddle of blood. Tran leapt to his feet and gently took the gun from Jade's hands, her face frozen in a very shocked expression. Tran stepped in front of Jade, turned, and trained the gun on Father Patrick who lay gasping for breath as he looked up at Tran.

"On your face with your hands behind your back, Jin Feng!" Tran yelled breathlessly.

Jin Feng/Father Patrick exhaustedly flipped Tran off with his middle finger. Tran immediately responded by firing a shot into his arm. Jin Feng erupted in a loud roar of pain.

"Think hard, Jin! You're either leaving with us or they'll find your charred remains when they sift through the ashes. That's more than you offered us downstairs. You've got enough evidence to take down several powerful organizations. The government will probably grant you immunity and put you into WitSec. That's a far cry better than facing trial and prison, not to mention what your bosses will do to you. You're a liability to their organization now. You of all people know what the Liu Dynasty does to liabilities. At least by cooperating, you'll have a life."

Jin nodded in defeat and held up his hands clasped together.

"Wrong. On your face, hands behind your back."

Jin complied and rolled over. The smoke from the front of the house was, mercifully, being blown out the open front door by a breeze that began when Hu had burst through and left open the back door; however, the fire at the front of the house was drawing closer. Tran fished a couple of zip ties out of his pocket and handed them to Jade.

"Look at me, Jin!" Tran ordered.

Jin turned his head and looked up at Tran.

"Jade is going to secure your wrists. If you so much as twitch, the first round is going right through your eye. Do you hear me?"

Jin nodded. Jade looked at Tran who nodded back. She took a tentative step forward when the house shuddered with a loud groan. Suddenly, the floor gave way before them. Tran reached out and grabbed Jade by her sports bra and pulled her back with them as the floor crashed into the basement amidst a flurry of sparks and new flames.

With a loud scream, Jin Feng plunged into the flames below followed by Hu's lifeless body.

Jade recoiled in horror while Tran quickly assessed the situation. They were now cut off from the front and rear doors by the fire which was quickly eating up what was left of the floor. He knew it would only be seconds before they joined Jin and Hu in their fiery death. Tran grabbed Jade's arm and launched her toward the stairs.

"Keep going up until you hit the roof! It's our only way out!"

Heeding his warning, Jade urgently started up the stairs, taking them two at a time. Her light figure shot up the stairs with Tran right behind her. The smoke was beginning to funnel up, but it cleared as they hit the third floor. Tran heard a loud crash below and prayed the stairwell wasn't about to give way with them in it. They rounded the corner, ran the short distance to the next stairwell, and high-tailed it up onto the roof. The young man who had been standing guard was still where Tran had left him. Tran removed the utility knife to cut him loose only to discover he was slumped over with a bullet hole in his forehead. Likely the handiwork of Jin Feng trying to eliminate all liabilities. Tran bit his lip in disappointment. He may have proven useful as a witness when the time came.

"Let's go!" he said as he began to lead Jade across several rooftops.

Tran was careful to remain at the center of the roof and out of direct eyesight of those on the street below. Blaring sirens emanated from below as several police cars began to arrive. In the distance, the high-pitched wails of fire engines could be heard as they raced to the scene. Tran wasted no time as he led Jade to the roof access-way of the townhouse at the end of the block. Tran tried the knob but the door was locked. He gave it a once over and saw it was a steel door in a wooden frame. Tran took a step back and began to kick the door with the heel of his boot. After four tries, the doorjamb splintered and gave way. Together, they rushed down the stairs. The third floor was empty, but they nearly crashed into a balding, heavyset middle-aged man emerging from a bedroom on the second floor.

"There's a fire a few doors over!" Tran yelled as they blew past the confused man in a flash. "Get out while you still can!"

In Darkness Light Shines

They plunged down the last stairwell and reached the front door. Tran unlocked the door and then causally led Jade outside and down the steps. They ignored the gathering crowd of onlookers and headed in the opposite direction, not stopping until they reached Tran's Ninja motorcycle over a dozen blocks away.

Chapter 70

Washington, D.C.

"Director Snyder. Director Snyder!"

Snyder opened his eyes and immediately regretted it. His office remained unlit but the light emanating from the anteroom nearly blinded him. His next realization was that his head felt like someone had drilled a hole in his forehead. *Wait? Why am I in my office?* Snyder looked down at the hand gently shaking him and followed it up to see his personal secretary, Marjorie Boland, looking down at him with a look that bordered between concern and contempt.

It was starting to come back to him now. He had met with the priest last night, if he really was a priest. He had instructed Snyder to fly to Georgia and meet up with SAIC Winkelman to conduct an interview of Victor Tupolev who would give a statement confessing to his involvement with President Galan. Tupolev would testify that he had accompanied several of his prostitutes to Belize as part of a trap for Senator Fowler. In exchange for his testimony, Fowler, when president, would have Tupolev deported back to Russia where he would be tried and found innocent. His days as a crime boss in America were over but he would at least be free.

The guilt had been steadily clawing at Snyder since he had woken up in that hotel room Sunday morning. He should have just confessed what had happened to his wife and ridden out the ensuing storm. It might have resulted in a painful divorce and a shameful stamp on what had otherwise been an exemplary career but at least he wouldn't be in the position he found himself now. He was already guilty of several felonies and the further this went, the more he was being asked to do. There was no turning back now. If he didn't continue to play along, he would either end up in prison or be found lying dead in a field somewhere with a bullet in his head. Rather than try to decide which was worse, he had escaped into a bottle of Jameson but here he was with the same problems and, now, a piercing hangover.

"What time is it, Marge?" his cotton-mouthed voice croaked.

"It's six o'clock in the morning, sir," she said in a serious tone. "You're due to brief the president at nine. I cancelled your eight o'clock appointment so you would have time to go home and make yourself presentable."

Snyder closed his eyes and exhaled. "I can't go home. I'll have to shower here." *No way can I go home now!*

"Are you out of your mind?" Marge chided. "You can't appear before the President in a rumpled suit smelling like a distillery."

"I can't go home, Marge!"

Marge's steely blue eyes narrowed in response to his tone before she shook it off. "Alright, then give me your clothes and I'll get them dry cleaned for you."

"How are you going to get that done in time for me to head over to the White House?"

"What? You don't think I've made a few connections of my own over the years? You're not the first person to have spent the night in his office. And you're not the first director to have landed himself in some hot water either."

"Excuse me?" Snyder asked as he swung his legs off his couch and stood up.

"You heard me," Marge said looking up at her boss.

Snyder towered over his little pixie of a secretary, but she didn't budge as she stared up at him in a challenging manner.

"Is it that obvious?"

"Yes. You've been sneaking off without letting me know where you're going, keeping odd hours, acting like someone's looking over your shoulder, and now, getting pickled and sleeping in your office."

"What are you, my mother?"

"No, because if I were, I'd belt you one for the way you've been acting. Now you want to tell me what's going on or am I gonna have to pry it out of you?"

"Are you allowed to talk to me like that?"

"Probably not, but you won't do anything about it."

"Why won't I?"

"Because you need me around here," Marge said assertively.

"Man, you're a pushy old gal," Snyder sighed.

"I've been here since Hoover ran the place which means I've been around a whole lot longer than you, bucko. Over that time, I've developed a sixth sense for what's going on and my instincts tell me that you're being blackmailed and that you've already crossed the line. Now you wanna tell me about it or do you want me to tell you what I think is going on?"

"What do *you* think is going on?" Snyder asked.

"I think you fell into a honey trap, and someone is holding the evidence over your head and forcing you to fix the investigation in a manner that implicates President Galan."

Snyder gawked at his spunky and often abrupt secretary. "What makes you say that?!"

"Because I happen to know the president is a decent and honorable man who would never do all the things the press and Fowler are accusing him of; therefore, I know the sudden surge of supposed evidence against him is a crock and the only people who could orchestrate this need someone like *you* to do it for them, only *you* are also a decent and honorable man who would never do such a thing, or at least you were, which is why someone set you up so they could blackmail you into fixing the investigation. How am I doing so far?" she asked, staring up at her boss with a penetrating stare.

"It's not like that," Snyder said looking away.

"Oh?" Marge persisted. "Then tell me what *is* going on then?"

"I can't," he said still unable to meet her gaze.

"Why not?" She pressed.

"Because it's complicated and it's classified."

"Oh, don't give me that!" Marge said disgustedly. "My clearance level is just as high as yours."

"I know that, Marge. It's not that. It's just, it's a need-to-know issue."

"And I don't need to know," she said with a tone of incredulity.

"Something like that," Snyder said with his eyes closed.

"Is that so?" Marge said with her eyes narrowed. "Well let me tell you something, mister. This office is bigger than both of us. My obligation is to this office, not to you. As it should be for you. I may not know everything you're wrapped up in, but I *can* tell you it's eating you alive. Whatever it is, if you want to make it out of it with your dignity, you'd better make sure you are walking the straight and narrow. You're one of the most honorable men who has ever presided over this bureau. Don't change now. You owe it to this office and to the nation you swore to protect."

Snyder nodded. "Thank you, Marge."

"Don't thank me. Just do the right thing," she charged. "Now leave your things on the couch after I step out. I'll get them dry cleaned in a jiffy and have them send some gym clothes up here for you to wear until I get back."

Chapter 71

Washington, D.C.

Tran stood under the hostel's shower with his eyes closed. The last two days had been demanding to say the least. Were it not for his training and experience as a Navy SEAL, he and Jade may likely have not survived to this point. As things stood, they still weren't out of the woods yet, but Jade was emotionally and physically spent, and they needed a little time to recover after last night's ordeal. Tran had allowed himself a couple hours of necessary sleep. The day ahead of them promised to be just as hectic and he would need to be sharp.

He soaped up for the second time. After Jade had fallen asleep, he had washed their clothes in the bathtub in attempt to get the worst of the smoke odor out of them. He hoped the shower would get rid of the rest of it. No doubt the authorities had discovered the dead bodies by now and were scouring the city looking for anyone that may have been associated with a fire. They had definitely suffered from some smoke inhalation and should have gotten themselves evaluated at an emergency department but, in Tran's estimation, that risk far outweighed any benefit. Jade had seemed stable, physically at least, emotionally, everything had come to a head and it took him a while to calm her down until she, mercifully, fell asleep in his arms. Tran was sore and exhausted, but he had been through worse and knew he could push on.

He glanced at his Garmin Tactix watch and noted the time. He turned off the shower and began to towel off. They would have to get moving soon. His backpack followed Jin Feng down into the flames last night. In it were both his and Jade's laptops and cellphones. Every bit of evidence Jade had collected had been in there. They would have their work cut out for them. La Rosa had coughed up a lot of information, literally, but it would help if they could find some material evidence to fortify the case. He hoped Jade could resurrect everything. He had asked her last night, but she had been too emotionally distraught and he couldn't get a straight word out of her. He desperately hoped she would be calm and level-headed this morning. Tran pulled on his spare pair of black boxer briefs, he had gotten out of his hastily thrown together go-bag and padded down the hall to their room.

Jade lay on her side sound asleep. Tran wished he could have left her to sleep longer but they had an enormous task ahead of them and time was of the essence. He gently shook her awake. Jade rolled onto her back and stretched as she looked up at him.

"What time is it?" she asked sleepily.

"Six-thirty," Tran answered as he pulled his cut-up shirt off the radiator and assessed that it was still damp.

"Oh! We need to get moving, don't we?"

"Yes," Tran said handing her a towel and then turning his back. "But you need to take a shower first. We can't go around town smelling like we were in a fire. I washed your clothes after you fell asleep. You were going on about being at the coffee shop when they opened but you were so emotional, I couldn't follow what you were saying. What's at the coffee shop?"

There was no answer.

"Jade?" Tran asked, hearing movement and glancing over his shoulder only to see her running out of the room.

*****

Jade walked into the coffee shop and looked around. There were only a few people seated by the window and only two in line ahead of her. When it got to her turn, she ordered a caramel macchiato and paid for it before heading over to the booth she sat in last night. She took a seat and pretended to look over the breakfast menu while she waited on the barista. With her other hand, she probed along the crevice where the backrest met the seat cushion. Within a few seconds, her finger contacted an object. She pulled it out and looked down to see the jump drive she had used to save Joe's video last night. She placed it into her pocket, stood, and walked back up to the counter to collect her order. Once outside she walked a couple of blocks to where Tran was waiting by his Ninja.

"Please tell me it was there," he said.

"It's in my pocket," she beamed as she handed him the coffee of which he took a few sips before handing it back. "I just need a new laptop."

"We'll have to use one of our cards to do that," Tran warned. "Once we do that, we'll pop up on the grid. It's risky."

"Do you have a better idea?" She asked.

"Actually, I do," Tran said as he fished a cheap burner phone out of his side pocket.

"You had an extra phone?"

"Yep," Tran nodded as he powered it on. "Actually, I kept two of them back at the room in addition to the ones we were using last night."

"I get it," Jade said nodding her understanding.

"Yeah?" Tran said looking up.

"Yes, Tran, for the same reason I sent copies of the video to your phone, my cloud, and this jump drive. You always say, *One is none, two is one…*"

"…and three is just enough," Tran finished with a smile.

He dialed a number from memory and held the phone to his ear.

"Yes, this is SO1C Truk, Echo Five for Commander Moslander please…"

Chapter 72

Alto, Georgia

"Fifteen seconds, Hannah. You got this!" Christy encouraged as the two finished their final plank. "And five…four…three…two…one…done!"

Hannah collapsed in a breathless heap on their cell floor. She rolled over onto her back and heaved a sigh of relief.

"Man! I'm so out of shape!" She exclaimed to the ceiling. "Are you trying to kill me?"

"Almost, but you'll pass out before you die," Christy said with a serious tone.

Hannah turned her head to look a Christy with an incredulous look. "Really?"

Christy laughed. "I'm kidding. You did great. It's misery at first but, after a month, your body will be craving exercise. The endorphin release of a good workout will be the only drug your body will ever want again."

"I hope so," Hannah said quietly.

"How are you feeling today?" Christy asked.

"I'm okay," Hannah said as she pushed herself up to a sitting position facing Christy. "The Suboxone is keeping me from craving, but I still feel like there is an 800-pound gorilla waiting to jump on my back."

"Yeah, and her name is Randy," Christy quipped. Together they shared a laugh.

"If that isn't the truth," Hannah remarked. "But, seriously, does that feeling ever go away?"

"The 800-pound gorilla?" Christy asked.

"Yeah," Hannah said nodding while she wrapped her arms around her knees and pulled them to her chest.

"It becomes less and less of a thing, but I think it's always going to be a fact in your life. Not that that's a bad thing, Hannah. Knowing it's out there will help you keep your guard up which you will *have* to do. You're going to have to set boundaries as to where you can and cannot go, who you can and cannot associate with. Just like an alcoholic shouldn't hang out at a bar. You will have to avoid situations that could tempt you."

"That's easier said than done, Christy. Those temptations are everywhere, especially in here."

"I didn't say it would be easy. You have to learn to look past them. Look to something bigger and better."

"Like what?" Hannah asked.

"Let us fix our eyes on the author and perfecter of our faith, who, for the joy set before Him, willingly endured the cross…"

"That's scripture, right?"

"Yes," Christy answered. "Hebrews twelve verse two."

"Well, no offense, but I'm not so sure bible verses will work for me."

"Well, setting aside the fact that that's how Jesus defeated Satan when Satan tried to tempt him in the wilderness, I quoted that verse because there are two great lessons in it that I use in my life. The first one is keeping our eyes on Christ. Do you remember the gospel account of when Jesus walked on the water?"

"Yes," Hannah nodded.

"Was He the only one who walked on the water that day?"

Hannah thought for a second before replying. "No, Peter did as well. He got out of the boat and walked on the water too. Right?"

"That's right," Christy acknowledged. "However, Peter also sank after he had walked some distance on top of the water. Do you know why he sank?"

"No," Hannah shrugged.

"Because he took his eyes off of Jesus," Christy answered. "There was a raging storm going on, but as long as Peter kept his focus on Jesus, the storm was of no consequence, nor was the physical reality of gravity for that matter. Peter was able to overcome both obstacles to do the miraculous simply by focusing on Christ. It was only when he let the storm distract him that he sank."

Hannah nodded slowly as she considered what Christy had told her.

"Anyway, that's just one of many things I do," Christy said uncertain how receptive Hannah had been to her advice. "I also set short-term and long-term goals, you know, a destination with waypoints in between. Things like that help too."

"You said there were two lessons," Hannah prompted.

"That's right, I did," Christy acknowledged. "The second part of that verse mentions a joy that led Jesus to *willingly* endure the cross. He was terribly beaten, whipped, spat upon, and mocked *before* they nailed Him to the cross and hung him up to die an excruciating death. Do you think there was any *joy* in that?"

Hannah quietly shook her head.

"Then what was the joy that verse speaks of that would lead Him to die a painful death on the cross."

"No clue," Hannah shrugged.

Christy leaned and spoke earnestly. "Hannah, that joy is you."

Hannah skeptically squinted her eyes and tilted her head.

"Yes, Hannah," Christy continued. "By going to the cross, He paid the penalty for your sins, my sins, and in doing so He opened up a way for us to receive forgiveness and be reconciled to God through Him which is something we can never do on our own. Only Jesus could do that by paying the penalty for us. Something he *willingly* did. That *joy* is the foreknowledge Jesus had of every redeemed life, your redeemed life and the vision He has of you being victorious over drugs, having a relationship with Him, and spending eternity with Him, Hannah!"

"But I've done so many terrible things," Hannah challenged.

"It doesn't matter what you've done, Hannah, it only matters what He's done, and He offers His forgiveness to you but you have to willingly accept it."

"I'll think about it," Hannah said with a grown as she stood up, "but right now, I'm starving. Let's go get breakfast."

"Sounds good," Christy said as she stood. "Let me just throw on my jumpsuit real quick."

Christy walked over to the stainless-steel sink and splashed some cold water on her face. She toweled off and stepped into her white prison jump suit. She buttoned it up and turned to walk out of their cell only to find Hannah wasn't there. Christy walked out into the hallway and looked around. Hannah was nowhere to be seen. A heavyset black female walked up to her.

"Randy said that you got one minute to meet her in the showers, else she gonna kill Hannah.

Chapter 73

Alto, Georgia

Christy ran down the hall to the communal shower. She felt everyone's eyes upon her. They all knew what was happening. Christy did too. It was a trap. She was about to enter the snake's hole but what choice did she have? Randy was a known killer, devoid of a conscience, and would butcher Hannah if Christy didn't show up. This was no bluff.

Christy arrived to find the door guarded by two of Randy's minions. Christy ignored them and charged into the room. As she entered, she encountered Randy standing behind a crying Hannah. Randy, her bruised and swollen face giving her a near subhuman look, held a prison shank made out of half a pair of scissors with medical tape wrapped around the handle. She held it to Hannah's throat as she smiled menacingly. They were surrounded by Randy's lieutenants including a short stocky gal whose name was Sally Grimstead but went by the name "Sally Grim." Another was a very obese Hispanic female with a high and tight haircut who was known as "Fluffy." Christy guessed it was because she looked a lot like the comedian, Gabriel Iglesias. The obese Black woman with the big Afro she had fought the other day stood there as well, sneering at Christy. Randy's messenger ran in behind Christy and stood off to the side, an expectant look on her face.

"Let her go, Randy!" Christy said sternly.

"Screw you, Storkleberry," Randy spat. "This little filly was my property to begin with until you showed up. I'm just takin' back what's mine. Unless of course you want to work a trade."

"A trade?" Christy asked skeptically.

"Yeah, Einstein, a trade," Randy said in in an exasperated manner. "Your life for hers."

"No, Christy!" Hannah pleaded through tears. "She'll kill you! Don't do it!"

"Mouth shut, little girl!" Randy growled at Hannah through clenched teeth as she pushed the blade of her shank into Hannah's throat for emphasis.

Hannah gasped in silence but continued to shake her head.

"You're kidding me, right?" Christy asked as a stall measure.

She knew Randy was serious. Christy had not only kept Hannah from being abused and pimped by Randy but had embarrassed Randy in front of the entire prison. Randy would be desperate to salvage her reputation as "Barn Boss" and restore the fear she used to intimidate everyone into doing her bidding. Killing Christy would accomplish both of those things in dramatic fashion. Taking on Randy with a shank would be challenging enough but there was no way Christy would stand a chance against all of them.

"Nope. It's her or you. What's it gonna be hero?"

"Then let's do this," Christy said taking a step forward. "Let her go."

"No! Christy! Please don't!" Hannah cried desperately.

"Sally Grim!" Randy yelled as she cast Hannah aside. "Shut her up!"

"Christy! I'm so sor…" Hannah was cut short by Sally Grim's backhand slap.

Sally Grim dragged Hannah into the corner, sat her down with and arm wrenched behind her back and forced her to watch. Fluffy and Randy's other minions all circled around Christy like a pack of ravenous wolves. Christy looked around and laughed.

"What's so funny, stork?" Randy asked, annoyed.

"I just think it's funny that, even with a knife, you're afraid to fight me one on one."

Randy's brow furled. "You think I'm afraid to fight you?"

Christy made a show of looking around at Randy's entourage and then nodded to Randy with her lips pressed together and eyebrows raised. "Yep."

"Screw you, princess!" Randy replied angrily.

"Oh! Well now!" Christy said feigning astonishment, "That vicious reply will convince everyone. Yes ma'am, Randy, as long as you have your minions to gang up on everyone, you'll continue to be the top dog around here. That is until someone calls your bluff and challenges you, but then, rather than fight anyone one on one, you'll just sic your bulls on them, won't you?"

Fluffy and a couple of the other sidekicks began to look at Randy questioningly. Randy began to notice.

"I don't need them!" she blurted defensively.

"And yet here we are," Christy gestured around her while staring defiantly at Randy.

"Fine then!" Randy blurted. "Girls, take a seat!

"Still want a piece of me?" Randy taunted with her shank as the minions sat against the wall.

"Not really," Christy answered. "In all honesty, I'd prefer you just let me and Hannah walk out of here."

"See! I knew you didn't want any of this." Randy smirked. "Too freaking bad, Stork. You've been a thorn in my side since you got here and it's time for you to go. Now c'mon!"

Randy began to slowly walk toward Christy, holding the knife out front with a menacing glare. Christy took a step back and kicked off her prison issue Crocks. Now that she was in bare feet, she was able to get up on the balls of her feet where she could be more agile. Randy slowly advanced and the onlookers began to shout their encouragement. Christy slowly sidestepped, circling around as she waited for Randy to make her move. Randy stepped closer and lashed out with the knife in attempt to scare Christy back, but Christy knew she was too far away and didn't flinch. Randy feigned a lunge and backed off, followed by another lunge and back step. Christy kept her poise, remaining coiled and ready to spring. Randy lunged forward, this time with intent to strike but Christy sidestepped, pivoted toward Randy, and delivered a palm strike to her head that nearly knocked her off balance. Randy recovered and turned toward Christy. She switched her grip on the shank, changing for an overhead strike, and it a seething rage, charged toward Christy. Christy waited for Randy to strike and then thrust her left forearm out into Randy's right forearm, stopping it in mid strike. Christy, simultaneously, delivered a palm strike to Randy's nose which was already broken from their fight two days ago. Randy cried out in pain, momentarily stunned. Christy wasted no time and followed through by quickly windmilling her left arm around Randy's arm, grabbing her forearm and pulling her hand inward until Randy's wrist was bent, allowing Christy to force the shank out of her hand.

Christy tossed the shank aside, delivered a heel strike to Randy's right knee and twisted her arm behind her back, forcing her face first onto the hard tiled floor. Christy pounced on Randy's back, grabbed her ears, and began to slam her face into the floor over and over. Christy sensed Randy going limp and let up. Without warning, she was blindsided by the large Black woman from the other day. Christy and the woman rolled across the floor, each fighting to gain the advantage. The woman wrapped her arms around Christy's back and began to squeeze hard, forcing the air out of Christy, who countered by wrapping her legs around the woman's ample belly and delivering a head-butt to the woman's face. The woman howled in pain but did not loosen her grip. Christy's arms were pinned to her sides as she desperately tried to land another headbutt but her opponent kept her head turned away making Christy's attempts fruitless. Her hands still somewhat free to move, Christy grabbed ahold of the lower part of the woman's huge belly, dug her nails in and squeezed with every ounce of strength she could muster. The woman screamed in pain and her grip loosened enough to allow Christy to be able to wriggle free enough to get a leg under the woman and push her off to the side. She quickly swung her legs over the woman's chest and throat while grasping her arm and pulling it back into an arm bar. With a loud crack, the woman's humerus snapped as her elbow dislocated. She cried out in pain and was out of the fight.

Exhausted, Christy rolled to her side only to see someone's foot swinging rapidly for her face. Christy instinctively brought her arm up as she tucked her chin and the foot connected with the side of her head. The impact left her seeing stars as another foot connected with her back. Then another. Then more people joined in kicking and stomping. Christy had no recourse. The only thing she could do was to curl herself into a defensive ball with her head tucked and arms wrapped around her face.

The rabid group continued to kick and stomp as others began to chant; *Kill her! Kill her!*

Something sharp pierced her behind her left shoulder.

The shank! Christy realized. Someone had just stabbed her with it. Another painful stab, this time in the base of her neck. She was completely exposed on the back, but she couldn't break her defensive ball. She would be even more vulnerable if her face and chest were exposed. Another stab struck farther down. By the white-hot jolt of pain, Christy knew that one had connected with a rib. Had it missed the rib, it would have taken out her lung or something even more vital like her aorta. Another piercing stab landed between her shoulder blades and while a foot connected with her head and then everything went black.

Chapter 74

Alto, Georgia

Christy's first sensation was that of a throbbing headache. She felt the hard tile floor beneath her as she realized she was no longer curled up in the fetal position but, rather, laying on her back, her head cradled in someone's lap. The kicking and beating had stopped. The crazed shouting had been replaced by moaning and a few urgent voices. Whoever was holding her was sobbing. Christy felt tears cascading onto her face. She opened her eyes and looked up to see Hannah's tear-stricken face.

"Hannah," Christy whispered as she reached up and gently placed a hand on Hannah's forearm.

"Christy!" She exclaimed. "Oh, thank God! Are you okay?"

"I've been better," Christy replied.

"I thought you were dead!" Hannah blurted out through tears. "I watched them stab you over and over while they were kicking you. They were holding me down, Christy! I'm so sorry! I'm so sorry, Christy!"

"It's okay, Hannah," Christy said gently patting her cellmate's forearm. "I'm here. I know they were holding you down."

"I'm so sorry, Christy," Hannah persisted. "This is all my fault. You didn't have to do this."

"I wasn't going to leave you, Hannah. Now help me sit up."

With a grunt, Christy sat up. Pain shot all through her neck and upper back, reminding her that she had been stabbed several times before being knocked unconscious. She looked down and saw a fair amount of blood on the ground but not as much as she would have expected had a major artery been hit. She seemed to be breathing alright, which led her to believe her lungs were relatively intact. While she conducted a quick self-survey of her injuries, it suddenly dawned on her that, for some reason, the fighting had stopped. Christy looked around and saw the room was filled with over dozen inmates. A couple of Randy's minions lay on the floor moaning. Christy looked around.

"What happened to Randy?" She asked.

"She's over there," Hannah said tossing her head over her shoulder. "You messed her up pretty bad."

Christy looked around at Randy's minions strewn about the floor. Just minutes ago they had been mercilessly beating and stabbing her.

"What happened to *them*?" Christy asked bewildered.

"She happened to them," Hannah said pointing up.

Christy looked up and saw a tall slender Black woman standing over her. She recognized her as the same mahogany-skinned woman she had noticed studying her in the chapel service as well as the infirmary and cafeteria this week.

"She burst in out of nowhere and tore the place up," Hannah explained. "She saved your life. They were going to kill you."

Christy looked up at the woman in awe and nodded. "What's your name?"

"Jacqueline," the woman answered.

"I don't know how to begin to thank you," Christy said shaking her head.

"You did a long time ago," Jacqueline replied as she spotted a patch of floor without blood and sat down next to Christy.

"I'm afraid I don't understand," Christy said, her face registering a look of confusion.

"You don't remember me, do you?" Jacqueline stated more than asked as she cradled her knees to her chest.

"I saw you in chapel on Sunday and you looked familiar, but I just can't place how I know you," Christy stated.

"A couple a years ago, I came to your ER in Duluth. I was whacked out on crack and suicidal. You took the time to sit down with me, you listened to my story, and you prayed for me."

"Jacqueline Sharpe!" Christy exclaimed as the connection was made. "Now I remember you! You look so different now. Better. In fact, you look great!"

"I am better," she said reflectively. "I was a mess back then. You helped get me into Adult and Teen Challenge."

"Yes!" Christy said excitedly. "And I've been praying for you ever since but when I tried to visit you, they said you had left the program."

"I did," Jacqueline nodded shamefully. "I got stupid and walked out. Had a friend come and get me. I was hitting the crack pipe as soon as we pulled out of the parking lot. I went right back to the street life until I ended up here with a life sentence for double murder and armed robbery."

"I'm so sorry," Christy replied.

"Don't be," Jacqueline said placing a hand on Christy's knee. "This is exactly what I needed. I hit rock bottom and it made me get my life straight. I got right with the Lord, and I've been clean for almost a year now. I'm in here for life but I'm more free than I've ever been and when the Lord takes me home, I'll be free for eternity. I might not be able to say that if it weren't for you."

"That was God working in your life, Jacqueline, not me."

"Yeah, but He used you to get it all started. You planted the seed, Dr. Tabrizi. I might already be dead had you not pointed me in the right direction."

"Well, I'm sorry you're in here but I'm glad to know you're doing well. I noticed you looking at me this week. Why didn't you come up to me sooner?"

"I guess I was afraid of what you might think of me."

"Jacqueline, I'm proud of you and I'm eternally grateful. You saved our lives in…"

"Face down on the deck! Everyone! Now!" Officer Singletary ordered as she burst into the room with a squad of Crisis Response Team (CRT) officers who were wearing body armor and carrying weapons.

Christy, Jacqueline, and Hannah all obediently sprawled out on the floor in prone positions as the officers fanned throughout the room looking for any remaining threats. Officer Singletary called for additional medical teams as the first team of medics entered the shower room. Spotting the blood, they waded their way through the prone bodies to Christy. They knelt down beside her and went to work with their field assessment.

"Ma'am, can you tell us what happened?"

Christy explained what happened while the paramedics began to look over her injuries and obtain her personal and medical information. When they learned she had been kicked in the head multiple times and knocked unconscious, they tried to place her in a cervical collar, but Christy refused.

"Ma'am, you could have a spinal injury. You have to wear the collar," the older medic insisted.

"Sir, with all due respect, I'm an emergency medicine physician, I can assure you my spine is not injured, and I'd just as soon not have to wear a collar or get stuck on a spinal board."

"Fine, ma'am, but you have multiple stab wounds, you've lost a lot of blood and you have a head injury. We're going to need to transport you to the trauma center."

Christy snorted, "If it means I get to leave this place for awhile, you can wrap me up in duct tape for all I care."

A paramedic team rolled in with a stretcher. The prison medic relayed Christy's injuries and condition to them and then moved on to assess Randy. Christy heard one of the paramedics requesting air transport as they rolled up with the stretcher.

"Guys," Christy began. "I don't think any of my stab wounds penetrated to anything vital. I don't think we need to use a helicopter for this."

"Ma'am, your injuries meet trauma criteria, and the nearest trauma center is on diversion. We're gonna have to fly you down to the trauma center in Gwinnett County."

"Oh," Christy said as she hid her smile.

Christy looked over at Jacqueline as the medics helped her into their stretcher.

"Thank you," Christy said as their eyes met. Jaqueline nodded.

She looked at Hannah who looked back at Christy. Tears were, once again, running down her cheeks. Christy gave a reassuring smile as Hannah mouthed a thank you in return.

The paramedics buckled Christy onto the stretcher and placed a pulse ox probe onto her left index finger. One of the medics then pressed a red button that activated the hydraulic lift which raised the stretcher with a grating, high-pitched whine that Christy was all too familiar with, hearing that same sound several dozens of times per shift. Christy winced.

"You okay, Dr. Tabrizi?" one of the medics asked.

"I'll be fine," Christy said as she leaned back and closed her eyes. "I just hate that sound."

Chapter 75

The White House

Snyder mopped his brow as he looked up at Leutze and Johnson's 1851 painting of Washington Crossing the Delaware that adorned the wall of the West Wing Lobby. His knee bounced erratically, a product of his nerves and his hangover. The depiction of Washington and his limited troops crossing the icy river on Christmas night where they would surprise and defeat Johann Rall's Hessian troops added shame to Snyder's list of maladies this morning.

He had always identified with patriots like Washington, Adams, Jefferson, and Lincoln. Men who dedicated their lives to building this nation into a place of freedom and opportunity. Now, not even a week later, he was a traitor. One alcohol fueled indiscretion had changed everything. He was now owned. The thing about it was that he didn't even know who was ultimately pulling his strings. He had his ideas. Fowler's party and their backers on the front end, but someone else was involved. A big player with a globalist vision. He suspected the Liu Dynasty, but it could be any number of players or an unholy alliance of same. Not that it mattered. Whoever it was, he was now firmly in their control. Marge's scolding had given him pause, but only for a moment. As right as she was, there was no turning back for Snyder. He had already broken several laws and committed several acts of treason. To confess now would, at best, get him a prison sentence but, more likely a bullet in his head, if not that of his family as well.

He desperately tried to steady his knee. Jorge Galan was portrayed by the media as a knuckle-dragging grunt Marine, but Snyder knew he was anything but that. President Galan was extremely well read, intelligent, passionate, and an excellent judge of character. Snyder didn't know whether or not the man played poker, but if he did, he probably cleaned up with his ability to read people's faces. Snyder knew there was no way he could brief the president with his nerves on edge and not be seen as the treasonous sham he had become. He had considered having a couple of belts to calm his nerves before he came over, but Marge had been hovering around his office up until it was time to come over. The more he thought about it, the faster his knee bounced and now his hands were beginning to sweat.

Maybe I should just make up an urgent reason to leave? There will be hell to pay but I can't go in there like this!

Snyder gathered his thoughts and his briefcase and stood.

"Director Snyder, if you will follow me; the president is ready for you."

Snyder took a deep breath, dried his right hand on his trousers and followed the young female intern into the West Wing corridor. She led him to the Roosevelt Room where President Galan was seated at the head of the table along with Attorney General Jacobs, Chief of Staff Embry, Assistant Chief of Staff Espinoza, the White House counsel and several other key personnel. President Galan, as was his custom, stood and greeted their new guest with a firm handshake.

"Thank you for joining us this morning, Frank, please take a seat and bring us up to speed," Galan said warmly as he gestured to the open seat at the other end of the table.

Snyder managed a thank you while hoping Galan didn't notice how sweaty his hand was. He placed his briefcase on the table and took his seat. He removed several folders, each a duplicate containing the details of his briefing in writing and passed them around the table.

"Mr. President, as I'm sure you're aware, we've had several, um, developments since we last met yesterday. I'm going to do my best to brief you in on what the Bureau knows at this point."

Snyder paused and looked up to see President Galan's reaction. Galan stared back stone faced and gave a slight nod. He sat with his back to the fireplace, above which hung the famous painting of Teddy

Roosevelt on the back of his horse charging up San Juan Hill. An act of valor for which he was posthumously awarded the Congressional Medal of Honor, which was displayed on the wall next to the door Snyder had just entered through. It seemed as though everything was serving as a reminder as to level of greatness this nation demanded of those who dared to serve. Snyder cleared his throat and looked down at the open file before him.

"I'd like to begin with the raid that was conducted earlier this morning at Quisenberry Farms. As you all know, there was a high level of suspicion that this was the loading point for the truck used in the Charlotte bombing yesterday. A joint raid was conducted by agents of the FBI, Homeland Security, and ATF. In short, it was a big nothing, sir. While there were some farming supplies found on sight that could be used to make explosives, they were nothing out of the ordinary for a farm of that type and nothing of the magnitude required to pull off an explosion of the magnitude that was seen in Charlotte."

"Frank," Galan began, "is it possible that they could have been tipped off and cleared the place out before our agents arrived?"

"Yes, sir, it is possible, but we have no evidence to support that theory at this time. Several agents and experts are combing through the location as we speak, but as of right now, we have nothing to go on. The details of the raid are spelled out in the briefing I gave you; I can go over them if you like but I'm trying to be mindful of your time and remain brief and to the point. Suffice it to say, we are still trying to find those who were behind this."

"Understood," Galan nodded. "Where do you stand on this being a cartel backed bombing?"

"Well, sir," Snyder said while drying his hand on his pants leg beneath the table, "as of right now, that's where our limited evidence leads and we are certainly pursuing it, but we are also looking for other explanations. It's certainly possible that the evidence we have was planted to point us in a certain direction, but in no way are we limiting ourselves on this matter."

"Fair enough, Frank. Considering this, do you have any reason to believe the Liu Dynasty could be involved with this incident or any of the incidents of the past week?"

"Well, sir, while I certainly acknowledge that Liu Shunyuan's reach is extensive and would not be surprised to learn of his involvement in many geopolitical affairs, other than their indirect ownership of the farm, we have no evidence to raise suspicion of their involvement in these particular matters at this time, sir."

"And what can you tell me regarding the supposed memo found on my secretary's computer in which I reportedly ordered the CIA to sheep-dip the Navy SEALs and ordered them to conduct the raid in Belize with an order to kill Senator Fowler?"

"Sir, all I can say is that is exactly what was found."

"And *I* can tell you that I never gave such and order, that no order came from this administration and that, whatever you found, is blatantly false and an obvious plant. I do hope you have your best computer forensic analysts investigating this and that we will set the record straight soon. *Someone* very close to this investigation leaked this to the press and I would hope you are looking into that as well!" President Galan said with his voice slightly heated.

"Mr. President," Snyder said clasping his hands together to keep them from trembling, "as much as you want the truth in these matters to come forth, I can assure you, sir, that I, the director of the FBI, want to pursue the truth and bring the right people to justice even more. That is what my entire career has been about, and I will not rest until justice is served."

President Galan stared at the FBI director with a contemplative look.

"You're a lousy liar, Frank."

"Excuse me, sir?"

"You were once an honorable and trustworthy man and you have not only spewed one lie after another, but you have betrayed your office, the Bureau, this administration and our nation," Galan said evenly. "How did they get to you?"

"Sir," Snyder said clenching his hands so tight they turned white. "Could you please tell me what you are inferring?"

President Galan nodded to a female Secret Service agent standing by the door and she disappeared out into the hallway. He turned his gaze back to Snyder and stared icily without saying a word. Snyder looked at the door when the agent reappeared a moment later with an Asian man and woman in tow.

"Director Snyder, are you familiar with Petty Officer First Class Tran Van Truk and the CIA's Jade Nguyen?"

Snyder looked the pair over. He had no idea who they were, but his instincts were setting of warning sirens inside his head.

"I don't believe so, no, Mr. President," he managed weakly.

"No?" Galan said feigning surprise. "Well, perhaps you haven't, but you should really hear their story. You see, Petty Officer Truk is a member of Echo Platoon, SEAL Team Four. When he learned his commanding officer and platoon chief had been arrested for allegedly attacking an island in Belize under my orders, he didn't believe it. He knew both men had been on leave and, in fact, Lieutenant Commander O'Shanick had already rotated out of command and was still on medical restriction from an injury he suffered during a mission over the summer. Furthermore, and let me stress this point, SO1C Truk knows their *character*. He knew there was no way they would ever be a part of an assassination attempt on a United States senator, no matter how crooked he may be. Rather than sit back and watch the politicians and the media railroad his teammates, SO1C Truk took matters into his own hands and began to conduct his own investigation. Only that drew the attention of some rather unsavory characters including this man," Galan picked up an 8x10 photo of Father Patrick and held it up for Snyder to see. "Do you know who this man is?"

"A priest?" Snyder said trying to hide the panic in his voice.

"Yes, a priest, Frank." Galan said with a hint of bitter sarcasm. "But not just any priest. This man happens to be Jin Feng, a Chinese national who works in the Diocese under his cover name of Father Patrick Santos. He also happens to run an assassination squad for the Liu Dynasty, and they targeted Mr. Truk and Ms. Nguyen for having the audacity of looking into what they suspected to be a frame job. Over the past two days they've been shot at, tortured, chased, and nearly burnt alive but through superior skill and the grace of God, they not only managed to survive, but emerge with the evidence they were looking for. Quiet convincing evidence, I might add."

Galan paused and looked at Snyder to gauge his reaction. Snyder willed himself to remain stoic although he now believed it was a futile gesture.

"So, Frank, it leads me to ask the question; why is it that *they* succeeded, despite running for their lives, while you, the director of the FBI, one of the top law enforcement offices in the nation, continued to lead us down the rabbit hole?"

"Sir, I…"

"Stow it, Frank!" Galan said sharply. "You've done nothing but lie to me since you stepped in here this morning. You've done nothing but lie to me all week. Perhaps you'd care to explain this," Galan said holding up a couple of 8x10 photos showing Snyder entering and exiting the confessional booth the other night.

"I was going to confession," Snyder shrugged.

"Is that a fact?" Galan asked with mock sincerity as he held up another photo showing Jin Feng aka Father Patrick leaving the confessional booth. "Confessing your sins to a priest who runs an assassination outfit for the very organized crime syndicate that has been orchestrating every sordid event of this coup attempt, including the death of a decorated Navy SEAL, the planting of false evidence, not to mention blowing up a building which killed two innocent people?"

"Mr. President, if you will allow me to explain…"

"I can't do that, Frank," Galan answered. "Because you must first be advised of your rights."

"Sir?" Snyder asked confused.

"Gentlemen," Galan said as he nodded to two federal marshals who had quietly entered the room.

"Francis Snyder," one of the marshals began, "you are being charged with 18 U.S. Code 2384 conspiracy to commit sedition, 18 U.S. Code 1510 obstruction of a criminal investigation, and 18 U.S Code 1519 tampering with and destruction of evidence. You have the right to remain silent…"

The entire staff looked on as Snyder was read his rights, placed in handcuffs, and escorted out of the room. Two new marshals appeared at the door.

"Come in, gentlemen," Galan said pleasantly before turning his attention back to the room. "The person in question is seated along the wall," Galan said pointing to his assistant chief of staff.

"Martin Espinoza," one of the new agents spoke, "you are being charged with 18 U.S. Code 2384 conspiracy to commit sedition, 18 U.S. Code 1510 obstruction of a criminal investigation, and 18 U.S Code 1519 tampering with and destruction of evidence. You have the right to remain silent…"

"Martin," Galan said holding up the photo Tran took of him in the church, "I would never have believed it. You've been with me since I was the governor of California. I've relied on you and trusted you. This photo is the actually the final nail in the coffin. Attorney General Jacobs has been poking around behind the scenes and had enough probable cause to get a surveillance warrant on your phone and computer. The real raid on Quisenberry Farms happened last night when we planned a raid in your presence. The agents, who conducted the raid, found ample evidence to go after the Liu Dynasty while you fell right into the trap and sent a text to Jin Feng confirming your involvement. You had a very promising career, son. I don't know what derailed you, but I doubt it was worth it."

Once the marshals had escorted Espinoza out of the room, President Galan addressed Tran and Jade.

"Petty Officer Truk and Ms. Nguyen, we rushed through things earlier to make these arrests happen. Would you please join us at the table so that we may go over everything you have in detail?"

"We'd be honored, sir," Tran said as he held Jade's seat for her and then took his own seat.

"Can I get you two anything?" President Galan asked. "Something to drink, perhaps?"

"We're fine, sir, but if I could make one request before we get started?"

"By all means, sailor," Galan gestured with hands spread apart. "What can I do for you?"

"Sir, the same people that killed Lieutenant Commander Harrison are out to kill Lieutenant Commander O'Shanick, Master Chief

Ramsey, Dr. Tabrizi, and the others who were involved. Can we see to it that they are looked after until we can get them exonerated?"

"You asked me that earlier, when we first met, son. I've already given the order."

Chapter 76

Atlanta, Georgia

Fowler's 757 touched down smoothly on the tarmac at Atlanta Hartsfield International Airport. Fowler impatiently unbuckled his seatbelt and stood. They were still taxiing to a private area away from the large airport terminal, but Fowler didn't care. The day was full of engagements; three campaign rallies in three different cities including an appearance on the steps of Philadelphia's Museum of Art. He looked forward to the day. The adulation of the crowds was intoxicating. The closer they got to Election Day, the more electric the crowds were becoming. They would finish the day in Austin, Texas and stay overnight at a plush downtown hotel where Theron had promised him there would be throngs of young female co-eds.

This stop was the only unpleasantry of the day. It was a campaign stop, true enough, but not one Fowler relished. He glanced at his watch. In thirty minutes, he would give a campaign speech in the Atlanta Convention Center in which he would announce he was naming Georgia Governor Judith Maynard-Worthington his pick for Secretary of State. Theron had pleaded the case in addition to Senator Williams' pleading earlier in the week. Despite having nearly been drowned by La Rosa the other night, Williams remained undaunted. He assured Fowler that, if Maynard-Worthington were named to the cabinet, Ramsey and O'Shanick wouldn't be alive by day's end.

As the airplane slowly braked to a stop, Fowler bent down and looked out the window. He could see Williams standing alongside

Maynard-Worthington in front of the gathered crown of onlookers and television crews. Both were snappily dressed in honor of the momentous - to them anyway - occasion. Fowler's part was to wave victoriously to the crowd, descend the mobile staircase without falling down, woo the crowd with a few quick remarks, and get into the motorcade that would take them to the convention center.

The flight attendant opened the door and waited for the mobile staircase to get into position. She then waved for Fowler to make his appearance. Fowler habitually straightened his tie and stepped toward the door. As he emerged onto the stairway, the crowd roared its approval. Fowler smiled and waved triumphantly in all directions for a set amount of time and then carefully walked down the stairs. Several sets of television cameras were filming him, so he beamed his brightest smile as he continued to wave. He stepped down onto the red carpet and began to walk to the opposite end where Williams and Maynard-Worthington were waiting along with the Mayor of Atlanta and several congressmen from his party. A fit attractive female, wearing a flattering navy blue business suit, and an equally fit and well-dressed Hispanic male emerged from the crowd and walked toward him, intercepting him before he reached the podium he was due to speak at.

"Senator Robert Fowler, I'm Special Agent Katie Huggins, FBI and this is Special Agent Javier Gomez," the woman said as she held up her FBI credentials. "We are here to place you under arrest…"

Chapter 77

Atlanta, Georgia

"We're gonna have to find another way over to the camp," Joe spoke quietly as he entered Ramsey's cell.

"What are you talking about, Joe?" Ramsey asked looking up from his bunk.

"I just talked to Condor, he said everyone wants those work details. It gives them first crack at what the camp inmates bring in from the outside. To get one of those slots, you have to pay a tax to the guys who pick the details."

"So we tell them we will. We'll be long gone by the time they come to collect."

"I thought of that but there's still a waiting list. Some guys have been waiting for two years to get a slot over there."

"Well, if we can't go through the wall, we will have to go over the wall," Ramsey replied. "It won't be the first wall we've navigated."

"We're talking a smooth concrete wall over thirty feet high, Rammer. No handholds. It would be easier to free solo El Capitan," Joe argued.

"I know, but there's not much up top. We just need to figure out a way up there. Maybe we could start working on a caving ladder. We've boarded ships that high."

"The problem there is getting the materials and assembling it which would take some time and then we would have to keep it hidden. That's a tall order," Joe said with his arms crossed as he leaned against the wall.

"It's something, anyway," Ramsey countered. "Not like we have anything else to do."

"Guys!" Condor said from the cell entrance. "The news just said President Galan is about to make an announcement about this SNAFU y'all are goat-roped into."

Joe and Ramsey exchanged curious looks. Ramsey sat up, swung his legs onto the floor, and stood up. They turned and followed Condor out and down to the day room where the usual crowd of older inmates and bikers spent most of their time. Joe felt a dozen pairs of eyes on them as they made their way through the tables to where the television screen was mounted in a protective Plexiglas case. A hearing aid commercial finished running and the twenty-four-hour news station resumed. An attractive, blond-haired blue-eyed broadcaster led off the noon hour with breaking news that President Galan was due to address the press with an announcement at any moment. She used the time to quickly recap the events of the week and the charges that had been leveled against him. The screen behind her showed the White House Press Briefing Room where the empty podium stood in front of a multitude of reporters all scrambling to their assigned seats.

President Galan suddenly emerged from the left side entrance and took the stage with a purposeful stride. Absent the uniform, he looked every bit the seasoned Marine Corps NCO he once was with his tanned face, close cropped dark hair, granite jaw, and fit physique in a black suit with white shirt and scarlet red tie. He gripped the lectern on both sides as if he was about to rip it off the stage and hurl it to the side.

"Good afternoon. By the tireless efforts of several dedicated and selfless people, our Justice Department has obtained a great deal of information that will bring to light what actually transpired during the incident in Belize involving Senator Fowler and the subsequent events that have transpired this past week. I'd like to begin with a brief video which I think will be self-explanatory."

President Galan stepped to the side of the stage as the screen, at the back of the stage, began to play the contents of the video Joe had filmed during their rescue mission in Belize.

Joe and Ramsey exchanged wide-eyed glances in response to what was unfolding in front of them. Tran had done it! Joe worked hard to suppress his grin as the video played out to a captive audience. Joe's voice was clearly heard, and it was readily apparent that he was wearing the camera on his chest while Fowler confronted him with Victor Tupolev, the Russian crime boss, stood to one side and Pedro Cardenas, the head of *Los Fantasma Guerreros,* stood on the other side with a rifle pointed at Joe behind the camera. Ramsey could not be seen but he had been right next to Joe during this moment.

Several of the inmates uttered choice words of disgust when Fowler smirked at the camera while proudly revealing to Joe and Ramsey that he had leaked the information that had enabled the LFG Cartel to shoot down a helicopter killing half of their platoon a year earlier during a rescue mission in Honduras. Much more was revealed by the arrogant senator, all of it incriminating, before he ordered Cardenas to kill Joe and Ramsey. A flurry of activity ensued that could not be made out on the video. Joe and Ramsey had desperately lunged for Cardenas and his gunmen. The camera cut out during the ensuing scuffle. Cardenas had actually been killed by Gary Lee, one of Clay Whitmore's top investigators, with an exceptional head shot through the window from over a hundred yards away just. President Galan returned to the podium and looked out at the cameras with a grim expression.

"My fellow Americans, it saddens me to have had to have shown this video; however, it saddens me more that a serious attempt to throw an election in favor of a criminal, backed by a criminal enterprise, was carried out in our country. The fact that a video of this horrific magnitude had to be shown to overcome a false narrative should serve as a wake-up call to all of us. Equally sad and appalling is the fact that several good people, including the brave men who were nearly killed in this video, were victimized with false charges and thrown into jail as pawns in a larger political game. I have asked Attorney General Jacobs to arrange for, effective immediately, the release of Lieutenant Commander Joseph O'Shanick, Master Chief Matthew Ramsey, Dr. Christine Tabrizi, Mr. Clay Whitmore, Mr. Chuck Springer, and Mr. Charles Courtnall to their own recognizance. These brave and selfless individuals bear no threat to anyone and are to be commended for their acts of valor in rescuing the fifteen young woman who were being held captive and used as sex slaves by the LFG cartel. I am certain the evidence brought forward today will result in their quick exoneration. Their lives were heinously disrupted and threatened at the hands of a corrupt political entity all for the sake of seizing power over our nation and the free world."

"Additionally, in the past few hours, the Justice Department has made several arrests, among them Senator Robert Fowler, FBI Director Francis Snyder, Special Agent in Charge Andrew Winkelman from the Atlanta Field Office, and are pursuing several more for their connections in this conspiracy which the evidence also suggests led to the murder of Navy SEAL Lieutenant Commander Patrick Harrison as well as the bombing of the office building that housed Whitmore Investigative in Charlotte yesterday. A complete and thorough investigation will be conducted, and we will keep you updated as the information is made known. It will be our mission to bring every person involved to justice. Please join me in praying for the restoration of our electoral process and for the healing of our nation. Thank you and may God bless the United States of America."

President Galan turned and strode off the platform. A cacophony of shouted questions trailed him out the exit. The news anchor appeared back on screen and began to give a recap of what the watchers had just witnessed.

Ramsey turned to Joe with a look of elation. "It's over, Joe! Mother trucker! It's over! We're gonna walk out of here free men!" He emphasized by slamming his fists down on Joe's shoulders.

"We sure are, brother," Joe replied pulling his friend in for a hug. "All of us. We're *all* going home."

Condor and at least a dozen of the bikers, most of them veterans, all gathered around Joe and Ramsey with congratulatory handshakes and slaps on the back for what they had done in Belize. Many of the other inmates stood and clapped.

"I knew that self-righteous Fowler was a crook!" Condor shouted over the noise into Joe's ear. "You guys just saved the country from a colossal Charlie Foxtrot! Someday, I might get out of here and I'd like to hope it's still a free country when I do!"

Something caught Condor's attention. Joe turned to see what Condor was looking at. All along the corridor, balls of flaming debris and other items began raining down from the upper tiers. Inmates were shouting and hurling objects. On the main floor, fights were breaking out. Condor swore loudly.

"What's going on?" Joe asked loudly so as to be heard.

"Free for all," Condor yelled back. "Something big is about to go down. One of the gangs gets the other gangs and the rest of the inmates riled up as a diversion."

"A diversion for what?" Joe asked.

"Usually a big hit, carried out by the entire gang. First, they distract the COs, and then they tie them up and barricade the doors. You see any CO's?" Condor asked.

"No, I don't," Joe answered.

"Then it's about to go down!"

Chapter 78

Atlanta, Georgia

"You see?" Condor nodded down the corridor. "Here they come in force."

Joe looked and saw a horde of sinister looking Latino gang members marching toward them. They were all shirtless, displaying their myriad gang tattoos which seemingly covered every square inch of skin up to and, in a few, including their faces and scalps. Their look was demonic. Most carried shanks or some kind or weapon or club. Joe estimated there to be around thirty.

"Looks like platoon strength," Joe commented. "They're here for me and Rammer, aren't they?"

"I'd say that's a good guess," Condor drawled. "That's La Gran Familia, kind of a parent outfit for all the various Mexican street gangs in here."

"Rammer!" Joe called.

Ramsey, surrounded by a group of laughing and animated bikers, looked over at Joe and immediately sensed something was amiss. Joe subtly bobbed his head in the direction of the Mexicans heading their direction. Ramsey was instantly by his side.

"They here for us?" he asked.

"Affirmative," Joe answered.

"Right when we're about to walk out of this place," Ramsey commented. "I'd say there's about thirty of them and two of us. How you want to handle it, boss man?"

"Identify the leaders," Joe answered. "We take them out first. If these guys are a bunch of sidewalk warrior randoms, they might scatter, and we'll walk out of here. If they're true believers…"

"Then we're hosed," Ramsey said completing the thought. He spat an expletive and cracked his knuckles followed by his neck. "No escape. Murder. Rape. Doin' time on the wild side. Let's get at it, Joe."

The demonic horde approached. The chaos continued behind them down the length of the corridor.

"Watch their eyes, Rammer. They all keep looking to the two in the middle. The one with the facial tattoos and the one next to him who looks like Satan."

"I got em'," Ramsey acknowledged. "I'll take the guy whose face looks like a graphic comic book."

"And I'll get Satan. Disarm them and get as many as possible."

"Roger that, Joe," Ramsey said as they squared off and locked on with their targets.

"*¡Largarse, tonto!*" Condor shouted from behind Joe.

"We got this, guys," Condor said as he and the other bikers stepped in front of Joe and Ramsey.

"Condor," Joe said placing a hand of restraint on his shoulder, "we appreciate it, but this is our fight."

"That ain't the way we see it," Condor replied in his deep drawl. "Y'all are the good guys, framed and targeted for death by a bunch of corrupt, limp-wristed, dip-wads. Y'all are the kind of people we picked up a rifle for in the first place. We know you guys are lethal but there's thirty of them and only two of you and we ain't about to stand by and let you two get shanked by these dirtbags; besides, every now and then we need to show the other gangs who's boss," Condor grinned.

Condor turned back to the Mexican gang and addressed them in Spanish. Joe and Ramsey, both fluent in Spanish, listened in with amusement as Condor told them in no uncertain terms, what would happen to them if they didn't walk away right then. He also called into question their limited endowment which led them to, en masse and armed, go after two unarmed men. The gang leader argued back, and a verbal back and forth ensued.

"I think this is what you call a Mexican standoff," Ramsey whispered.

Joe chuckled in response. "It's sure setting up that way. They don't sound like they're backing down."

As if to emphasize the point, Condor turned to his cronies, "Y'all get ready to fight!"

Joe and Ramsey tensed, ready to spring into action. Joe sighted in on the leader he had dubbed "Satan" looking for vulnerabilities. He held a prison shank in his right hand with an underhand grip. Joe planned to let him strike out with the blade, disarm him quickly, and disable him just as fast.

Suddenly, several whistles began to blow. Joe looked up and saw dozens of armed COs, covered in protective riot gear, masks and helmets, flooding into the cell block. Inmates immediately began dropping to a face down position with arms and legs spread out where they could be seen. The few who didn't were mowed down by the leading group of COs as they ran past while others stayed behind to ensure no one got back up. Condor and the bikers all hit the deck as did the La Gran Familia soldiers. Joe and Ramsey did so as well.

"That's them over there!" a large CO shouted, pointing toward Joe and Ramsey.

Two officers formed up with the big man, who Joe recognized as Officer Trenton, the former Marine who had processed him in what was only five days ago but seemed like an eternity. The three ran over and pulled Joe and Ramsey up to their feet.

"You fellas come with us!" Trenton ordered as he turned and took off in a run.

Joe shot a quick look back at Condor. Their eyes met and they shared a silent look of respect.

"Look us up when you get out," Joe said. "We'll make sure it's still a free country."

Condor flashed a thumbs up in response. Joe and Ramsey turned and ran after the officers.

Chapter 79

Duluth, Georgia

Bless the LORD, O my soul, and all that is within me, bless his holy name! Bless the LORD, O my soul, and forget not all his benefits, who forgives all your iniquity, who heals all your diseases, who redeems your life from the pit, who crowns you with steadfast love and mercy, Who satisfies you with good so that your youth is renewed like the eagle's. The LORD works righteousness and justice for all who are oppressed.

With tears of joy, Christy read the psalm aloud, over and over. The ordeal was over. The news continued to play on the TV up in the corner, but she had muted out after watching replays of President Galan's presser for nearly an hour in stunned elation. The corrections officers who had accompanied her to the emergency room had already departed. An official from the prison had driven down with Christy's few belongings and processed her paperwork in her treatment room. Being a physician in the same emergency department, once Christy's trauma evaluation had been completed, her room had seen a constant stream of colleagues and co-workers dropping in to express their relief and happiness that she was out. Eventually, all the well-wishers had returned to their work allowing her a little time to take it all in. Christy had used the time to pray and give thanks. The sudden turn of events seemed nothing short of a miracle to her.

The ER Director Dr. Chip Jenkins, Christy's boss and friend, popped in through the curtain with his trademark Georgia country boy smile. He was in his early forties, average height, slim build with short blond hair parted to the side. He wore his trademark work boots, gray Carhartt work pants and a navy blue scrub top with his stethoscope draped around his neck.

"CT scans are all negative, Christy. Head, neck, and chest are all clear."

"I told you they would be," Christy said with a smile.

"I know," Jenkins said holding his hands up on mock surrender, "but I wasn't leaving anything to chance with one of my all-star docs. I need you back on the schedule!"

"If I can get one day to get things in order, I can be back on the schedule after that."

"That won't be necessary," Jenkins drawled. "We're covered through the weekend, and I want you to take a few days off. You were originally scheduled for Monday through Wednesday; you can just start then."

"That's perfect. Thanks, Chip," Christy replied.

"Alright, then. I just need to irrigate your wounds and throw in a few sutures and we can let you get out of here," Jenkins said as he began to open the suture tray. "I counted five stab wounds altogether on your neck and back. That sound about, right?"

"I have no idea, Chip," Christy quipped as she swung her legs over the side of the bed and sat up with her back facing her colleague. "My head doesn't turn around that far."

"You don't remember getting stabbed?"

"Oh, I do, but I kind of lost count. I was getting my head kicked in at the time," Christy answered. "Are any of them big? As in multiple sutures?"

"Nah," Jenkins answered. "I'm just doing loose approximation. One stitch each."

"Then let's just forego the Lidocaine," Christy suggested.

"I hear ya. I'm the same way," Jenkins agreed. "For one or two stitches, it ain't worth enduring the shots. Alright, I'm just gonna clean these with some Betadine first before I irrigate them."

"Boy, I'll tell ya, Christy," Jenkins bristled as he began to clean her stab wounds. "Any one of these could have done some serious damage. I can't believe they didn't get your lung and this one on the side of your neck *had* to have come close to your carotid artery. Dang, girl. Someone was watchin' after you!"

"In more ways than I can count," Christy said gritting her teeth as the Betadine stung her wounds.

"Alright, we're gonna get a little wet here," Jenkins announced as he filled a large syringe up with saline solution and attached a plastic IV catheter at the end.

"Have at it, Chip."

Jenkins inserted the plastic catheter tip deep into the first wound and ejected the saline solution deep into the wound. Christy felt a sting as the solution filled the wound and washed back out to flow down her back. Jenkins repeated the process several times and the moved on to the next wound. He continued to ask her about her experience over the past week taking more interest in what they did down in Belize. Thirty minutes later, all the wounds were irrigated and loosely sutured.

"You need me to go over wound care instructions with you, Christy?"

Christy laughed with her colleague. "Just let me go home, Chip."

"How *are* you gettin' home?" he asked.

"Stacy Morgan's going to drive me," Christy answered. "She's finishing up her last case now and then meeting me down here. I appreciate everything y'all did for me."

"What's the first thing you're gonna do when you get home?" Jenkins asked as he finished cleaning up and discarding all the suturing materials.

"Stacy and I are going to find Joe and Ramsey and then we are going to get an early dinner out and spend the rest of the night sitting around a fire by the lake. That's what we were doing the night were all arrested."

"Somebody say my name?"

Christy looked up and saw her close friend, Dr. Stacy Morgan, standing in the entrance. Stacy had already changed out of her surgical scrubs into an ankle-length navy blue Mexican print skirt with a white tank top. Her shoulder length blond hair appeared to have received some attention as it did not have the mussed up look one would expect after having worn a surgical cap.

"Yes!" Christy exclaimed. "Are you ready to leave already?"

"Yep, my last case was just a simple tubal ligation," Stacy smiled. "Were your scans okay?"

"Yes, thank God," Christy answered.

"You got her all patched up, Chip?"

"Best as I can do," he answered. "But I'm gonna need you to stay on her about staying out of the lake for a week or two."

"I'll try but you know what lousy patients doctors can be, especially ER docs!"

"True enough," Jenkins laughed along with Christy and Stacy. "Alright, I've done all I can do here. Christy, I'll have you discharged in a couple of minutes. I know you've got somewhere else to get to."

"Thank you, Chip, for everything. I really appreciate it."

"I'm just glad were gettin' you back," Jenkins said with a nod and a smile before turning out of the room.

"So have you heard from Joe?" Stacy asked excitedly.

"No," Christy said briefly making a sad face. "But who knows how long it will take them to get discharged from the prison. It's a federal prison. Probably like trying to move a patient through the VA."

"Ugh! At that rate, we won't see them until next week!" Stacy said as she pulled the privacy curtain closed. "But let's hope not, so get dressed!

"I hear that!" Christy said as she tore off her hospital gown and opened up the prison bag with the clothes, she had been wearing the night they were arrested. She pulled on her black workout leggings and gray University of Tennessee Volleyball t-shirt and slipped into a pair of running shoes. A metallic knock came from the other side of the privacy curtain.

"Come on in!" Christy said cheerfully.

The curtain was pulled partially open and, Mitch Williams, one of the hospital security guards, carefully peaked around the side.

"Dr. Tabrizi, ma'am?"

"Yes, Mitch?"

"There's a paramedic crew in the ambulance bay that heard you were here and would like to say hello, ma'am."

"Thank you, Mitch," Christy said pleasantly.

"You're never lacking for admirers, are you?" Stacy teased.

"Oh please!" Christy said dismissively with a laugh as they walked out of the room, "Like you aren't either? This is the south. Petite, perky blonds like you are what every guy is looking for down here, not tall half-Iranian brunettes."

"Whatever," Stacy said giving Christy a playful shove.

A sensor in the ceiling detected their approach and the sliding doors of the ambulance entrance automatically opened up. They stepped out into the covered ambulance bay and froze. There, before them, stood Joe and Ramsey. Christy squealing with delight then ran and jumped into Joe's arms while Stacy did the same with Ramsey. Joe spun Christy around in a tight embrace. Christy, with tears in her eyes, wrapped her legs around Joe, grabbed his face in both hands, and began to kiss him over and over. Joe smiled and took it all in as he continued to hold her tightly. It had been an emotional week for both of them. The release was cathartic and neither cared who was watching. A minute later, Christy disengaged and hopped down onto her feet. She looked up at Joe as they continued their embrace.

"I never lost faith," Christy began, the tears still in her eyes, "but part of me really thought I would never see you again."

"And I'm told you they tried to stab and beat you to death just a few hours ago," Joe said looking into Christy's eyes with concern. "Are you okay?"

"A few minor cuts and bruises but I'm good now," Christy smiled and pulled Joe in tighter. "I'm very good now," she said softly.

"Joe! Gun!"

Ramsey's heated warning came a split second before a loud pair of gunshots pierced the inside of the ambulance bay. Joe reacted immediately, instinctively dodging to the side and pulling Christy with him as he used his body to shield her. There was no cover out here. He and Ramsey were unarmed. Their only play would be to run. No matter how skilled the shooter, beyond a few yards, a moving target was difficult to hit with a handgun, which is what Joe's trained ears had already communicated to the tactical part of his brain.

"Christy! Stacy! Parking lot! Run!" Joe yelled as he shoved Christy forward while keeping himself between her and where his auditory sense told him the shooter was. His back had been turned when the first shots were fired.

"Go! Go! Go!" Ramsey yelled following close behind Stacy who was trying to run in sandaled shoes.

More gunshots rang out. Joe felt the sonic crack of a round as it flew closely past his right ear. Christy had hit her stride, her long legs putting considerable distance behind her in a hurry. Without breaking stride, Ramsey scooped up Stacy and kept moving. Joe shot a quick glance over his shoulder but couldn't see the shooter. More shots rang out. A round struck Joe in the back, and he collapsed to the pavement.

Chapter 80

Duluth, Georgia

"Joe!" Christy screamed.

Joe lay on his back looking up, wide-eyed, at Christy and Ramsey. He desperately tried to take a breath, but his lungs wouldn't move.

"Joe! Are you hit?" Ramsey asked.

Joe, unable to move air to speak, nodded with his mouth open.

"I don't see anything on his front," Christy stated as she performed a quick assessment. "Get his c-spine, Matt, and let's roll him. I'll check his back."

"Roger that!" Ramsey said as he positioned himself on his knees behind Joe's head and grabbed a hold to stabilize his cervical spine.

Christy knelt at Joe's side and positioned her hands on his shoulder and hip. "On your count, Matt," she said as her clinical side kicked in.

"One, two, three," Ramsey counted.

Together, they rolled Joe up on his side. Christy leaned over and inspected his back.

"I see one! Right upper back," she proclaimed. "That's all I see. Let's lower him, gently, Matt. On your count."

Ramsey counted off and they gently lowered Joe onto his back. Stacy came running out of the emergency room entrance with Chip Jenkins and a team of nurses with a stretcher in tow.

"Christy, what happened?" he asked.

"He was shot!" she exclaimed. "Right scapular area. I only see one wound but he's not moving air. We've got to get him inside!"

The nurses gathered around Joe. Ramsey spotted a petite nurse wearing a Mennonite prayer cloth and skirt and asked her to stabilize Joe's head while he lifted Joe onto the stretcher. They quickly got Joe onto the stretcher and made their way back into the emergency room.

"Clear Trauma Three, Jenkins spoke loudly. We need radiology stat! Call a level one trauma and get CT surgery down here now!"

They wheeled Joe into the trauma bay and went to work. A tech began hooking Joe up to the monitor and pulse ox while another tech attached a blood pressure cuff. Nurses began prepping each of his arms for IV's while another used a pair of trauma shears to cut Joe's shirt off. Jenkins picked his way around the staff, quickly working his way through a physical exam.

"Take some deep breaths, Joe," he requested as he listened with his stethoscope.

"He's a little shallow but they sound equal, Christy," he said looking up.

Christy nodded while she stood next to Joe, overseeing the whole process.

"Good strong pulses in his wrists and feet too," Jenkins pronounced. "Blood pressure is 128 over 76. Moving all four extremities well, neurovascularly intact."

"Thank God!" Christy exclaimed as she let out a breath.

"Okay, I see another wound on his upper arm here. but it looks old," Jenkins said pointing to Joe's Triceps.

"Um, that was from a gunshot last week," Joe said finally able to move enough air to speak.

"You're kidding me?!" Jenkins looked at Joe with an amused expression.

Joe simply shrugged and shook his head. He immediately regretted shrugging as the movement caused pain to shoot through his shoulder.

"Well, alright then, all I see, otherwise, is the one wound on his back," Jenkins continued. "Lift your arms for me, Joe."

Joe winced as he raised his arms over head.

In Darkness Light Shines

"Okay, we have another wound in the right axilla," Jenkins stated as he continued to look Joe over. "I don't see anything else. Hopefully, we're looking at an entrance and exit wound. Let's get an upright chest X-ray, please. He may still have a pneumothorax."

"Wouldn't be my first," Joe commented wryly.

They raised the head of the bed until Joe was nearly upright. The radiology tech placed an X-ray cassette behind Joe's back and then positioned the X-ray machine. The rest of the staff stood out of the room for a few seconds while she snapped the image. Christy and Jenkins both stepped in to view the image as it materialized on the X-ray machine's control panel. They both were silent as they studied the image.

"I don't see a pneumothorax," Jenkins observed.

"No, me neither," Christy agreed. "Nor do I see any foreign bodies. I think it *did* go through and through!"

"Unless that bullet's hiding, I agree," Jenkins said. "We need to check the rest of him now. Make sure we aren't missing anything."

In the case of gunshot wounds, a proper trauma exam consisted of a head-to-toe evaluation, examining every crevice and square inch of skin. Once a bullet enters the body, it can take an unpredictable path, such as entering the upper back and exiting the pelvis. There is a lot a valuable real estate between those two points and a thorough evaluation was necessary to avoid missing a potentially lethal injury.

"Yes, you do," Christy nodded. "I'll turn my back."

The nurses pulled Joe's shorts and boxer briefs down and rolled him on his side. Jenkins performed a quick examination of the pelvic region and found no additional wounds. They rolled Joe onto his other side, and he repeated the process. There was nothing. They lowered him to his back and helped him pull his shorts back up.

"He's all clear, Christy."

Christy turned around. "So it looks like just the one?"

"Yeah," Jenkins answered. "I think we oughta scan him as a precaution, but I doubt we'll find anything. My guess is the bullet struck his scapula at an angle and skipped off, exiting under his arm."

Christy clasped her hands in front of her and closed her eyes. "Thank you, Lord."

A knock came at the entrance. Joe looked up to see Ramsey and Stacy looking in.

"C'mon in," Joe invited.

"You can talk," Stacy commented hesitantly before looking at Christy. "I'm hoping that means good things?"

"He's fine," Christy replied. "We think the bullet deflected off his scapula but didn't do any real damage. We're getting a CT scan to make sure."

Joe smiled wearily when he saw the instant look of relief come over Stacy and Ramsey. "Didn't mean to scare you like that. I think it just knocked the wind out of me. What happened to the shooter anyway?"

"Critter got him," Ramsey stated plainly referring to Christy's neighbor, Tom Crittendon, the former Army Ranger who owned a gun shop.

Unable to get ahold of Christy, Ramsey had contacted Crittendon to pick them up from the prison. Crittendon had later heard from Stacy that Christy was in the ER and offered to drive Joe and Rammer over.

"Security told him to move his truck and he was walking back when he saw the shooter pull up in his car and get out with a gun."

"Is the shooter dead?" Joe asked.

"Very."

"Where's Critter now?"

"Outside talking to the police."

"Shoot, we might all be dead were it not for him," Joe observed reverently.

"Dang straight," Ramsey agreed. "The best way to stop a bad guy with a gun is a good guy with a gun. Freaking legend."

"Well, daggum," Dr. Jenkins said upon entering the room, "there's so many news people and cops out there it looks like somebody kicked over an ant hill!"

"Great," Joe commented. "The last thing we need is any more publicity."

"Well, you kinda had to expect this would generate some news, I guess," Jenkins replied. "Anyhow, your CT was read. Darnedest thing, everything else looks good, but they're seeing some bullet fragments just above your left pelvis."

"Yeah, I took round there a few years ago in Afghanistan," Joe said nonchalantly. "Does this mean we get to go home?"

"It does, but tarnation, son! How many times have you been shot?" Jenkins asked.

"This'll make three," Joe answered plainly.

"And you also survived going over Niagara Falls?"

"Yeah, but that was just one time," Joe quipped with a grin.

Chapter 81

Duluth, Georgia

"So when do you guys have to return to Virginia Beach?" Stacy asked as she added a moderate amount of Sriracha sauce to her bowl of Pho.

They had all been asked to provide statements to the police and did not leave the hospital until late afternoon. The events of the day had caused them all to miss lunch, so they decided their first stop was to their favorite Vietnamese restaurant, Saigon Fusion. They had invited Crittendon, but he needed to get back to his gun shop and politely bowed out. Before leaving, he had told them he was planning on having a fire by the lake and invited them all to join him. That suited everyone nicely, but the first order of business was this early dinner.

In response to Stacy's question, Joe and Ramsey shot each other looks of surprise and eventually shrugged. They hadn't given it a thought.

"I'll call in tomorrow and see what they say," Joe answered while looking at Ramsey. "I think they know what we've been doing.

"Do you think they'll let you stay through the weekend?" Christy asked.

"Maybe. Neither one of us is currently on operational status. We'll have to get back soon, I would think. I'll have to have a medical eval for my two gunshot wounds before I process out."

Christy shared a quick smile with Stacy upon hearing Joe's mention of processing out of the Navy.

"So are you both still planning on moving here and starting a tactical course?"

"A man's got to do something for a living these days," Joe said with a humorous smile.

"Dyin' ain't much of a living, boy," Ramsey in his best Clint Eastwood impression.

"What?" Christy asked perplexed.

"Nothing," Joe said reassuringly, "just a little gunfighter humor. I take it you've never seen *The Outlaw Josey Wales?*"

"I've heard of it," Christy answered. "I think my brothers have watched it."

"What's that?" Stacy asked.

"*What's that?*" Ramsey reacted with mock outrage. "Only the greatest western ever made!"

"Second greatest," Joe interrupted.

Ramsey responded with a questioning look bordering disapproval. "What's number one?"

"*Tombstone*," Joe said matter of factly as he took a bite of his spring roll.

"I'm your huckleberry," Ramsey replied.

Stacy rolled her eyes. "Ugh! Boys! Can you just tell us what you're both planning to do?"

Christy laughed at the interplay. It was so good to be laughing with her friends again.

*****

They had lingered after dinner, simply sharing their experiences of the past week and savoring a good meal with each other. Just that morning, none of them could foresee when such a moment would happen, if ever. Talk had turned to the future during the ride home in Stacy's SUV. Joe and Ramsey had both accepted the fact that their days as operational Navy SEALs were over. Time was not a friend to SPECWAR operators, and both were being put out to pasture, so to speak, albeit not by choice. Ramsey had a full twenty years of service under his belt and could retire with a pension. Joe, on the other hand had only ten years in, but, if he couldn't lead an operational platoon, he was ready to consider other options.

The best option was sitting right beside him, currently talking to his mother on her phone. He and Christy had openly talked about getting married and having a family one day. They had even talked about adopting two teenage girls from Central America where each had played a role in rescuing from human sex trafficking rings. There were a few details he wanted to iron out regarding his future employment, but he was ready to ask Christy to marry him and he knew she was ready as well. He had actually planned to drive up to Nashville, on the sly, to ask Christy's father for her hand in marriage this past week. Unfortunately, their arrest and imprisonment had thrown a monkey wrench into those plans. He would have to see what team headquarters demanded of him and figure out a time he could follow through on visiting Christy's father. It was time to get on with their future.

Christy bid his mother goodbye and hung up her phone.

"I think she's more relieved you're out of prison than she is I am," Joe teased. Christy and Joe's mom were kindred spirits who hit it off the moment they met. They spoke weekly on the phone and texted often.

"That's cuz' I actually talk to her on a regular basis, Joe O'Shanick," Christy teased right back.

"I call her when I can," Joe said defensively, "It's not like a work a nine to five job."

"Don't listen to him, Christy," Ramsey yelled playfully from the front seat. "I tell Joe to call his mother every day!"

Christy gave an accusing nod to Joe.

"Just like I remind him to call you!" Ramsey added.

"What?!" Joe objected.

Christy delivered a sharp backhand to Joe's midsection.

"Oh! That felt good," she said wincing as she used her right hand to rub her left shoulder.

"Pull one of your stitches?" Joe asked.

Christy nodded. She then looked out the front windshield and her face brightened. Joe looked up and saw they were turning into her driveway.

In Darkness Light Shines

"Home," she said quietly, her tone a mixture of hope and relief.

"Welcome home, neighbor," Crittendon greeted while walking over from his house as they all piled out of Stacy's SUV.

"There's our hero!" Stacy greeted back.

"Nah," Crittendon said waving her off. "Just in the right place at the right time. I'd be a miserable wreck had that turned out any differently. Can't stand the thought of losing the best neighbor I've ever had."

"Well none of us might be standing here if it weren't for you, Tom," Christy said as she and Stacy sidled up on each side of him, each kissing him on the cheek.

Crittendon looked at Joe and Ramsey, his eyes lighting up with a mischievous grin on his face as he pulled Christy and Stacy in tightly and held them. "Careful now! I'm a lonely old man. Y'all are gonna get me worked up into a lather," he laughed.

"Well, I'm gonna work on that," Christy said as they turned walked toward her front porch, both still arm in arm with her neighbor. "I have a nurse friend that I know you would like."

"My lady, you have me intrigued," Crittendon said smoothly. "Just so long as she's not one of them bossy Nurse Ratched types."

"Oh, shoot! I don't have my keys!" Christy exclaimed.

"I got it," Stacy said holding up the spare key Christy had given her.

Stacy unlocked the door and the five entered. Christy breathed a sigh of relief upon entering her home. Even this morning, she wondered if she would ever see it or Joe or any of the people with her now ever again. Now she stood in her house with some of the closest people in her life. She slowly walked around, taking it all in: her kitchen, her great room, her spectacular view of Lake Lanier. Then something struck her. Something was off? No that wasn't it. Something was different. Christy turned around and looked at her friends.

"Didn't we leave this house a mess? And wasn't my front door kicked in during the raid?"

"Yeah, that's right. It was," Joe answered.

Christy looked around in perplexed amazement. "The front door works fine, and the house is immaculate!"

Stacy and Crittendon secretly stole a glance and smiled at each other.

Chapter 82

The White House
Six weeks later

"Welcome honored guests!" the cheerful young female intern greeted as she walked into the West Wing reception area. "President Galan is pleased you could join him. If you will follow me, please," she turned and led them out into the well-appointed hallway.

They were led down a hallway where an ornate door stood open. Stacy gasped as she realized what room they were about to enter. The intern gave a courtesy knock at the door and led the group in.

"Mr. President," the intern began upon entering the room, "it is my honor to present to you Lieutenant Commander Joseph O'Shanick, Dr. Christine Tabrizi, Master Chief Petty Officer Matthew Ramsey, Dr. Stacy Morgan, Petty Officer First Class Tran Van Truk, Miss Jade Nguyen, and Mr. Tom Crittendon."

President Galan smiled as he stood by one of two chairs seated in front of the fireplace. He looked regal wearing a black suit with white shirt and royal blue tie. Standing in front of the other chair was Charles Courtnall. Standing also was Clay Whitmore and his assistant, Chuck Springer. All three were sharply dressed in dark suits. Joe, Ramsey, and Tran were dressed in their Navy dress blue uniforms. Christy wore a black knee length business skirt with a cream-colored silk blouse. Stacy wore a navy blue formal skirt with a light blue blouse and Jade wore a navy blue business suit with a white blouse. The intern stood aside as President Galan stepped forward and greeted all of the new arrivals who were greeted by the other guests in turn.

"Please everyone, have a seat," President Galan said graciously. "There's coffee and tea on the table in front of you and if anyone would care for something else, Senior Chief Nelson will be happy to accommodate you," he said gesturing toward a tuxedoed Navy steward.

Once everyone was situated on the twin couches, President Galan leaned forward, resting his elbows on his knees, hands clasped in a gesture of earnestness.

"I wanted to convey my gratefulness that you all were willing to set aside the time and make the effort to be here today. It is by no small measure on each of your parts that I have been honored with another four years in this office. You each suffered tremendously at my expense and nearly paid for it with your lives. I want you each to know how eternally grateful I am. I owe you each a debt of gratitude that I will never be able to repay."

"Not at all, sir," Joe spoke for the group. "It was our honor and, if I may, sir, it's an honor and a *relief* to still have you as our Commander in Chief." Ramsey and Tran nodded their agreement.

"Well, gentlemen, to hear that from three of America's finest naval special warfare operators means more to mean than anything. It's praise from the praiseworthy and the honor is mine."

"So," Galan said excitedly as he leaned forward, "I'd like to bring you all up to speed on where we stand with the investigations."

Galan went down a roll call of all the principal members of what truly had been a conspiracy to throw the election through a trumped-up October surprise. Sal La Rosa had still been unconscious in his bathtub later that morning when federal agents had come to arrest him. The confession Tran had gotten out of him could not be used as evidence, but it had led to several investigations that had turned up substantial evidence implicating several key players including La Rosa, Frank Snyder, SAIC Winkelman of the Atlanta FBI Field Office, and Senator Williams from Georgia among other key players. La Rosa had cut a deal with federal prosecutors and had given up a lot of party secrets including their deep ties with the Central American cartels, Russian organized crime, and the Liu Dynasty. Despite his deep involvement, La Rosa would likely serve a minimum sentence when all was said and done but he was done with any party business and his reputation in the dark underworld of organized crime was permanently scarred now that he had turned snitch. He would have a mounting legal battle to retain his assets, and would spend the rest of his life looking over his shoulder. As much as Galan wanted the man to rot in prison, he didn't think La Rosa's life on the outside would amount to much knowing people were out to kill him.

Frank Snyder had begged to confess and to turn witness but, with La Rosa a virtual treasure trove of evidence, Snyder paled in comparison and was facing decades in prison if found guilty on all of his charges. Deputy FBI Director Wickenheiser currently faced no charges. Although investigations were ongoing, nothing had been found to directly implicate him. He was either the innocent Boy Scout between Snyder and Winkelman or he had been able to keep the evidence pointing elsewhere. Katie Huggins had replaced Winkelman as the acting SAIC for the Atlanta Field Office and she had named Special Agent Javier Gomez the new agent in charge over the organized crime division. His first task was the dismantling of the Tupolev organization. Tupolev remained in prison and had yet to say a word. Russia, or more likely his oligarch benefactor, was suing the United States to deport Tupolev back to Russia but Attorney General Jacobs had a team of attorneys fighting to keep Tupolev stateside to face his own trial and likely imprisonment.

Federal agents were rolling up the Liu Dynasty for their involvement in the Charlotte bombing, the hit on Lieutenant Commander Harrison, and several other charges including espionage. Unfortunately, both Liu Fan and Liu Shunyuan had fled the country and were back in China. The Chinese government wasn't exactly cooperative with the United States, and it was unlikely that either Liu would be deported to face trial but the investigations into their organization continued.

Senator Fowler was still trying to wriggle off the hook. He and the party had an army of lawyers filing lawsuits in just about any court that would hear them. They went to the press daily to garner support; they amazingly had their party faithful bending over backwards to cast doubt on his actions while creating spin on the ones that could not be refuted. It had mattered little. It was too late to change the election ballot and Galan had won in an electoral landslide. Having been arrested while in Atlanta, Fowler was still being held in the Fulton County Detention Center. It wasn't USP Atlanta where Joe and Ramsey had been held but it was no country club either. His attorneys had fought to have him released on bond but DOJ attorneys argued that Fowler had used a body double, on more than one occasion, to elude his Secret Service detail to fly off to various sexual romps, including the incident in question down in Belize, proving him to be a flight risk and in jail he remained.

The investigations into Fowler would continue for months before initial trial proceedings could begin. His involvement in nefarious and treasonous activities ran deep and wide; thus, it would be some time before he faced trial which would be sure to capture national attention. In the meantime, the media circus continued with many trying to call into question the legitimacy of Galan's election while demanding a new election be held. It wouldn't. They had picked their candidate and he had been exposed as a treasonous criminal in bed with foreign entities, not to mention sex-trafficked women.

"Mr. Crittendon," Galan said after finishing his recap. "This hasn't been released to the public yet because I wanted to present it to you first, but we can now confirm that the shooter you dropped last month happened to be the same guy that killed the former SAIC of the FBI's Atlanta Field Office, Cliff McPherson."

"Is that so?" Crittendon responded, his eyes wide in surprise.

"It certainly is," Galan answered. "His name was Nikolai Sivakov. Former Russian Spetsnaz. He was a close associate of the Tupolev organization, but he also did a lot of freelance work. It's estimated he has racked up over three dozen kills and those are just the ones we are relatively certain of. You not only saved your friends that day, but you rid the world of a very dangerous killer. Well done, sir."

"Well, gee, sir, I uh, well, thank you," Crittendon stammered with genuine humility.

Christy, seated between Joe and Crittendon, patted her neighbor on the knee in appreciation.

"Now that brings me to the next item I wanted to discuss with you all," Galan continued. "The DOJ has concluded their investigation into each of your involvement with this incident. They have concluded that each of you acted honorably and reasonably within the law under the purpose of rescuing several women whose lives were in danger. All charges against you have been dropped. In fact, you are all to be commended for your bravery and heroism. This nation needs more people like you. People who are still willing to put others above themselves. People willing to do the right thing. That's what this nation was built upon and that's what has sustained us."

"Thank you, Mr. President," Joe said along with the others.

"Please don't thank me," Galan said holding his palms up, "I meant every word. Many young lady's lives and those of their families would be far different were it not for your selfless actions. Our nation is better off as well.

"To that end," Galan continued. "I am in need of your services and would like to discuss a proposition with you, if that's alright," Galan said looking at Joe and Ramsey.

"We are at your service, Mr. President," Joe responded.

"Excellent," Galan smiled. "Well then, if it's alright with everyone, I will have Jenna escort everyone else to the dining room where we will reconvene in a few minutes for lunch. I'd like to have Lieutenant Commander O'Shanick, Master Chief Ramsey, and Petty Officer Truk remain here with me and Mr. Courtnall."

"Everyone, if you will follow me," the young intern spoke from the door.

Christy and Joe exchanged curious glances as they all stood. The party filed out of the Oval Office while Joe remained behind with his two teammates.

"Gentlemen, please have a seat," Galan said as he and Courtnall sat back down.

Joe sat back down on the now vacated couch. Ramsey and Tran sat on the opposite couch. They all looked at President Galan with awkward curiosity.

"Gentlemen, it has come to my attention that, I'm losing two of you to the civilian world," Galan said eyeing Joe and Ramsey.

"Yes, sir," Joe answered. "Master Chief Ramsey and I have reached the end of our operating days and, rather than be put out to pasture, we are exploring some options of our own."

"Well, I'd like to see if I can change your minds."

Chapter 83

Washington, D.C.

"Last mile...and go!" Christy directed.

Together, she and Joe increased their pace from a light jog to slightly faster than Christy's normal long-distance pace. This was the fifth and final mile of her grueling mile repeat run routine which consisted of a mile warmup followed by five fast paced miles, each separated by a half mile light recovery jog for a total of eight miles. Although Joe could maintain a faster pace, he preferred running beside her; besides, Christy's pace was impressive, and he was still breathing heavy enough to know he was getting a good workout.

With athletic grace, the two ran down the large sidewalk that paralleled the National Mall. The late afternoon sun had warmed the air to the low sixties and the winds were light as was the crowd. It was a perfect day to run in the nation's capital. The Washington Monument loomed ahead while the Capitol Building faded behind. Joe knew the last mile would end at the Monument. Christy had mapped out their run earlier with the monument as their finish. She loved planning her workouts and following all the metrics: pace, heart rate, cadence, and more. She hadn't said it out loud, but Joe was beginning to suspect she was setting another Ironman triathlon on her horizon.

"Quarter mile," she said between breaths as she poured on the speed and pulled ahead. "C'mon, frogman!"

Joe smiled. Christy's striking beauty was matched by her humble, caring, nurturing personality. She could quietly light up a room while at the same time making each person feel admired and appreciated. She had patiently helped Joe work through his spiritual agnosticism and introduced him the real Christ, the Lamb of God who is also the Lion of Judah. Christy reflected so many of His qualities. She was a healer and a peaceful harbor to her patients during times of great distress. She never thought twice about pouring her life into the abused women she met at the woman's shelter ministry she and Stacy served in. Over the past six weeks, she drove up at least once weekly to Alto to visit her former cellmate Hannah and came back beaming with pride over the young woman's progress to stay drug free; however, she also contained a playful yet competitive spirit. Whether they were playing Euchre with Ramsey and Stacy or out for a workout, Christy's love of competition always found its way to the surface. Her brothers told him she had been a fierce volleyball player in high school and later at the University of Tennessee but always the selfless teammate, the first on the floor at practice, the last to leave, and the first one under the net to shake hands with the other team when the game was over.

But Joe was competitive too. He had been a three-sport athlete in high school; football, swimming, and lacrosse and had gone on to play Division One Lacrosse at the Naval Academy. He lingered behind Christy for a brief moment, enough time to appreciate her graceful form. Her silky black hair, pulled back into a loose ponytail, matched her black running leggings which were accentuated by a neon green running shirt. Her ponytail swayed rhythmically with her long stride as she slowly increased her speed. Joe shifted into overdrive and began to reel her in. Christy seemed to sense his approach and opened up her throttle even more. Joe matched her increase and began to overtake her. He so wanted to give her a playful smack on the rear end as he passed her, but they had established boundaries and that was a no-go zone until they were married. *Soon,* he hoped. They just had to work a few things out.

As the Monument approached, they were in a near sprint. Joe matching Christy stride for stride. They pulled even with the famed obelisk and simultaneously slowed to a brisk cool down walk. Both clasped their hands behind their heads as they caught their breath.

As they neared the Lincoln Memorial, Joe grabbed Christy's hand. "Let's sit on the steps and take in the view," he said.

"You read my mind," Christy said as they began to climb. "Race to the top?"

"I would, but not here. This is kind of a sacred place."

"Good point," Christy said as she gave his hand a squeeze.

They reached the top and took a few minutes to quietly admire Lincoln's large statue and read the inscriptions of the Gettysburg Address and Lincoln's Second Inaugural Address that were carved into the marble walls. Afterwards, they sat down on the top step and looked out over the Reflecting Pool. Joe wrapped his arm around Christy's slender waist and pulled her in close. She rested her head on his shoulder. Joe smiled contentedly.

The Capital Building's rotunda hovered in the distance beyond the Washington Monument and all the memorials between. Joe marveled at the incredible history of the founding of the United States, the amazing land of freedom and opportunity it had become, and the memorialized names before them that helped preserve the nation. He cringed at the thought of so many self-serving, corrupt politicians who would try to exploit this for their own gain. Playing a role in putting Fowler away had nearly cost Joe and the others their lives but they had emerged relatively unscathed and, looking out over the nation's capital while sitting beneath the memorial to one of its greatest leaders, Joe concluded it had been worth it.

"I saw you engaged in conversation with the president and first lady after lunch today," Joe said breaking the silence.

"Yes! Oh, she's a doll!" Christy exclaimed as she picked up her head and looked at Joe, her emerald green eyes full of animation. "She reminds me so much of your mom."

"Really?" Joe replied with a contemplative tone. "Yeah, I guess I can see that. She certainly seems genuine. So what were you guys talking about?"

"They had asked about my time in prison, and I told them about Hannah. They seemed to really care. They worked with an inner-city church in San Diego for years before he was elected governor. They get it. And guess what?"

"What?"

"I told them I was worried about her safety and asked if he would be willing to commute Hannah's sentence if she would be willing to enroll in Adult and Teen Challenge."

"Did you really?" Joe asked. "What did he say?"

"He's giving her a full pardon! Isn't that something?"

"Wow! I'll say! That was a great thing to do, Christy. You are such a source of light in her life. I love that about you."

"Well, I just hope she completes the journey she is on. She was in such a dark place when I first met her."

"Hmm," Joe mused aloud.

"What?" Christy asked.

"Well, a thought just occurred to me," Joe began. "You know how you always say that when God permits bad things to happen, there is a reason? You know, how He will work something good out of it, Romans 8:28 and all that?"

"Yes," Christy answered. "His permissions always have a purpose. What are you suggesting?"

"Well maybe one of the reasons we were allowed to endure that whole ordeal, you in particular, was so that you would be put in Hannah's life? I mean, all things considered, we came out of it relatively okay, but she may have been given a whole new lease on life."

"You're absolutely right, Joe. It's something I never care to go through again, but I can definitely see the purpose in it looking back."

"So would you say it was worth it, Christy?"

Christy grinned and placed her head back on Joe's shoulder. "Definitely."

They sat together in silence. All was right in their world. After a few minutes, Christy broke the silence.

"So what did the president want to talk to you guys about?"

Joe paused as he thought about how best to answer her question.

"Oh," she said. "Is it classified?"

"No, not at all," he said as he caressed her side. "He tried to convince Rammer and I to stay in the Navy a while longer."

"Oh?" Christy asked sounding surprised. "I would think it would be difficult to say no to President Galan. So what did you tell him?"

"I told him the truth; that if I can no longer operate, then I'm ready to move on and, more importantly, that you and I are starting to make plans for the future."

Christy looked up at Joe and smiled in a conspiratorial manner. "And what did he say to that?"

"He said he knows you could get a job anywhere but asked if that was something we'd be willing to even consider. He wasn't forceful. He was simply asking."

"And you know I would, Joe. I've told you that. I'm totally willing to move anywhere you go if you want to stay in the teams."

"I know that," Joe said patting Christy's thigh appreciatively, "and I appreciate that more than you know, but I really like the idea of starting up that security firm and tactical course with Rammer and I told him that. And then he said that would actually fit into what he has planned for us."

"How's that?" Christy asked.

"He wants to establish and NGO-type operation whose purpose is to locate and rescue human trafficking victims. Just like what we did in Belize. His original idea was to have us based in Coronado where we would operate under cover as BUD/S instructors which would allow us to train regularly and slip away when a mission arose. But after hearing about our plan to operate a tactical course in rural Georgia, he said that could work too. We would have a way to train that wouldn't draw unwanted attention and we could get to just about anywhere in the world from Atlanta. He said Rammer and I could pick our own team; we would report directly to his task force on human trafficking and have full government funding, intel, support, and logistics."

"It sounds like you're at least considering this," Christy surmised.

"I'll be honest, Christy, it has a lot of appeal but, and I'm dead serious about this, you're my first priority. I'm not doing this if it in anyway doesn't sit well with you or could come between us."

"Then tell him, yes," Christy grinned.

"What? Really? Are you serious?" Joe asked astonished.

"Yes," Christy said with a serious tone. "Joe O'Shanick, you were made for this. God made you a warrior. You've saved my life on more than one occasion, and you've saved countless others. I know you're not going to do this forever, but for the time being, I believe it's His will for you."

"But it's not without risk, Christy," Joe cautioned. "Some of these ops could still go kinetic like what went down in Belize."

"I know that," Christy replied. "But I also know that you are safer *in* God's will than you ever could be were you *not* to be doing His will. I have total peace about this. In fact, I'm excited about it!"

"Alright," Joe said curiously, "so let's say we do this, where would you want to live?"

"I would *love* to live on Coronado but there's no way we could afford it, even with what I make," Christy said. "I think we would have to stay here."

"Not so fast," Joe said smiling.

"What? Oh, we could live on base?"

"Yes," Joe answered, "We could, but our options have been opened up. We can live anywhere we want."

"What are you talking about, Joe?"

"Who else was asked to stay behind when you guys got up to leave?"

"Matt, Tran, and Mr. Courtnall," Christy answered. "Why?"

Joe grinned. "I've been waiting all day to tell you, but I wanted to surprise you."

"What?!" Christy demanded.

"Mr. Courtnall," Joe said.

"What about Mr. Courtnall?"

"Mr. Courtnall expressed the fact that losing his daughter put everything into perspective for him. That all of his vast wealth meant nothing and he would have gladly traded it to get Tracy back. He said he can never repay what we did for his family and what you did for him, personally. He also said he was devastated over what happened to us all being arrested and nearly killed. He knows none of it would have happened had we not volunteered to help get Tracy back. In response, he cited the biblical reference of when kings used to offer up to half their kingdom and without telling us, distributed half his wealth evenly into accounts for you, me, Ramsey, Tran, Jade, Clay, Chuck, and his associates who helped with all of this."

Christy gasped in astonishment. "Joe! We can't accept that! We volunteered of our own free will. We got involved because it was the right thing to do. I *never* expected so much as a dime for doing that."

"I know," Joe answered. "And I told him the exact same thing, but he not only insisted, he also said it was a done deal and that the accounts were already established."

"Just how much are we talking about?"

"A lot," Joe answered. "The annual interest off just one account would eclipse what you make as an ER physician."

"So you're saying we are set for life?" Christy asked still in disbelief.

"That's exactly what I'm saying, if you can believe it," Joe grinned. "So that puts Coronado back on the table. Where would you like to live? Keep in mind, I don't have to do this."

"No, you don't," Christy said, "But I still think it's what you were meant to do, and for that reason, you need to. You and I are both called to serve. Money or not, this is our path. With that in mind, I think Coronado makes the most sense."

"Really?" Joe asked.

"Yes. I think you and Matt would make excellent BUD/S instructors. Plus, I remember sitting on the waterfront and watching all the sailboats sailing up and down the bay. I would love to spend some out there. I can picture us getting a sailboat and doing the same thing," Christy said dreamily. "So when would you have to be out there?"

"It's still in the conceptual stages," Joe said as he stood and stretched his arms, "but President Galan said probably sometime late spring."

"Oh, well that gives me time to find a job and get my house sold," Christy said. "And not to be overly practical, but we can't live together until we are married. I know we've talked about it, but we really need to think about that. Do you have a plan?"

"Not really," Joe answered plainly.

"Joe O'Shanick, that's not like you. Every time I ask you if you have a plan you *always* respond with *I'm working on it,"* Christy said making quotation marks with her fingers.

"Well, this is different," Joe answered.

"Why do you say that?" Christy asked looking up at him with peaked curiosity.

"Because, this time, I don't have a plan," Joe said looking around. "Are you aware that almost sixty years ago, a great man stood on these very steps and gave a speech in which he said, 'I have a dream'?"

"Yes, I'm quite aware of that," Christy answered, her curiosity blending with confusion. "But why are you dodging my question?"

"Because, I don't have a plan," Joe said followed by suddenly dropping to one knee before Christy, his eyes gazing at her intensely as he held a simple yet elegant diamond ring before her. "I have a dream."

The End

About the Author

John Galt Robinson is a practicing emergency medicine physician. He weaves his experiences from the exciting, tragic, and sometimes humorous world of emergency medicine into a much larger story with intriguing characters who tackle relevant social issues in a fast-paced adventure. John grew up just upriver from Niagara Falls on Grand Island, New York. He earned his medical degree at East Tennessee State University after a previous career as a certified athletic trainer. He lives in South Carolina with his wife and family where he is an active sailor and triathlete.

His first three books, *Forces of Redemption, Power City,* and *Lost Angels* have been well received.

Author's Note

Dear Reader,

My first novel, Forces of Redemption, was intended to give the reader a glimpse into the horrors of human trafficking. In Lost Angels I attempted to delve much deeper into the domestic aspect of human trafficking. In reality, the horrors are far worse and far more widespread than can be explained in the context of a novel. Human trafficking is an enemy that must be fought on both a grand and individual scale. Nations and states must rise in defense of those who cannot defend themselves but we, as individuals, can contribute as well. Neighborhood awareness, serving in a ministry or shelter, and community involvement are great places to start. Donating time or resources to a ministry or charity that fights these battles is another great option. While conducting research in preparation for Forces of Redemption, I learned of an organization made up of volunteers who locate and rescue victims of human trafficking. They are retired Navy SEALs, private investigators, law enforcement investigators, and other public servants. Their organization is named Saved in America. If you would like to learn more about them or financially support them, please visit their website: www.savedinamerica.org.

    I have also recently partnered with another organization named Lighthouse for Life that helps women, who have been rescued out of the sex slave industry, rebuild their lives. Lighthouse for Life provides safe housing, counseling, education, job opportunities, and much more to help these women recover from their traumatic experience and to assimilate back into decent society. Please consider giving them your support at www.lighthouseforlife.org.

In each novel, I have referred to an organization named Adult and Teen Challenge that really exists and has scores of treatment centers nationwide, which serve to rehabilitate and train people who have walked the path of addiction or a troubled lifestyle. Adult and Teen Challenge houses and trains people to leave their troubled past behind them for good. Please strongly consider financially supporting this vital ministry. For more information, please visit their website www.teenchallengeusa.org.

One final note, I hope you have enjoyed reading this novel as much as I have writing it. As I write this, I am hard at work with the next novel in this series. Joe and Christy will be back in a new and different adventure along with some familiar friends and some new villains. As Christy learned, what she does matters. May this be said of each of you.

Thank you,

John Galt Robinson

Forces of Redemption

During a hectic Emergency Department shift, Dr. Christine "Christy" Tabrizi rescues a young Honduran girl from the gang that has been prostituting her and discovers the horrors of human trafficking tracing all the way back to the cartels in Central America. Christy volunteers for a mission in Honduras, to help rescue as many young girls as possible from the cartels that control them. Joe O'Shanick is part of a Navy SEAL platoon deployed in Central America and finds himself in the midst of hostile territory when the president of the United States, a man of Mexican American heritage who sympathizes with the human condition in Central America, declares war on the cartels. In the middle of a tense hostage scenario, Christy and Joe's paths collide, and they must rely on each other and their respective skills to escape with their lives.

Power City

A man is mysteriously swept over Niagara Falls. The city of Niagara Falls, nicknamed The Power City, finds itself in the shadow of a new power broker, the Catalano organization. This resurgent mafia family's rise to power leaves a trail of death and corruption in its wake. Navy SEAL Joe O'Shanick is their next target for execution, but the sinister reach of the Catalano organization extends beyond O'Shanick to his family and physician friend, Dr. Christy Tabrizi; however, this criminal organization forgot one thing: Navy SEALs leave no man behind. *Power City* explores the dark world of organized crime while weaving a story of faith and the selfless love of one's family and friends in a roller coaster ride of crime, medicine, military action, and suspense.

Lost Angels

A powerful organized crime syndicate is abducting young women from college campuses and enslaving them into human trafficking. Charles Courtnall is a wealthy investor willing to sacrifice his personal fortune to find his daughter. He hires Clay Whitmore and his team of investigators to find her, only to find out she is being offered to the highest bidder in a global dark web auction. Clay and his team are stymied at every turn by a sinister criminal organization that has deep government ties and stays one step of ahead of them. Dr. Christy Tabrizi, an emergency medicine physician, treats a young woman who managed to escape the human trafficking ring. Christy enlists the help of her close friend, Joe O'Shanick, a Navy SEAL, to locate and rescue the other women. O'Shanick and his teammate, Matt Ramsey, join forces with Whitmore's team in a desperate attempt to rescue the women before it's too late. They discover the corruption exceeds that which they imagined. *Lost Angels* explores the dark world of human trafficking, organized crime and political corruption while weaving a story of faith, selfless love, and heroic commitment in a suspenseful tale of crime, medicine, and military action.

KCM Publishing
a division of KCM Digital Media, LLC

Made in United States
North Haven, CT
20 January 2023